"I read the book with wonder and emotion. The love between Michaela and Rivi is depicted precisely and delicately, showing us both the white birds and the black ones. It's beautiful."
—Amos Oz

"Judith Katzir is a wonderful writer; her prose, so rich in detail and evocative images, manages to tether her unique characters to an entire country, bringing both vividly to life. In *Dearest Anne*, these complicated and enthralling relationships emerge in fascinating ways, and Katzir uses her exacting eye and an innovative form to bring this captivating and unpredictable story to the page."—Jennifer Gilmore, author of *Golden Country*

"More than anything else, the book is a temple of love to the imaginary, and to literature as an option for deep and vigorous living. . . . The story succeeds in arousing interest and emotion. . . . The greatness of the novel is understood only in retrospect, after reading it and tying all the threads, events, and vantage points together into one complete picture."—Ya'ara Muki, *Time Out* (Israel)

"Judith Katzir is by far the most talented of the so-called young Israeli women writers. It is really impressive how Katzir lets her protagonist trace these two decisive years in her life and to see the emotional depth and the poetic sharpness of her descriptions. *Dearest Anne* harkens back to her first novel [*Matisse Has the Sun in His Belly*], completes it, and gives it closure—a great literary achievement."—*Jüdische Zeitung* (Jewish Times)

"There is something addictive about Judith Katzir's writing: the ability to pour beauty and meaning into a fleeting moment, to catch it in the tangle of time and shape and polish it all in metaphoric language that is amazingly sensuous and precise."
—Miri Paz, *Globes*

"In *Dearest Anne* the author manages to get inside a fourteen-year-old girl without judging her, teaching her, or setting herself above her. Nature and human nature together celebrate a new beginning. This is Judith Katzir's best book."
—Nathan Shaham, author of *Rosendorf Quartet*

"Judith Katzir—a true writer—has produced a novel dealing with sensitive and difficult human material. With a skilled hand she transforms it into a sensual work full of love and sensitivity that touches the inner heart."—Haim Be'er, author of *Feathers*

"An absorbing and enjoyable book courageously written."
—S. Yizhar, author of *Preliminaries*

"Judith Katzir is an expert at describing everyday life in Israel. . . . As she describes modern women's self-understanding, a moving dialogue full of contradictory feelings develops. . . . Rivi's diaries are a record of becoming an adult, and the education of the heart. They record sexual initiation, erotic passion, and the power of fresh feelings; also doubts, loneliness, death, and the risk of love without morality. Judith Katzir's novel . . . breaks a taboo with sensitivity."
—Carsten Hueck, dradio.de

"Judith Katzir describes a decisive period in the life of two women poetically, silently, and with immense power to absorb her readers. The novel is credible precisely because Katzir does not reserve questions about guilt and abuse."
—*Mannheimer Morgen*

"Katzir shows her ability to describe the process through which a great love enriches the lover's life and the lives of those around him or her."—Shulamit Lapid, author of *Nunia*

"Katzir has made good on all her promises, justifying all the praise she received. . . . *Dearest Anne* is a wonderful book, carrying the best of Katzir's genetic structure in every sentence. . . . She tells a deeply private and personal story that is at the same time universal. It is a deeper, more multilayered psychological picture than there is in any psychology book. If you will, it is *A Portrait of the Artist as a Young Woman*, done with great artistry, in beautiful language that brings together the pain and the beauty. Pure pleasure."—Eilat Negev, *Yedioth Ahronoth*

"When the author touches the reader, there may be a measure of consolation. Perhaps it gives us life. Judith Katzir tells us all this . . . through mastery of the basic tool of her craft. . . . Her descriptive powers are outstanding. Portrayals of the physical surroundings and of the adolescent girl's tangled web of emotions are thoroughly convincing. Katzir listens to her readers and seems to know them well. The delicate tonality and the materials she chooses to weave into the novel will confirm her place as a major writer."—Ioram Melcer, *Ma'ariv*

"Body language and poetic language are powerfully fused. Poetry rouses love, and love rouses poetry. . . . Acts of love are described with amazing directness and sensuality. The scent of secrecy and of the forbidden enhances love and gives it a dizziness and a separateness that go beyond the qualities of the normative world. . . . Judith Katzir describes wonderfully the feast of the awakening body, and arouses compassion through her portrayal of the immense insult of its end."—Pnina Shirav, *Yedioth Ahronoth*

"Dear Judith, I want to tell you that this beautiful love of two women for one another, and of each of them for books and images and words, filtered into the depths of my heart. In this book you have been a splendid teacher, telling me in delight and in bitterness about myself, about literature and about life. . . . This is the most feminine book I have read this year. Romantic love, love for books and words—these Katzir describes beautifully with so much talent and sensitivity."—Rana Verbin, *Ha'ir*

"Judith Katzir has written what turns out to be one of the most beautiful love stories in Hebrew in recent years, and without a doubt the most beautiful . . . [and] the first single sex-love story in Hebrew, because it distils the beauty of homosexuality and does not fall into the temptation of interpreting it by means of 'straight' instruments. . . . If someone is capable of speaking to the dead, it is Judith Katzir."—Aviad Kissos, *Walla*

Dearest Anne

The Reuben/Rifkin Jewish Women Writers Series
A joint project of the Hadassah-Brandeis Institute
and The Feminist Press

The Reuben/Rifkin Jewish Women Writers Series, established in 2006 by Elaine Reuben, honors her parents, Albert G. and Sara I. Reuben. It remembers her grandparents, Susie Green and Harry Reuben, Bessie Goldberg and David Rifkin, known to their parents by Yiddish names, and recalls family on several continents, many of whose names and particular stories are now lost. Literary works in this series, embodying and connecting varieties of Jewish experiences, will speak for them, as well, in the years to come.

Founded in 1997, the Hadassah-Brandeis Institute (HBI), whose generous grants also sponsor this series, develops fresh ways of thinking about Jews and gender worldwide by producing and promoting scholarly research and artistic projects. Brandeis professors Shulamit Reinharz and Sylvia Barack Fishman are the founding director and codirector, respectively, of HBI.

Dearest Anne

A Tale of Impossible Love

Judith Katzir

Translated from the Hebrew by Dalya Bilu
Afterword by Hannah Ovnat-Tamir

The Feminist Press
at The City University of New York
New York

Published in 2008 by The Feminist Press at The City University of New York
The Graduate Center, 365 Fifth Avenue, Suite 5406, New York, NY 10016
www.feministpress.org

Library of Congress Cataloging-in-Publication Data
Katzir, Judith.
[Hineh ani mathilah. English]
  Dearest Anne : a tale of impossible love / by Judith Katzir ; translated from the
Hebrew by Dalya Bilu. — 1st ed.
  p. cm.
  ISBN 978-1-55861-575-5 (trade paper) — ISBN 978-1-55861-579-3 (trade cloth)
  I. Bilu, Dalya. II. Title.
PJ5054.K345H5613 2008
892.4'36—dc22
                                                2007033834

Text and cover design by Lisa Force
Printed on acid-free paper in Canada by Transcontinental

12 11 10 09 08   5 4 3 2 1

The beginning, the worst of beginnings,
is better than the best of endings.
—Shalom Aleichem, *The Song of Songs*

When I die
Passing into another nature
The invisible Carmel
Which is all mine,
The core of happiness,
Whose pine needles, cones, flowers, and clouds
Are engraved in my flesh—
Will separate from the visible Carmel
With the avenue of pines that descend to the sea.
—Zelda, from *The Invisible Carmel*
Translated by Tova Weizman

Let Me Begin

After it was all over I walked down the dirt track leading from the new cemetery to the old cemetery, leaving behind my back the mountain with the low white houses of the village of Kababeer planted on its summit, huddled in the shade of the stone mosque with its chalky dome and two twin minarets. Before, when the stretcher tilted sideways and your body wrapped in white slid into the pit, I opened my eyes wide and forced them to look. Afterwards they wandered to the line of the mountain ridge, trembling against the background of the silvery porcelain sky of early autumn. Yes, you had come home, to the sea and the Carmel mountain you loved, your view from now on.

I parted from your son last, briefly touching his clammy, lifeless hand, avoiding his eyes, and he nodded with a kind of mechanical pecking motion, his two blue beetles blank as ever. What did he feel? What did he understand? Only twenty-two years old, and already his fair hair was growing thin, and his body was stooped as if he bore the weight of a lifetime on his shoulders. A boy with autistic traits, a strange, alien child, a retarded infant robbed of his mother, who had seen far more than he should have; a fetus whose little body was crushed under

3

that heavy burden and whose legs kicked in protest, a spermatozoon that met an egg in a little hotel in Paris, a misconceived idea.

A hand light as a wing came to rest on my shoulder. I turned my head to the tall woman with the gray hair cropped short in a boyish haircut, and in front of my eyes the slender curly-haired girl of once upon a time emerged, with the high cheekbones and the two clear scraps of sky above them, and the beaky nose, which had now turned red. In her hand she held a bunch of wildflowers. "I've just arrived, I'm so sorry I'm late," panted Osnat, blowing her nose on a white tissue.

"It was the same as it always is," the words fell heavily out of my mouth.

"But she wasn't like anyone else," her eyes stared at me in surprise.

"No, she was completely herself."

"Did you speak?" she wanted to know. "Did they ask you to say something?"

"They didn't ask. I read a poem."

"Did he say Kaddish?"

"He stammered something, in an American accent, Yoel helped him."

"I'll go and say hello to them and give her the flowers."

"They're lovely. She would have liked them," I said, and remembered another bunch, that you gave to Osnat, your best friend, on her fifteenth birthday, after not speaking for months, and the two scraps of sky opened up to you then in huge delight.

"Did you come by car?" she asked. "You can drive back to Tel Aviv with me. You live in Tel Aviv now, don't you?"

"Yes, but I'm staying here. I have a few ends to tie."

"Visiting relatives?"

"That too," I nodded, remembering our family plot in the old cemetery, my grandmother and grandfather under one stone, my mother by herself, between them and the path.

"I read somewhere that you had a daughter," said Osnat.

"In the meantime I've had another one. Carmel will be eleven, and Noga's two. And you?"

"My children are already grown up," she smiled. "Tamar's studying art in New York, and Roi is in the army."

The only time I saw her she wasn't planning to get married. When was it? The summer of seventy-nine, twenty-two years ago.

"Are you writing something new for us?" she asked. "I've read all your books, they always take me back to Mount Carmel, with the wind and the cyclamens and the pinecones."

"Lately I've mainly been erasing," I apologized. Once, when I was young, my words were quicker and wiser than I was. With the passing of the years I've gained in wisdom and maturity, while the words, tired and bewildered, trail behind.

Suddenly she embraced me. "You should write about her," she whispered in my ear, "about the two of you."

"Yes," I hesitated, "my memory is covered with white spots. I have to find the diary I wrote then. It's buried somewhere."

Yes, that's where I'll go, to the disaster area, to the place where the fire flower was born and where it was buried alive. I'll go down to the wadi, to our dwarf pine, and look for the hiding place under the flat rock, and dig for the notebooks, even though there's almost no chance of finding them after twenty rainy winters. Now that your body's resting in the earth I'm free to resurrect those years that I've never written about, or spoken about to almost anyone. I myself could hardly believe that they were what they were, that the two of us were what we were, and I buried them deep within me and I knew that it was forbidden to wake them up.

"Will you call me, Rivi? I'm in the phone book. Let's meet in some cafe?" Osnat's hands were holding my shoulders, and the scraps of sky, which time had not dulled, examined my face sorrowfully. "That time when we met you were still really a child. How time laughs at us, I can't believe that I'm already fifty."

"I'll call," I said, and I knew that she too knew that I wouldn't.

Osnat stroked my arm as if to console me, and I looked at her ungainly figure walking down the path and kneeling next to the mound of earth covered with stones and flowers, surmounted by a little wooden sign with your name on it.

The gate to the old cemetery is open. I pass under the ornamental inscription. "Righteousness shall go before him." The iron letters leave no room for argument. The black funeral board is empty, with chalk marks, as if wiped by a tired teacher's hand at the end of the day. I climb the asphalt path, which in recent years has become my way home, and here they are, the three of them, resting in the shade of the cypress tree; Grandma and Grandpa under one marble slab, above them the high, broad headstone in "natural" stone, with the inscription in elongated, rather fancy letters, "Lipkin," and underneath it the names Emanuel on the right and Rivka, who waited for him almost thirty years alone under the stone, on the left. Mother next to them in a single grave inclining slightly towards theirs, like a little girl creeping into her parents' bed after having a nightmare, and they moved a little to give her room.

Her headstone is identical to theirs, and the letters too; at the top only the first name, Carmela, like the notice on door of my daughter's room, "Carmel's room," and below, in smaller letters, "Shenhar, born Lipkin."

For eleven years we've been coming here every 24th of Nisan—Oren, Noam, and I. I arrive first and sit down on her cold stone, leaning my back against the headstone and letting the wind cool my face burning in the khamsin. It's pleasant here, in the shade. Nowhere else have I heard the birds sing like this, in real joy. In front of my eyes is the back of the Schwartzbergs' headstone, polished black marble, in which every year I see my changing reflection: long hair, short hair, brown, blond, highlights, sunglasses, prescription glasses, contact lenses, thinner, fatter, twice pregnant, age spots on my arms and face. Only like this, with my body very close to what remains of her body, I relax and feel at peace. Without words I tell her what's happened to me, only the important things, so as not to disturb her rest; you know, Mother, I got married, you have a granddaughter, I wrote a book and another book, you have another granddaughter.

Once life stuck to me, people fell in love with me, I fell in love, my heart raced to the edge of the abyss and crashed, again and again, like James Dean's red racing car. In recent years nothing sticks to me, I do everything with my own hands, my family, my books. Today life no longer succeeds in surprising me, only death. It arrives at unexpected times and gathers to itself the people I loved: Grandfather Emanuel, Mother, Aunt Tehiya, and now you too.

When Oren and Noam arrive—two tall serious men who were once my little brothers—I stand up, remove the cellophane paper from the flowers I bought in Tel Aviv and dragged with me in the train, and put them down on your single bed. A few of them I scatter on Grandma and Grandpa's double marble blanket. For long moments we stand around her in silence, just the three of us, we don't need anyone else, each of us with his own account to settle, the account of the anger and the pity, the insult and the forgiveness, the guilt and the atonement. Each of us with his love. When the ritual is over, we leave and go to the beach and sit in one of the beachfront restaurants to eat hummus and drink beer, and talk about our children and our work, and sometimes also about her.

But today is the sixteenth of Elul, the fourth of September two thousand and one, the beginning of autumn. I came here alone, to inform you of her death; you know, Mother, the woman you detested so violently is already under the ground as well, I'm the only one left above it, at long last free of both of you.

But what will I do with this freedom, I think in alarm, what

7

will I do here alone, and suddenly I long to curl up next to Mother, in the narrow space between her and the path. I look around me; most of the graves next to the path are double, crowding against the curbstone, and perhaps there's room for an extra plot here too, and if it's free maybe I'll acquire it. Carmel and Noga will enjoy coming here, sitting on top of my deteriorating body in the shade of the cypress tree and listening to the birdsong.

Decisively I stride to the gatekeeper's little whitewashed booth and knock on the door. An elderly man opens it, a white kaftan, black skullcap, wispy gray beard.

"Yes, miss?"

"I want to inquire about purchasing a plot. "

"Who for? "

"Me. "

"For you?" He examines me suspiciously. "How old are you, if I may ask."

"Thirty-eight. "

"Thirty-eight? " he repeats in astonishment. "Sick, God forbid?"

"No, not yet, it's just that my family are buried here, and I thought of buying next to them . . . so I'll have it, you know, for any eventuality."

"Ah," his face clears in a smile, "come in, come in, what's the section and plot?"

I squeeze into the tiny office, where the air is thick with sour sweat, and recite the numbers of the plot and section.

The gatekeeper opens a long ledger with a black cover, reminiscent of a class attendance book, and turns the pages.

"Yes, I see there's a place here, next to the deceased Shenhar, a place reserved for a woman."

"Why for a woman?" I wonder.

"A strange man is not buried next to a woman, only her husband is permitted." He gives me a rebuking look.

"Yes, that's logical," I try to placate him. A strange man

buried next to a woman is shocking licentiousness. And since both my mother's husbands are married to other women, it's hard to imagine that either one of them will want to acquire the plot and lie next to her for eternity. No, this has to be my plot.

"Carmela Shenhar is my mother, of blessed memory," I confess to soften his heart, "how much will it cost me to purchase the plot next to her?"

"It's written here," he points to the modest cardboard notice hanging on the wall behind him, "a plot in the old part, twelve thousand, a plot in the pantheon—twenty." I look closely at the notice, crooked handwritten letters, like an ice cream stall, small cone—twelve shekels, big cone—twenty.

"Where's the pantheon?"

"Where your late mother is, may she rest in peace," he explains while his long fingers play with his beard, "the plots close to the entrance. The mayor Abba Houshi is buried there, Almogi the head of the Labor Council, all the old leaders."

For years I've been coming here, and I didn't know that my grandparents and my mother were buried in the pantheon. A family of gods. Zeus, Hera, and Aphrodite. Twenty thousand shekels for the right to be buried in spitting distance of Abba Houshi.

"Too dear," I say as if I'm bargaining for a secondhand car.

"That's the situation, there are hardly any plots left here. Today people are buried only in the new cemetery."

But there are no trees in the new cemetery, I implore him in my heart, it's all exposed and glaring in the sun, and I want to be here, in the old one, to curl up next to my mother in the shade of the cypress trees. And what about the new computer I was planning to buy, and the laser operation to correct my vision, and the new bed for Carmel?

"You know what," the gatekeeper softens, "I'll write your phone number down here, and if anyone wants to buy the plot next to the deceased, may she rest in peace, I'll get in touch with you first."

9

"Thank you," I smile at him in relief, "you've been very helpful."

I walk down the path, pass the water fountain, and emerge on the road, almost tempted to raise my hand and hitch a ride, like years ago, when Racheli and I would return from the sea with salty loofah hair, skipping barefoot from the shade of the trash can to the shade of the bus stop, with our sandals dangling from our jeans bags and the pavement burning under our feet like life itself.

A taxi stops next to me, and I open the door and climb into the air-conditioned interior. "To the Carmel Center, please, to Panorama Street."

The landscape here hasn't changed; like a child's drawing, tree and earth, sun and sky, but where is the house with the red roof and the blue door and the two windows open like eyes, and the chimney with the curls of smoke? In its place there's a white space on the page.

Our two-storied childhood home in the pine stand on the corner of George Eliot and Panorama Streets we sold years ago to a contractor who wiped it off the face of the earth together with the pine trees, and replaced it with a block of luxury apartments overlooking the view of the bay. With the money we received we built three other houses, to make a new life for ourselves in them. In my new house I sew and patch, stitching Mommy to Daddy, Daddy to Carmel, Carmel to Noga, Noga to Mommy, over and over again, day after day, night after night, hour after hour, diligently, bleary-eyed, with the pricked fingers of two left hands, just so it won't come unraveled.

The bay sticks out a giant tongue of sea at me, pierced with earrings in the shape of ships, and I turn my back to it and cross the road, and go on walking up the hill to the school, panting, my heart pounding. The blue iron gate gapes and a few boys with peroxide spikes burst out of it. Colored tank tops expose tattooed biceps. A crowd of older boys and girls, twelfth graders presumably, cluster around a fancy motorbike, smoking and laughing. And here are two girls of fourteen or fifteen, one fair and slender with a Slavic face, and the other short and suntanned, an orange tank top clinging tightly to little breasts that touch your heart, exposing a flat, smooth chocolate stomach. What children they are, I marvel to myself, soon Carmel will look like them, how is it possible that I was like them then, so very very young.

I wait a little longer, perhaps a little girl will come out of the gate in a sky-blue uniform shirt, with two braids and glasses in square plastic frames, and at her side her blue-eyed friend, whose wheaten hair reaches to under her ears, and who address each other in the male gender; and perhaps Galya the nature study teacher will come past, or Miss Hardona the history teacher, or perhaps Hourgi the headmaster, whose name I saw in the newspaper two years ago, in a notice announcing his death; and perhaps coming towards me I'll see a young teacher with freckles and a bronze-colored ponytail, and she'll smile at me with burning brown eyes, and climb up the hill to an eggplant-colored Mini Minor. But it's late now, past two o'clock, and the school day is over.

I drag my heavy feet away from there and go on climbing up Wedgewood Street, passing the post office, which has been redecorated in red and white, resisting the temptation to climb the steps and see if my phone booth, my little-house-in-the-post-office for two years, is still there. Today everybody has a cell phone. I pass Max's stationery store, where I once bought the second notebook of my diary, the one with the photo of Mike Brandt on the cover. In those days, at the beginning of the school year, the stationer's would be crowded with children, but now it's no longer there, replaced by a fashionable shoe store. Koestler's cake shop is still here, on the corner of President Avenue and, as then, it breathes aromas of chocolate and cinnamon into my nose. I peek into the old pharmacy next door, expecting to see the high wooden cabinets with the glass doors enclosing pale yellow potbellied bottles of powders with labels lettered in black Latin, but the pharmacy has refurbished its appearance and its smell, and it now resembles many others of its kind. I cross the street and look over the fence at the wadi I would slide down to the scouts' den, a little girl in a khaki uniform and a blue tie, her hands clutching at bushes and her fingers unwittingly crushing a yellow broom flower, or the leaf of a mastic tree.

At the pedestrian crossing opposite the gas station I stop and wait for the green traffic light. Even though the street is empty of cars the people stand and wait for the light to change, not like in Tel Aviv, where I usually wait alone, betraying my Haifa origins. Afterwards I walk past the blank gray building of the auditorium, on whose steps we would sit barefoot, Racheli and I, stirred to the depths by Bergman's *Persona* or Truffaut's *The 400 Blows*, which we had seen in the basement Cinematheque.

The pine trees at the bottom of Hatzvi Avenue, mute witnesses, still lean towards each other from both sides of the pavement, and their tall crests arch together over the street in a living green cathedral vault. I remember once saying to you, they're probably whispering about us, and you were silent for a minute and then you said, trees don't whisper and waves don't whisper, only people whisper, and their whispers sound like a scream. In those days the indifference of the trees reassured me. Now I want to shake them until they shed their cones in a black shower of pine nuts, to torture them until they agree to talk. Open your mouths and tell me how we were, when we walked beneath you in the afternoon, a young woman and a girl, and in front of them, racing down the hill, a dog as red as a flame. Remind me what we wore, what we said, if we laughed, if we wept, if the woman laid her hand on the girl's shoulder, under the braid. Tell me how the time was and how the love was.

In your house, on the corner of Kalaniot Street, everything

is as it was; the honeysuckle creeping over the gateposts, and the pine tree bowing its dark foliage to your porch. I'll open the low gate with a practiced hand, I'll climb the steps with the blue railing and the geranium planters, I'll ring the bell, and already I'm in your arms, my face in the hollow of your neck and Dulcinea's front paws digging into my blue-shirted back. The Germann family are still here too, on the dark green mailbox. Only the label with your names on the blue mailbox, "Michaela Berg, Dr. Yoel Rosen," has been exchanged for another, "Dr. Moshe and Nitza Tavor." And what would I do, a woman heavy in weight and years, in the arms of Mrs. Doctor Moshe Tavor?

I turn into Nitzanim Street and go down the dirt path to the edge of the wadi, dislodging stones under my shoes, which are soon covered with dust, and my heart leaps into my throat. Here's our pine tree, its trunk short and thick and its crest flattened out and spreading luxuriantly sideways, like a dwarf's hair. Under it the flat rock, which covers the hiding place. I hold onto the tree trunk and sit down on the rock. Nearby, under the mastic bush, someone has left an old mattress with a dirty woolen blanket and a battered suitcase tied up with a rope. Presumably a homeless person who made himself at home here. For a moment I am seized with envy—now all of this is his.

The beauty of the place hurts me—the silvery triangle between the curves of the mountain; the smell of the pines growing more intense in the afternoon hours, when the sun beats down on them with the last of its strength and sucks the oil from the pine needles; the wind, which stirs the vapors of the sea with the breath of the plants and the resin and tosses them at my nose.

All these were once mine, and today they are strangers, they don't remember, as if I had never existed.

All these were once yours, and you will never see them again.

My hand gropes for the mineral water bottle in my bag, and

I pull it out and drink. All these hours in the sun I haven't felt thirsty, but now I pour more and more tepid water into my throat, and splash some into the palm of my hand and wet my blazing face. I look for a strong dry pine branch to start to dig; here, under a projecting bit of the rock, was the opening of the hiding place, a kind of coney or some other rodent's lair, into which Dulcinea liked poking her damp nose. Little stones and dirt tumble down the hillside, and I dig the stick in again and again; from time to time I pour water from the bottle, to soften the soil, I tear up old roots and suddenly I panic, afraid of scorpions, but then I carry on stubbornly, digging with my hands, and doubt creeps into my heart like the dirt getting under my fingernails, how is it possible that you'll find the notebooks you abandoned here a lifetime ago, and even if you find them, and even though you wrapped them in five or six plastic bags and tightened the bags around them with rubber bands—it's almost certain that they will have been completely ruined by the rain and the insects and the rodents, because if the body rots and disintegrates in the ground, how will the words survive?

My hand gropes, and already there's an opening big enough for three fingers, wriggling around to widen the space that has opened up, and in another minute the whole hand is inside, groping blindly between the walls, hitting the floor and ceiling again and again, but the womb is empty, the hand comes up empty. My heart freezes within me, the notebooks aren't there, a stranger has found them without meaning to, twenty years ago or only yesterday, and his eyes have plundered them of that young girl and of the fire flower. The gate is locked, and the flaming sword bars the way.

"Have you lost something?" I turn around in alarm and see a man, or is he an animal, rising from behind the bushes, wild gray hair and beard hiding his face. How long has he been watching me. He comes closer at a swaying ape-like gait, wearing a black turtleneck sweater and over it a long sheepskin coat, and his narrow brown eyes look out at me from the tangle of hair, and his mouth stretchs in a wolfish yellow-toothed smile. Where do I know this man from?

"Yes, I have."

"What have you lost? Love?" His voice is strained, as if he hasn't used it for a long time.

"Yes, and mainly myself."

"Yourself . . ." he repeats after me, scratching his nose with a black nail. Is he mocking me? And suddenly I know who he is, it's Joe the wolf-man, Joe-ten-lira, who used to hang around the plaza of Rothschild House, passing the freaks sitting on the auditorium steps and asking everyone, maybe you got ten lira for me? I used to wonder where he lived. Then his long hair was black, and his beard too. So time hasn't spared him either.

"Come," he whispers with a cunning gleam in his eyes, "I want to show you something."

You follow him, what have you got to lose? He goes up to the suitcase lying next to the mattress, unties the rope, and opens it. Then he takes out one of the swollen plastic bags and hands it to me, "You must be looking for this."

I take the dusty shopping bag with the logo "Rauch Haber-dashery," trying not to betray my eagerness, and when I peep into it the blood leaps in my veins; they're there, all four of them, and they look undamaged, the binder with classical Europe, and the one with Mike Brandt on the cover, and the notebook with the leather binding from England, and the Virginia Woolf notebook. My fingers yearn to touch, my nose to smell, but I restrain myself, now I have all the time in the world.

"When did you find them?"

"Don't know, a long time ago."

"When, a month ago, a year, ten years?"

"Don't know, don't understand time, I was waiting for you."

"Do you know me?" It can't be that he remembers too, that

he recognizes in me the barefoot fifteen-year-old with the long hair, sitting among the freaks on the steps.

"Of course, you're Anne."

"Why do you think that I'm Anne?"

"The letters are to Anne, I kept them for you, I knew you'd come."

"Did you read the letters?" I whisper in alarm.

"It's not nice to read other people's letters," he sends me his ingratiating wolfish smile, and I let it go. What do I care if he read them?

"Maybe you got ten lira?" he suddenly remembers.

"Sure." My hand rummages urgently in my bag, pulls out my purse, and I hand him a note for fifty. Prices have gone up after all.

"Ahh . . ." He hesitates. "I haven't got any change."

"I don't need change." I'd be happy to give you a thousand shekels safekeeping fee, twelve thousand. Twenty thousand.

"Thanks, Anne." The note swallowed up in the pocket of the sheepskin coat, and he pulls out a crumpled Marlboro packet, and offers me one too, with narrowed eyes, "You smoke?"

"No, thanks, and I'm not Anne."

"You're not?" He's disappointed. "Then who are you?"

"I'm the other one, I wrote the letters to Anne."

"And where's Anne?"

"Anne died. A long time ago."

"Pity," he bows his head in sorrow. He's been waiting for her here for years. "So she didn't read your letters?"

"No."

"What did she die of?"

"The Nazis killed her."

"Ah." His look clears. "Where, in the Holocaust and heroism?"

"Yes, in the Holocaust and in heroism."

■

I walk back up the dirt path to Nitzanim Street, the black handles of the plastic bag searing the palm of my hand. In another minute I'll sit on the green bench opposite your house, I'll let my heart stop galloping and slow down and I'll take the notebooks out of the bag. First I'll breathe in the old paper smelling of dank earth and turn the pages urgently, with clumsy fingers, to check if they're all whole. Then I'll open the first notebook, a binder the color of the bench, and here's my handwriting from then, strained blue letters, squashed up against each other, lines rocking up and down at uneven intervals, and in the afternoon light filtering through the canopy of the pines, in the fragrance of the honeysuckle, I'll turn time back, to the beginning.

Monday, Passover week, 4.4.1977

Dearest Anne,

Let me begin. That's how you opened it, on the twentieth of June, forty-two, your diary in the form of letters to Kitty, your imaginary friend, who you took with you into hiding soon afterwards. The diary with the red-and-white checked cloth cover, which you received from your father on your thirteenth birthday, stretched out in front of you like a morning at the beginning of summer, bright and full of promise, with the smell of fresh paper and with endless pages waiting to be filled; here I am, Anne Frank, beginning to write, here I am beginning the exciting adventure that is my life; and you couldn't know that your beginning wouldn't have a continuation, and that it was so close to the end.

And here, thirty-five years later, in a golden-blue spring morning, I too am beginning; our literature and composition teacher, Michaela Berg, who's young and amazing and a fantastic teacher, gave us a Passover holiday assignment to read your diary and to write you a short letter. She promised that whoever

17

wrote the best letter would read it to the whole school at the Holocaust Memorial Day ceremony. The book *Anne Frank: The Diary of a Young Girl* has been lying next to my bed ever since I got it for a bat-mitzvah present, and even though I've already read it three times, I read it again now, and I spent two days working on the letter. I haven't shown it to anyone, but I think it came out quite well, and I'm holding thumbs for Michaela to choose me to read it at the ceremony. (If she says it's any good— I'll copy it for you.)

When I wrote the composition, I discovered that I liked writing to you, to your sharp, delicate face, which couldn't be called "pretty," but which glows with a kind of moonlight; to your smile that's mischievous and a little shy; and to your big slightly protuberant eyes that shine with curiosity and intelligence (in the pictures they look black, but it's hard to tell, because your pictures in the book are black-and-white; perhaps they're dark brown or green). I especially like talking to your brave, stormy soul, "a bundle of contradictions," as you wrote, because I feel the storms and the contradictions inside me too, and mainly the passionate longing for what doesn't yet have a name, which may be nature and may be love and may be God and may be life itself.

I love writing too, and dream of being a writer or a poet one day. When I write a poem I'm filled with a special kind of excitement, a kind of inner warmth and intense concentration, and then nothing can hurt me, sometimes it seems to me that the world is speaking to me in hints, the sea is blinking in Morse code, the wind is whispering secrets to me, nothing is what it seems, everything is actually a sign of some other, hidden thing, and the poems I read, or write, are keys that help to understand these hints, to connect them and decipher them, in order to reveal something true and important to the soul.

When I was little, before I learned to write, I would sit for hours in the wood behind our house and arrange little flowers and pine-nuts and leaves and pine needles on old tiles I found in the storeroom, changing the order again and again, until it seemed the most beautiful and the most right, creating entire worlds for myself. When I was five years old, my mother taught me the alphabet, and since then I like arranging words. Once I still let her read my poems, but about a year ago I stopped. I showed her a poem called "A Red Rose in a City of Ice," which I worked on a lot and I was proud of, and she read it and immediately asked if it was about her, and I wasn't thinking of her at all when I wrote it, or about myself either, I was just writing a poem, and she didn't even say that it was beautiful.

In poems I can't say everything that happens to me and what I think, and since nothing seems real to me until I trap it in a net of words, I've decided to write a diary. (And maybe I'm just deluding myself, because how is it possible to trap the depth of the sky after the rain, the precise color of the evening, the touch of the wind on your skin? Sometimes the holes in my net are too big, and lots of things fall out. . . .) The diary will also give me a chance to practice, a kind of little laboratory where I'll perform experiments, and improve my style.

I know that if you were, let's say, a girl in my class, I would want us very, very much to be friends. I've got one good friend, Racheli Rubin, smart, sensitive, and bit withdrawn, like me. We're both kind of loners, and we don't really care what people think of us. I can tell her *almost* everything, but with you I can be completely frank, and I can be sure you won't tell my secrets to anyone. I try not to think about the fact that you're actually dead, and that if you'd been saved and remained alive, you'd be almost forty-eight, much older than me, even older than my mother, who's forty (but she won't let me tell, because she wants people to think that she's much younger). In your diary you've always remained thirteen to fifteen-and-two-months—exactly my own age. (I'm thirteen and a half. In November I'll be fourteen.)

What I'd like most—now I'm taking a deep breath and saying it—what I'd like most is to be your Kitty, the one for whose eyes and heart you wrote your diary. At the beginning of the year we learned in Michaela's class the poem by Zelda "Each Man Has a Name." The poem begins: "Each man has a name given to him by God and by his father and mother" and it goes on with everyone who gave this person a name: the mountains and the sea, his sins, his blindness, and his longing, his holidays and his work, his enemies and his love, and so on. I don't have love yet, or work, or enemies (I hope), and for the time being I haven't managed to sin a lot, and so I choose to call myself by the name you gave me. And so that you can decide if I'm entitled to it, if I'm worthy of your friendship and your trust, I need to write to you about myself completely honestly, without embellishing or beautifying, as you wrote about yourself, "plain and unadorned."

(I've only just begun, and already I'm flaunting the fancy Hebrew thanks to which I've always been the favorite of literature and composition teachers, and of course you wrote and read in Dutch, and you knew German and a little French and English too.)

So here I stand before you; Rivi Shenhar, student in the eighth grade, living in Haifa on the Carmel, a girl with a lot of faults and a lot of secrets.

First of all, I'm not pretty. When I was small people actually said I was. In the first grade the girls from the top grades would stroke my head in recess and call me Snow White. Menahem, my grandfather's friend, who's an amateur painter, always said that I looked like a little girl in a Renoir painting. When I was six, I sat opposite him for a few Saturdays in my white dress with the sailor collar and my black patent leather shoes, and he painted me in gouache, and when he was finished he gave me the picture as a present and wrote on the back: "To Rivi—a chestnut crown of curly hair, eyes two lakes, open and fair, crimson lips with pearly teeth, a dimple in each apple cheek, from Menahem the painter, who writes terrible rhymes." A year ago Menahem had a stroke, and ever since then he's been paralyzed in half his body and he can't paint, he just sits in a wheelchair in front of the window and smokes his pipe and looks at the sky and the clouds. But the painting is still hanging in my room above my bed. Sometimes I look at it and think sadly how I've lost my looks since then. In the third grade we were playing "The boys on the girls" in the school courtyard, and Avner the bully chased me until I fell on my face and broke my two top front teeth—a big unsymmetrical gap in the middle of my mouth. Ever since then I've gotten used to smiling with my mouth closed. When I laugh I try to cover my mouth with my hand. In the fourth grade I failed in my efforts to hide from the teacher Edna the fact that I couldn't see what she wrote on the blackboard, not even from the front desk. My mother took me to the optician next to her travel agency in Hadar, and together we chose a square plastic frame, blue-gray like the color of my eyes. And so the "open lakes" turned into two framed puddles, and the "pearly teeth" into the entrance to a cave between jagged rocks. My open face turned into a hidden face.

So far the external flaws. In addition I have two inner defects: I only hear in one ear, the right one (in the left one the auditory nerve is damaged, from birth). Racheli has already grown used to sitting or walking on my right, but with strangers I'm ashamed to say anything, and when they're on my left I have to turn my head and make an effort to hear them, and even then I don't always hear, I only pretend to. I've also noticed that when I don't wear my glasses I hear a lot less well. Isn't that funny?

The last defect is attacks of rapid heartbeats, which happens when I have a high fever, or when I get overexcited, and sometimes for no reason. When I was small I took medicine to slow down my heartbeat, but over time I invented breathing exercises for myself, with whose help I succeed in getting the pace back to normal. In any case, the doctors have forbidden me to go to clubs, or parties where the music is too loud (in order not to lose the hearing in my only ear), and I'm not allowed to drink coffee, cola, and hard liquor, or to smoke cigarettes (because alcohol, nicotine, and caffeine make your heart beat faster). It seems I'll have to spend my youth as a total square; drinking carrot juice (to improve my eyesight) and reading books. I don't really care, I've been a certified bookworm from the age of five. When I was small, my father used to check out books for me at the Borohov Library in Hadar (apparently he still cared about me then) and since then I've devoured the primary school library and another two libraries in the Carmel Center (the old one in Keller Street and the new one in Hanasi Avenue). Sometimes I imagine that I've gone to live in the library in Hanasi Avenue, which is beautiful and spacious, and flooded with a pleasant light in the afternoon, as if it's shining out of the books. I could sleep on three chairs pushed together, or clear the broad lower shelf of the encyclopedias and dictionaries, and fix myself a bed on it. There's even a little fridge in the library, and quite decent toilets too. You'll laugh, but whenever I'm looking for a book I have to take a crap. Once, as soon as I found the book I was looking for (*Three Men in a Boat*, by Jerome K. Jerome), I couldn't keep it in and I snatched the book from the shelf and took it with me to the toilet. I started reading and apparently I become so absorbed that I laughed out loud without realizing it, because when I came out I bumped straight into Tirza, the strict old librarian, who was waiting for me outside the door. She barked at me and threatened that if it happened again she would cancel my subscription. I wanted to tell her that compared to all the kids who scribbled in the books and wrote dirty words and tore out pages in the most exciting parts, what I did was really not so terrible, maximum a bit of a smell, but I knew that cheek was the last thing I needed in this situation. (You see, I really am telling you everything. . . .) If I lived in the library I could read all night long, including the books in the not-for-your-age section. Tirza never lets me take out books from that highly desirable section, but with Hava, the young librarian who looks like a half-blind mole, I'm bold enough to lie that they're for my mother, and she writes them on my card and doesn't say anything. This way I got to read *The Arrangement* and *The Exorcist* and *Fear of Flying*, which have quite provocative passages. But unfortunately I don't live in the library, but in our house in George Eliot Street, named after the English woman writer who chose a male pseudonym.

Our house is at the bottom of a steep hill, opposite the primary school I went to until two years ago, on the corner of Yafeh Nof Street, which was once called Panorama Street. From the big windows of our living room you can see the whole of the bay, the ships anchored in the harbor and the smoke stacks of the oil refineries.

I live with my mother Carmela, and my two little brothers, Oren and Noam. My father Yehuda, who teaches political science at the university, doesn't live with us anymore. They got divorced a year ago, when I was in seventh grade. My grandfather, Emanuel, lives one floor below us, and sometimes I go down to visit him in the afternoon. He makes us tea with biscuits, and tells me about his mother, who was the most beautiful girl in Petah Tikva, and about his childhood in Haifa in the days of the Turks, and in Alexandria during the first world war, and about the Reali High School, where he studied in one of the first years of its existence, and about Grandma Rivka, who was "an exceptional personality, beautiful and clever and independent." Grandma worked as a teacher in the Leo Baeck school, and she was my mother's teacher from first to fourth grade (Mother told me once that she had to call her "teacher" like all the other children, and that it was very hard on her). She died in Grandpa's arms of breast cancer, at the age of fifty-five, a year before I was born, and she left me her name, which I hate, and the fear of her disease. I know that Mother is afraid too—once I caught feeling her breast in front of the bathroom mirror—and maybe that's why she never mentions her mother, and also I guess because she misses her, and the memories are painful for her. Once a year, two weeks before Purim, she lights a memorial candle in front of Grandma's picture on top of the television, and she and Grandpa go down to the cemetery and meet Aunt Tehiya, Grandma's younger sister, and Amos and Nathan, their big brothers, and after the memorial service they all come up to our place for coffee and cake, but even then they don't talk about her, but about their children and grandchildren and their trips abroad, and once, when I asked to go down with them and see the grave, Mother said dryly, "There's nothing to see, it's just a stone."

I like listening to Grandpa, even though his voice is hoarse and his Hebrew flowery, and sometimes he throws in words in Yiddish or Arabic, which I don't understand and he has to translate for me; even though he doesn't really talk to me, mainly he enjoys listening to himself. After tea he puts on his jacket and one of his fancy caps—he has a collection of caps to match his jackets, checked wool for winter and pale cotton for summer, to protect his bald head from the rain and the sun—and goes to visit his girlfriend Bracha, who Mother says is vulgar, but in my opinion she's actually nice and full of life. Bracha has been divorced twice and widowed once, and Mother won't let Grandpa marry her, maybe because she's afraid that Bracha will want to even up the number of her widowhoods to the number of her divorces, and maybe because she thinks it's a betrayal of Grandma Rivka.

Grandpa lets me stay in his apartment, and I walk around the rooms, open the bar in the sideboard and breathe in the smell of the whiskey and the cognac and the liqueurs and the smell of the wood, and sometimes I pour myself a drink of cherry brandy in a little crystal glass and take small sips, and my face grows hot and life suddenly seems glamorous. In the study I look at the albums and sniff the old books, and sometimes I leaf through a volume of the *Hebrew Encyclopedia* and read all kinds of entries, and in the bathroom I like sniffing his shaving brush and the blue bottle of aftershave. It's only the smell of the bedroom that I can't stand, unaired bed linen, medicines and old age.

Grandpa owns a travel agency in Hadar, which started off

in the fifties as an internal tourism agency that organized holidays in convalescent homes for Holocaust survivors, paid for by the government. But in recent years, ever since Mother started working with him, the office has expanded and organizes overseas trips, mainly to Europe, for survivors and even for ordinary people. The travel agents are on the first floor, next to the entrance, with glossy-colored posters on the walls behind them of windmills and sunlit fields and snowy mountain peaks. Grandpa's and Mother's office is on the second floor, and in the room next to it are iron cabinets with big cardboard files, black and white, with the names and addresses of the clients on their backs. Between the cabinets is a door leading to a little storeroom with a broken-down photocopying machine, a vacuum cleaner, a pail and broom, and piles of dusty brochures advertising tours that were over long ago. After reading your diary, I thought that in an emergency, this storeroom could serve as a hiding place, with the door hidden by one of the filing cabinets.

In the meantime, until I buy a special notebook with a lock, like your diary, I've started to write to you on the backs of the papers that Mother brings from the office, describing the various tours, "Classical Europe in Twenty-One Days," "The United States from Coast to Coast," "From the Canals of Venice to the Lights of Paris" and so on. Mother and Grandpa travel quite a bit, but I've never been abroad. I read the descriptions of the tours, and imagine myself riding on a red double-decker bus in the gray, foggy streets of London, feeding the traditional pigeons in Saint Mark's Square in Venice (that's what it says. Do you think that they wear little skullcaps on their heads?), or visiting a Dutch windmill. In the "Classical Europe" tour, one of the mornings in Amsterdam is devoted to visiting your hiding place, and after that they have free time for shopping.

It's getting late and I'm tired, I'll go on tomorrow.

Yours, your old-new friend, Kitty

P.S. Perhaps I'm lying to myself, and deep down I hope that someone will find this diary, and read it and see how intelligent and sensitive I am?

Tuesday, 4.5.77

Dearest Anne,

I want to tell you about our first meeting: I received your diary as a bat-mitzvah present, I don't even know who from—when I opened the wrapping paper there was no card inside it. It must have fallen out, or else they forgot to put it in, but I like to think that the book somehow arrived on its own, a present from you.

Actually I haven't told you about my bat-mitzvah party, which was a year and a half ago. When I think about the stuffy affair my parents organized for me it seems to me that I wasn't there at all, it was some other girl, whom I observe from a distance, trying to find early signs of their divorce, less than three months after that Saturday:

The girl stands in the garden of the house and receives the guests. Her parents have organized a big reception in the back garden—at lunchtime for the extended family, in the evening for their friends. The buffet is spread on long trestle tables hidden under white sheets. Plastic chairs and tables are dotted around among the pines. Chains of colored lights hang from the branches. Waiters in black and white circulate among the guests, carrying trays of little sandwiches, bits of pickled herring on toothpicks, burekas and sausages. It's very hot outside, on the radio it said ninety degrees, and her mother wails, who would have thought we'd have a khamsin like this at the beginning of November? She asks the waiters to cover the salads on the buffet—the flies are already circling above them, landing on the edges of the bowls and rubbing their forelegs in anticipation of the picnic—and gloomily predicts that the Waldorf salad and the egg salad will spoil, because mayonnaise doesn't keep long in the heat.

The girl is wearing a mauve maxi skirt with a pattern of little flowers, and a blue knit blouse with wide, drooping sleeves. These garments were bought a few days ago at the "Maskit" handicrafts shop, as a compromise after quarrels and tears—her mother wanted her to wear a dress, and she wanted to wear jeans, and in the end they agreed on something that neither of them liked. It's very hot in the knit blouse, which sticks to her body and reveals the bumps of her budding breasts. (When she feels them they hurt, and she's been afraid for some time now that she has cancer. She knows that every day could be her last; every book she reads, every movie and every swim in the sea. And this bat-mitzvah too is her last birthday. At night before she goes to bed she opens the window and prays to the black sky, if you don't let me be sick I'll believe in you as long as I live and I'll even become an Orthodox Jew. And only the year after, when she turns thirteen, she'll feel that she can't keep the secret imprisoned inside her any longer, and will burst into terrible tears and tell her mother, and her mother will take her to her gynecologist, and the elderly bespectacled doctor with the white hair and the powerful smell of aftershave, will touch her chest with long, delicate fingers, and reassure her that they are only growing pains, little girls of her age never get breast cancer, and she'll know that she has received her life as a gift, and on the bus home she'll remind herself to thank God before she goes to bed, but in the end she falls asleep and forgets.)

Around her neck is an enamel pendant of a bird in a burgundy color that she got from her mother for her last birthday. She's wearing glasses with blue-gray frames, the color of her eyes. Her hair is combed in two bunches, but with a side parting, so that the bunch on the right is too fat, and the one on the left too thin. Her grandfather, in a cream-colored safari suit and shoes with holes punched in them, his bald head covered with a summery cap and his complexion ruddy, films her with a "Super 8" movie camera. No photographs were taken of the party, only that movie, which the next day they watched once, and after that it got lost among the movies her grandfather took on his trips abroad. And nevertheless that day will flicker in her memory without sound, and in the unreal colors of a home movie.

The girl smiles at the guests with her mouth closed, and receives the gifts with shy pleasure, and she is surprised at the size of the affair, at the exaggerated efforts invested by her parents. She doesn't know yet that in three months time her childhood will be felled. She kisses the wet cheek of Grandma Pnina, her father's mother, who has beads of sweat hanging from the red lipstick slipping off her lips, because she climbed from Hadar to the Carmel on foot, to save the bus fare. The girl refuses to take the damp crumpled envelope her grandmother thrusts into her hand, and she mumbles, give it to Daddy, he's collecting them. (In the movie you can't hear the words, but the girl can lip-read, and she remembers every detail too.)

Grandma Pnina explains that Grandpa Ya'akov didn't come with her because he isn't well, and she was afraid the heat would be bad for him. (He had to have his legs amputated as a result of an accident when he was working as a building worker, and ever since then he's been in a wheelchair.) Then she drags her heavy body to the table where her son Itzik is sitting with his wife Sima. Itzik, who is a traffic cop, is the girl's only uncle, because her mother has no brothers or sisters.

Later on, one after the other, two gray-haired stalwarts drive up in their big pickup trucks, Amos and Nathan, Grandma Rivka's brothers. Each of them is carrying, in addition to the bag with the gift, a wooden crate full of Valencia oranges from their citrus grove in Rehovoth, and the girl knows that however many of these oranges they eat and squeeze for juice, most of them will shrivel up and rot all winter long at the bottom of the fridge, sprouting white and green patches of mold, and in the end they'll be thrown into the trash. And here comes the lemon-colored Beetle belonging to Aunt Tehiya, who lives in Ramat-Gan in a house with a huge garden, surrounded by flower beds and fruit trees. When the girl was small and her parents went abroad, she spent her holidays with her, a wild child who climbed all the trees and read all the books left by Aunt Tehiya's children, who had grown up and left home. They sailed together on the Yarkon river—Aunt Tehiya rowed the boat with her strong arms—and visited the Planetarium and the zoo in Tel Aviv and the wax museum in the Shalom Towers and went to matinees at the Oasis cinema, including movies for grown-ups, and Aunt Tehiya let her sleep with her in her bed, in the place left empty by Uncle Moshe, who died years ago of a heart attack.

"Well, Monkey, have you got your period yet?" Aunt Tehiya asks soundlessly without moving her lips, sticking her elbow into the girl's arm, and she smiles at the beloved face, brown and lined from working in the garden, and says, "Not yet, what do I need it for, I have time."

Grandma Pnina gets up heavily and goes to greet the relations from Rehovoth and Ramat-Gan, who were born in the country, true "sabras" who spoke Hebrew without an accent, and none of whose family had perished "over there;" thirteen years ago when Yudeleh, her clever son, met the delicate blond Carmela Lipkin from Panorama Street at the university and married her—they had become her family. She too has not yet guessed that in two months time Yudeleh will come back to her with one suitcase, and that whole marriage will seem to her one big mistake.

The girl's mother, who is considered one of the most beautiful women on the Carmel, is laughing with her cousins. In a short purple dress with a slit up the side, she crosses her pale, slender legs and holds a cigarette between the red spots of her nails, which look to the girl like pieces of petals torn off a rose. Her father is wearing black trousers and a snow white shirt like the waiters, and sandals, and one of the arms of his glasses—whose thick lenses shrink his eyes into two blue pinheads—is broken and stuck together with scotch-tape. He is standing behind the bar and serving the guests, pretending to enjoy the role of barman, which he undertook for reasons of economy.

29

Does he still not know that this winter he will have to leave his home and his children and return to his parents' home in Hadar with one suitcase?

Her two little brothers, fair-haired like their mother—Oren's curly and Noam's straw that gets into his eyes—are playing soccer with Uncle Itzik's sons. The pine trunks are their goalposts. They too, of course, don't guess that their sister's bat-mitzvah is nothing but a grandiose and hypocritical farewell party to thirteen years of marriage.

In the early evening a stray breeze from the sea finds its way into the garden, and the heat lets up a bit. The colored lights are lit, the pine needles flare up in red, yellow and blue, and the little wood behind their house is transformed into a fairy forest. Two loudspeakers tied to the trees like megaphones at a Scouts camp, spray out hoarse music, and her parents and their friends dance on the paved terrace, waltzes and tangos and rumbas, and to the crooning of Sinatra and Elvis, also cheek-to-cheek slow-steps. Areleh, her father's friend from the "Alliance" school, who always talks to her with his face too close to hers, unconscious of his bad breath, and likes running his finger down her back, to see if she's already wearing (she's not!) a bra, invites her to dance, and she says "No thank you, perhaps later on."

She watches her mother and father dancing, and something in the picture doesn't seem right. Her father is looking at his big feet, careful not to tread on her mother's toes in her pointed shoes. The inside of her wrist touches his waist, a cigarette between her fingers, and her eyes above his shoulder are dry and empty. The girl breathes in the sounds and the lights and the warm scented air, and says to herself that she must feel and remember everything, this is her evening after all, a unique, special evening that will never return.

When she realizes that nobody is paying any attention to her, she goes up to the house.

On the carpet of her room she opens the presents that have been heaped up there since the afternoon, impatiently tearing off the flowered wrapping paper, disappointed to discover boxes of jewelry and letter paper and photo albums of Jerusalem and Masada and the Yom Kippur War and archaeological discoveries in Sinai, and she continues frantically searching for one thing that will please her. And here it is—a book titled *Young Poetry: An Anthology*—with a coffee-colored cover and little black-and-white photographs of the poets, mostly men, and among them four or five women too. For a moment she feels surprised, the book seems to her too modest, too cheap for a bat-mitzvah present, and she opens it and reads the inscription from Tamar, her mother's friend from the Reali school, whose straight black hair frames her long white-powdered face and her green-gray eyes, outlined in black; who always wears a dark purple velvet top, and smokes a lot, and speaks high-flown Hebrew in a hoarse breathy voice; and who once told the girl that she writes poetry herself, and two or three of her poems were published in literary supplements. Tamar is bringing up alone the son born to her out of wedlock, and the girl's mother says that she's a beatnik and weird, and she hardly ever invites her over on Friday nights with the other couples—who drink alcohol, eat olives and peanuts, and squares of cheese on matchsticks, as well as quiches and cheese blintzes and two kinds of cake, and on Saturday mornings she and her brothers raid the fridge and polish off the leftovers—but she herself thinks that Tamar is interesting, not like their other friends, who spend most of their time talking about trips abroad, their own and mainly other people's.

And she opens the book and holds it up to her nose, and then she reads the first poem, "Delight" by Dalia Ravikovitch:

There I knew a delight beyond delight,
and that was the Sabbath day
when all the branches reached up to the light.

Like a bubbling river, the light streamed everywhere,
and the wheel of the eye desired the wheel of the sun.
Then I knew a delight beyond delight. . . .

31

And she trembles inside with the joy of the meeting between shadow and light and between cold and heat, because the delight is red and hot, and the boughs of the trees are green and cool, and the light is yellow and hot, and the river is green-gray like Tamar's eyes, and the sun is orange, and everything flows and washes and rolls, everything is in motion, the light turns the cold shady green into a river of liquid copper, and yellow water lilies devour the ripples hurrying by and the floating blade of grass, because when you feel such delight the light triumphs over the shade, and the heat triumphs over the cold, and you have to move and you have to devour, and even your head can turn into a Valencia orange.

And in the end she opens the last present, which has no note attached to it, and discovers the black cover of *Anne Frank: The Diary of a Young Girl.*

And ever since then your diary and the *Young Poetry* anthology have been on my bedside table, and I read them almost every night before I go to sleep.

Yours, Kitty

P.S. Do you think they decided to throw that grandiose bat-mitzvah party for me out of a guilty conscience?

Wednesday, 4.6.77

Dearest Anne,

This is how it happened: one night two months after the bat-mitzvah I woke up and heard them talking in quiet voices in the living room. My mom asked, and what will happen to the children, and my dad, like he always did, said to her, whatever you want. I remember that I got up and closed the door and went back to bed and pulled the covers over my head and shut my eyes tight so as not to hear. In complete silence my life smashed to smithereens, like the silent movie of the bat-mitzvah, in silence and also in slow motion, because after that conversation nothing happened, just ordinary days of school and work, and I told myself that they'd changed their minds, but today I realize that all the time there were little signs that I didn't want to see. For instance, the Italian course that Mom began attending at Rothschild House, twice a week, three hours at a time. She said that it was important for a travel agent to know languages, and she liked Italian in particular, because it was such a melodious language, but when she opened the book at home to prepare her homework, she would repeat the days of the week over and over again, until I too knew them off by heart: domenica, lunedi, martedi, mercoledi. . . . I asked her how come that was all they'd learned in a whole month, and she smiled a little smile to herself and said that it was always best to do things slowly but thoroughly. One evening the doorbell rang, and it was a delivery boy with a bunch of blood-red roses. On the note it said only "To Carmela Shenhar" without any signature. I asked her who had sent the flowers, and she said, "I have no idea, maybe some client of the agency." Dad raised his head from the paper and muttered, "I suppose they're from your lover," and Mother laughed too loudly and said, "Who would want an old rag like me." A few days later she bought herself an easel, canvases, and oil paints, and started painting on the laundry porch. Over her clothes she wore an old gray smock, which was immediately covered with paint stains, and around her head she tied a bright silk scarf, like the woman painter we once saw in a French movie. The laundry porch stank of paint and turpentine, and the smell permeated our clothes as well. Mother painted red and yellow blotches on a turquoise-gray background. Every few minutes she lit a cigarette and stepped back from the painting, and surveyed it through the smoke. I told her that the painting looked like a river with whirlpools and water lilies, and that she could call it "Delight," but she said that it was an abstract painting. She painted two canvases like that, like two identical twins, and then she grew bored. She put the easel and the paints away in the broom cupboard on the porch, and decided to register for a course on transcendental (what a long word) meditation, and persuaded me to go with her. For a few weeks we took the bus to Neve-Sha'anan every Tuesday evening. There we sat in circle in some apartment with another eight or ten people, closed our eyes opposite a picture of the smiling Maharishi with his white beard and long hair surrounding his bald pate and the fly in the middle of his forehead, and kept quiet. I don't know why she dragged me to that course and not, for example, to a psychologist, where you can talk and not just keep quiet (Mother doesn't believe in psychologists, she says they're all disturbed and full of complexes themselves); perhaps she wanted to bring me closer to her, so I wouldn't be angry with her, so I'd be on her side. Perhaps she thought that the meditation would help me to relax in the difficult period ahead. At the end of the course there was a ceremony—each of us went into a room smelling of incense, knelt down in front of a picture of the Maharishi—who went on smiling that smile of his, content with life and with himself, not caring about anything or anybody, because he had already reached Nirvana a long time ago—and sacrificed flowers and sweet fruits that we'd brought from home to him, dates and bananas wrapped in a white handkerchief; and the teacher whispered each of our secret personal mantras to us. I felt like laughing, but I controlled myself, and I swore to the picture of the Maharishi never to disclose my mantra to anyone.

The day after the ceremony, Wednesday, when I went to school, I told Yael Brosh, my best friend since fourth grade. She'd done the course a few weeks before, with her mother, who's a beautician and all the women on the Carmel go to her. I suggested to Yael that I would tell her and only her my secret mantra, and she would tell me hers. She was silent for a moment, and then she said that she was sorry, but she couldn't. She couldn't be my friend anymore.

"But why?" I demanded in dismay.

"I can't tell you." Her face, where I could always read what she was thinking, was now sealed.

"Is it because of the mantra? Because of the meditation? Are you angry because I went to meditation too?"

"No, it's not because of the meditation," she said patiently, and for a moment I thought she was taking pity on me, "and it's not because of you either."

"So what is it then," I pleaded.

"It's because of your mother. My mother won't let me talk to you because of your mother."

"But why, what's my mother done?" My beautiful, perfect mother. It had to be a mistake.

"I'm not allowed to tell you, and don't ever ask me again," Yael decreed and walked away.

I didn't ask again. We didn't become friends again. I didn't dare ask Mother either, but I sensed that it was somehow connected to the Italian lessons and the mystery of the bunch of roses.

On Saturday, on Arbor Day, Dad took Oren and Noam, who were then seven and five, to play soccer on the school playing field, and I stayed at home to help Mother fix lunch. She was standing next to the sink, peeling zuchinnis, and leaning her blond curls against the pale yellow Formica doors of the dish-drying rack, as if unless she supported it her head would fall into the sink together with the vegetable peels. I stood next to her. The pine branches beat against the narrow window above the sink and the wind whistled. The wind always whistles like a kettle in winter, and sometimes it howls like jackals. Quietly, in her driest voice, Mother said the words, and I, after beginning to hope that they'd changed their minds since that night when I overheard them talking, asked if it was final.

"Yes, I think so," she replied with her eyes on her hands that went on peeling the zucchini.

I asked her which of them wanted the divorce, even though in my heart I knew. Mother kept quiet for a moment and then she said, "Both of us." And she added, "That's the way it is, sometimes people who live together don't get on." I wanted to tell her that she was lying, to remind her of the roses, but I didn't dare. I asked her where we would live. She said, "You children will stay here with me."

In the end I said, "If you don't love Daddy, why did you marry him in the first place."

She thought for quite a long time, and then she said, "Your father is a good man, but people change."

I went to their bedroom and closed the door. I lay down on the bed and covered myself with the down quilt, I was shivering all over. I curled up like a fetus, with my hands between my thighs, to warm up, and I thought that all my practicing since I read *Lottie and Lisa* and imagined that they were getting divorced and I had to decide which of them I wanted to live with—hadn't helped, because nobody even asked me. I tried to connect the signs, which previously I hadn't really wanted to understand, and I knew that it had been hanging over us all the time, because the air between them had always been as brittle as glass.

After some time Daddy came in. I prayed in my heart that he would sit down beside me, but he walked around the room with his hands in his pockets. I asked him if it was true. He said, "Yes, but you don't have to worry, I'll always be your father, I'll come and visit you and invite you to come to me."

Mother called us to come and eat. I said I wasn't hungry, and shut myself in my room. I hid in my bed and cried all day long, depths within depths within depths until rock bottom, until there were no tears left in me. Late in the evening I came out. Daddy wasn't there and Oren and Noam were sleeping. Mother was sitting alone in the living room, smoking a cigarette and staring at the television. I sat down to watch a program of songs for Arbor Day with her, and after that an episode of "McMillan and Wife." McMillan and his wife got on my nerves, because they looked so much in love, and I knew that they would never get divorced.

On the following nights Daddy slept on the living-room sofa. In the evenings he would go out, and I would wait for him, trying not to fall asleep, until I heard the grating of the key in the lock. One day, when I came home from school, I saw that his underwear drawer was open and empty. I remember feeling relief. Mother was lying in bed with her eyes closed and a wet towel on her forehead. Nothing was said. As if nothing had happened.

A few days later Mother went on a trip to Italy for a week, and Grandpa moved in to sleep at our place. I asked her who she was going with, and she said that she was going alone, on business. I'm sure she went with the-bunch-of-blood-colored-roses, whom she may have met in the Italian lessons and he promised her a trip to Italy as a gift in honor of the divorce. I told her it was a good thing she'd learned a little Italian, and the Italians would be pleased that she knew how to say all the days of the week in their language, and she looked at me intently for a minute and said, don't be cheeky.

Daddy went to live with Granny and Grandpa in Hadar, and for a few weeks we didn't see him. After that he began coming to visit, but usually he doesn't come up, he stands under the window of Oren and Noam's room and calls them. They go down and he takes them to play soccer on the school field. He never calls me. Maybe he thinks that I don't like football (actually I do. I don't like volleyball, because I'm afraid the ball will hit my glasses and break them). Sometimes he stays in the yard, and they help him to wash his Susita with the garden hose, and then Mother sticks her head out of the window and yells, as if she's talking to me, "Your father thinks I should pay for him to wash his rattletrap, but he never remembers to deposit the check in time." I don't know if Daddy can hear her yelling, because he, like me, is deaf in one ear, and only hears what he wants to hear.

Only rarely, when it rains, he comes upstairs. At first he would open the unlocked door without ringing the bell, as if it was still his home, until Mother grew angry and changed the handle. Now you can't open it from the outside, and he has to knock. Sometimes I let him in and he mumbles a greeting and looks at the floor, and goes straight to Oren and Noam's room and they play dominoes or chess. I know how to play chess, he taught me when I was four, but he doesn't play with me, and he never comes into my room, or asks me anything. When he calls, and I happen to answer the phone, he says right away, "Give me your brother." I call Oren, and every time a salty wave rises in my throat.

A few months after the divorce he turned up suddenly on Saturday morning and took the three of us for a sail on a big boat from Haifa to Acre. There were a lot of people on the boat, including Batya, a youngish woman of thirty something, with thin auburn hair and a pale face and sunglasses. She's the secretary of his political science department. Batya tried to be nice to me, and she asked me about school and Scouts and about my friends. I answered her politely, but I didn't feel like smiling at her. When we reached Acre we went to eat at a restaurant, and Daddy ordered hummus and salads and *shishlik*, whatever we asked for, maybe so Batya would be impressed by his generosity. On the way back he stood by himself in the stern, leaning his hands on the rail. I went to stand next to him, in the hope that he would say something to me or ask me something, but he didn't ask me anything, he just looked at the two lines of foam trailing in the wake of the boat, and I didn't know if he was smiling to himself, or just narrowing his eyes against the glare. A month later he married Batya, and he didn't invite us to the wedding. I suppose he wanted to save on three helpings of food. Now they live together in her apartment in Hadar, not far from Granny and Grandpa, and Oren and Noam go to visit them sometimes, but he never takes me. Granny and Grandpa have divorced me too, they never come up to the Carmel anymore, and I haven't seen Uncle Itzik and Sima and their children since the bat-mitzvah, so that I've lost half my family, like the people who came from the Holocaust, and I only have my mother's family.

Maybe Daddy thinks that I blame him for the divorce, and that I'm on her side. Once I heard her telling her friend Ruth, "Rivi doesn't care about him at all, she doesn't even say hello to him," and there was pride in her voice, as if she'd won some contest, and I wanted to burst into the living room and tell her that he was the one who should have talked to me and taken me to his place, even by force, like when I was small and trailed behind him in the street, because his legs are long and he takes big fast steps, and he lost patience and grabbed hold of my arm with steel fingers, and lifted me and dragged me behind him, and my legs hovered helplessly over the pavement, and afterwards I discovered red and purple marks above my elbow.

Sometimes I want to remind him of our conversation the Saturday before the divorce, and his promise that he would always be my father. I want to remind him that I'm his firstborn child, his only daughter, and how proud he was of my poems that were published in the children's supplement of the newspaper, which he himself had typed on the green typewriter and put into an envelope and licked the stamp and sent off, and how he had bragged about my poem about the war that was published in the book *Children Write and Draw the War of Judgment Day*. Daddy and I traveled to Jerusalem together, to the meeting of the children whose poems and drawings had appeared in the book, and we met the Minister of Education and Culture, and Daddy said to him, let me introduce my daughter, one day she'll be a poet like Rachel, and I was chosen out of everybody to read my poem into the microphone, and it was even broadcast on the radio, but I don't know how he'll react if I remind him, because he's probably forgotten everything.

Not long ago I saw a science fiction movie on the television, about somebody who had all his insides removed and he was left with only the shell, the body, and he turned into a robot in the form of a man, an android. Sometimes I think that this is what happened to him as well; they opened him up and removed the father I once had—who carried me on his shoulders and taught me to swim and helped me with my homework and sang funny songs to my girlfriends (when Yael Brosh still came to play with me he would sing to her "On Top of the *Brosh* [cypress tree] in the Yard" and to Mother he would sing, "There's a gorgeous girl in Haifa, she lives in a street called Panorama")—and left only a hollow body. Like the wax figures in the museum in the Shalom Tower in Tel Aviv, that look almost real, and sometimes they speak too, like Ben Gurion who reads the Declaration of Independence, and Gideon Hausner, the frightening prosecutor in the Eichmann trial, who points at the glass cage and says in a shrill, trembling voice, that in the place where he stands six million accusers stand. Sometimes I think that it would be better if he were dead, preferably in some war. At least with a dead father you can love him, you can miss him, but how can you miss a father that you see at least once a week, and he never sees you?

At school I didn't tell anyone about the divorce. There aren't any other kids in our class whose parents are divorced. In the parallel class there's one boy, Avshalom, whose father was killed in the Yom Kippur War, and ever since then he's half an orphan and his mother's a widow. Every year, on Memorial Day, he reads "Here Our Bodies Lie" and the teachers shed a tear. I don't know if I didn't say anything because I was ashamed, or because I didn't want them to feel sorry for me. I'm sure they all know anyway. Because most of the mothers, and the teachers too, are clients of Malka Brosh, who always hears all the gossip, and takes care to pass it on while she removes the blackheads from their faces. I've started working at school, and I've become a really good student, because I didn't want the teachers to think I was going downhill because I'm a child from a broken home. Towards the end of seventh grade I made friends with Racheli, and one Saturday, when we went to the beach together, I told her. I asked her not to tell anyone, not even her parents, because I was afraid they'd tell her to break off relations with me. Racheli told me in confidence that her mother had once been married and divorced, and Nurit, her elder sister, was actually the daughter of her mother and another father. I was glad to discover that we're not the only family with complications.

I don't know if I'm allowed to feel this, but sometimes I really envy you because of your bond with your father, Otto, who you nicknamed Pim, who loved you and cared about what happened to you, and who you could always talk to about everything.

It's already late, I'll go on tomorrow.
Good night, Kitty

Friday, 4.8.77

Dearest Anne,

Since they got divorced I've tried to help my mother as much as I can, because I can see how hard it is for her; in the morning she makes us sandwiches and takes Oren and Noam to school, and then she goes to work, and comes home at half past three. She has something to eat and lies down to rest. At five o'clock she has coffee, and then she goes out to do the shopping and prepares lunch for the next day, cuts out patterns from *Burda* and sews herself clothes on the electric sewing machine, hangs out the laundry, takes down the laundry, folds the laundry, irons, and rearranges the closets, changing winter clothes for summer clothes.

My main task is to heat up lunch for Noam and Oren, lay the table, and afterwards clear the table and wash the dishes. Ever since Mother started working at Grandpa's office, when I was three, we had a maid who cleaned and cooked and looked after Noam and Oren. Her name was Annette, and she was dark and beautiful, with a black light shining from her face. After lunch we would sit together on the porch, she would tell me about her city of Casablanca, and her husband, who she married when she was sixteen, and her ten children at home on the small-holders farm, and I would smell the detergent mixed with her sweat. Sometimes Daddy would come home to have lunch with us. Annette called him Monsieur Shenhar, and they spoke to each other in French, which she knew from Casablanca and he knew from the "Alliance" school. Even though I didn't understand a word, I loved listening to the sound of the language, like the fresh smell of lemons. Mother didn't say anything, but I could see that it annoyed her not to understand. A few weeks after the divorce she quarreled with Annette, and yelled at her for never cleaning the skirting tiles, and after working for us for ten years, she dismissed her as if she were thin air. Today I think that the skirting tiles were only an excuse, and that Mother gave Annette the sack because she knew all kinds of secrets about her. After Annette we had a few other maids, but none of them lasted more than a month. The three of us drove them crazy, like Jane and Michael in the movie *Mary Poppins*; we refused to eat what they cooked, because we only liked Annette's rissoles and chips, and we would hide their clothes and shoes. After the fourth maid we decided that Mother would cook and I would heat up the lunch, and the maid would only come once a week to clean. I regret it a bit, because sometimes I feel like going to Racheli's after school, and I don't go because I know that Noam and Oren are waiting for me at home, hungry.

In the evening Mother makes us omelets and salad, and washes the dishes. Sometimes she has to help Oren with his homework, which he never remembers to do. And then she sees that Oren and Noam get their schoolbags ready, and shower, and she makes their beds. Even when she watches television her beautiful hands, which are smaller than mine, are busy knitting or mending clothes, sewing on a school badge, or a button, or fixing a hem. Her hands are always in motion. Even when they're resting, she has a cigarette between her fingers.

I would like to know how to do things with my hands, like her, but I have two left hands. In a whole year of handicraft lessons I succeeded in sewing one apron, of green material, with a purple zig-zag ribbon around the edges, which came out quite crooked, and two cherries embroidered in chain stitch, above which I embroidered "To Mother, your ever-loving daughter, Rivi." She actually wears the apron sometimes, but I know that she's disappointed in me. She would have liked a daughter who was more like her, like the little sister she always dreamed of having, who she could talk to about clothes and shoes and her favorite television series, like "Upstairs Downstairs," "The Pallisers," and "The Onedin Line." Instead she got someone who was too serious, slow, always with her nose in a book, dreaming, writing poetry, always dropping things. "Butterfingers" she sometimes calls me. She complains that I don't lift a finger to help her in the house, and that I shut myself up in my room too much and I'm not sociable. It's true that I shut myself off from her, hiding from her X-ray eyes that know everything, judge everything, see right inside me. Sometimes I'm not even sure that she loves me. Once, when I was small, I was afraid that she was putting poison into my food or my chocolate milk, and after I ate and drank and nothing happened to me, I was ashamed of being so bad and so ungrateful to her.

Mother doesn't get on too well with Oren either; he's quite a disturbed child, he doesn't like school, he hangs around with a gang of little toughs from the neighborhood and steals candy from the supermarket with them; when he's at home he's mean to Noam, the apple of her eye. She's always hugging and kissing Noam and calling him "my baby" even though he's almost seven, and dragging him with her wherever she goes. When Oren bothers him Noam wails and Mother runs after Oren with a belt in her hand, or she throws shoes at him and yells, "You'll be the death of me." Sometimes she locks him in the bathroom, to calm down, and he screams and kicks the door, until she lets him out. With all the noise and pandemonium the three of them create, the house turns into a lunatic asylum, and then I have to shut myself into my own quiet little haven, to read or write or just to dream. Sometimes I brim over with all the things whirling around in my head, and the blood begins racing through my veins at top speed, as if it's trying to catch up with my thoughts, and then I have to daydream for hours at a time, with my eyes shut tight, or open wide, and I reconstruct things that have happened to me and imagine what I would like to happen, like a movie that I screen to myself over and over again, until everything soaks into my body. When Mother opens the door (lately she's learned to knock, at least) and finds me lying in bed and staring at the ceiling, she asks, what are you doing? And I say, "Can't you see? I'm growing up."

On Saturday mornings Mother gives herself "beauty treatments;" she plucks the hairs from her legs with strips of white cloth smeared with red wax, soaks her feet in a basin of lukewarm water and chalk stone, and scrapes the hard skin off her heels with a special instrument, files her fingernails and toenails, and paints them with a dark red nail polish, whose smell pervades the house (she doesn't really tear up rose petals and stick them to her nails, like I thought when I was small), and she shampoos her hair and rolls it around pink rollers. Ever since Malka Brosh broke off relations with her, she applies her own "masks"—she smears some green stuff onto her face and walks around with it for hours. It isn't enough for her to be one of the most beautiful women on the Carmel. I think she goes to all this trouble to look her best for her mysterious boyfriend. Almost every evening, except for Friday and Saturday, as if she's under some spell, she goes down to the white car waiting for her opposite the house like a whale in the dark, and disappears into the silhouette of the man whose name she refuses to disclose. One day, after all three of us nagged her, she said angrily, "What difference does it make to you what his name is, let's say his name's Moishele."

Every morning, at exactly half past seven, his suave voice smelling of aftershave comes over the phone, "May I speak to Carmela?"

"Just one moment please," I answer politely, and call, "Mother, Moishele's on the phone."

She speaks to him quietly and briefly, and I know that

they're making a date for the evening. After she goes out, we watch "All in the Family" with Archie Bunker and his dopey wife Edith, and their blond daughter Gloria with her miniskirt and her big tits and her husband Meathead, or else we watch "What's My Secret" with Uri Zohar. If there's nothing interesting on the television we play a game where you're not allowed to touch the floor: I arrange the chairs from the dining nook between the dining table and the living-room coffee table, in two lines and with big intervals between them. This creates a kind of circle of furniture, where you have to jump from one to the next, and anyone who falls and touches the floor loses. I almost never lose, because my legs are longer than theirs. Two weeks ago Noam fell off a chair and hit his forehead hard on the corner of the table. He cried terribly and I didn't know what to do and where to look for her. I went down to Grandpa's and knocked on the door, but he wasn't home either, because he'd gone to a concert with his girlfriend. Oren suggested calling our father. I told him I wouldn't call him even if Noam had cracked his head open. In the end I took a knife and pressed the blade to his forehead so he wouldn't get a bump in the place where he'd hurt himself, and he more or less calmed down and went to sleep. I waited up for Mother and dozed off on the sofa, and I woke up when I heard her high heels on the stairs. When she opened the door and saw me her face fell.

"What are you doing up at this hour, go to bed."

"Yes."

"Should I wake you up as usual?"

"Yes."

"Goodnight then," she said from the passage, on her way to her room.

"Goodnight then."

Yesterday we didn't play keep off the floor, because we were watching the game between Maccabi Tel Aviv and Mobilgirgi Varese, in the finals of the European basketball championship. In the last minutes, which were the most suspenseful, because the score was really close, there were suddenly disturbances in the reception, and the picture moved to the top of the screen with maddening stripes in the middle. I used a trick I'd learned from my father when he was still living with us—first you treat the television set kindly, you switch it off and let it rest and cool down. After a minute you switch it on again and if it hasn't calmed down yet you give it a good thumping on the top and the sides, which usually brings it to its senses. So we missed the end of the game, and when the picture steadied we saw the sweating Tal Brody accepting the cup and waving it in the air and shouting that we were on the map, but the important thing was that we'd won by a lead of one point, and the European cup was ours!!! For the first time in history!!! Later on that night people went wild in the streets.

Sometimes Mother doesn't go out for a few evenings, and then she shuts herself in her room and argues with Moishele on the phone. She reminds him that he promised her long ago to leave his wife, like she left her husband, instead of which he stays in hotels with her for all kinds of seminars and conferences to do with the bank. So now I know that he works in a bank. One afternoon I went into the three bank branches in the Center and tried to guess which of the clerks was Moishele, and then I thought that maybe he worked in some branch in Hadar or Neve-Sha'anan, or maybe he was the bank manager who sits in the closed room with the little window, and maybe this wife is the one who works in the bank and not him. After Mother slams down the receiver, I hear her crying behind the closed door, and I can taste the salt in my throat. I want to go in to her room and sit down next to her on her bed and put my arms around her. It feels strange to think that my mother, who I've known ever since I've known myself—her skin and her voice and her smell—has a secret life that I know nothing about. But I'm sure that she won't tell me. She never talks to me about real things that you think or feel, only about what you should do and what you shouldn't do.

When I start feeling sorry for myself, I think about how you too had a hard time with your mother and your sister and all the grownups around who tried to educate you, but you never had the possibility of going out, or friends you could talk to, or television. The only place you could escape to was your diary, your hiding place within the hiding place. And then I say to myself that my situation really isn't so bad.

Yours, Kitty

P.S. They said on the news that Rabin resigned as Prime Minister, because they discovered that his wife had a bank account in America. My mother was glad, because she hates the Labor Alignment. She says they're all corrupt. She supports the Heruth Party, Menachem Begin, and the Greater Land of Israel.

This is a new poem that I wrote for her last night (but I won't show it to her).

I'm twelve and a half years old,
holding on to the railing of the porch,
watching you slip out to the white car and
vanishing into the shadow of the man inside it.
Abandoned and adoring I wait for you in time that stands
   still,
until you return to me from the darkness—
your eyes the eyes of a tame animal,
waking from a dream of the rain forests.

Monday, 4.11.77

Dearest Anne,

The Passover holidays are over, and today we went back to school. I handed in the essay I wrote about you to Michaela, and I'm waiting to get it back with her comments. She promised to read the essays quickly, because the Holocaust Memorial ceremony is on Thursday. (If only, if only! Hold thumbs for me.) Michaela is a wonderful teacher, and I could talk about her for hours, but I haven't got anyone to talk to, and so I'll describe her for your patient ears; she has thick, rich chestnut hair, down to her shoulders, sometimes tied back and sometimes loose. Her complexion is fair with a few freckles, her brown eyes are big and burning, and they can pierce and smile, look angry and caress and wink, they're the most beautiful eyes I've ever seen in my life. Her face is small, but her features are big—high forehead, thick eyebrows, a funny, too big nose, a wide mouth. Sometimes you can smell the cigarettes from it, but I don't care. All I can see is the smile of inner joy when she talks about a story or a poem. She isn't tall, and she's quite thin, her breasts are small and so are her hands. Sometimes she sits on her desk, and then you can see that she's got great legs. She's got a lovely voice, deep and warm, like the sound of a cello, like night, or velvet. Even when she bawls us out she's so cute that I want to hug her. When she comes into the classroom light streams from her like the sun, and my stomach turns over as if I've eaten too much chocolate spread. I love watching her as she walks between our desks, her hands draw pictures in the air as she talks, and she turns the beam of her smile and her eyes on us, grimaces, winks, raises her eyebrows, puffs out her cheeks, flares her nostrils, wrinkles her brow—her feelings are written on her face every passing moment. I follow the changes in her face, riveted, reading her thoughts on it. I have always been surrounded by people whose faces don't betray anything. My mother's perfect face. My father's wax face. My own face is in hiding too, it has learned to betray nothing. Michaela's face doesn't hide, she lets it be open and generous.

I liked Michaela the first time I saw her, on the second day of the school year. She entered the classroom with a light, gliding step, the black attendance book under her arm, smiled at us, and with a quick movement gestured us to sit down, as if the ceremony of standing up for the teacher seemed pointless and old-fashioned to her. Then she stepped up to the platform, put her bag down on the chair, slammed the attendance book with both hands onto the sloping top of the teacher's desk, to silence our whispers, and said, "Good morning to you, I'm Michaela, and we're going to study literature and expression together."

Racheli, who was still sitting next to me then (in the meantime she's been banished to another desk for chattering), whispered, "She's pretty, isn't she?" And I made a "so-so" movement with my head. I tried to guess how old she was and I couldn't decide, she looked young to me but also old, she looked ageless. At break Yael Brosh told us (her mother's Michaela's mother's beautician too) that she's almost twenty-six, and she's getting married to a resident from Rambam Hospital, called Yoel Rosen.

Michaela opened the attendance book and called the pupils' names, letting her eyes rest on each of us, to engrave us in her memory. When she called, "Rivka Shenhar," I said, "Yes, Rivi," and our eyes met for the first time; her open brown eyes and my secretive gray eyes.

Afterwards she took a slender little book out of her bag, sat on the edge of her desk, tucked the skirt of her blue tricot dress between her thighs like a waterfall between two rocks, and said, "I want to read you a poem I love." She read a poem by Leah Goldberg, "April Khamsin," as if she were giving birth to it as she read, and I didn't know what held me spellbound, the words or her voice, which has depth and darkness, as if it's coming from a big sound box.

I know that day was a day that had no parallel,
a day when nothing happened, nothing at all,
and what distinguished it from other days
no evil omen, no sign of grace could tell.

And every line was a key that opened more eager, thirsty little mouths in me,

Except that the sun gave off a jasmine smell,
except that the sands of the shore had lips that kissed,
except that a heart in the stone pulsed as in a wrist,
except that the evening burned like an orange's golden
    shell.

And something swelled inside me as if I was going to cry,
because I knew that it was all true, and I only wished that one
day I too would be able to capture all this in words,

How to remember that day—anonymous, vague as mist?
How shall I preserve the grace that suddenly fell?
How shall I believe that on that day alone
every flutter and scent came from my marrow bone?

The book was in her hands, but she didn't need it, because
she knew the poem by heart. Her gaze circled the room, on the
lookout for a spark, a lightning flash. I offered her mine, behind
the lenses of my glasses. She smiled at me, and poured the last
verse slowly into my eyes,

For every tree in the wind was a trembling sail,
and silence had the eyes of a little girl,
and tears the odors of the blossoming grove,
and the name of the city resembled the name of my love.

When she finished reading there was a silence. Our class,
grade 8E, is a "homogeneous" class. Last year, at the beginning of
the seventh grade, they concentrated the best pupils from the
three elementary schools entering our middle school in it. The
teachers say it's a pleasure to teach us, and kids from the other
classes call us mockingly "the genius class" or the "grinds' class."
And nevertheless, when Michaela asked, "Who wants to tell us
what the poem is about?" no one dared to risk it. Her gaze hovered between our heads, over the blue shirts stiff with embarrass-

ment, returned questioningly to my eyes, and retreated from them in disappointment. More than anything I wanted to tell her what the poem was about—about time passing relentlessly, about the rare living moment and how to capture it like a goldfish in a net—but I couldn't find the words. They climbed up my sides, crowding, jostling, pushing, and knocking each other down.

Michaela smiled to herself and said, "You're right, I shouldn't have asked what the poem is about, but what you felt when you heard it. I remembered the jasmine bush in my parents' garden, and how at the end of every summer I would go out at night to smell it, because I knew that soon it would be winter and all the flowers would fall off."

"You could have picked a few flowers and pressed them," said someone, Michal or Anat. (The girls in the class, except for me and Racheli, who inherited the moldy old names of our grandmothers—are called Michal, Anat, or Yael.)

Michaela reached for her bag, pulled out a packet of cigarettes and lit herself a long cigarette, and I noticed how beautiful her hands were, supple and delicate, with small manicured unpainted nails, and with two gold rings, one broad and the other narrow, set with a green stone. When her arms move they look like swans' necks. She said, "I could have pressed the flowers, but then they would have changed, the color, the smell, it would be like embalming a living thing in a can of preserves."

"She could have written a poem," I whispered to Racheli, and Racheli whispered back, "So say so."

"No, you say so," I said, and Racheli raised her hand and said, "You could have written a poem about it."

Michaela beamed at her, her eyes moving between us, and said quietly, "I tried lots of times, without much success. It's a good thing that there are people who know how to distill sensations into words, like getting the essence of a smell into miniature bottles, and they write the poems for us."

And then I asked myself for the first time, if I would ever have the courage to show her my poems.

In the Sukkoth holidays I discovered that I missed her. In the first days after the holidays she didn't come to school, and Yael Brosh said that she'd gotten married to her doctor, and they'd gone on honeymoon to Greece. In the first lesson after she came back tanned and radiant, she was pushed into the classroom by a torrent of little girls congratulating her and asking to see her new ring. I didn't go up to her, wedding rings don't particularly interest me. In any case after a few years people throw them into the lavatory and pull the chain, like my mother did on the day her divorce came through.

Michaela climbed onto the platform, and without any introduction, as usual, she read another poem by Leah Goldberg, and then she wrote it on the blackboard in her open, vigorous handwriting:

Teach me, God, to bless and pray
For the luster of a ripened fruit, the secret of a wilted leaf,
For this freedom: to see, to feel, to breathe,
To know, to wish, to fail.

Teach my lips a blessing and a hymn
At the renewal of your time with morning and with night,
Lest my day today be like yesterday,
Lest my day become habitual to me.

She told us to take out our composition notebooks, and to write a composition inspired by the poem: "For this freedom—what can I do so that my days don't become habitual to me."

I wrote that I wanted to learn, to know and to read as much as I could. That I aspired to contemplate life and the world around me with a lucid mind, a clear gaze. That I wanted to remember the sights and the sensations, and to put it all, feelings, impressions, thoughts, into writing. At the end of the composition I wrote that I was ashamed that the things that were important to me were so selfish.

As I wrote I suddenly felt a light hand touching my hair. I raised my eyes and saw Michaela standing next to me. She smiled as if she were about to burst out laughing, and said, "There's a tail sticking out of your braid, should I fix it for you?" I nodded my head, too excited and embarrassed to speak. She undid the braid, combed the hair with her fingers, and braided it again. All this time I breathed in her scent, which had a marvelous smell of tea, and I didn't want it to come to an end. Her hands felt so good. When she was finished she said, "Now it's fine," and smiled her wonderful smile at me, with her beautiful white teeth, straight into my eyes. I could hardly manage to say thank you. She was so adorable, I could have killed her with kisses!

A few days later she gave back the compositions. When she put mine down on my desk, she stroked my back with her hand and said quietly into my ear, "It's not in the least selfish, what you wrote, it's the most that an artist can aspire to." I didn't say anything. I felt that my face was on fire. That my ears were on fire. That my stomach was burning up. I wanted her to ask if I really wrote, if she could see my poems, but she didn't ask. It looks as if I'll have to find the courage to show her myself.

Michaela doesn't give us marks. She says that numbers are handed out at the HMO clinic. At the bottom of the page she wrote to me: "Memory and imagination are the main tools of the writer. It's no accident that Mnemosyne, the goddess of memory in Greek mythology, is the mother of the muses. You should read *Portrait of the Artist as a Young Man* by James Joyce, I think there's a copy in the library," and she signed it Michaela Berg (why "Berg" and not "Rosen"? Maybe she hasn't gotten used to being married yet). Naturally I ran to the library the minute the bell rang for recess and took out the book. Even though it was quite hard going I made an effort and read it to the end, so that I could go up to her after class and talk to her about it, but to this day I haven't found the courage to do it . . . miserable coward that I am. I carry the composition around with me in my pocket and try to read her character in her signature (anyone would think that I'm an expert in graphology . . .) and kiss it again and again. Now too the page is folded up in my pajama pocket.

Goodnight for now, yours, Kitty

Tuesday, 4.12.77

Dearest Anne,

This afternoon, when I climbed down the wadi on my way to Scouts, I had an attack of rapid heartbeats. My heart stopped for a minute, and the world spun and darkened, and then it started beating again at terrific speed, as if horses were running amok in my throat and all over my body. I sat down on a rock under the broom bush and did the exercises I invented to slow down my pulse; I hold my breath as long as I can and strain as if I'm taking a crap, and then I take a deep breath and hold the air in my stomach, and let it out slowly. I did this a few times, until it suddenly stopped all at once, and then I lay down to rest, with my head on the rock in the sun, and looked at the deep blue of the sky through the yellow flowers, and breathed in their sweet smell, which may be the smell of the sky, and I picked one of the flowers and stroked my nose and lips with it, and narrowed my eyes in order to trap the colored needles of light between my lashes, and then I closed them tight and everything turned orange. I would have gone on lying there in the sunshine and pleasant breeze and thinking about Michaela, instead of going to the Scouts, but the orange suddenly turned black, and when I opened my eyes I saw that the sun had disappeared, and in its place, in all her length, Lilach Miller from grade 8D was standing above me in her scout's uniform. She asked me what I was doing, and I sat up and told her that I lay down to rest for a minute because I didn't feel well, and she made a kind of movement with her mouth as if she were chewing sour gum, and said, "You're a little weird, aren't you?" I didn't answer her. I got up and we walked together without speaking until we reached the den.

When I was small I used to have these attacks often. Today I know it's called "tachycardia," but once I used to say to Mother "My heart's going tick-tock," and she would put her hand under my blouse to feel my heartbeat, and I would stand still and try to breathe as little as possible, so as not to get in the way of her examination. Sometimes I would tell her it was going tick-tock even when it wasn't, perhaps because I wanted to feel her hand, but then she would take it out quickly and say rather crossly, "You're just imagining it, there's nothing wrong with you."

Once, when I was about four years old, I had an attack that lasted for hours, and they took me to the hospital in the middle of the night. I remember that they dressed me in disgusting green pajamas (after I got better and went home I refused to sleep on sheets the color of those pajamas, and to this day I never wear green). I lay on a high bed, and a lot of people I didn't know touched me, doctors and nurses, and especially one nurse, Bruria. I was sure she was a witch, because she had purple hair. I knew that normal people had brown or blond or gray hair, but no human being had hair like hers, straight and purple, cut through the middle by an exact part and turned up in two rolls above her white gown. Her face was sharp and freckled and quite pretty, and her eyes were green with white sparkles, and she had long nails painted silver, and she gave off a sweetish kind of smell mixed with the poisonous smell of the hospital. Every morning she stuck a needle into my finger and squeezed it hard between her fingers until blood came out, and twice a day she rolled up my pajama sleeves and trousers and smeared a cold liquid on my arms and legs with cottonwool, and pinched them with big cold pincers that were connected with red and blue wires to a big machine that was called an ECG, and afterwards she unbuttoned my pajama jacket and smeared the cold stuff onto my chest as well, and pinched me under my armpit and next to my nipple with brown siphons like the ones that make soda water in the "Sipholux," which were also connected to the machine, and I lay like that for a long time, with my hands and legs tied up, shivering with cold, smelling the sharp smell of the liquid, and the machine shivered too, and made strange noises, and spat out a huge paper snake full of lines that looked like pointed mountains.

I remember that all the time I wanted my mother to come. Bruria explained to me that Mommy and Daddy were at work, and that they were only allowed to visit me in the afternoon, in the visiting hours, but I waited for them from the minute I woke up, and someone pulled down my pajama pants and pushed something cold up my bottom, and I knew it was a thermometer, and I waited for it to warm up and then for them to take it out, and after they took it out they forgot to pull up my pajama pants and I pulled them up by myself, and I prayed in my heart that Bruria wouldn't come with her needles, and that she wouldn't take me to the room with the machine, and not to the dark scary X-ray room either, where you have to drink a dense liquid before you go in, from a glass like her nail polish, which nearly made me vomit, and then you have to take off your top and press your chest to a freezing iron plate and stand still, because it's strictly forbidden to move.

All day long I sat in bed and looked at the door, waiting for Mother's face to appear, with the bright, slightly worried smile, and when more and more time passed and she didn't come, I started to cry, and a big boy came up to me and asked me, why are you crying, and I said, I want my mommy, and the boy put his hand into the cloth puppet of the Red Indian that I had then, with the pink felt dress, and the black wool braids and the huge nose, and pushed it into my face and laughed, here's Mommy, here's your mother, and I, choking with insult and tears, shouted, that's not my mother, my mother's real and much more beautiful.

I remember too that after I came home from the hospital I refused adamantly to stay alone in the kindergarten, and Daddy stayed there with me all day, and I bragged to the other children that he was the kindergarten policeman (then I thought that being a policeman, like Uncle Itzik—who I sometimes saw in the Center directing the traffic when the traffic light broke down—was much better than some old lecturer at the university). At least I have some memories of him left.

That's it for now, "Starsky and Hutch" is starting in a few minutes,

Yours, Kitty

4.13.77

Dearest Anne,

Her childhood, from before the time when her father left home and his own body and turned into an android, sometimes seems to her like the lost continent of Atlantis, or like a shipwreck—into which she has to dive to rescue all the treasures that she can, before time buries them beneath the sands of oblivion. It's not only the sweet memories that she wants to bring up from the depths, but also the bitter ones, because they're all equally important.

She wants to remember the frightening and amazing height that lifted her onto its shoulders, and the whole world swayed, and her little fingers clung to his hair, and his huge hands gripped her thighs. Or in the sea, riding on his dolphin back sliding through the waves, with her arms wound around his neck and her mouth on his wet salty skin. And when he came home from work she liked to press her face to his suede jacket, to which the smell of gas from the Susita stuck like thorns, and after he showered and put on short pants and sat down to read the newspaper, she climbed onto his lap and breathed in the smell of soap from his chest.

She wants to remember the time when he saved her life. She was four or five years old, and they were sitting in the living room playing chess, and her father who was a champion chess player and had two broken trophies in his closet that he'd won when he was young, was teaching her how to open with the

57

pawn and where to jump with the knight and when to castle the rook, and then her black king suddenly fell and rolled on the red carpet under the table, and she bent down and reached out her hand to pick it up, and was alarmed to discover that it had grown legs and a long tail, and two horns curving over its head, and she said, Daddy, my king has turned into a giant cockroach with horns, and her father bent down and said, move away, it's a dangerous scorpion, and she climbed onto the sofa and said in surprise, I didn't know that my sign was dangerous, but her father didn't answer, he just took off his giant sandal and hit the scorpion again and again with his face twisting and turning red from the effort, until the black tail stopped twitching, but he went on hitting her sign even when it was squashed completely flat and in the end he scooped the scraps of mangled flesh onto the folded newspaper and went to the kitchen and threw them into the trash, and when he came back he bent down again and found her real king, which had rolled under the sofa, and said to her, let's go on. But she didn't want to play anymore, because all the black chessmen looked to her like dangerous scorpions, and ever since then she never played chess again, and her father played against himself, with the whites and the blacks, until Oren grew up a bit and turned four, and he taught him everything again from the beginning.

And there were the three times that he hit her, each of which she remembers with painful clarity (her mother slapped her frequently, but she doesn't remember any of those slaps). The first time was when she was five and she wanted to take the bag of chocolate eggs wrapped in colored gold paper that she had received from Aunt Tehiya to kindergarten to share with the other children; and her father, who was sitting in his undershirt at the kitchen table, bending over a brimful cup of coffee, said no, because there weren't enough chocolate eggs for all the children, and she argued, so I'll just share them with my friends, but her father, who usually didn't have an opinion of his own and said about everything, ask your mother, insisted this time on saying no, and her mother, who was leaning against the door post and smoking, laughed dryly and said, "Your father's a Mapainik, with them it's like Russia, to prevent anyone being deprived they prefer everyone to go without," and the little girl didn't know what a Mapainik was or where Russia was, but she smiled at her mother, who smiled back, and then she stole up behind him and pinched his stubborn neck, digging her fingernails into the flesh as hard as she could, and he reached behind him with his hand and closed his steel fingers around her wrist, and pulled her and lay her on his lap and pulled down her pajama pants and spanked her bare bottom with his huge hand, and she heard his hard, rapid breathing and she yelled, "Stop it, stop it, I won't take the eggs to kindergarten, I'll be a Mapainik like you," but the hand couldn't stop and it went on and on, like a machine, and the little girl cried, I have to go to the toilet, and her mother said quietly, "Let her go, in a minute she'll shit herself here in the middle of the kitchen."

The second time she was seven or eight. Like on every Friday they went down to Hadar, to Granny and Grandpa Shenhar, and they saw the Friday afternoon Arab movie together on television, and she—who didn't understand how they could watch the same movie every week, with the same plump black-haired actress, fluttering her long eyelashes and wailing at every little thing with her whole face and body and both her hands; and with the same actor with the glistening hair and the black mustache and the cigarette between his fingers and the thick ring on his pinkie; and with the same sobbing music and the same belly dancer—sat in the green armchair next to the bookcase with the glass doors and read *Tevye the Milkman* again, because the other books were volumes of *The Talmud* in black covers, and *Passover Haggadot*, and books in Polish and the works of Marx and Engels, which her father had bought when he was young, and two or three books of Yiddish poetry by Ephraim Fishelson, who was a distant cousin of Grandpa's, and Granny and Grandpa said that he brought a lot of honor to the family. Afterwards she read a little of *Les Miserables*, which she already knew, because her father had told her the story about Jean Valjean, who stole a loaf of bread because he was starving and they put him in a prison called the Bastilles, and about the French revolution and Marie Antoinette, who told the poor, starving masses that if they didn't have bread they should eat cake, and because of that they chopped off her head in the guillotine.

After the Arab movie they switched off the television and sat down to eat the gefilte fish, and the soup with *lokshen*, and the *polkelach* with rice, and the compote; and she and her mother stayed in the living room and ate an omelet with bread and a few olives, which Granny Pnina prepared especially for them, because her mother was a vegetarian and preferred not to see other people eating meat, and the little girl wasn't a vegetarian, but the soup with the yellow chicken toes floating in it revolted her. After they drank tea from glasses in silver holders, and ate the apple cake that Granny Pnina had baked in the "wonderpot" on top of the stove, she decided to collect in a plastic bag the skin and gnawed bones and the chicken toes from everybody's plates, in order to feed them to the cats in the yard, and she planned how she would whisper "Psss psss psss," which was their secret password, and they would come to her in droves, from their yard and the yards of the neighbors, black and white and gray and ginger, and she would divide the leftovers between them equally, like Daddy had taught her, and she would be the Marie Antoinette of the cats, only generous and fair.

When they got home it was already dark, and she whispered the secret password, but the cats didn't come, not even one, and she couldn't find them, and her mother wouldn't let her keep the plastic bag in the fridge, in case the smell of the chicken invaded her vegetarian food, and then the little girl thought for a minute and came up with a solution, she would leave the bag in the car until the next day, and in the morning she would go down to look for the cats. But her father objected and said angrily, "My Susita isn't a rubbish bin," and she regretfully threw the bag into the big bin in the yard, in the hope that the cats would find it for themselves, but when they entered the house her father suddenly began to hit her and shout, "What do you think, that my car's a rubbish bin," and she cried, it isn't fair, it isn't fair, because she had never had any such thoughts about their old Susita, which they called the rattletrap. She had only wanted to be the Mapainik Marie Antoinette of the cats.

(Now I think that Daddy isn't really a true Mapainik, because if the Mapainiks believe in liberty, equality, and fraternity, like in the French Revolution, and sharing out everything equally, without depriving anyone, then how come he only shares out himself to Oren and Noam, and deprives me?)

The last time, when she was ten, she lost a ten lira note, and she was afraid to tell them but she knew that she must, and she went into the living room with her stomach turning over as if it were in a washing machine, and told them, and her father got up and stood over her with the face of a stranger and pushed her so that she fell on the carpet, and he kicked her on her legs and her back, and her mother cried out in alarm, have you gone mad, what are you doing, leave her alone, stop it, but he went on kicking her stomach and her legs and all over her body and yelling, "You think money grows on trees, at your age I was already earning my own money," and when she stood up, supporting herself on the wall, and went convulsed with weeping to wash her face, she heard her mother's whisper cracking like a whip, "Is it the child's fault that you grew up in the gutter," and this word, gutter, hurt her even more than his kicks, and when she raised her face from the sink she suddenly discovered the folded pink banknote lying innocently on the marble counter.

That's all the treasure I managed to bring up from Atlantis for you this evening,

Yours, Kitty

P.S. I'm such an idiot, I forgot to tell you the most important thing: today we got our essays back, and guess what? Michaela asked me to read my composition about you at the Holocaust Day memorial ceremony tomorrow, in front of the whole school!!! Can you believe it? She made a few corrections here and there (she even added an entire sentence of her own . . .) and she said that it was very mature and moving. I told Mother and asked her to come and hear me, and she promised she would. Before I go to bed I'll practice, so as to read without mistakes, and to remember to raise my eyes from the page from time to time, like Haim Yavin and Dalia Mazor when they read the news.

Thursday afternoon, 4.14.77

Dearest Anne,

Oren and Noam are knocking on my door and nagging that they're hungry, but before I get their lunch I have to tell you about the strange Holocaust Day I had. When I woke up this morning, I remembered that the participants in the ceremony have to wear white shirts. I took my white shirt down from the laundry line, and I thought of asking Mother to iron it for me, but I knew that she'd be annoyed and complain that everything with me has to be at the last minute, so I didn't ask her. Before she left for work I made her swear that she would come at a quarter to ten, and she said that she would reschedule a meeting she was supposed to attend, or send Grandpa instead. The shirt didn't look too creased, so I wore it as it was, and quickly combed my hair, because I was going to be late for the rehearsal. Outside it was cold and drizzling, so I put on a sweater as well, and I prayed that it would stop raining before the ceremony began. I didn't want anything to spoil our day, mine and yours.

At twenty to ten I was already waiting for Mother at the gate, and she arrived on the dot. I saw how the kids, from the higher classes too, looked at her, and through their eyes I saw again, as if for the first time, how beautiful and elegantly dressed she was, and how she gave off a scent of narcissi from the Diorissimo she bought in Italy. I tried to catch Michaela's eye, because

I wanted her too to see what a beautiful mother I had, and I planned to introduce them to each other after the ceremony was over. Mother looked me up and down with her critical gaze, and told me to go and comb my hair. I wanted to go on standing next to her, but I didn't argue. I took the little hairbrush she fished out of her bag and went to the toilets. The minute I returned the sirens went off, and I joined my class, who were standing close to the stage. The sirens died down, and our principal, Ephraim Hourgin, who everybody calls Hourgi, went up to the stage and announced in the solemn voice he keeps for ceremonies and speeches, "I am honored to call on Mr. Yitzhak Levy, a Holocaust survivor, to light the memorial torch."

Noam Bloch whispered "A Brand Saved from the Burning" and a few boys began to giggle. Unbelievable how infantile boys in the eighth grade can be. Yitzhak Levy, the school janitor—who on ordinary days is just plain Itzik, dragging his short leg in its built-up black boot down the corridors, always dressed in shabby khakis, holding a pail and broom in his hands, while Hourgi gives him orders, Itzik fix this, Itzik clean that—this Yitzhak Levy now stood erect on the platform, in black trousers and a pressed white shirt, as befitting a Holocaust-Day-janitor, lit the torch, and sang from the depths of his stomach, "*El-malei-rahamim*," his eyes tightly shut and his body swaying.

Hourgi made a speech about the heroism of the partisans and the Warsaw Ghetto Uprising fighters, and the establishment of the State of Israel and the Israeli Defense Force, and concluded by saying that it was up to us, the youth who would be drafted in the coming years, to continue to strengthen our gallant army, in order to ensure that never, never, would we go like lambs to the slaughter again. The school choir sang "Never Say that This Is My Final Journey" and "Brothers There's a Fire," and a few boys from the eleventh grade read a letter by Mordecai Anielewicz. I knew that after "My God, my God, may it never end" it would be my turn. It stopped raining and the sun came out quite strongly. I started to sweat, from nervousness too, and before I went up to the stage I quickly took off my sweater and gave it to Racheli to keep for me. Hourgi said, "I call on Rivka Shenhar, from grade 8E, to read the composition she wrote about Anne Frank." I went up to the microphone and began, trying to keep my voice steady:

"Dearest Anne,
"Before the war you were an ordinary girl, like me, with parents who sometimes got on your nerves, and a big sister, and a cat called Moortje, and girlfriends and suitors. You loved laughing and chattering in class, riding your bike, ice skating in winter, reading books, and watching movies, and you collected pictures of movie stars. On your thirteenth birthday you got a diary in a red-and-white checked cloth cover from your father, and you began to write in it. You dreamed of being a writer one day, when you grew up."

I raised my eyes for a minute, and looked from my mother, who was standing stiffly with her arms folded on her chest, and Michaela, who smiled at me encouragingly from the other end of the yard.

"And then your country was occupied by people who decided that you had no right to all these things: no right to study, to move freely about the streets of your town, to laugh, to breathe the air of the world, to grow up, you had no right to live, all because you were Jewish. You were forced, you and your family, to hide. You took your diary with you to your hiding place, and for two years you went on writing in it, describing your daily lives in the shadow of the war and the fear. In hiding you continued to learn, to develop, to dream, and to plan your future, you observed the others and your own inner self, you learned a lot about the human soul and about yourself, and you and Peter Van Daan found consolation in each other, you knew young love.

"And perhaps because of this your dairy is so shocking, so heartrending: because of the cruel contradiction between your young, brave, sensitive spirit, all vitality and hope, believing in human goodness and striving to grow and contribute to humanity, and the dark hearts and minds of those who decided to exterminate you.

"Until I read your diary, I didn't know much about the Holocaust. The nameless and faceless "six million"; the blue numbers tattooed on the forearms of a few of the adults I know; the face of Hitler may-his-name-and-memory-be-blotted-out with his little mustache and forelock, and the terrible curse, may you be buried in his black grave; the wax figures of Eichmann in the glass cage and of Gideon Hausner the prosecutor; and Hannah Szenes the heroic parachutist. The parents and grandparents of many of us who survived the hell and whose families perished, are not in the habit of speaking about those times."

Suddenly I noticed that Mother was turning around and beginning to walk towards the gates with a brisk, firm step, and I almost shouted into the microphone, Mother, wait, I haven't finished yet, why are you going, but I just swallowed the lump choking my throat and carried on:

"Your diary gave a name and a face to one of the six million dead, and thanks to it we know that all the others too had names, faces, voices, memories, loves, hopes, and wishes, and that each of them was a world and the fullness thereof. Now it is up to us to gather them one by one, names, pictures, life stories, because until we collect them all, to the last one, six million men and women, children, babies and old people, six million worlds—we will not be able to begin to understand the dimensions of the loss, the dimensions of the catastrophe.

"'If we bear all this suffering,' you wrote, 'and there are still Jews left in the world, one day the Jews will no longer be sentenced to extinction, but an example to the world. Who knows, maybe it will be our faith that will teach the good to the world and to all the nations, and to this end, this end alone, we have to suffer.'

"You were right in your prediction, we are no longer sentenced to extinction, we have a flourishing state defended by a strong army, but are we an example to the world? I'm not sure. Have we learned the lesson and made it a rule to respect the other, the weak, the stranger living in our midst? Even between ourselves there is no respect and no peace. I believe that every person living in our century, in the middle of which is a huge gaping wound that refuses to heal—never mind if he's a Jew or an Arab, German or Dutch or Thai, because we were all created in the image of God—has to decide between his self and his conscience that as long as he draws breath he will not join those who rob others of their humanity, hurt them and deprive them of their rights, that he will not identify with them, but oppose them with all his strength.

"For your suffering, which was not in vain, for the diary that you wrote, in the light of which so many young people have been educated, from which so many have derived hope and strength, for the example that you were and will continue to be, I, an Israeli girl living safely in Haifa, want to thank you from the bottom of my heart."

When I finished there was a silence. A few pigeons took off from the schoolyard with a beating of wings and landed on the roof of the gym. I stood looking at the sea of students and teachers, and tried to engrave the moment in my memory, so that I would always remember it as a moment of triumph, but inside I felt that everything had been spoiled. I stepped down from the platform, and Racheli whispered to me, "You read wonderfully, I was terribly moved," and all I wanted to do was cry. Throughout the singing of the national anthem I racked my brains to try to understand what it was in my composition that had made my mother so angry, maybe what I said about parents who got on your nerves. After "Hatikva" the ceremony came to an end and everyone dispersed. Kids of all ages came up to me and said things, but I wasn't listening. I shut myself in the toilet and cried quietly, and when I calmed down I washed my face with a lot of water, to get rid of the red blotches, and then I went to the secretary's room and asked if I could use the phone. Mother was already back in the office and Dvora, her secretary, told me that she was in a meeting. I asked her to put me through to her urgently, because I had been hurt. When she came on the line, I shouted in a whisper, so the secretaries wouldn't hear, "Why did you leave in the middle, you promised me you would put your meeting off." I felt the tears flowing again and I turned to face the wall. Mother said in a stern voice, "We'll talk about it at home," and I yelled, "No, tell me now." And then, in her dry voice, she said that since she didn't hear a word of what I was reading anyway, she had decided to return to the office.

"Why didn't you hear, the microphone was working perfectly," I asked in a choking voice.

"Because I saw how the entire school was looking at my slut of a daughter, standing on the platform at the Holocaust Day ceremony in a creased shirt, like some orphan child without a mother to take care of her," she spat out without raising her voice. "When I was your age I was already doing my own ironing, but for you it's too much of an effort even to ask me to iron your shirt for you. A butter-fingered slut who doesn't even know how to button her shirt properly."

I looked down and discovered that the right side of my shirt was hanging out lopsidedly over my jeans. I must have buttoned it wrongly in the morning, because I was in a hurry and because I was excited, and the mistake was hidden under my sweater, until I took it off and went up to the stage, and the whole school saw me in a creased, crooked shirt. I wanted to tell her that the people freezing from cold in the camps didn't care if their shirts were creased, and when they sent them to the gas chambers they were completely naked and their heads were shaven, and that it wasn't fair that the composition I had worked so hard on and was so proud of, was less important to her that some silly mistake in buttoning my shirt, but I knew there was no point in arguing with her. I muttered, "Okay, see you later," and put the phone down, and hurried out past the secretaries, who pretended to be busy as if they hadn't heard.

I stood in the corridor blinded by tears, with a taste of salt in my mouth, and suddenly I felt a soft hand on my shoulder. Michaela. I couldn't help smiling at her. She took my face between her hands. "Why are you crying, you read wonderfully, and your composition was wonderful," she smiled into my eyes and wiped my tears away with her thumbs. I told her haltingly about my mother, and the shirt and the button and the sweater. Michaela laughed, "You shamed your mother in front of the whole school, oh dear, how well I know that story."

I wanted to ask her where she knew it from, and if her mother was like that too, but then Hourgi emerged from his room, surveyed us suspiciously, and asked Michaela to come inside. She whispered to me, "We'll talk later, wait for me at the gate after class."

I passed the time in Mr. Jacobs's English lesson in experiments with drawing Stars of David in one line, without raising my pen from the paper. When the bell rang I threw my things into my schoolbag and ran to the gate. Michaela was already waiting for me there, a cigarette between her fingers. "I see you've calmed down a little." I nodded. A new bout of tears choked my throat. If I hadn't been ashamed to, I would have thrown my arms around her neck and wept on her shoulder. Not only about Mother and the button, about everything.

"What did Hourgin want with you?" I dared to ask.

Michaela didn't answer. Her shoe played with a little stone on the pavement. Her head was bowed. In the end she raised her eyes. "He thinks I shouldn't have chosen your composition to read at the ceremony. I told him it was the best composition, ten times better than the others, and he said that the composition might be well written, but how was it possible to say that the Jews weren't an example, he thinks that the State of Israel is definitely an example to the whole world." She frowned and mimicked Hourgi's low voice: "'The student Shenhar is nothing more than a pipsqueak who hasn't yet done anything for the state, and she has no right to judge it.' In his opinion it's inconceivable to claim that all human beings, Jews and Arabs and Germans and Thais, are the same. This sentence is an insult to the Holocaust survivors and an insult to all of us, who are still fighting for our survival surrounded by millions of enemies who want to destroy us. I told him that in my opinion the opposite is true, and he cut me short and said that he didn't have time to conduct philosophical arguments with me, and that next time he would go over all the material for the ceremony himself, and not rely on the poor judgment of junior teachers."

I succeeded in smiling at her, and the corners of my lips trembled, "So are you sorry you chose my composition?" Michaela looked into my eyes and two tiny flames flashed in her pupils, "How can I be sorry," she said quietly, "I chose it with my mind and my heart, just like you wrote it. I chose it with all my might." She gave me a long, warm kiss on my forehead. "And you can tell your mother, that clothes are only intended to cover us, but in words we reveal ourselves."

She turned around and returned to the school building, and I crossed the road and walked down the hill home. I thought about her words, how she was revealed in them, and also in her eyes and her movements and her smiles and her voice, and I knew that never, in all my life, would I love another person the way that I loved her. I consoled myself with the thought that it may have been for the best that Mother had walked out of the ceremony, because the last part of the essay would no doubt have infuriated her too, maybe even more than the shirt and the button, and I knew that I wouldn't tell her what Michaela has said, because there was no chance that she would understand it.

And you too, I know, are smiling at me forgivingly,
And I hope that you're a little proud of me.
Your Kitty

P.S. Soon they're going to show the drama they made about you on the television. Ronit Porat is playing you, and Gideon Shemer is playing your father. I saw it last year and two years ago as well, and now I'm going to see it again, because every time I see it I feel as moved as if it's me there in the hiding place.

Thursday, 4.28.77

Dearest Anne,

Today I followed Michaela and I found out where she lives! The truth is that I started spying on her two weeks ago, a few days after the kiss on Holocaust Day: I waited in the schoolyard after classes, I hid behind some book, and lay in wait for her. When she walked out of the gate I started following her at a safe distance, and then I saw her getting into an eggplant-colored Mini Minor. The car coughed and slid towards me with a smile, and Michaela saw me and waved.

After that I surveyed the street every day in the hope that the car wouldn't be there. Today my efforts bore fruit; I didn't see it in front of the school, or in the streets nearby. After the last class I hid in the toilets on the first floor, knelt on the lavatory lid and watched the gate through the little window. When I saw her hair, shining in the sun like a bronze horse's tail, I rushed down and started following her innocently, keeping to a fixed distance.

As if with an invisible cord she pulled me behind her up the hill in the direction of Rothschild House, along the paths of the Manya Shochet Park and down Hazvi Avenue, under the pines whose crests meet above the road in a green tunnel leading to the wadi at whose feet the sea gleams like a broken piece of mirror. At the corner of Kalaniot Street she pushed the garden gate open and went in, and I bent down and hid behind a car. After a few minutes I gathered the courage to walk past the fence, as if by chance, and with a quick glance I snatched my booty: an iron gate painted white, with honeysuckle twining around its posts, a blue mailbox with their names, Michaela Berg and Dr. Yoel Rosen, and next to it the green mailbox belonging to their neighbors, the Germann family. And beyond the hedge with the sky-blue flowers which I had once, when I was small, stuck to my ears for earrings, I took in the view of the house and fixed it in my memory: two stories painted white, the front door on the first floor made of dark wood, with clay pots luxuriant with ferns on either side of it. Steps with a blue iron railing and planters full of red geraniums climbing to an identical wooden door on the second floor. Three pine trees in the front garden shedding dry needles onto the tiled porch of the ground floor apartment, where a white iron table stands with a few chairs made of wrought iron in a leaf pattern. On the second floor one of the pines bends its head to a porch crowded with pot plants where two deck chairs covered with floral mattresses rest. The closed plastic blinds separating the porch from the apartment open two rows of eyes to the street, as if keeping watch that nobody disturbs the afternoon siesta of the occupants. For a moment it seemed to me that the blind moved and there was somebody standing behind it and watching me. I took fright and hid again. Could she have noticed me following her? Luckily for me, nobody walked past. I must have looked rather strange, imagine the picture: a drowsy spring afternoon, a girl with glasses and

71

two braids, a blue shirt with its sleeves rolled up and jeans with flares and stickers, bending down and hiding behind a car. Thin shafts of sunshine pierce the canopy of the pines. Calm descends on the street, the house. Only the girl's heart races.

I don't know if Michaela lives on the bottom or the top floor, and I imagine her going in at both doors and sitting on both porches.

Yours, Kitty

5.3.77

Dearest Anne,

In the afternoon, when she comes home from school, she lies on her mother's bed in a square of sunshine. Her eyes are half closed and she tries to trap colored needles of light in her lashes. Her face grows hot, the frames of her glasses burn, and so does the blue sweater of her school uniform. Her armpits perspire, she feels as if steam smelling of her body is rising from her. She thinks about her literature teacher.

Once, when she was three or four years old, in her previous life in the lost continent of Atlantis, the earliest that she can remember—she knew that if she lay on her belly and joined her thumb to her forefinger and pressed them into the inner fold of her thigh, and rocked forwards and backwards with her eyes shut and her toes stretched tight, it would be warm and sweet there, and in the end there would be a kind of fluttering of little wings, like the bird she once saw, shaking the rain off its feathers. Every day after she came home from kindergarten with her mother, and they ate lunch, her mother would go to rest in her room, and the little girl would switch on the radio and listen to the children's program, and then she would take off her clothes and lie on her stomach on the cold balustrade of the balcony, her body pressed against the black railings, which she sometimes imagined were prison bars, the sun burning her back and the backs of her legs and her buttocks, and the wind brushing her skin—and she would rock to and fro with her eyes closed and her legs tensed, until she felt the fluttering of the little wings and her heart beating fast down there, and her body grew warm and relaxed, as if a big smile had spread through it, and sometimes she would fall asleep like that, naked in the sun and the wind.

She liked putting things down there, the corner of her blanket or a smooth cool building block, and feeling how her peepee grew cooler and the block grew hotter, until they were the same, and once her mother woke up from her afternoon nap and saw the lump in her panties and asked, what have you got there? And the little girl said nothing, just a block, and took it out and showed it to her, and her mother yelled, don't you know that you mustn't put things there, it's dirty, and the little girl didn't understand what it was forbidden to put there, just the block? And the corner of the blanket, was that allowed? And her hand? And what was dirty, the block or her peepee? She was confused, and from then on she tried not to let her mother see her putting things into her panties. And once the big boy from the house next door saw her from below lying on the balustrade and he yelled at her, I'll tell your mother on you, and she didn't know what he was going to tell her or why, because it felt so nice, and it wasn't anything bad, but after that she only did it on her bed, under the covers. She didn't ask herself if other little girls did it too, she just rejoiced in her body that felt such sweetness.

And when she was already in school, in the second or third grade, she discovered that when she did it she thought about other people, imagined them touching her, stroking her, or kissing her, like her teacher Edna, and sometimes smacking too, like the handsome and crazy Avner, who grabbed hold of her arms from behind at recess and forced her screaming and laughing to the ground, and told her, now you're my prisoner.

And during the Passover holidays in fifth grade Yael Brosh smuggled her big brother's copy of the book *Everything You Wanted to Know About Sex* out of his room in the Monopoly box, and they read it together, and she already knew what a man and a woman were supposed to do in bed, and she stole looks at her father when he came out of the shower naked, and she couldn't understand how such a big thick thing would ever be able to get into her little hole, which from Yael's brother's book she knew was not the hole you peed out of, but that there were two, one for peeing and one for men and babies; and even stranger and more frightening was the thought of a gigantic baby ever coming out of that little hole.

And how was she ever going to reach the climax of pleasure, which in the book they called an "orgasm," if the little organ called the "clitoris" was at the top, and the hole for the men was at the bottom, and there was also the hole for peeing between them as well?

She didn't dare ask Yael, because she was sure that she was the only one in this situation. In all the other girls, and the women too, the clitoris was right at the opening of the hole for the men, so that their penis could rub against it, like it said in the book, and stimulate it to orgasm. Only in her case had there been an unfortunate mistake, and God, or his angel in charge of sticking on the clitoris, had stuck hers on too far from the hole. She would never have an orgasm.

She wanted to study the book again and have a good look at the pictures, but Yael had already taken it back home in the Monopoly box, because she was afraid her big brother would discover that it was gone, and when she asked her to read the whole business about the orgasm again and explain it to her, Yael said decisively that she remembered, there were two kinds, a good orgasm and a bad orgasm; the good one was when the man put his penis into the woman and stimulated her inside, and the bad one was when only the clitoris was stimulated, which was a childish orgasm. And then she said to herself that perhaps her wing fluttering was actually the bad orgasm, and she knew that because of the mistake in the location of her clitoris she would never have a good orgasm.

And when she was twelve, and went to spend the summer holidays at her Aunt Tehiya's in Ramat Gan, she found a *Patrick Kim* detective story that belonged to her son Rami, where it said that when women had an orgasm they sprayed out some kind of water or juice, and there was one woman in the book who was tortured and injected with some red stuff that gave her more and more orgasms, and even when she begged for it to stop, because she couldn't stand it anymore, her torturers refused to inject her with the green stuff to make it stop, until she gave away the hiding place of her lover Patrick Kim. She read this chapter over and over again, and touched herself under the covers until she felt the fluttering, and for the first time she noticed that the hole-for-the-men was wet in her too, but her juice didn't spray out to a distance, like with Patrick Kim's mistress, and only stained her panties a bit.

And two months before her thirteenth birthday she discovered a dark brown stain on her panties. It was after a gym class, and she and Racheli were changing their clothes in the toilets, and she asked Racheli to come in to her stall for a minute and look at the stain and tell her if it was really it, and Racheli who was six months older than her and had already started a few months before, examined the stain and said that she thought it was. At recess, when they were sitting in the yard, she dared to ask Racheli if her clitoris was close to the hole-for-the-men, or if it was on top, and Racheli said that with her too it was on top, and in her too the hole for peeing was in between them, and she relaxed. She wanted to ask her if she also touched herself until she felt flutterings, and if with her too it was like a bird's wings, or like butterflies or the waves of the sea or like the rain, or maybe like something else, but she was shy.

All day she didn't tell her mother that she'd started, she wanted to keep it to herself a little longer, and only the next morning, when she woke her up to go to school, she said, "You know what, I got my period yesterday, but don't tell anyone, especially not Daddy," and her mother smiled at her, and there was a strange gleam in her eyes, maybe from happiness, and she kissed her cheek and promised that she wouldn't tell anyone "and definitely not your father, who I don't think would be particularly interested," and she searched the drawers in the bathroom closet, and gave her half a packet of sanitary towels, and explained to her how to put them in her panties, and said that on no account should she flush them down the toilet, because it would block the drains, and she had to wrap them in old newspapers and throw them away in the trash can in the kitchen, because otherwise they would stink the whole bathroom out.

Ever since then the girl has been wearing these sanitary towels, that slip sideways, and in the end the stain comes out a bit on the towel and a lot on her panties, and sometimes it seeps through to her jeans. Racheli is already using tampons (mini), and she says they're very comfortable, they don't make a bulge in the seat of your pants like the sanitary towels, and you can even wear a swimsuit. Maybe I'll try them too.

Yours, Kitty

5.18.77

Dearest Anne,

Yesterday there were elections to the Knesset, and we didn't go to school, which was turned into a polling station, (Mother and Grandpa voted there, Mother for the Likud and Grandpa for the Independent Liberals). In the morning I went down to the Carmel beach with Racheli, for the first time of the season. The water was still a bit cold, but when we got used to the cold, our bodies stopped feeling it, and then it was wonderful. I like swimming far out, to the place where the waves are like big whales, rising and falling slowly and apparently calmly. I lie on the back of a whale, waiting for it to rock me up and down, and suddenly I'm right inside the wave with my eyes shut, and it slams me forward with a loud noise of crashing surf, like in Hawaii 5-0, and my limbs are upside down, legs up and arms down, and all the water is above me, and for a moment I panic that this is it, I've had it, and then the wave moves ahead without me, and my legs flail until they find the sandy bed, and I stand up swaying, with the taste of salt in my mouth and water pouring out of my nose, and push the curtain of wet hair out of my eyes, to look for Racheli and make sure that she too is alive.

Afterwards we lay on our bellies at the edge of the water, letting the waves wash over our bodies and retreat, with the foam tickling underneath us, from our chests to our stomachs and between our legs, where it feels especially delicious. Our chins on the back of one hand, the other hand digging in the wet sand that dribbled between our fingers making little castles, which were washed away and destroyed by the waves. We talked about our mothers (Racheli hasn't been getting along with her mother too well either lately). I said that I admired my mother for choosing not to remain in a loveless marriage, and for working so hard and bringing us up by herself, but I didn't like the fact that she was so critical and mocking, which made it impossible to ever talk to her about anything. Racheli said that her mother was domineering and controlled her father, to whom she herself was very close and who she loved. I said that I didn't think I would ever get married, because people who were stuck with each other for years got sick of each other in the end and only stayed together because of habit and the house and the children, and also because they were afraid of being alone with themselves, because perhaps deep down inside they didn't really know who they were. Racheli said that she would definitely get married, because she wanted children and children needed a father. I told her that not long ago I had read in the evening paper supplement *Days and Nights* an interview with a French woman writer called Simone de Beauvoir (I had even cut the interview out and kept it). This Simone de Beauvoir said that motherhood was the real slavery of our day, and that if women wanted a child anyway, they should have it without getting married, because marriage was the biggest trap of all. She herself didn't have any children, because she chose to devote herself to her writing. She was the philosopher Sartre's girlfriend, and all their lives they lived in separate apartments. She also said, that the ideal was bisexuality, and a woman who wanted to be liberated should be willing to love a man or a woman "without anxiety, without compulsion, without obligations." I remembered this sentence, which I really liked, perfectly. Racheli said that she didn't think she could be with a woman in a relationship like the lesbians. I was silent for a minute and then I said I didn't think I could either, even though I wasn't sure. I think that anyone who wants to be an artist or a writer has to be open to experience everything. You wrote in your diary too, that once, when you slept over with a girlfriend you had a strong desire to kiss her, and you did so, and you suggested that you touch each other's breasts, but she refused. You wrote that you went into ecstasies every time you saw the naked figure of a woman, like the statue of Venus in the "History of Art": "It seems so wonderful and beautiful to me that I have to stop myself from crying. If only I had a girlfriend!"

All this doesn't mean that you were a lesbian, because afterwards you kissed Peter and you dreamed about boys, all it means is that you were sensitive and inquisitive, and curiosity about the world and the people in it, about the whole range of human experience, is in my opinion the most important quality for a writer.

After we finished philosophizing we felt hungry, and we went to the kiosk to buy falafel and grape juice. After that we walked along the beach until the sun beat a copper path from the horizon to the shore, when we went to the locker rooms to change. In the shower Racheli closed her eyes, and I peeked at her body, which is slimmer than mine and with bigger breasts too, and thought about whether I would like to kiss her and touch her breasts, whose nipples had stiffened from the cold water. And I knew that the answer was no.

In the evening Mother didn't go out, and we sat down

together to watch the election results, which were a big surprise, an "upheaval" as the presenter said—the Likud and Menachem Begin have taken power! Mother was so happy that she jumped and danced like a little girl, and sang, "The river Jordan has two banks, and both of them are ours." She says that we shouldn't give the Arabs an inch, because they have seven huge countries, and we have only one little country, and they want to throw us into the sea. I think that part of her happiness is revenge against my father, who's a passionate supporter of the Alignment, still from the days when it used to be called Mapai.

This morning the class was divided in two camps, the delighted and the disappointed, and I was in the delighted camp, not because of Menachem Begin, but because we had a class with Michaela. She looked at me and Racheli and our faces that looked like traffic lights, and smiled and said, "I see that some of you voted yesterday for the sea."

Yes, no question about it, I definitely vote for the sea.

Your Kitty

P.S. Tonight I wrote a new poem, "You," dedicated to Michaela. It describes the way a sunbeam coming in at the classroom window dances in her red-gold hair and sets it on fire.

6.7.77

Dearest Anne,
Yesterday afternoon I went with Racheli to her art class in Hadar. (Racheli has a crush on her art teacher and she wanted to show him to me. He really is cute.) After the class we went to buy popsicles at the kiosk on the corner of Herzl Street. Above the kiosk window a rope was stretched, and hanging from it on pegs were extremely well-developed naked girls, some photographed from the front with the legs apart, and some from behind, on their knees, wearing only tiny lace panties tucked into the cleavage of their buttocks. We decided to go halves and

buy the only magazine in Hebrew, *Bool*, whose pictures were in black-and-white. We couldn't decide which of us would get it first, so we tore it in two, right down the middle; I got the naked girl's right tit, and Racheli got the left one. When I got home I shut myself in my room with my half of the magazine, but when I came to the story about the young girl whose psychologist tells her to lift up her dress and pull down her panties and kneel on the carpet with her face in a cushion, I discovered that the continuation, which described what the psychologist did to the girl on the carpet, and which would have been the most exciting part—was on page 34, with Racheli. I called her up and asked her to bring her half to school today. At recess we made the exchange under the desk, but it turned out that the pimply Gidi Lehman was standing behind us and peeping, and suddenly he snatched both halves of the magazine and jumped onto the teacher's desk and waved the two halves of the naked woman in both his hands and shouted, "See what Rivi and Racheli read, everybody, look and see what Rivi and Racheli read!" All the kids coming back into the classroom after recess burst out laughing, and we didn't know where to bury ourselves, but we pretended that we didn't care. And then Galya, our nature-study and homeroom teacher, who's in an advanced stage of pregnancy and looks like a hippopotamus dressed in a circus tent, came in and yelled at Gidi to get off her desk, and she picked up the two halves of the magazine, and joined the two halves of the naked woman together, and made a face as if she were going to vomit, and asked who it belonged to, and a few of the kids told on us, and Galya said, "You two are the last I would have believed it of. If the mighty cedar sheds its leaves, what of the hyssop on the wall?" I wanted to tell her that she'd made a mistake in the saying, and point out that as a nature-study teacher she should know that cedars don't shed their leaves, because they're evergreens, but I knew that we'd already gone too far and cheeking her into the bargain was not a good idea. She didn't return the magazine to us, but folded it up and put it in her bag, and now she'll get to know what the girl and her psychologist did on the carpet, but I'll never know. Racheli said that Galya would tell Hourgi on us and show him the magazine, and I said that she would take it home and get off on it in secret. Racheli wrinkled her nose and said, "How can she? She's pregnant." What do you think, Anne, do pregnant women have desires? It's a pity that it wasn't Michaela who found the magazine. I'm sure she would have laughed and given it back to us. In two weeks time the long vacation starts, and I won't see her for more than two months, how sad. . . .

Yours, Kitty

Wednesday, 6.8.77

Dearest Anne,
This evening I went down with Racheli to the "Book Week" fair in the forecourt of the municipal theater. I love walking around the illuminated stalls with all the books spread out in front of me. I feel the book with my fingers and raise it to my nose and breathe in deeply, and read the blurb on the back cover, and the first page, and if my heart begins to race and my face begins to burn, I know that this is it, and I take out my purse and pay, and the desired book is in the plastic bag in my hand, and it's mine forever and ever, until somebody borrows it and forgets to give it back. I'm never mean about books, they belong to the whole of humanity, after all, not just me, and I don't write on the title page "stolen from Rivi Shenhar" either, like a lot of the other kids do, because why on earth should I write my name in a book written by somebody else? One day, when I'm a poet or a writer, they'll invite me to stand inside the stall, next to the sellers, and I'll sign my name in my books (the name given me by my craft . . .); but in the meantime Yael Brosh, for example, has four books that I lent her when we were friends, *Little Women*, *Anne of the Island*, *Kajtus the Magician* and *Lottie and Lisa*, and now I'm embarrassed to ask for them back, because

she's probably forgotten by now that they belong to me, and she'll think that it's only an excuse to talk to her, and all I can do now is miss my books, or buy new ones, which would be quite a waste, considering the stacks of books I haven't read yet.

Mother gave me eighty lira, and I knew it would only be enough for three or four books. Racheli only got fifty, and she bought *Narcissus and Goldmund* by Hermann Hesse and *Jonathan Livingston Seagull* by Richard Bach. I want to read them too, and I'll get them from her (Racheli isn't mean with books). I bought *The Bell Jar* by Sylvia Plath and *Poems* by Yona Wallach, who I'd never heard of before, but when I opened the long book with the red flowers that look like wounds, rare butterflies flew out of it straight into my heart. In the end I had twelve lira left, which were just enough for a little purple booklet *All Your Breakers and Waves* by Dalia Ravikovitch, my favorite poet.

As we were walking towards the exit with our bags of books, I suddenly saw, in the middle of crowd of people next to one of the stalls, a ponytail the color of bronze and an ear with a pearl earring, and my heart jumped into my throat. I said quietly to Racheli, "Look, there's Michaela," and she asked, "Are you sure it's her?" I said, "Yes, I'm sure" and I started making my way through the sweaty bodies, until I was standing almost next to her, pretending to look at the books and leaf through them, and suddenly her right hand, the one with the broad ring, shot out over the piles of books and caught hold of my hand. I raised my head to the wonderful smile with the shining eyes and the fan of little wrinkles, and she went on holding onto my hand like some precious treasure, as if she were afraid of losing me, until we escaped from the crowd together.

Michaela said, "How nice to meet you here," and then she noticed Racheli and said, "How nice to meet you both," and demanded like a curious little girl, "Show me, show me what you bought." We opened our bags and she peeked into Racheli's and said that she too, when she was our age, had read all Hermann Hesse's books, but then she had discovered Thomas

Mann, compared to whom Hess had suddenly seemed crude and childish, and she asked if we had read anything by Thomas Mann, and we said no, and she said that we should, and that most of his books had come out in Hebrew, and the translations weren't bad, and she recommended starting with the short stories, "Tristan" and "Death in Venice," and then go on to the novels, some of which, including *The Magic Mountain* and *The Confessions of Felix Krull* were in the school library.

And then she looked into my bag, and I breathed in the tea smell behind the ear with the pearl earring, and she smiled into my eyes and said, "I see that you're interested in poetry and in women." I almost let slip, "Because I write poetry myself," but I heard myself say instead, "Yes, I have a collection." Michaela wrinkled her brow and asked, "What collection?" And with trembling lips I invented on the spot, "A collection of women writers and poets, because in school, apart from poems by Leah Goldberg and Zelda, and the story by Dvora Baron about Raizele and the cow, all the works we studied were by men."

Michaela raised her eyebrows, as if this was news to her, and said, "You're right, I never thought about it, it's the Education Ministry curriculum, it was probably written by men." She asked me what I already had in my collection, and I said that I had *your* diary, and *Little Women* and *Anne of the Island* (although Yael's got those books it's enough that I read them and loved them for them to be mine), and the poems of Dalia Ravikovitch, and *In the Fifth Heaven* by Rachel Eitan (from the "People's Library" that my father once had a subscription to through his work), and *Daniel Deronda* by George Eliot, whose street I lived on, and Simone de Beavoir (even though I hadn't read her book, only the interview with her in *Ma'ariv*, I still felt that she too was mine), and *Fear of Flying* by Erica Jong, and a few more, which I couldn't remember at the moment.

Michaela laughed and asked, "Have you really read *Fear of Flying*?" and said that my collection wasn't very big, but it was interesting and varied, and that the books I'd bought this evening seemed to her an important addition, and then she opened her bag and showed us *Mrs. Dalloway* by Virginia Woolf, and said that she'd read it in English, and she was interested in checking the translation, and if it was any good she would let us know, even though it was always worthwhile to make the effort to read in the original language, "and then you can add Virginia to your collection."

Suddenly I envied her for reading English and having the whole world of books open to her. I promised myself to concentrate more in Mr. Jacobs's classes, so that I too would be able one day to read English like I read Hebrew, and really feel the taste and color of the words inside me.

Michaela smiled again and said, "I'm going to walk around some more and satisfy my greed, see you on Monday," and she pressed our hands holding our bags with a gentle pressure of her hand, and pushed through the people crowding around the stalls and disappeared, and her bronze tail vanished without a trace, and I thought that we only had three literature lessons left until the end of the year, and how much I wanted to give her a present, or write her a letter.

On the bus to the Carmel I consulted Racheli, and she said that a present was complicated, because I didn't really know her taste, and I didn't have a lot of money either, but she would definitely be glad to get a letter.

I know that a polite thank-you letter from a diligent student would be like lying to her face; and writing the truth—that I woke up with her in the morning, and thought about her every minute of the day, and dreamed about her at night, and admired and loved her more than I would ever have imagined possible— I couldn't write that, because it would scare her. So what the hell can I write her?

Your Kitty

Addition—Thursday morning:
Tonight I dreamed about Michaela again, and I'm writing it

down quickly, before I forget it. I'm riding on the Carmel underground train to Hadar, to the book fair or someplace else. I look out of the window, and instead of seeing my reflection against the background of the darkness of the tunnel, I see Michaela's face. She looks at me seriously and says something, but I can't hear her because of the window separating us, and the noise of the train. I know that what she's trying to tell me is supremely important to my soul, to my very existence, and I try to read her lips, but I can't, and she shakes her head sadly and puts her hand on the windowpane. I put my hand on hers on the other side, and we look into each other's eyes, and our hands are so hot that the glass melts like jelly, and for a split second our hands actually touch, and then Michaela suddenly dissolves and vanishes. I woke up very agitated, with a rapid heartbeat and a dry mouth, and with a sweetness in my stomach and all over my body, which I can't find the words to describe.

6.21.77

Dearest Anne,

The long vacation has begun, and I have a lot to tell you. Yesterday we finished school and received our reports. Mine is quite good. I have six "very goods" (two from Michaela, for literature and composition), three "goods" and three "quite goods" (for English, crafts, and gym). Mother of course pulled a face. Why don't I try harder in English? Did the crafts teacher find out that I have two left hands? She always has to see the empty half of the glass. Even if the whole report had been very good, apart from one good, she would still have had something to say. I don't care. The subjects I like I learn for myself, and with the rest, like English and math, I make an effort, because I know I'll need them in the future.

In the last class with Michaela, which was also the last class before the end of the term, we didn't study. Michaela brought chocolate balls covered with coconut that she made herself (delicious!), and anybody who wanted to spoke about a book that they liked and recommended it to the others to read in the holidays. I spoke about *The Bell Jar*, which over the past few days has sucked me in completely. Even though Esther Greenwood, the heroine of the novel (who is Sylvia Plath herself, when she was young), is already nineteen, and I'm not yet fourteen, I identify with her completely—with her voracious appetite for reading and writing, her ambition to be an important poet one day, with the knowledge that I feel things more deeply and more strongly than most other people, and with the need to dam these feelings with words, so they won't drown me, and also so they won't escape from me into the lands of oblivion.

I outlined the contents of the book, and I said that the extreme sensitivity of Sylvia Plath, whose father died when she was nine, caused her to try to commit suicide, after which she was hospitalized in a mental hospital, and in the end, when she was thirty one and the mother of two children, she killed herself by turning on the gas. Michaela said that the connection between art and madness had become a romantic myth in the culture of the West, but that it wasn't necessary to be mad in order to be an artist, Mozart and Picasso and many others had created wonderful things and they were perfectly sane, even though each of them had possessed certain eccentricities. I said that if all the oversensitive people had artistic tools by means of which they could cry out their mental wounds, perhaps there would be less mentally ill people in the world. The only sick ones left would be those whose sensitivity was so great, and whose wounds were so deep, that nothing could cure them. Michaela smiled and said that my attitude was romantic too, and that research had already shown that insanity was often simply a question of chemistry.

Most of the kids weren't listening. Michaela and I were conducting a private conversation, and I felt that the air between us was taut and vibrating, and suffused with the sweetness in my dream.

After me other kids spoke about the books they liked, but I wasn't listening. My stomach was squeezed tight with indecision about whether to go up to her after class, and what to say to her, and how to part. (Because the letter didn't come out in the end. I wrote a lot of drafts, and none of them seemed right to me. Some of them seemed too phony and disguised, some too frank and exposed, some too chatty and slapdash. If I'd had the courage to give her the letter I really wanted to write, there would be apart from her name and mine, only three words. . . .)

When the bell rang Michaela said, "Enjoy the holidays, read a lot," and everybody rushed out, jostling at the door like horses scenting the fields, shouting, "Have a good time," and "See you next year."

Three kids went up to her to complain about their marks (we received our reports from our homeroom teacher in the previous lesson), and she spoke to each of them patiently. One of the things I like about her is that always, even when she's in a hurry, she listens attentively and explains slowly, as if she had all the time in the world, like a real lady. After they left too, I went up to her, and she took my left hand in her right hand and held it gently. My lips trembled as I said, "I wanted to thank you for all this year," and Michaela looked at me for a moment, and then she said, "I thank you too—and the thanks of a teacher, and the satisfaction of a teacher, stems from knowing that the student is with her, and you were with me all the time, your eyes and your look were with me." She went on holding my hand in hers and smiling at me with her whole self, and suddenly she brought her lips to my forehead in a long kiss, warm and soft (not wet), a maternal, heartfelt kiss. When she removed her lips from my forehead and smiled at me, I had to hold back my tears. I thanked her again (for what, for the kiss?) and said see you later, and my lips trembled in a faltering kind of smile. Michaela said, "See you, Rivi," and I felt that she really meant it. I left the classroom and leaned against the wall, because my knees had melted like a double popsicle-de-luxe on two sticks.

So my collection of kisses from Michaela has grown (I have two, together with the kiss on Holocaust Day), and I am beside myself with joy. Except that I won't see her for two months, and by then I'll probably die of longing.

Good night, your Kitty

P.S. Last night on television I saw Menachem Begin's first speech as our new Prime Minister. He spoke like some biblical prophet, and said that too much blood, Jewish and Arab, had been shed in the region, and suggested putting an end to the bloodshed, and called on King Hussein, President Sadat, and President Assad "to meet with me, whether in our capital cities or on neutral ground." I wonder if anything will come of it.

Friday, 7.1.77

Dearest, dearest Anne,

Guess what fun I had today? Who I went to visit? Michaela!!! And I'm not bluffing and not fibbing, it really happened!!!

Racheli came around to my place this morning and in the afternoon I walked her home. (After Mother called me into the kitchen and hissed, "Hasn't your friend got a home? She's been hanging around here for hours." I wanted to tell her that Racheli had a home and how it was much more normal than ours, but I held my tongue.) I persuaded her to go via Hatzvi Avenue, even though it was longer. On the way I transmitted a telepathic message to Michaela, please come out, I want to meet you. I repeated this lots of times to myself, and once I also said: And I want you to invite us in. When we came to her street, everything was quiet and still. I told Racheli that I was tired, and maybe we could sit down on the bench for a while to rest. She said, I know why you suddenly felt tired exactly here.

We sat opposite her house and watched the ants bearing their burdens and scurrying around on the pavement as if they were the only creatures on earth. We sat there for a long time, and I had already despaired and was about to suggest to Racheli that we carry on, when suddenly I saw her coming out of her gate and walking towards a white car parked further down the road, apparently her husband's. She opened the door and took out a black James Bond briefcase. We approached her and she saw us and asked in surprise, "What are you doing here?" Without thinking I said, "I'm seeing Racheli home, and we're doing research on the life of ants." Michaela smiled and asked, "Why ants of all things?" And I stammered, "We saw a whole lot of ants, one of them was carrying a watermelon seed on its back, it must have been awfully heavy." Michaela looked at me intently, as if I had said the most fascinating thing she had ever heard in her life. She said, "I live here," and pointed to the house. I said, "Really? What a lovely house." She said, "Will you come and visit me?" I said, "If you invite us." She said, "Would you like to come now?" I said, "If you invite us." She suggested we come up for fifteen minutes. Her huge ginger dog called Dulcinea jumped up to greet us. She leaped on Michaela and almost knocked her down. Michaela apologized for the mess (there wasn't a mess at all), and invited us to sit down, and she went into the kitchen and returned with a jar of lemonade and three blue glasses. She asked what we planned to do in the holidays, and if we were going to the Scouts' camp. We told her that we'd decided to leave the Scouts, because the activities were boring, and that the day after tomorrow we were going to Jerusalem, to a summer camp for art-loving youth. Michaela told us that she had been there too when she was a girl, that there were fleas in the bed, and that the drama teacher had gone mad. We laughed. Her husband came into the living room, he was tall, bespectacled, and slightly balding. She said, "This is Yoel, and these are two of my most serious students." I was in the middle of taking a sip of lemonade, and I choked and started coughing. (After we left, Racheli said that he looked a bit of a bore, but it's hard for me to believe that Michaela would marry a bore.) Dulcinea jumped up on the sofa and ate the flowers in the vase on the table. Racheli played with her, grabbing hold of her ears and kissing her nose. The phone rang, her husband answered and said, "Michaelush, it's for you." She went to the phone in the entrance hall, and to my great surprise, spoke in German. Usually I don't like hearing this language (I know that you didn't like it either. Even though it was your mother tongue you refused to speak it, because of the Nazis), but on Michaela's lips it sounded as soft and sweet as fresh rolls. In the meantime I looked around, trying to impress every detail on my memory: a beige sofa with cushions with Arab embroidery, a stereo and tons of records, an antique-looking piano, a dark wooden cabinet with glass doors holding porcelain, crystal goblets, and bottles of liquor, and beautiful paintings on the walls. I especially liked one of a little girl in a white dress, with straight brown hair to the lobes of her ears, sitting in a park on a rounded white wooden bench. On the end of the bench sat an elderly woman, apparently her nursemaid, with gray hair and a long white apron, busy with knitting or embroidery. The woman is looking at the little girl, who is looking into a grand white baby carriage, and you can't tell if there's a baby inside it or a doll. At the forefront of the picture, in strong strokes of greens and reds, is a big bed of tall gladioli, hiding the feet of the little girl and the woman, and you can actually smell them, and also the thick lawn, and the light flooding everything. Michaela said the artist's name was Max Liebermann, and her father, who had an art gallery in Hadar, had bought the painting in Berlin in the thirties, before he fled the Nazis and came to Palestine, and a few months ago he had given it to them as a wedding present. In the next room, the study, I could see an antique desk with lots of drawers and compartments that you could close with a kind of folding lid, a huge library, a red-and-black carpet with a few big cushions on it, a window with a transparent white curtain through which you could see a cypress tree and behind it the wadi and a little triangle of sea.

Michaela came back to us and said, "That was my mother.

90

She wanted to make sure that we're coming for Friday night dinner at seven." After that she asked if my parents were local products, and if we spoke another language at home. I told her that on my mother's side I was the eighth generation in the country, and on my father's side the second generation, and that the only language my parents spoke to us was Hebrew. (I didn't tell her that they were divorced, and that my father didn't speak to me in any language. . . .) She asked Racheli about her parents, and Racheli said that her father was from Poland and her mother from Holland, and they were both Holocaust survivors. She also said that her mother had known you in her childhood, that you were both in the same class, and that later on she met you in Auschwitz. (I already knew that, of course. Whenever I go to Racheli's house, I nag her mother to tell me more about you.) I said, "If Anne Frank had survived, perhaps she would have come to Israel and lived on the Carmel, and her daughter would have been in our class, and we would have gone to her house and met Anne, who may have changed her name to Hannah, and would surely have been a fantastic writer." Michaela looked at me with a smile and said, "You keep a diary, don't you?" I nodded my head and blushed, as if she could have known that I wrote it to you, and that most of the diary was about her. Afterwards she spoke to Racheli about her painting classes, and said that she had painted too when she was younger. Her eyes followed the smoke ring spiraling from her cigarette, and she said, "When I was your age I played the piano, danced, painted, wrote poetry, and went to drama classes. People always said that I had been blessed with talents. Today I know that being a little talented in a lot of fields is more of a curse than a blessing. I wish I had had a lot of talent in just one field."

I wanted to tell her that there was one field in which she was terrifically talented, that she was a wonderful teacher, but I felt as if somebody had closed my lips with a clothes peg. It felt so good being there in her house that I didn't want to leave, I could have gone on sitting there for years. And then Michaela suddenly said, "Now I'm going to send you home," and I felt sad, like in the tea party on the ceiling of the laughing uncle's house, when Mary Poppins says it's time to go, and everybody stops laughing and lands on the floor. Michaela saw us to the door, said she hoped we enjoyed the summer camp in Jerusalem, and looked at me with her special look, which crinkles the little wrinkles at the corners of her eyes, penetrates me, and caresses me all over. When we came out I wanted to hug the trees and dance and shout, I was in her house! Instead I'm writing to you. Your paper ears absorb everything.

Yours, Kitty

7.7.77 (amazing date . . .)

Dearest Anne,

I'm writing to you from Jerusalem, from the summer camp for art-loving youth in the "Bayit v'Gan" youth hostel. I'm sitting on the roof. The air is pink and clear and the smell of the pines here is drier and sharper than in Haifa. Soon it will be evening and it will begin to get cool.

We're seven girls in a room. Racheli and I sleep head to head on the top bunks of two double-decker beds and we talk until two in the morning. Tonight I confided in her that I dream about Michaela, write about her in my diary, and think about her all the time. I didn't dare tell her how I thirst for the touch of her hand on my hair, on my shoulder, and that I document every touch in my diary, deliberate or accidental. Racheli said that she knows, she sees my face in Michaela's classes, the way I blush when I talk, and the way my eyes sparkle, and how I sat reverentially on the edge of the sofa when we were in her house, as if it was some kind of temple.

She asked me what I wanted to happen. I thought for a minute and said, "I want to show her my poems."

"And what else?" whispered Racheli, "do you want to be friends with her?"

"Of course I do," I whispered, "but why should she want to be my friend?"

"I want to be your friend."

"Yes, but she must have friends of her own age, married friends, why should she want to be friends with a kid?"

"You're not a kid." Racheli's eyes shone at me in the dark, "You're a devil."

I laughed, burying my face in the pillow, "If I'm a devil then so are you a devil."

At that moment the old names we had inherited from our grandmothers were forgotten, the one who had perished in the Holocaust and the one who had perished from cancer. We were two devils, talking to each other in the masculine gender.

Each man has a name given to him by his best friend. . . .

But to you I am as always, Kitty

7.20.77

Dearest Anne,

Home again, in my old familiar room. Leonard Cohen revolving on the record player and whining about Suzanne. The window's open and not a hint of a breeze. You can die of the heat. In a little while I'll melt and turn into a puddle. Here are a few more experiences from the summer camp for you: on Sunday morning they took us for a tour of the Old City, we went to the "Augusta Victoria" to hear a mass sung by a Danish choir accompanied by an organ. I closed my eyes, breathed in the incense, and let the music fill my body. Afterwards we walked through the bazaar and ate delicious bagels with sesame seeds, dipped in wild thyme in a twist of newspaper. I bought myself an embroidered top with flared sleeves made of a stiff burgundy material, and ever since I came home I've been wearing it all the time. Mother pulls a face and says, "When are you going to take that Arab rag off? Soon we'll have to scrape it off you with a spatula."

Over the past few days I've been copying my selected poems into a notebook, to give them to Michaela at the beginning of the school year, or even, if I succeed in gathering up my courage and phoning her up, during this long vacation. I copied down "Last Khamsin," "Morning Hour," "Wanderer's Anthology," "The Dark Fruit," "Desert Mirages," "Not Exactly from Here and Now," "Eucalyptus," "The Mermaids," and "Gum Arabic." I'm still making up my mind about "The Wind's Story," "Autumn Song," and "On Friday Night." Obviously I won't give her the poem "You" that I wrote to her, it gives too much away. Yesterday morning I made up my mind to call her. I locked myself up in my mother's room, picked up the receiver, dialed the first four numbers (my stomachache grew worse with every number . . .), and with the last one I returned my finger as slowly as I could. And then I heard her soft "Hello," with a question mark at the end of it, as if she were waiting for something to happen, for some surprise, and I couldn't utter a sound, and I put the phone down. I think I'm going to have to wait until the beginning of September.

Michaela, Michaela, Michaela, why can't I stop thinking and dreaming about you? What is it about you that attracts me so much and makes me love you to insanity?

Yours, Kitty

8.5.77

Dearest Anne,

This morning Racheli came to visit me, and just now I accompanied her to the Center. We parted with hugs and tears, and afterwards I stood and watched her receding into the distance as she walked down Ocean Road; her slender figure, her thin legs in the short jeans, the blond hair reaching to her earlobes. Tomorrow she's going to Amsterdam with her mother and she'll be there to the end of the holidays. Her mother's sister lives there with her husband and her two sons. (The two sisters were together in Auschwitz, where their parents died, and after the war Racheli's mother decided to emigrate to Eretz Israel, and her sister returned to their childhood home, not far from the street where you lived, and she lives there to this day.) I envy her of course, both for the flight (I've never flown yet), and for all the things she'll see, which I only know from the descriptions on the back of my letters to you, with the "Classical Europe" of Mother's tourist agency; sailing on the canals, the cathedral, the flower market, the windmills, the yellow cheeses, and most of all I envy her for walking down the streets you once rode down on your bicycle, with the wind in your face, and your life, which had only begun still seeming to you as full of surprises as a birthday table, and as long as eternity, and of course—for the visit to your hiding place. I made her swear a thousand oaths to bring me back all the pictures and souvenirs possible, and also to photograph the hiding place, if it's permitted, and she promised.

Everybody's going overseas. My mother's leaving in a few days too, this time for Spain (presumably with Moishele), and Grandpa's going to America with his Bracha. I think he feels the need to compensate her for the fact that they've been together now for over ten years without getting married, or even moving in to live together, and that's why he takes her with him on all his trips, and also I suppose because he enjoys her company, because she's quite amusing.

Oren and Noam will go to Daddy, and perhaps he'll take them to Eilat, so that I'll be left by myself, as usual, and I'll go to Aunt Tehiya in Ramat-Gan, and help her in her garden, and we'll probably go to the sea and to matinees, but mainly I plan to read (I took *Death in Venice* and *The Confessions of Felix Krull* by Thomas Mann out of the library), and perhaps I'll give birth to a few new poems there. It goes without saying that I'll take you with me too.

Yours as always, Kitty

Dearest Anne,

I'm sitting under the mango tree and reading the wonderful
Felix Krull. (I've already finished *Death in Venice.* He writes brilliantly, but it's a little hard to believe that an old man could
really fall in love like that with such a young boy.) The elongated, orange, ripe-to-bursting fruits are hanging above my
head, and from time to time I raise a lazy hand and pluck one,
cut it open on both sides with a knife, and slice the shining flesh
lengthways and sideways, fold the peel over like a tortoise's shell,
and bite into cube after cube, and my mouth opens up to the
festive, orange taste, the taste of sun, the taste of life, and the
juice runs down my chin. Finally I suck the hairy pit, which is
the sweetest of all, and lick my fingers thoroughly, and get up to
wash my sticky hands and face with the garden hose, and go on
reading and playing with my tongue with the little hairs stuck
between my teeth.

Sometimes I think that I drew whatever strength I possess
from this garden, from the red soil with the beds of lilies and
nasturtiums and birds-of-paradise, and from the big lawn, where
the sprinkler with its outstretched arms practices pirouettes
every evening, and from the trees surrounding it—nearly all of
which I once climbed, when I was small: the loquat and the
guava, the pecan and the pomelo, the mango and the blood-
orange, the only one I didn't climb was the shadowy avocado
with its big leaves, because its branches start too high up on its
whitewashed trunk.

And this heavy house gives me strength too; Grandma Rivka's and Aunt Tehiya's parents built it over fifty years ago, and it
hasn't changed since then. The same open veranda, whose tiles,
divided into two triangles, dark brown and light brown, were
my very first memory from the age of two or three, even before
I knew the colors, but I felt the tiles, warm and dusty, under my
bare feet, and Uncle Moshe, with his bare chest and khaki
shorts, lifted me up to look into the orange crate standing on

the balustrade, and said, look at Kitzi's new kittens, and I saw the cat lying there with the kittens crowding up to her, pink and bald and blind, and I breathed in their smell, which wasn't nice, but has remained in my nose since then as the smell of newborn life.

And the folding wooden shutters with the *menshelach*, they too are from then. And the dark hearts of the ivy running riot over the walls of the house all the way up to the roof. And there's always food I like here for me, and old books, and quiet to read and write and dream, and starched sheets and towels, and dozens of smells from my childhood, from the lost continent of Atlantis.

And I drew strength especially from her herself, from Aunt Tehiya, who we call Auntehiya, as if the aunt is part of her name, and she calls me "monkey" (each man has a name given to him by his Auntehiya . . .), and who looks herself like a strong tree, with her muscular brown legs and upright back and the black braid set on her head like a crown. When I was born she came to live with us, to help my mother take care of me, and when I was two years old she lifted me onto her shoulders and took me down to the wadi, and taught me the colors from the colors of the cyclamens and the anemones and the wild chrysanthemums, and I know that she loves me not because I'm her dead sister's granddaughter, and not because I'm my mother's daughter, but because I'm me.

Aunt Tehiya is the only person I know who always says exactly what she feels. If, for instance, I left the bathroom in a mess, or took things out of the fridge and forgot to put them back, she looks me in the eyes and says quietly, I'm cross with you, and explains why, not like my mother who punishes by silence and by ignoring me for days on end, not answering me even when I ask her for something, as if I don't exist, until I can't stand it anymore and I cry and apologize for everything, even for things I didn't do.

Aunt Tehiya is capable of talking about some acquaintance

of hers and saying, "She really hurt my feelings" or "I'm sorry for her," and also, "I really love her"; and when someone leaves her, like her son who lives in America, or like Uncle Moshe, whose heart suddenly stopped seven years ago, she says, "Sometimes I miss him so much," and her nostrils redden, and to me she says, "I think about you a lot, every night before I go to sleep I worry about your mother."

It's so right, simply to say what you feel, that's what they invented words that express emotions for, so why don't they exist in my parents' dictionary?

Yesterday evening, when we were eating together on the veranda (fried eggs and salad cut fine and black bread with Bulgarian cheese, and bitter olives and delicious brown baby eggplants that Aunt Tehiya pickles herself), I told her that sometimes, in the dark before I fall asleep, I remember that one day I'm going to die, like everybody dies in the end, and my heart begins to race in fear, and reaches a record speed, because how is it possible that the whole world will still be here and only I won't be, what, the sun will go on rising and setting without me, and at nine o'clock they'll show "Today's News" on television? How is it possible that the eyes that see the trees and the sky and read books will suddenly stop seeing, and these hands with the long fingers, which are so much me because I've grown used to them ever since I was born, even though I could have had other hands, will lie under the ground and won't be able to move, and the same goes for the face that I see every day in the mirror, and which I've also somehow gotten used to, even though it seems completely accidental to me (and sometimes I even manage to imagine for a minute or two that I have somebody else's face); and especially how can it be that my brain—which is the only thing that isn't accidental, because it is me—that remembers so much, and even knows its own death—will simply switch off one day and stop working, like a broken television set?

Aunt Tehiya slowly chewed a slice of bread with Bulgarian

cheese and listened, and I said that sometimes I can't go to sleep for hours, because death is like a riddle that I have to make a supreme effort to solve, like that Hungarian cube that's made of lots of colored blocks that you have to turn around and around until each side of the big block comes out the same color, or like that famous picture by Escher, of a hand drawing a hand.

"Take another slice," Aunt Tehiya passed me the bread basket, and I put my hand on my stomach and said, "I can't, I'm bursting."

"That's how I sometimes feel about life," she said reflectively, "as if I've eaten too much and I haven't got room for another crumb, and all I want to do is lie down somewhere and sleep, and be left in peace. But you're just beginning now, and your appetite is still big, and so is the fear that the meal will suddenly come to an end. You'll come to see that after the first course your hunger is already somewhat appeased, and after the main course you're so full that you don't really care if dessert is served or not, and after dessert there's no room at all for anything else and all you want to do is lie down and rest."

"And so you stop being afraid, because in any case you've lost your appetite," I suddenly understood, "that's quite reassuring."

"You've lost your appetite, and your teeth to chew with too," she smiled at me with her brown eyes, "but the difference between a meal and life is that in life you eat the sweet dessert at the beginning, and all the rest comes afterwards. You're eating the dessert now."

"So why does it sometimes seem to me that I'm eating bitter herbs?" I poked my fork into the remains of the salad, turning a piece of tomato from side to side.

"We both know why. Your parents haven't given you an easy time." Her long-fingered hand with its brown spots, and the line of earth edging her nails, rested on mine, "But it doesn't matter so much what you eat, what's important is that your sense of taste is still sharp and capable of experiencing the whole range of flavors, and the same with your sense of smell and all the other senses, which grow dull with age. That's why we long all our lives long for the food of our childhood, the landscapes of our childhood, the music we heard when we were children. It's not because this eggplant," she fished a baby eggplant out of the pickle jar, "is tastier than the pickled eggplant you'll eat in twenty or thirty years time, but because your mouth is still young and inquisitive and unspoiled, and the same with your eyes and ears and heart, especially your heart."

With regard to my heart—I wanted to ask her—do you think it's all right that for almost a year now there's been a certain woman, a teacher, living inside it, like in the nursery rhyme about the woman who lived inside a pumpkin shell? But instead I asked her quietly, "And you, aren't you afraid of dying? You're not so old yet, you're only sixty."

Aunt Tehiya stacked the plates and bowls into a tower and said, "I'm not afraid. There are still a few countries I'd be happy to visit—China, for example, could be an interesting dessert—but I've already eaten my main course, down to the last scrap, I devoured it like a lioness, blood and skin and bones and all."

Yes, that's what I should do, I said to myself as I followed her upright back to the screen door leading to the kitchen holding the pickle jar in my hands; devour life boldly, like a lioness, with blood and skin and bones and all, like the adventurer Felix Krull.

Soon we'll drive in her yellow Beetle to Tel Aviv, we'll go down to the beach to see the sunset, and then we'll go to see the new Woody Allen movie, *Annie Hall*, showing at the Seagull Cinema.

Goodbye for now, Kitty the Lioness

Now it's midnight, we just got back from Tel Aviv, and I have to tell you about *Annie Hall*—what a great movie! Wise and funny and romantic and touching! At the beginning of the movie the character played by Woody Allen tells a joke about two old ladies in a hotel, and one of them says to the other one, "The food here's terrible," and the other one says, "Yes, and the portions are so small. . . " He says that this is how he feels about life—full of loneliness, suffering, misery, and sorrow, and all over too soon. Aunt Tehiya and I looked at each other in the darkness and started to laugh, because we felt that Woody Allen was speaking to us, as if he'd overheard our conversation yesterday.

Hidden on the Ocean Floor

The sun has already gone down behind the mountain, leaving behind it a cold, murky light and the dark canopy of the pines. The Carmel always looks sad to me when evening falls. I close the binder on my knees, and my hand digs into my bag for the crumpled tissue I used at the funeral. Aunt Tehiya didn't tell me everything at that supper on her porch; she didn't tell me how the days grow shorter as their numbers increase, and how the weeks, months, and years shrink as you grow older, like the Valencia oranges of my childhood in their compartment in the fridge. The insulting shrinkage of time she left me to discover by myself. Now I know: all the time time keeps shrinking, and soon my body will follow suit, and whatever I devoured I devoured, and whatever I left I left, and Aunt Tehiya is no longer alive for me to tell her what I ate and what I left, and neither are you, who devoured and left nothing.

A middle-aged woman in a floral dress is walking down the road, dragging a swollen checked shopping cart behind her. She lashes me with a suspicious look and pushes the gate, and I recognize her as Mrs. Germann, your downstairs neighbor, whose porch we would steal past in Indian file, and once she and her husband went on holiday and left you the key to water the plants, and we fled to their apartment and hid from Yoel and the baby screaming in his arms.

How long have I been sitting here on the bench opposite your old house, unable to pick myself up and move, to begin the journey back to Tel Aviv. I glance at my watch and am alarmed to discover that it's already a quarter to seven, and take the cell phone, which I switched off during the funeral and forgot to switch on again, out of my bag, and call home. Yair's worried voice, "Where are you, I tried again and again and it was switched off."

I'm tied to them by an umbilical cord with an infinite capacity for stretching, a hundred kilometers and more. Even to the ends of the earth. "I'm still in Haifa, I got held up, I'll take the next train back."

"You remember that there's a parent-teacher meeting at the school at eight." Rebuke in his voice. I forgot all about it. The beginning of the year teacher-parents meeting in Carmel's class. To meet the new homeroom teacher. I'll never make it in time. "You'll have to go on your own, maybe you can get the neighbors' daughter to babysit."

"Whatever you say," he grunts, betraying his hostility to this whole trip, to you, and to our story that accompanies my life like a shadow.

"Have the girls eaten?" I make an effort.

"We're eating now." We is the three of them. I'm outside, on the bench opposite your house, up to the neck in a past that threatens to engulf me entirely.

"Okay," I give in, "I'll be there in a couple of hours, I don't remember when the next train is. Tell the girls I send them kisses."

He tells them, and I hear their birdlike lip-smacking. The kisses are the stitches; when we get up in the morning, and before we leave the house, and in the afternoon when we come home, and in the evening before we go to bed. We are joined to one another by chain stitch.

I take hold of the handles of the shopping bag, pull myself up from the bench, and trail down the street in the direction of Ocean road. My hand goes out to stop a cab, "To the Carmel beach railway station."

Racheli's old house, on the corner of Ocean road and Tamar Street, is in darkness. Her father died four years ago, and her mother always saved on electricity. The Saturday before last we drove to Upper-Modi'in, where Racheli lives with her husband, a born-again Jew like her, and their five children. The two wheaten braids hidden under a purple bandana, and the Dutch eyes—bluer-than-blue circles painted on Delft china—had not dimmed.

We sat at the kitchen table. Racheli breast-fed her new baby whose head was a golden patch on the hill of her swollen white breast, and I told her about your illness that had spread hopelessly, and the tears gathered on her lashes, and suddenly one of her neighbors came in and asked for a glass of boiling water, because their hot-water urn wasn't working and they couldn't fix it until after the Sabbath, and Racheli wiped her eyes on her sleeve, gave me the sleeping baby, and said naturally, addressing me in the male gender, "Devil, hold her for a minute," and I took the baby from her arms, a bundle of warmth smelling of baby-shampoo, and said, in the same gender, "I'm holding her, Devil, don't worry," and the neighbor's eyebrows frowned suspiciously under her headscarf.

The radio is on, it's the seven o'clock news. The elderly taxi driver, bald headed and mustached, puts out his hand and turns up the volume. Twenty wounded in the bomb that went off this morning in the street of the Prophets, in downtown Jerusalem. The suicide bomber dressed up as an Orthodox Jew. The Police Commander of the Northern district has concluded his evidence before the commission of inquiry into the events of October last year, when thirteen Israeli Arabs were killed by policemen. A little girl of six was forgotten in a closed school bus and suffocated to death. The old lady who had come back to life during her own funeral last week was released from hospital and returned to the old age home. A further drop in the heat load was expected.

The taxi driver switches off the radio and half turns his head to me. "It's all the opposite of what it's supposed to be, children die and old people come back to life, and where it's supposed to be dark it's even darker than it should be, sometimes I feel like taking a big hose-pipe, like the kind on fire engines, and cleaning out the whole country, religious, secular, Arabs, settlers, everyone, mopping them all up with a lot of water, like the story of Noah's Ark, and beginning everything from the beginning again."

I nod at him and make an effort to smile. Yes, I want to go back to the beginning too, to the first page of a notebook with a new smell.

The seven twenty train is already waiting at the platform. If I don't hurry I'll miss it, steal myself a little more time, but I'm already in the coach in the gloomy neon light, searching for a table with four vacant seats; on one of the seats I sit down, on the seat next to it I put my bag and the shopping bag, to prevent any possibility of a stranger sitting next to me. Two woman soldiers, in navy uniforms, one with cropped fair hair, and the other with dark hair in a ponytail sprawl out on the two pairs of seats next to the table across the aisle. They rest their heads on either side of the window and get ready to go to sleep. The train jerks forwards and backwards, and then it suddenly takes off and begins moving heavily. In a minute I'll take out the second notebook, with Mike Brandt on the cover, walking in a field of yellow tulips with his hair dancing in the wind.

Thursday night, 9.1.77

Dearest Anne,

In honor of the first day of the ninth grade I've started to write to you in a new notebook. I bought it yesterday afternoon in Max's shop, with my school supplies. I looked for a notebook with a lock like yours, but I didn't find one. It was crowded and stifling there, with all the kids who put it off till the last moment, and I couldn't stand there making up my mind forever. In the end I bought a rather ridiculous folio notebook with a picture of Mike Brandt on the cover, striding through a field of yellow tulips with his long hair flapping. Even though it smells new, it must be an old notebook, from before he killed himself. I'm not into Mike Brandt, I don't really know his songs (except for one they play all the time on the radio "*Laisse moi t'aimer*"), but his face looks nice and smiling, without a hint of suicidal tendencies. After my parents' divorce I would imagine killing myself by jumping from the Shalom Tower in Tel Aviv, and everyone, even the android, crying and being sorry, but I've never succeeded in really understanding why healthy people commit suicide. Because even in a time of suffering they can hang onto the hope that things will get better, like you wrote in the darkest days in your hiding place: "There's always some beauty left—in nature, sunshine, freedom, in yourself . . . look at these things, and you'll find happiness and regain your balance." Even if I live another seventy or even eighty years, I'll have the whole of eternity to be dead in, and until then a few interesting things can still happen to me. . . . I punched holes in the "Classical Europe" pages from Mother's office whose backs I wrote on in the eighth grade and put them into a green binder.

Today at twelve noon all the students from the middle school were assembled in the gym hall for the ceremonial opening of the school year. The long vacation had no effect on the usual stink of rubber, dust, and sweaty gym shoes. Me and Racheli—who only got back from Amsterdam yesterday, and brought me a few postcards with pictures of you and the hiding place—sat down at the side, with our backs to the wooden ladders. I looked for Michaela, and suddenly I saw her, and my heart began to jump. She was standing at the back with the other teachers, but apart from them, leaning with her shoulder against the wall and smoking, even though it was forbidden to smoke in the hall. She had her back to me, and I couldn't catch her eye. She was tanned and she had a new dress on, pale lilac with little blue flowers and narrow shoulder straps, her hair was cut to just under the ears, exposing her long, slender neck.

Hourgi, his angular face tanned, in a snow white shirt and black trousers, brushed his silver forelock off his forehead, tapped the microphone with his finger, cleared his throat, and said in an authoritative baritone, one-two, one-two-three. And then he put his brown, muscular hands on his hips, and made a speech about the loss of values in the youth of today, "Nothing interests you, except for Elvis Presley," rolling the "r" and spraying the people sitting in the first row with saliva. Racheli and I raised our eyebrows and tried not to laugh. Neither of us were too upset over the death of Elvis, who had died of cardiac arrest two weeks before while sitting on the lavatory and trying to shit. (My mother was actually quite upset. They're about the same age, and when she was young she liked "Love Me Tender" and other songs like that.)

"Who is this Elvis anyway," continued Hourgi in sacred rage with his arm cutting the air, "a drug addict, a junkie with a guitar."

I stole a glance at Michaela and managed to catch her eye. She crinkled her eyes and sent me a long smile, at the bottom of which lay something I was unable to decipher, and then she dropped her cigarette butt onto the floor and crushed it with her sandal. She really smokes too much, even more than my mother. After that we left the hall and I didn't see her again, but tomorrow we have a literature lesson!

Yours, Kitty

9.15.77

Dearest Anne,
This year all of Michaela's classes are in the last hours. I have to go through seven purgatories of history, geography, math,

biology, Bible, and gym, in order to reach one o'clock and see her coming into the classroom—the burning eyes, the smile, the freckled shoulders, the ponytail, the blue sandals, the smell of cigarettes mixed with a faint smell of hand cream, and here she is, as large as life, as if she has just popped out of her home in my heart to give us a literature or written expression lesson, after which she will immediately return to her permanent abode.

In one of her first classes she asked us to write a composition on the subject of "A biblical character who appeals to me" for homework. In the evening I got into bed with the Bible in the leather binding with the zipper, which my mother received from her parents on her thirteenth birthday together with the not-very-original dedication "And thou shalt meditate therein day and night."

I meditated all night and continued to meditate the next day on the question of which character to choose. I knew it would be a woman, because women are far deeper and more interesting, and I don't really understand men. At first I thought of writing about Jephthah's daughter, I opened the chapter in the Book of Judges to remind myself, and read how her father, the son of a harlot who kept the company of vain men, made a stupid vow, that if he won a war he would offer up as a burnt sacrifice whatsoever came out of his house to greet him, and how his only daughter, whose name we are not told, came out to greet him with timbrels and with dances, and Jephthah, instead of explaining to God, and mainly to himself, that he hadn't intended to sacrifice a person, but only some sheep or cow, rents his clothes as if he's the victim here, and says, "Alas my daughter thou hast brought me very low" and "thou art one of them that trouble me" as if it's her fault, and tells her about his vow and expects her to solve the problem for him, and she tells him that she's prepared to sacrifice herself and die, and only asks him to allow her to go to the mountains with her friends and weep for her virginity and the life she would not have, the love she would not know and the children she would not bear, and suddenly I felt tears trickling down my cheeks, because it was so cruel, far more cruel than the story of the binding of Isaac. God stopped Abraham's hand holding the knife, and Isaac remained alive; but he didn't stop Jephthah, perhaps because God prefers boys and he doesn't care too much about girls, and perhaps because he didn't ask Jephthah for the sacrifice in the first place. And I knew that I wouldn't be able to write this essay, because I would never be able to understand how she could have agreed to sacrifice her life for him, when she went to the mountains she could have run away, it must have crossed her mind, and her friends could have helped her, but she chose to return to this terrible father and let him offer her up as a sacrifice; and I didn't understand either how her mother, Jephthah's wife, who isn't mentioned in the story at all, let him sacrifice their only child.

Afterwards I paged through the Book of Kings, and I came to the story of Jezebel, daughter of Ethbaal the king of the Zidonians, a spoiled princess who thought she had everything coming to her, including the vineyard of Naboth the Jezreelite, and she got Naboth killed so that Ahab her husband could take possession of his vineyard. And I went on and read how Jehu the son of Jehoshaphat killed Joram King of Israel, the son of Jezebel, and Ahaziah the king of Judah, the grandson of Jezebel, and then he arrives in Jezreel to kill Jezebel as well, and Jezebel, who already knows that her son and grandson have been killed, and that it's her turn now, doesn't hide or run away, but paints her face and fixes her hair and stands at the window in regal pride to greet the man who is about to kill her, and even finds in herself the strength to mock him, "Has Zimri peace, who slew his master?" I knew that I understood her pride far better than the submissiveness of Jephthah's daughter, and I felt a little sorry for her, too, after all she came from a strange land and a different religion, and the prophets Elijah and Elisha didn't respect her belief in Baal, and they hated her for being a strong masterful woman, and they turned her into a scapegoat for their religious war, and I thought that even someone who had done wrong didn't deserve to die in such a cruel way: her eunuchs, who were supposed to be her most loyal servants, threw her out of the window, and Jehu's horses trampled her underfoot, and she wasn't even buried, for the dogs had eaten her, just like Elijah wanted, and then I decided to write about her, a foreign queen, proud, hated, and misunderstood. I knew that nobody else would write about Jezebel. The other girls would write about predictable, positive characters like Deborah, Sarah, and Rachel. Racheli said she was going to write about Eve. I asked her why, and she thought for a minute and said, "Because she was the first mother in the world." I bet she'll have a million children one day. In any case, when I sat down to write the essay, it suddenly came out as a poem. I think it's not bad. I handed it in to Michaela and now I'm waiting. Maybe after this poem she'll ask if I've written other poems, and I'll be able to give her the notebook at last.

Yours, Kitty

9.22.77

Dearest Anne,

Today Michaela returned our essays. She went from desk to desk, handing out the pages, and she said, "Most of you wrote satisfactory essays, some of you wrote stuff and nonsense, and one of you wrote a poem."

She asked me to stand up and read the poem out loud. I held the page and felt my face burning and my hands trembling. I tried to read without my voice trembling too:

Jezebel

On that fateful day
when you lost your son,
the kohl blackened your cheeks
and the crown of your hair scattered in the wind.

And when you were thrown from the window
by those you trusted,
all the gods of Sidon
listened silently to your lament, queen.
Only their hearts were pierced by the cry,
and my heart, thousands of years later, too.

Are you still crying, woman?
Desist, everyone is satisfied now:
the dogs licking up your blood,
and the prophets too.

When I finished I felt that my face was boiling and my
blouse was soaked with sweat. A few of the kids clapped, and
Yuval Shalev said in his reedy voice, "I didn't know you were
such a Bialik," and Amnon Neuman said, "Not Bialik, Leah
Goldberg," and Gidi Leiman said, "Rachel," and Noam Bloch
said, "Zelda," and everyone laughed. And then Gil Klein, who
had once, when we were dancing "slow" at a party in the seventh
grade, tried to press up against me with the fly of his jeans, and
I pushed him away, complained, "It's not fair, I sat for three
hours on a five-page composition, and she scribbles some poem
in five minutes." Michaela waited for everyone to calm down,
and all the time she looked into my eyes over the heads and
smiled at me. I thought that she would talk about the poem but
to my surprise she didn't say anything. She asked Gil to read his
dry-as-dust five pages about the prophet Samuel, perhaps so his
feelings wouldn't be hurt, and Racheli whispered to me, "He's
such a bore."

When the lesson was over and everyone left, and Michaela
was still busy writing something in the attendance book and
organizing her briefcase at her desk, I decided to approach her.
My stomach hurt as if I needed to go to the lavatory. Michaela
raised her head, as if she sensed me, standing there, and smiled

at me. I said, "You didn't say anything about the poem," and she bowed her head and said, "Everyone has moments when it's hard to find words." She said that when she read the poem at home she was very moved and she even showed it to her husband, and that she was especially impressed by my ability to feel compassion for Jezebel. She lifted my chin with her gentle fingers, looked deep into my eyes, as if she were reading my heart, and said, "You should lift up your head and straighten your back, because you're taller than all of them," and suddenly she brought her lips to mine and kissed me gently on the mouth. I was a little frightened. I'd never thought about her like that. With burning lips I asked, "Would you like to see more poems?" Her eyes lit up as if she'd won a prize, "Of course, of course I'd like to." We made a date for me to come to her house during the Sukkoth holidays. I'm so happy and confused that I probably won't be able to sleep all night. I go over everything again and again, her fingers under my chin, her lips on mine, which are still stinging like a burn. I try to understand how the poem could have given rise to such excitement in her, perhaps even to love for me, as if the words I write have a power of their own, a frightening magical power over which I have no control.

I probably won't sleep until Sukkoth.

Your Kitty

Sukkoth, 10.3.77

Dearest Anne,

This morning I went to Michaela with my poems. I met her getting out of her car and trying to hold down her dress that was flapping in the wind. She was untidy and she wasn't made-up, but she was as cute as ever. She smiled at me and asked, "Do you know Rocinanta?" I said, "Do you mean Dulcinea, your dog?" And Michaela patted the roof of her car and announced, "Please meet Rocinanta, my trusty rattletrap, who takes me wherever I want to go, and sometimes wherever she wants to go."

I said that as far as I remembered Don Quixote's horse Rocinante was a he and not a she, and Michaela laughed and said, "My Rocinanta is definitely a she."

When we went inside we were greeted by Dulcinea, who jumped onto Michaela with her front paws on the low neckline of her dress and almost pulled the whole thing off. I sat down on the sofa in the living room, and Michaela went to the kitchen and came back with coffee and cookies. She sat down and lit a cigarette. Suddenly, without any intention, the words escaped me, "What do you get out of that shit?" and she asked, "What shit?" I said, "The shit you're holding in your hand." Michaela said, "Apparently it does something for me," and asked me why I was so aggressive. I said that I hated it when people knowingly harmed themselves. She said, "And don't you ever harm yourself? You're doing yourself a lot of harm with that aggression," and she imitated me, "'What do you get out of that shit?' It closes doors, instead of opening them, and if someone has the door shut in his face he may not knock again. We build fortresses around ourselves in order to protect the things that are important to us, and we forget that what's really important to us is the connection with other people." I bowed my head and nodded.

"I know that you like yourself," she said, "but you have to work on yourself. You don't need those defenses. You're delicate, I know, but you're also strong." Dulcinea jumped on the plastic bag with the notebook of poems, and Michaela grabbed her by the collar, moved her to the other side of the sofa and scratched her neck. I took the notebook out of the bag and gave it to her. She read slowly, attentively, and her lips drew the words voicelessly. Every now and then she smiled and said quietly, "They're really very mature for your age," as if she were talking to herself, but she knew very well that I was anxiously watching her every movement. When she finished reading she asked me if I could leave the notebook with her so that she could read the poems again. I said, "It's for you to keep. I copied the poems for you." She smiled broadly and looked at me with that kind, maternal look she reserves for special occasions. She put the notebook down gently on the table, and then she looked at me in silence. Tears choked my throat. The impressive speeches I had prepared at home were forgotten as if they had never been.

"Strange," I said, "I came to talk to you, and suddenly all the fine words have flown out of my head." Michaela looked at me again with the same special look that narrows the fan of wrinkles at the corners of her eyes, penetrating me and caressing me all over on the inside. And then she shook herself and said, "Tell me a little about yourself." I told her that my parents were divorced, and she looked as if she'd received a slap in her sweet face. She asked me when they got divorced and if I understood it. I said that I could understand why my father divorced my mother, but I couldn't understand why he divorced me at the same time. I told her that he didn't talk to me or take me to his house, only Oren and Noam, and she said quietly, "I can't understand either how he could give up a wonderful girl like you. Perhaps he can't cope with your growing up?" She suggested that I try to talk to him. I said that I'd given the part of my heart meant for my father an anesthetic a long time ago, and I no longer felt anything there, like a local anesthetic at the dentist's, and that if I tried to talk to him it would no doubt come back to life and begin to hurt. I also said that he had always been good at talking about politics and big ideas, but never about the things you feel, and maybe that was why my mother had grown tired of him, even though she never talked about feelings either. Actually both of them were quite dry people, in that they were actually compatible, but maybe they each had a different kind of dryness. Michaela smiled and asked if I had older boyfriends, if I was interested in boys, and if there was "anyone in particular." I told her about Arik from Netanya, who was two years older than me. I met him through "Penpals" in the youth supplement of the evening paper, and after we'd corresponded for a year he decided to come and study at the military academy in Haifa, and on Tuesdays, when he had leave, he would come to me and we would go to see a movie. Once, when we went to see *Love Story*, he tried to kiss me, but I turned my head away, because the wonderful, beautiful heroine was just about to die of leukemia and the tears were pouring down my cheeks, and also because he had rotten teeth and bad breath. I told him this, and he was hurt and said, so what, your teeth are broken too, and ever since then he stopped coming, but I didn't care. I liked going out with him, with the military academy uniform that looked like a real uniform, and once I even wrote him a poem "My Love the Soldier," but I didn't really love him. Michaela said that it was natural and understandable that I should have older boyfriends, because I was fourteen only on my ID card. I told her that I didn't have an ID card yet, because I was only fourteen, and she laughed. All the time we looked into each other's eyes. Michaela asked, "What are you thinking about when you look at me like that?" I said, "I could ask you exactly the same thing." "But I asked first," she smiled, and I said, "Maybe I'm thinking about what you're thinking." Suddenly I started to tremble.

Michaela asked if I was cold, and she held out her hand. I took her hand, which was warm. She asked me if I wanted her to switch on the heater. After that we sat on cushions in front of the electric heater, which gilded her face and hair, and we went on looking and talking, talking and looking. Michaela put on a record by a singer I'd never heard before, Marianne Faithfull, whose voice was hoarse and tortured as if it came from the deepest place in the pit of her stomach, and after that we listened to something classical by Debussy, which reminded me of sunbeams dancing on water. She asked me what kind of music we listened to at home. I told her that we never listened to any kind of music at home, only to the news and commentaries on the radio, which had a bit of music in between them, and on Saturday mornings, if we turned on the radio before the "News of the

Week" we heard a bit of the classical program. But a little while ago I had received my grandfather's old gramophone (he had bought himself a new stereo), and I began to buy records, among them the "Kaveret" band, Leonard Cohen, Stevie Wonder, and Manhattan Transfer, and Grandfather had given me the magical "Misa Criolla," which was already scratched from me listening to it all the time.

She asked me what classical music I knew, and I said very little, in fact nothing, and she said, "Okay, we'll take care of that." Afterwards she told me about herself at high school, and about Osnat, her best friend from then and to this day, who lived in Tel Aviv and illustrated children's books, and about her first boyfriend when she was seventeen, with whom she was madly in love, and who was shell-shocked in the Yom Kippur War, and ever since he had been hospitalized on and off in psychiatric hospitals.

I told her that Racheli and I sat and talked about her for hours, and at the beginning of the long vacation, when she met us on the bench opposite her house, it wasn't by chance. . . . She said that she also had a story I wouldn't believe: she had passed the corner of Panorama and George Eliot Streets several time and looked up. . . . I looked at her in surprise, and she said, "You're putting me to a new test, I've never taught a friend before." I felt the corners of my mouth trembling, but I managed to say, "I've never been taught by a friend." I said that if she passed George Eliot Street again, she could come up. Michaela said that it was usually at times when I wasn't at home, and in the evenings she had a husband. I asked what exactly he did, and she said that he was specializing in anesthesiology. I asked, "So if you suffer from insomnia at night does he put you to sleep?" And Michaela laughed and said, "No, I actually like being awake at night, when everything's quiet. You can hear your thoughts better." She put out her hand and stroked my back on top of my blouse and in the gap between my blouse and pants. I closed my eyes, and she asked, "Does that feel good?" I said yes. Again we looked into each other's eyes for a long time, and she said, "You don't know what I'm thinking now." I said, "It's not night now, so I can't hear your thoughts, and I'm not trying to either." Michaela said, "I know, you're caressing, you have all kinds of different looks." She said that my direct looks frightened people, and that our homeroom teacher Galya once said that it seemed to her that I knew what was going through her head, as if she were thinking aloud. I said that my direct looks were the result of being deaf in one ear, and reading people's lips to make sure I understood what they were saying.

How Michaela laughed! I had never seen her laugh so much, until the tears came to her eyes.

Afterwards she asked if I was hungry. I said a little, and she went into the kitchen. Again I noticed how pleasant and pretty her house was, with its clean smell, with the antiques blending into the modern furniture, the pale, calm colors, with splashes of brightness from the paintings on the wall, and the carpets, and the cushions with the Arab embroidery, and the little bunches of flowers. Every object stood in the place that seemed to have been ordained for it by nature, the light filtered through the milky curtains suffused everything to exactly the right degree. I rumpled Dulcinea's fur, she laid her head on my lap, and I thought that I couldn't remember when I had felt so comfortable. There are moments that I know I will long for even as I live them. Have you ever felt like that?

Michaela returned with two bowls of steaming homemade vegetable soup, which gave off an inviting smell of parsley. We ate and talked about children's books we both loved (Michaela loved *Little Women* and *Anne of the Island* too, and the books by Eric Kastner), about her university studies and the thesis she was writing for her M.A. on Leah Goldberg's love poems. She told me about Leah Goldberg, and about her great love for the poet Avraham Ben Yitzhak, who was almost thirty years older than she was, and who had published only eleven wonderful poems, collected in a slender volume. She stood up and went into the next room, came back with the little book, wrote something in it and gave it to me. I opened it and read the inscription: "To the lover of poetry, to the writer of poetry, in the hope that you will love Ben Yitzhak, due to him and due to you—and I will enjoy your love. From Michaela, autumn 1977." I felt my face flushing as red as a baboon's bottom. So that she wouldn't notice I opened the book at random and started to read one of the poems, and then I came upon the lines, which seemed to have been written for her, and I said, "Listen to how beautiful," and I read aloud, trying to keep my voice from trembling:

> "And while you sit so by the fire,
> its gold flickering
> across your chestnut hair as you lean,
> its gold flows along your fingers,
> the flames darting
> in the mirror of your black silk gown."

And Michaela who knew the poem by heart held my hand and continued in her dark velvet voice, and her eyes drank mine:

> "You and I,
> the rush of seas
> above us now,
> are hidden
> like two pearls
> in their woven robes,
> on the ocean floor.
>
> I didn't know what I wanted—
> and my desire drank the silence down. . . ."

We went on looking at each other, my hand in hers. I almost drowned in the burning brown lakes of her eyes. I wanted so much to embrace her and lay my head on her shoulder, but I suddenly stood up and said that I had to go. Michaela smiled and asked like a little girl, "Will you come to me again?" I said, "Sure." She saw me to the door and said how glad she was that I'd come, that she knew she'd gained a human being. My throat locked and I couldn't answer. She kissed me on the cheek, and I stroked her arm and left.

Yours, she who doesn't know what she wants

10.10.77

Dearest Anne,

The holidays are over and I'm back at school. All day long I waited for Michaela's class, with longing and a little apprehension too—would she hint that I'd been to her house, or treat me like a regular student, as if nothing had happened? We began to read Shalom Aleichem's *Song of Songs*—Shimek loves Lily, Lily loves Shimek and I love . . . during the course of the lesson she looked at me a few times with her eyes narrowed, as if she were trying to remember something. After the class I dawdled on purpose, taking a long time to arrange my schoolbag, and I saw that she was dawdling too. We remained alone in the classroom. Michaela came up to me, took both my hands in hers, and smiled into my eyes. Without thinking I said, "I have to meet you." She suggested that I come to her house, she would make us something to eat, and afterwards we would go for a walk with Dulcinea. I told her that I had to go home, to heat up my brothers' lunch, but that I could come afterwards. I ran home, laid the table quickly, and heated up their food (the soup not enough, the spaghetti too much, the ones at the bottom got burned). I didn't have the patience to wait for them to finish so I could wash the dishes, and I rushed out. I was so excited that I forgot to change my clothes, and I was already next to Rothschild House when I realized that I was still in my school uniform. When I reached her house the table was already laid with a checked cloth and pretty ceramic plates. We ate chicken breasts

119

in a mustard sauce and creamed potatoes together, and for dessert stewed apples made by her father, and afterwards we went out with Dulci.

"Remember yesterday's date, for it is a very important date in my life. Isn't it an important day for every girl when she receives the first kiss of her life?"—you wrote to your Kitty on 16.4.44, after Peter kissed you for the first time.

Today I can reply to your question—yes, the first kiss is very important, but I could never have guessed in my wildest dreams that it would happen like it did. I'll try to describe it to you:

On a clear golden autumn day the young woman and the girl go out for a walk with the dog. They walk down Hatzvi Avenue, under the canopy of pines, to Nitzanim Street, continue along the dirt path that goes down to the wadi, and sit down under a pine tree on a flat rock overlooking the wadi and the sea. Every now and then one of them picks up a stone and throws it hard down the slope. The dog, which has been standing at the ready all this time, one forepaw in the air and one ear pricked up, springs up and flies after it like a flame in the wind. The woman slides her hand down the girl's back in its blue school-uniform blouse. Afterwards she takes the rubber rings off her braids and gently undoes them. The girl looks questioningly into the bright brown eyes. The woman whispers, you don't know how beautiful you are. Suddenly the girl hugs the woman tightly. The woman's eyes grow big and her pupils dilate so much that the girl is afraid of being sucked into them. The woman holds the girl's face between her hands and tastes her mouth and drinks. Her lips are soft and her tongue pushes, probes. The girl's mouth fills with the taste of peppermint and smoke. Her broken teeth don't bother the woman. Gently she removes her glasses. The girl closes her naked eyes against the sun. Her eyes fill with orange. Hot orange in her mouth. Hot orange pulsing in her panties, in the seam of her jeans. The dog runs around them in circles and its tail wags wildly. It cocks its head and whines, aggrieved because they have stopped throwing stones for it. The girl's hands grope under the woman's thin sweater, they have to feel the damp breathing skin. When they encounter the soft roundness over the ribs they stop, not daring. The girl's heart climbs into her throat and pounds and pounds. There is nothing strange about this kiss. Nothing alien. Only something new and astonishing. Like a blind person whose eyes have been opened to see.

When I came home I found that my panties were soaking wet. I washed them in the sink and scrubbed them with lots of soap, so as not to leave any suspicious sign. I was afraid that my mother, with her X-ray eyes, would see immediately that something had happened to me, that I was a new girl, as it were. But in the afternoon she went with Noam to the grocers, and about an hour ago she went out with her Moishele. It seems that this time her "bionic eyes" didn't see anything.

Oren and Noam are in their room, pretending to be Steve McGarrett and Steve Austin, shooting at each other with the battery-powered guns Grandpa brought them from America— which make a terrible noise, but I don't care. I close my eyes, my lips remember her lips, my hands remember her slender ribs and warm damp skin under the sweater, and I can hardly believe that it really happened.

Yours as ever, Kitty

10.11.77

Dearest Anne,

The girl is at home in bed, she's ill. She has a sore throat and a low fever. Perhaps it's because of yesterday's excitement, and perhaps because the weather has changed and turned cold and rainy, and perhaps she's a little nervous about going to school. . . . Her mother made her a cup of tea with lemon and went to work. She lies in bed and waits for the phone. She knows it will ring soon.

At ten o'clock, in the long break, the teacher calls. The girl says she's sick. The teacher asks if she can come and visit her after the next lesson.

The girl hurries to the bathroom to brush her teeth and wash her face. Afterwards she goes back to bed and waits. She tries to see through the teacher's eyes the orange flowered wallpaper, the clumsy iron bed—the bed Grandma and Grandpa Shenhar got from the Jewish Agency when they immigrated to Israel, and when she was three years old her father brought it home for her to sleep on instead of her crib—and the scratched and wobbly desk, and the orange Formica closet with the picture of the singer Ilanit with long blond hair and a striped dress, from the first "Eurovision" contest that Israel participated in, which she had once cut out of a magazine. She notices that the books on the shelves are leaning sideways, exposing triangles of white wall, text books and novels and old books of her mother's, *Memoirs of the House of David* in five volumes, which her mother has been trying for years to persuade her to read, but they seem boring to her, and the four volumes of *Wonders of the World* in their faded red cloth covers stamped with the golden sun, that she liked to read when she was small.

She knows that her room is childish and tasteless, and she guesses that her beloved won't like it.

An hour later the doorbell rings. She jumps out of bed in her long T-shirt and opens the door. The teacher beams her smile at her in the red-and-green checked cape, which reminds the girl of forests, gnomes, and fairies. Her hair is tied back. In her hand she holds the book *Letters to a Young Poet* by Rilke, and a bunch of narcissi. The teacher enters the living room, looks around at the pictures, and lingers on the twin paintings, which look like whirlpools and water lilies against a greenish background, and remind the girl of the poem "Delight."

"My mother painted them," she says proudly, "aren't they beautiful?"

The teacher drops her eyes and smiles to herself, "They seem quite amateurish to me."

"Come and see my room," the girl says boldly. They go to her room. The teacher scans it with a quick glance. Her eyes come to rest on the picture of her as a little girl hanging over her bed.

"That painting's not bad."

"A friend of my grandfather's painted it once. When I was young and beautiful," the girl smiles apologetically.

"You've certainly grown a lot uglier since then, granny," the teacher winks at her, and they both laugh.

"You don't like the room, do you?" the girl asks in disappointment.

The teacher unbuttons her cape, smiles, and, quoting from Leah Goldberg's *A Flat for Rent*, she says, "'The apartment's just right, and having such neighbors will be a delight. . . .'"

"And the room?" the girl insists.

"The room?" The teacher looks around again. "Let's say that there's room for improvement."

Afterwards she sits down on the edge of the rumpled bed. The girl sits down too, and she doesn't really know what to say. The teacher looks at the view of the pine swaying in the wind and the scrap of gray sky, her left leg is crossed over her right leg, and her left foot, in the black suede boot hugging her ankle, revolves around itself in rapid circles. The air is heavy with the scent of the narcissi.

And then the teacher turns to the girl and pulls her to her, pushes a lock of hair off her forehead, and they kiss. The girl is sucked in again. Sucked in. Suddenly she stops, draws her face back, looks into the brown eyes, agitated as if by a storm of autumn leaves, and says, "I don't know if it's right, what we're doing."

The woman looks at her sorrowfully, almost helplessly, and says, "I don't know either, kiddo, all I know is that I love you." And then, as if she's telling herself, she whispers, "The love is erotic, that's obvious."

Instantly, like a flash of lightning, the girl understands that no one will protect them, that they are alone and that nothing will justify them, including their love. And she understands too that they are in great danger, the woman even more than her, the woman is in her hands. And in her heart she knows, like swearing an oath, that she will do everything in her power to protect her, and that she will never, never, even if they torture her, betray her to her enemies.

And then the girl asks if anything like this has ever happened to her before.

The woman thinks for a minute and says, "No, only with men, and it wasn't like this."

"How like this," asks the girl anxiously, although she already knows.

"Like this," the woman whispers, and the blood suffuses her lips, "so strong."

After Michaela left, I tried to read the Rilke, but I couldn't concentrate. I breathed in the bittersweet whiteness of the narcissi, which I put into jam jar (I'll tell Mother Racheli brought them), snuggled up under the down blanket, and thought that if anyone had told me a year ago, when I first began to love her, or even only a week ago, that we would be like this, she and I, I wouldn't have believed it. I'm sure that a lot of young girls love and admire their teachers, so how come the miracle only happened to me, and the woman I love fell in love with me?

Yours, Kitty

10.16.77

Anne Anne Anne!

That's it, today it happened. Our first time. My first time. Nothing will ever be the same again. I've changed, and the whole world has changed.

I'll always remember the time, an autumn afternoon, when the sky suddenly darkens and the rain belts down and stops, and the sun burns itself a tunnel through the clouds. I'll remember

the place too, her study, the carpet with its red-and-black diamond pattern. Michaela was wearing light brown flared gabar-
dine trousers, and her green velvet blouse that I love, with a
matching velvet ribbon in her hair. She looked like a slender
sapling; brown trunk and green crest. I was wearing my school
uniform, jeans and blue blouse, and lace-up blue boots. We
stood on the carpet, kissing, swaying, and suddenly, just as we
were, clothes and all, we fell onto the big cushions, clutching
each other and swaying like a ship. We went on kissing and
groping under each other's blouses, and this time I was bold
enough to touch her soft little breasts with the nipples stiffening
like cherry pits, and she, ever so gently, touched mine, because
neither of us wears a bra, and the sweetness between my legs
grew and grew, until I felt the fluttering of the wings inside me,
like always only much stronger, and the whirlpool drew us in
and covered us, and Michaela closed her eyes and screamed and
screamed.

I'll always remember how she screamed and how I looked at
her in astonishment. I never knew that people screamed like that.
I never knew their faces broke up like that and their eyes closed.
I never knew I had it in my power to cause such pleasure.

Afterwards we continued, with the same hunger, with the
same desire, and this time I screamed too. My love taught me to
scream. My love taught me to explode onto her with a scream.

When the storm subsided, we cuddled up together on the
carpet, nose touching nose and eyes as close as could be, the
autumn leaves sailing slowly over the lake.

"See how we're woven together like a braid," she whispered,
"like a Sabbath loaf."

"Like two fetuses," I whispered, "you're giving birth to me
and I'm giving birth to you."

I'll always remember how I climbed up Hatzvi Avenue,
light as the wind, swaying, drunk. Panting like an asthmatic I
swallowed air that smelled of rain. In front of my eyes the houses danced, rising and falling on waves of pavements and roads.

And in all the hours that have passed since then I've been looking at my eyes in the mirror, which have changed from a child's eyes to a woman's eyes, and saying to myself over and over again, yes yes yes, it really happened.

And I'm so happy, Anne, so happy and proud.

Your Kitty

P.S. Now I understand in every fiber and cell and pore, down to the deepest root of my soul, what Dalia Ravikovitch meant in the poem "Delight."

Saturday, 11.19.77

Dearest Anne,

I haven't written to you for a long time, and I apologize. Perhaps I have less need to write a diary, because I tell Michaela almost everything that happens to me, and that I think and feel. A month has already passed since our first time. During this time we went on discovering each other, eyes and soul and body. Many days went by until we dared to remove our blouses, until we took off our trousers, and it was only a few days ago, when my desire to really feel her, without any barriers, was already overwhelming, that we stripped off our panties as well, as if so long as the narrow strips of cloth separated us, so long as we had not been welded together flesh to flesh, we could say to ourselves that we were still within the bounds of the permissible. And perhaps we knew that we had to go slowly, for otherwise the expanses of naked skin would corrode one another like acid.

With every garment that we removed I was struck by wonder—wonder at the suppleness of the breasts with their prickly nipples, and the softness of the thighs, and the fullness of the buttocks, and the sweetness of the vagina in the wild growth of chestnut hair that licked my skin like fire, and the wonder of the sounds, and the smells.

For the first time in my life I am seeing a woman's body at such close quarters. Not counting my mother, who has a good body, with a narrow waist and everything, and nevertheless it embarrasses me a bit to look at her, and when I do look, not only when she's getting dressed but sometimes even during meals, she frowns and says, what are you staring at? And not counting the elderly women in the changing rooms at the sea or the pool, who I peek at in dismay—what, will I look like that one day too? No, it's impossible, and in any case I have a long way to go.

Michaela and I are the same height (five feet, four inches), and more or less the same weight (I'm three pounds fatter than she is . . .) and our build is quite similar too. When she's dressed she looks very slender, because her back and shoulders are narrow, and her breasts are small (more or less like mine, but the nipples are darker, like the beaks of two white doves), but when she takes her clothes off, she reveals the soft belly, which I like to kiss and where I like to lay my cheek, and the apple buttocks, and the generous thighs whose skin on the inside is smooth and pleasant to the touch as silk.

Imagine the picture: the darkened bedroom, my love is lying on her back and my hands are moving over her body as if drawing it in chalk and charcoal; in chalk—her belly, her breasts, her neck, her swanlike arms, her thighs. In charcoal—the delicate outlines, the nipples, the hollow of the navel, her hair spread over the pillow like Medusa's snakes, her lips with a dreamy-voracious smile hovering over them, her flared nostrils, the widening shadows of her pupils.

A few days ago I switched on the bedside light, rested my cheek against the inside of her thigh, and looked into the tangle of chestnut hair—everything there looked more or less like with me, only bigger and fleshier, with mysterious clefts and folds, and her clitoris is stuck in exactly the same place too. Michaela laughed, "What are you investigating so thoroughly there?" and said that I was the most inquisitive person she had ever met.

Afterwards she embraced me from behind in our favorite teaspoon position, and whispered into my ear, "What fairytale did you come to me from, tell me, do you really exist, or am I only dreaming you?"

Dulcinea was lying on the corner of the bed, her head resting on her forepaws, looking at us with her patient, understanding look that accepted everything.

"I exist like Dulc exists, like the world exists."

"Prove it."

"If I fart now," I couldn't resist laughing, "will that be proof?"

"Pig," she pushed the backs of my knees with her knees, "fart as much as you like."

"And like this," I assailed her, pushing her onto her back and pinning her arms to the mattress, "do I exist like this?"

"Enough, enough, I give up," she laughed up at me with the sunspots in her eyes and with all the freckles on her face and freed her arms from the fetters of my hands and pulled my head down for a kiss.

In class we pose as teacher and pupil, our performance is perfect. From my desk in the second row I watch her lips reading Tchernichowsky's poem "Dumplings," the lips that had drunk from my mouth; and her hands writing with chalk on the blackboard, the hands that had made butterflies fly from my skin.

I put my hand up and my beloved turns to me with a smile. I say clever things, I shine, I celebrate. Michaela makes an effort to shine for me too, she claims that I make her brains sweat. (We have prearranged signs: scratching the forehead—you were brilliant. Scratching the nose—you're talking nonsense. Touching the lips—I'm dying to kiss you. . . .) The other kids sense that there's a special connection between us, but none of them can guess. I only told Racheli a few days ago, and I made her swear that she wouldn't tell anyone, even if they tortured her with a thousand tortures. She promised, looking at me gravely with her Dutch eyes—blue circles on white china, like the windmills painted on the tiles they have in their sideboard.

"When you go to bed together what kind of pleasure is it?" she asked curiously, without embarrassment, "Is it like, say, reading an awfully good book?"

I laughed to myself. I didn't know how to answer her, how to bridge the gap yawning between us. "No, devil, it's something else entirely, when you have a serious boyfriend you'll probably understand."

Impatiently, like two colts with quivering nostrils, we wait for the last bell, and race outside according to a fixed procedure—Michaela goes first and climbs the hill to Rocinanta, while I hurry down the hill and wait for her around the corner. The car slows down, the door opens, and I jump in and immediately lie down on the seat, which is already inclined backwards, so the kids and the teachers won't see me on their way home.

Rocinanta, who has now changed into a Trojan horse, climbs in the direction of Ahuza and continues up the mountain. The houses grow fewer and the green spreads out. After the university tower she slides down one of the dirt tracks and comes to a halt on the outskirts of the forest. We get out and find ourselves a bed of pine needles. There we fall on each other with kisses and remove our sweaty jerseys, desperate to feel the softness of the breasts, the stabbing of the nipples, the prickling of the skin, desperate to coil around each other. At the sound of bleating and the distant chiming of bells we make haste to cover ourselves, but a few days ago, immersed in each other to the point of oblivion, the sheep came right up to us, and above us stood a barefoot Druze boy in a gray galabieh, his eyes astounded, like smoldering coals.

After the shepherd boy had receded with his flock, I asked Michaela why we had to drive to the forest even when she knew that Yoel wasn't at home, and she said that ever since her childhood she had loved to sense the sun and the wind on her skin, and to feel that her body was a part of nature.

At a quarter past two I hurry her up, we have to get up and

get dressed and get back, and we push our blouses into our pants and pick suspicious pine needles from each other's hair, because at half past two at the latest I have to be home, to heat up my brothers' lunch. Every day the task hangs over my head like a Damocles sword and leaves us only a snatched hour of passion. At half past three Mother comes home from work and finds them sprawled on the carpet opposite Steve Austin. The kitchen table is clean, the dishes are washed, and the model child is in her room, absorbed in a book, or busy doing her homework.

On the days when Michaela doesn't teach, I leave the house after finishing my lunch-time mission and call her from my little house in the post office, in other words the phone booth at the entrance to the post office on Wedgewood Street (I don't call from home, because my mother might come home suddenly, and my brothers could overhear as well). I shut the door behind me, insert a token, and dial, and at the sound of her happy, expectant "Hello," I collapse cross-legged onto the floor of the phone booth, my back to the door, so nobody can open it, and also so that nobody on their way into the post office can identify me. We talk like this for maybe half an hour, tell each other in minute detail about the events of the day and the dreams of the night. Sometimes I cry over some stupid quarrel with my mother or for no special reason (Michaela says I have "Weltschmerz," which is German for world-pain), and when I emerge from the booth, my face is full of red blotches, as if I've got measles, and then I go down to the wadi and hide between the bushes until the blotches fade and I can go home. Because when Mother sees me crying, she's sure I'm "putting on an act" to make her feel sorry for me, and she calls me a "malingerer," a "sourpuss," a "piece of work," and sometimes she gets angry and says "In a minute I'll give you something to cry about," as if she doesn't give me enough reasons as it is. . . .

Twice a week Michaela attends classes at the university till the evening, and we can't go to the forest after school. On those evenings I wait for her on the way down to Ocean Road, taking big gulps of the cold, violet air, so that our kisses will taste of rain and pines. And here's Rocinanta stopping next to me, and here's my love on the other side of the window, her eyes, her smile, her hand opening the door.

A few days ago she picked me up on her way back from the university, and we stopped not far from her house, in a small dark street. We started kissing, and suddenly I felt that my cheeks were wet, and there was a salty taste in her mouth. "What is it, Mishi," I said in alarm, wrapping her face in my hand, 'why are you crying?"

"It's because of Yoel." Her tears collected between my fingers. "Ever since we . . . haven't been to bed with him for a month, and he can't understand what's happening to me, and he's so sad."

Sharp as a razor the girl who's never known a man says the only thing that can protect their love from being exposed, "Go to bed with him tonight, you have to."

"I don't think I can, little one." Her head is in the hollow of my neck, and her narrow shoulders are trembling.

"Then force yourself," I mobilized the cold composure of a surgeon cutting into the living flesh to save a life. "You'll see that you can."

The next afternoon, when Rocinanta was puffing up the mountainside, Michaela smiled at me over the steering wheel, "Mission accomplished."

"Was it hard for you?" I couldn't resist it, lying on the back tilted seat, not sure what answer I wanted to hear.

She thought for a minute and said, "Not as hard as I expected. It seems that guilt and pity aren't bad as an aphrodisiac."

I try to avoid bumping into Yoel, who spends most of his time at the hospital anyway. But one afternoon he came home unexpectedly, just as I was about to leave. I smiled at him politely, avoiding his eyes, which were bloodshot after a long shift at the hospital. Like my father, he too looks to me like a robot in human form, a talking wax doll. I can't imagine him drinking from her mouth the night wind she had previously drunk from mine, and his white anesthetist's hands moving over her marvelous body, which is so much, so much mine.

Goodnight, Kitty

P.S. Last week was my fourteenth birthday. Mother bought me musk perfume in a cute little bottle with a purple ribbon, and Grandfather gave me four hundred lira "to buy yourself a nice dress," but I hate dresses, and I bought a jeans overall, blue suede clogs with platform soles, and a thin gold ankle chain. My mother pulled a face, "Ankle chains are a lesbian sign, aren't they?" I swallowed the lump stuck in my throat and explained to her that lesbians wore the chain on their right ankle, and mine was on the left, to reassure her. The android, as expected, didn't take the trouble to phone. From Racheli I got two pairs of colored stockings, and from Michaela the two volumes of *The Magic Mountain* and a letter. She wrote that until she met me she didn't know that it was possible to love with such tenderness, and that she woke up with me in the morning and went to the toilet and brushed her teeth with me, and fell asleep at night embracing me. I am before her eyes all the time, and my name is in her heart like its beating, like a soothing mantra. She wrote that I was her good fairy, that I had given her the biggest gift that a person can give or receive: herself. You can imagine how I cried when I read her letter.

P.P.S. Sadat, the President of Egypt, is arriving in Israel tonight on a historic visit, and tomorrow afternoon he's going to make a speech in the Knesset!

Thursday, 12.15.77

Dearest Anne,
For the past two weeks I've been eating Hans Castorp and drinking Hans Castorp and sleeping Hans Castorp and dream-

132

ing Hans Castorp and waking Hans Castorp and walking Hans Castorp and studying Hans Castorp. I read *The Magic Mountain* under my desk in class, on the way home, at meals, and in the lavatory. The book has swallowed me to such an extent that it sometimes seems to me that I myself am Hans Castorp recovering from tuberculosis at the Berghof sanatorium in the Swiss Alps, debating with the scholarly Settembrini, in love with the beautiful married Madame Chauchat whose face with its high cheek bones and narrow gray-blue eyes remind him of the face of the school fellow he had loved when he was thirteen. (Thomas Mann writes that this is the age when love is the most intense. . . .) I especially liked the fact that Hans asks her how she can love her husband who is so much older than she is, and she says, how can you not love someone who loves you so much.

Yesterday afternoon I asked Michaela if this was the reason that she fell in love with me, and she thought for a minute and said that she was enchanted by my love for her, but that she was even more enchanted by my soul, which was like a rare orchid, which if it was watered and fertilized and given warmth and light, would produce exquisite flowers. She said that when she was my age she dreamed of being a painter, a writer, a musician, or an actress when she grew up, but her mother had never encouraged her to be an artist.

"My mother thought that painting and playing the piano were nice as hobbies, but that anyone who wasn't really talented turned in the end into a frustrated artist, like my father, who in his youth studied painting in Berlin, and had to stop because of the Nazis; and that I should learn a practical profession. As far as my mother was concerned the whole world was divided into practical and unpractical," she puffed on her cigarette, "once I was angry with her, I thought that if I had been encouraged and believed in, I could have developed into an artist. Today I think that if I had been really talented, I would have made my own way, found the right teachers to guide me. Perhaps I didn't have the courage to go all the way, to take risks, to look inside into the depths of the abyss, and also to expose myself. Instead I became a teacher, and my greatest pleasure is to discover a soul like yours, open and thirsty and enthusiastic, and to give you everything that I didn't receive."

"I've never heard you play," I was suddenly curious, "why don't you play something for me."

Michaela said that she hadn't practiced for ages, that she was completely rusty, but in the end I persuaded her. She sat down at the piano and played Mendelssohn's "Autumn Song," which starts strong and dramatic, continues with sweet sorrow and longing for the end of summer, for everything that passes and perishes, and her playing was so precise, pinching the heart but not wringing it, not forcing it to feel. Afterwards she taught me a simple song for four hands, and we played it together, faster and faster, our hands kept colliding and we burst out laughing. And then Michaela put on a record of dance music and taught me the waltz and tango and foxtrot, and we whirled between the furniture, her face as close as could be to mine, and her eyes burning, and when we were already hot and sweating from dancing we began to kiss, and holding on to each other we lurched to the bed, shedding our clothes in the passage like the breadcrumbs scattered by Hansel and Gretel in the forest so as not to lose their way back, and then we discovered cords dangling between both our legs, a blue "O.B. mini" one between mine and a white "Tampax" one between hers, and again we were overcome by wild laugher. We went on making love without taking the tampons out, and the cords didn't bother us at all, only Dulcinea was disappointed; she likes our bodily secretions, and we always let her lick our fingers, and this time there was nothing to lick, it was all absorbed by the tampons.

Afterwards Michaela showered and got dressed up to go to a concert by the Philharmonic in the auditorium with Yoel. She put on transparent black stockings, which made her legs even sexier and more shapely, and a deep purple velvet dress, embroidered with little pearls, and burgundy-colored suede boots. I told her that she looked like the queen of the night. I sat on the lavatory lid in their bathroom and watched her in the mirror pinning her fiery mane up with a crescent-shaped ivory comb, and making up her face with delicate practiced movements, concealing the childish freckles with the makeup, and her face opened and glowed, and her eyes gleamed as if she had lit a little lamp inside herself. Before we left I carefully removed lumps of mascara stuck to her lashes and cleaned the lipstick from her teeth.

All night long I envied Yoel sitting in the auditorium next to my perfumed queen of the night with his elbow touching her elbow and his thigh touching her thigh, and hearing the music that she heard. I made myself a cup of tea and poured a little rum into it (I had discovered that it calmed me and improved my mood), and consoled myself with the last chapters of *The Magic Mountain*. At two o'clock in the morning, when I finished the book (720 pages!) I paged through your diary to see if you had read it too, and I found that you had permitted yourselves to speak and read all the "civilized languages," in other words—not German.

Today, in Michaela's class, we started reading the story "N'ima Sasson Writes Poems" by Amaliah Kahana-Carmon, about a Jerusalem girl in love with her literature teacher Ezekiel, who writes him a poem, "My Dear Teacher," and gives him her notebook of poems to read; and I stared at my dear teacher and imagined what we would do together after school, when we drove to the forest and spread the tartan blanket on the damp bed of pine needles, between the crocuses and the harebells and the wood sorrel, and the pale brown mushrooms sprouting at the foot of the trunks. I looked out of the window to make sure that it wasn't going to rain, and saw that the sun was forging a tunnel between the clouds, and I knew that it would warm the damp earth until it steamed with a living smell of grass and roots, which would mingle with the breath of the pine needles and our sweat, and suddenly a silly little poem came to me. I wrote it on pages I tore out of the middle of my literature note-book, and on the way to the forest I read it to Michaela, and she laughed:

My dear teacher

I love to see you getting dressed
I love to see you comb you hair
I love to see you paint your face
but most of all I love
to see you get undressed for me.

I love to hear you talk
I love to hear you play the piano
I love to hear you pee
but most of all I love
to hear you come because of me.

That's all for now, your Kitty Castrop

12.25.77

Dearest Anne,

For the past couple of weeks Yoel has been on duty at the hospital on Saturdays, and I've been leaving the house at ten o'clock in the morning and staying at Michaela's until evening. I ask her a hundred million questions, learning her and wanting to know everything about her. Yesterday she told me about her father, Ernst, who grew up in a family of prosperous merchants in Berlin, in a house with "Kinderstube"—which breathed art and theater and music—with his big sister, who studied architecture in the Bauhaus school. This aunt had died a few years ago, and Michaela had been very attached to her. She lived in Jerusalem and she never married, and Michaela would go there in her holidays, and they would go for hikes in the mountains and wadis, and sleep in the same bed. Her father and his sister were members of the "Wandervogel" youth movement, which worshipped youth and believed in simplicity and returning to nature, in the spirit of nineteenth-century Romanticism, and was based on the relationship between a young counselor and his or her charges of the same sex. They would go for hikes in the forests, swim naked in the lakes, put up tents and sing folksongs around the campfire. Their anthem "Rejoice young man in your youth—your kingdom in the country, in the town—song and laughter on your lips—see how good it is to be young" was later adopted by the Zionist youth movement Hashomer Hatzair.

Her father studied at the academy of art and intended to be a painter, but in the middle of the thirties the Nazis barred Jews from attending the universities, and he emigrated to Palestine with thirty paintings he had bought at bargain prices from Jewish painters, and opened the "Berg Gallery" next to the Ritz Cafe, under the municipal theater. Her mother, Martha, had grown up in a banker's family in Hamburg (Hans Castrop's city!), and she came to the country as a young girl with her sister. Their parents, who stayed behind, didn't get out in time and perished in Bergen-Belsen, and Michaela was called after her grandfather Michael.

"My mother always dressed me in the most beautiful dresses, cooked healthy, nourishing food, did my hair and cut my nails, and it was very important to her that I did well at school, but she wasn't the kind of mother you could curl up in bed with." It was a glorious, golden Saturday, with a washed sky and a mild winter sun, and we sunbathed in our panties on the deckchairs on the back porch, listened to Mahler's "Lied von der Erde" (Michaela persists in my musical education, and every time I come to her she plays me another classical work), and drank orange juice with a drop of vodka and little red umbrellas for decoration.

"I don't remember her playing with me or telling me stories, and I don't remember her ever hugging me. My father actually liked making up stories for me, especially one story, which I asked him to tell me every evening before I went to sleep. In this story I run a home for stray orphan dogs, whose names are Hans, Fritz, and Ursula, and also Ahmed and Fatmah, in order to fit into the Levant, and I dress them in capes and dresses and decorate them with ribbons and little golden crowns, and have tea parties and balls for them."

"I also once wanted to be the Mapainik Marie Antoinette of the cats," I said, and told her about that evening at Granny and Grandpa Shenhar's, and how my father hit me. Michaela listened to me, sucking on her cigarette.

"You weren't beaten because of the cats and the bones," she said quietly and her eyes burned with compassion, "you were simply the most convenient punching bag in the vicinity." Dulcinea stole onto the porch and lay at our feet, her coat electric with the radiance of the sun, "My father never hit me, but my mother always treated him a bit as if he were a child, she let him feel that he didn't really count. He wasn't at home much, he spent most of his time at his gallery, or on business trips to England. In recent years I began to suspect that he had another woman in London, because he's a warm, sensual man, and my mother's a perfect lady, with an uptight soul. You have no idea how I hated being left alone with her, when he was traveling. Every year when they asked me what I wanted for my birthday—and with us birthdays were a big deal, with piano playing and flowery speeches and a table for gifts—I begged them to give me a little brother or sister. I imagined how I would get up in the morning and go to the gift table, and find a baby with golden curls lying there, and she would open her blue eyes and smile at me. But my mother would laugh bitterly and say, the stork has no more presents for us. She was already quite old when I was born, thirty five. Now she expects me to produce a grandchild for her, but I'm tired of fulfilling her expectations, distinguishing myself at school, going to university, being a teacher, and marrying a doctor."

"She probably didn't expect you to fall in love with one of the girls in your class," I said to the glass in my hand.

"No," Michaela smiled, "I imagine she didn't expect that."

"So am I your adolescent rebellion?" I asked, nibbling the point of the umbrella.

"No, kiddo," her upper lip turned red, "you're a tremendous love that suddenly struck me like lightning."

"And you're not afraid that we'll be found out?"

"I am afraid," she said quietly, "if it comes out my whole world will be destroyed. Sometimes at night I pace the floor and tear my hair, what am I doing to you and myself and Yoel, but it's stronger than I am and stronger than the fear too."

I put my glass down and went to sit next to her, I hugged her body and collected the tears trickling down the sides of her nose with my lips, and thus we lay together on the deckchair on the porch, and when my beloved began to take off, I gagged her mouth with my hand, so the neighbors wouldn't hear her scream, and the sky spread over us like a canopy, and only God saw.

Afterwards we went inside and got dressed. Michaela made us spaghetti Bolognese, while I sat on my special chair in the kitchen, rested my chin on my raised knees, and watched her hands moving calmly and precisely, without a superfluous gesture. When we were eating, Michaela asked if my relations with my mother had always been difficult. I thought for minute and said that long ago, when I was really small, we had been close. I don't remember what we did together, we just were, child and mother, mother and child, in days that were so alike they seemed like one long day, with the square of light creeping under the big glass doors of the porch, and the warm smell of the ironing and something cooking, and infinite silence, or sometimes songs from the neighbors' radio, obla-dee, obla-da, and so on. When she was in a good mood, she would take me piggyback and read me stories and teach me the alphabet. After lunch she would go to lie down and I would turn on the big radio, one of those old fashioned ones with a green eye, and listen to the "Mother and

Child Corner." Once I asked her to listen with me, and I explained to her that the program was for mothers too, because if it was only for children, it would have been called "The Child's Corner," and she agreed and listened with me, but usually she shut herself in her room, and I played quietly so as not to disturb her, and waited for her to wake up and wash a peach for me, and cut it into yellow segments with red eyes.

She would get up at four o'clock, and sit at the table in the dining nook, with a cup of coffee and a cigarette between her dark red nails, and look out of the window, and she had a kind of little balloon in her mouth that she shifted from cheek to cheek, and I knew that she was thinking all kinds of thoughts, and she didn't see me sitting on the carpet at her feet, or remember that I had waited a long time for her to wake up. Perhaps she was remembering her life long ago, when she was young and her mother was still alive, and she had lots of suitors, and she didn't have to look after me and wash me peaches. Inside the smoke veiling her face, with one cheek squashed and crumpled from the pillow, she always looked a tiny bit old to me, and once I said to her, you're the oldest of all the mothers in the neighborhood, aren't you, and she turned her dry look to me and said crossly, do you really think so? She was about thirty then, the youngest and the most beautiful not only in the neighborhood, but on all the Carmel, and even though I apologized, she still holds it against me to this day.

And there was that afternoon when I got lost. Mother didn't permit me to go out of the garden gate, she was always afraid I would reach the road and get run over, but there was a new building going up next to our house, and there was a wonderful pile of sand on the site that you could slide down for hours, and one day I was playing there with two friends from the neighborhood, I was Wendy, and Gila—who was Tinkerbell—scattered fairy dust on my head, so I would be able to fly away with Peter Pan to the land of lost children at the foot of the hill. When it started to get dark Gila went home, and Talya asked if I wanted to come home with her, because they had a television set and we could watch Mickey Mouse on Lebanese television. She lived one street above us, opposite the convent, and I went to her house without telling Mother, but we didn't see Mickey Mouse, because the screen was full of flickering white spots, and Talya explained to me that it was because it was snowing now in Lebanon, so we went to her room and played a bit, and then I left. It was already quite dark, and I walked along the high convent wall and peeked in through the bars of the gate. I stood there for a bit and waited until I heard the solemn pealing of the bells, and saw the old nuns, grave and mysterious in their long black dresses with the crosses on their chests, and the gray head scarves hiding all their hair, hurrying to prayers with their heads bowed, like a herd of strange animals. Afterwards I crossed the yard of the abandoned building—which had once belonged to the British police, and people said that there was an old British policeman still living there, who had fallen in love with a girl from the Carmel and refused to return to England, and in the meantime the girl had married somebody else, a Jew, and had children, and probably grandchildren too, but the policeman stayed in the abandoned building, today he was quite old, his ginger hair was turning gray, and also his neatly trimmed mustache, and sometimes you could see him walking up and down next to the supermarket, erect, in a checked three-piece suit, waiting for his elderly love to do her shopping with an orange plastic basket—and I wasn't frightened, because I remembered the way home, and I knew that I was a brave adventurous little girl, and I took deep breaths of my new, immense, intoxicating freedom, and then I returned to our street, which was already pervaded by the smell of frying omelets, and all along it the neighbor women stood in the dim doorways of their houses and said hurry home, your mother's calling you, your mother's looking for you, your mother's worried, your mother's standing on the porch crying— and when I got home I was a bundle of tears and guilt, with my hair full of fairy dust, which had turned to sand, and this was the second time I had betrayed her, and I knew that for such a betrayal there was no forgiveness.

At about the same time Oren was born. I was disappointed, because I'd always wanted a sister, preferably a twin, but I could have compromised on a sweet little baby girl, and Oren was a difficult baby, always crying, and she looked after him all day long and at night as well, and she was tired and irritable, and two years later she gave birth to Noam, and I was disappointed again, and in honor of the birth I decided to cut off Oren's long blond curls so the guests at the reception wouldn't think he was a girl, and by mistake I cut the lobe of his ear with the scissors, and it bled a lot, and Mother got into a big panic, my father wasn't at home, and she had just come home from the hospital after giving birth and already she had to run with both of them in her arms to the HMO clinic, to get Oren's ear stitched, and this was another of my wicked deeds that could not be forgiven.

And Michaela listened to me with her whole self and said quietly, "Everything can be forgiven, kiddo, it's only a question of will and love," and I knew that she was wrong, that there were betrayals it was absolutely impossible to forgive, like the betrayal of Udi Adiv, for example, who spied for the enemy, or like falling in love with your literature teacher.

Now I know: love is when the person you love opens the door for you, and takes your hand and gives you a guided tour inside himself, like a house, which up to now you've only seen from the outside and now you're invited to get to know it from the inside, with its own special colors and furniture, and how the light falls on the objects, and also the shadows and the hidden corners with the curls of dust (for example your hiding place, which had a main floor and an attic, and the warehouse, to which it was the most dangerous to go down, and you went down only at night, so as not to get caught), and you go up to the attic and look out together at the view from the window (from the window of your attic you saw, you and Peter, the top of the chestnut tree, which was the only bit of nature you had to console you in two years of hiding, and there you also kissed for the first time), and then you go down hand in hand to the main floor, where the books and the records and the collections and the albums are arranged, and in the end you go down to the warehouse, and there—full of dust and cobwebs—the memories, dreams, and secrets are piled in a heap. And after the guided tour is over, the person who loves you lets you go on wandering around inside him at your will, to climb up and down the stairs to all the floors, to open the photograph albums, to rummage in the drawers, to taste from the saucepans on the stove, to tear the cobwebs from crumpled dreams, rusty as old tin toys, and even to upset the order.

This afternoon, when we sat under our pine tree with Dulcinea—two butterflies circled around her, white and yellow, and she couldn't decide which of them to chase, and only gazed at them spellbound—I told all of this to Michaela, and she hugged me and laughed, you certainly upset my order. Afterwards we got up to go, and Michaela whistled to Dulcinea, who refused to part from some abandoned lair she had found under a rock and pushed her nose into it and barked in excitement. And when we climbed up Hatzvi Avenue, after a thoughtful silence, Michaela said, the question is who washes the floor, and we decided that each one washes the floor in his own house.

Yours as always, Kitty

January 9, 1978

Dearest Anne,
Yesterday Michaela and my mother met! I'll tell you in the proper order, otherwise you won't understand anything.

When we had just started, and I went to Michaela's house in the afternoons or on Saturdays, I would tell my mother something close to the truth, "I'm going to my literature teacher to get a book," or "I'm going to my literature teacher to prepare something for the class."

143

The more frequent my visits to her became, the more suspicious my mother became, and one evening, a few days ago, she began questioning me.

"What do you do there all the time," her X-ray eyes bored into my eyes.

"Nothing, just talk," I made an effort not to drop my eyes.

"How old is she, this teacher of yours, thirty?"

"Twenty-seven."

"Single?"

"No," I said with suppressed triumph, "married."

"And when you go to her house, is her husband there?"

"Sometimes. Usually he's on duty. He's a doctor at Rambam Hospital," I boasted.

Mother refused to be impressed. "What does a woman of twenty-seven have to talk about to a child of fourteen, I don't understand."

"Books. She lends me books, and we talk about them. *The Magic Mountain* by Thomas Mann, for instance. You should read it if you haven't read it yet."

Mother pulled a face. She asked me for Michaela's phone number, and she called her. Michaela suggested that they meet to talk. They made a date to meet yesterday afternoon, at Koestler's Cafe in the Center. At the meeting, Michaela told me today, she mobilized her most pedagogic tone, and told my mother that I was mature for my age and that I had a rich inner world. I wrote, I was gifted, I needed care and guidance. She said that it was no less interesting to talk to me than to people of her own age.

"I told her the truth," she smiled over the wheel on the way to the forest, "but I felt as if I was lying brazenly."

Mother said politely that she understood, but the relationship didn't seem healthy to her. She asked Michaela not to invite me to her house anymore, and not to meet me outside school hours. She threatened that if the meetings continued she would go to the head of the middle school and also to Hourgin.

Michaela had no option but to promise her.

When Mother returned from the meeting she encountered a sphinx face. "Michaela's nice, isn't she?" I asked casually at supper, carefully cutting up my omelet.

"She's a *Yekke-putz*, no?" Mother said, using the term for a Jew of German origin who was putting on airs. She refused to be seduced b Michaela.

"No she's not, maybe her parents are but not her," I was obliged to come to the defense of my beloved. Mother had hated the Yekkes ever since she was a child; Grandma Rivka used to send her to Mintz's grocery store, and Mintz and his wife ignored her and served their Yekke customers first, calling them "Frau" and talking to them in German. The sting of that childhood insult had never dulled.

Mother didn't argue with me, she only said, "She promised me that you wouldn't meet outside school hours anymore, and I hope that the affair is closed."

All morning I waited impatiently to hear what Michaela had to say about the meeting. When the bell rang at the end of the last lesson we raced out as usual. On the way, driving up the mountain, I asked her how my mother had seemed to her.

Michaela said that she was very beautiful, and she seemed to love me in her way, but she didn't really know me. She said that my mother was a cold woman.

And then Rocinanta stopped on the dirt track and we found ourselves a corner in a field of cyclamens. Michaela sat down under a pine tree, her back against the trunk (afterwards, when we got up, I scraped little lumps of resin off her blouse with my nails), and I lay on a bed of pine needles with my head on her lap. She bent over me and we kissed. Her hand opened the buttons of my jeans and slid smooth and cool under my panties, to the core of sweetness, and all the time her warm lips kept sucking mine, until my legs stiffened and my whole body trembled.

When Michaela dropped me at the Center I said to her, "So we're going to stop meeting, right?"

Michaela smiled. "Absolutely. Now that Racheli knows, you can go to her place instead of mine."

From now on we'll have to be very careful. When I go to her I'll have to keep my eyes peeled because Grandfather's girlfriend Bracha lives in Nitzanim Street, and he drives through Hatzvi Avenue when he goes to see her. It's hard for me to lie to those green X-ray eyes. Lying corrodes the mouth, blackens the tongue, but I have no choice, I'll have to perfect the art of concealment. (I'd better find a good hiding place for you. All I need is for Mother to find this diary and read it. . . .)

There are so many things I don't know; I don't know why my mother and father stopped loving each other (if they ever did . . .), I don't know why my father stopped loving me, I don't know who my mother's mystery lover is. (Funny that she's having an affair with a married man, while I'm having one with a married woman . . .); there's only one thing I'm sure of: I love Michaela and Michaela loves me, so how can I even think of not meeting her anymore?

Yours, Kitty

P.S. I almost forgot; on the twentieth of February Michaela is turning twenty-seven, and I've decided to knit her a scarf. I went down to the wool shop next to the Orly Cinema and bought a pair of knitting needles and sky-blue and brown wool, the color of both our eyes. I told the saleslady that I'd never knitted anything before, and she taught me to do cable stitch. At the beginning the cables came out stiff and a little crooked, like the fingers of a child learning to hold a pencil, but as I proceed they're improving, and I'm really enjoying myself, and most of all, I'm proud of myself. Can you imagine Butterfingers sitting in her room every evening and clicking her knitting needles like some granny with years of practice behind her? I sit on the floor with my back to the door, so nobody can open it, and when anyone knocks I quickly hide the knitting under my mattress.

Dearest Anne,

Michaela strokes me and her hands are like clouds. She strokes for hours without getting tired, and surrounded by the stroking I dream, and turn into whatever I want, I can be a girl or an animal, male or female, a baby or an old woman, a mortal or a goddess. Sometimes I fall asleep while she's stroking me, and her hands go on and on, like the sea, which is never still, like lying on the edge of the water and letting the foam of the waves flow onto your body and ebb away from it, flow and ebb and flow until the end of time.

And in the endless stroking, with Dulcinea lying at our feet, breathing heavily and warming our feet with her fur, we talk. I discovered that love is greedy, it wants to swallows the beloved and all her life, her childhood memories and former loves. I have no former loves with which to feed our love, and I ask Michaela to tell me about hers.

A few days ago, entwined in the light of a winter afternoon, she told me again about Shaul, her first, a charming ruddy boy with gleaming cat's eyes and a fair, slender body, and long fingers that could paint and sculpt and play the clarinet, and were expert at rolling the joints they smoked between fucking, with Bob Dylan and Janis Joplin and the Beetles in the background, until he was drafted and was taken to the war from which he returned burned-out and bitter.

And she told me too about Phillip, with whom she lived for a year in Paris. He was studying film and she was studying art and French, and combing all the museums. And I—a girl whose mother was a travel agent, but who had never left the country, and for whom the Paris of books and films was an object of yearning for what seemed to her real life—accompanied them in my imagination on their walks through the Luxembourg Gardens, along the river Seine (Michaela says "Sen" like a true Frenchwoman), and watch them kissing on the bridges with long wool scarves around their necks, and sitting in cafes with their icy hands wrapped around piping hot cups of chocolate.

And Michaela slips naked out of the warmth of the down quilt and melting bodies and makes her way to the cold dark study and comes back with photograph albums and switches on the reading lamp over the bed, and opens the album, and here they are in the snow in blue duffel coats and wooly hats and scarves. And here is her slender silhouette in front of the window, because Phillip pursued her to photograph her in the nude, and she would draw him, and here are the drawings in a brown envelope: a young man, solid and curly-haired, sitting or lying in all kinds of poses, and his long penis is uncircumcised.

And here's Michaela on her twenty-first birthday, smiling over a huge bowl of spaghetti, with a lit candle stuck in the middle, because at the end of every month, when her monthly allowance from her parents ran out, Phillip would cook spaghetti and make a sauce from all the leftovers he found in the fridge.

"So why did you split up?" I asked. Phillip seemed a lot more romantic to me than Yoel.

"I missed Israel, my father, my friends, my mother nagged me to come home already and start going to the university so that I would have a profession—and Phillip didn't want to come here with me."

"And when you came back, you met Yoel?"

"Not exactly, I'd known Yoel since we were children, our parents were friends. We would go on holiday together, the two families, to pensiones in Nahariya and the Judean hills. He was also an only child, his mother called him "Yoelshin," a shy, skinny kid, he hardly opened his mouth, I never thought there would be anything between us. But after I came back from Paris and met him at some party, he was already in his fourth year at medical school, tall, not bad looking, and suddenly I felt like seducing him, so I asked him to drive me home, I was living with a roommate then, and I invited him to come up. He was quite scared and sweating all over, I think I was his first, but somehow I managed to guide him in the right direction, and that was it, since then we've been together, to the great delight of our parents."

"And who did you like going to bed with the most?"

"With Phillip. He was without a doubt my best fuck."

"Better than me?" I was offended.

Michaela laughed. "Of course not, nobody's better than you."

"How can it be," I tried to understand, "that you always loved men, and you enjoyed being with them and everything, and suddenly you love me?"

Michaela pulled a cigarette from the pack next to the bed and lit it. "It's a mystery to me too," she said at last, "you revealed new things about myself to me."

"Do you think that I'll be able to be with men too one day," I asked timidly, "or that I'll be . . ." I had difficulty in pronouncing the word that was never spoken between us, "a lesbian all my life?"

A ripple of pain crossed her face, and she gathered me into her arms, "I'm sure you'll love men," she said firmly into my eyes, "and men will love you madly. I'm already jealous of whoever will have you in the future."

I tried to gain reassurance from her words, but the fear that I'll always be like this didn't go away, because sometimes, when I'm lying on top of her, and her breasts are so soft and provocative, and her face breaks up below me with delight, I feel like a man, a young boy conquering a woman. So maybe I really am a masculine girl and I'm destined to be attracted only to women?

That night I wrote a long poem, "In the Name of Love," and I'm copying the first verses for you:

Sometimes I stand and wonder
at the desire of your body to expose you
to the eye of the sun
to the eye of the sea
to the blind eye of the earth,

if you could you would strip your soul too,
to let me look at the light.

Should I tell you the pain of the fruit
Yearning to ripen before its time?
Tell me first what the sun feels
Drinking its fill of the sour-sweet sky
and letting it taste
the nectar of kisses.

Come let us live the spring of the body,
come let us die with the quiet heartbeats
and with the rushing waves
breaking on the shore.

Today it is winter again.
The only evidence of yesterday's spring
a small pale-green fig leaf,
and a newspaper with the weather forecast
blowing in the wind.
Two witnesses are enough.

What do you think? I think it's not bad. Perhaps I'll give
her the poem for her birthday together with the scarf that I keep
on knitting diligently every night.

Your Kitty

February 22nd

Dearest Anne,
I've just begun, and already the tears are dripping from my eyes
and leaving wet spots on the paper. This afternoon I went to
Michaela's with the new scarf (her birthday was on Saturday, she
celebrated it in a restaurant with Yoel and both their parents).
The scarf came out fantastic, long and wide and soft, with thick

tassels. In addition I copied the long poem into a notebook with a purple cover for her, together with everything I'd written about her in my diary when I loved her without her knowing.

Michaela was so happy! She immediately wrapped the scarf around her neck and said how nice it felt, and now she would always be able to feel as if I was hugging her. I gave her the notebook too, and she read it, and there were tears in her eyes. She said that although I had already told her how I'd felt about her last year, ever since I met her—she never imagined the extent. She took my face in her hands and whispered, "How did I deserve to be so loved by you, kiddo, I must have done something really, really good once."

Afterwards we got undressed and slipped under the cool quilt. Her hands wandered tirelessly over my body along the routes of pleasure, giving birth to joy and yet more joy, covering expanses of skin, mending and healing and bewitching, awakening my desire, and I got on top of her and rode her thigh, pressing down on the mouth of her erupting volcano until my fingers melted, and my eyes sought her eyes straining to stay open for me, until they clouded over and closed, as if to keep her soul from flying away, and her whole glorious body pulsed, held fast in the palm of my hand.

Afterwards we lay welded back to stomach under the quilt, watching the clouds sailing behind the cypress tree.

And then we heard the grating of the key in the keyhole. Her body froze for a moment against my back, and in an instant she sprang out of bed, snatched up my clothes and threw them onto the bathroom floor, and whispered like a whiplash, "It's him, get dressed quickly and go." I went into the bathroom and through the crack of the door I saw her shooting into her jeans and blouse, running her fingers through her hair, and hurrying barefoot to the front door, to release the latch, which she never forgets to lock.

I locked the bathroom door and sat naked on the cold rim of the tub, my whole body covered with prickles of goose pimples. I loathed the figure in the mirror with its damp blotchy face. I washed my face and hands, to rid them of her smell, and I cupped my hand and filled it with water and drank more and more, to drag out the time. Then I got dressed slowly and I heard their hushed voices behind the door.

"Is she here again?" Yoel complained in a tired voice.

"What can I do," she said lightly, with pretended despair, "she has problems at home. She comes to pour her heart out to me."

All of a sudden my beloved had turned into a stranger.

When I emerged into the passage, Yoel looked at me with pity mingled with suspicion. I mumbled, "I have to go, good-bye," and escaped. I walked heavily up the hill, my ears straining for the sound of her treacherous footsteps, which did not hurry after me to mend the wound.

In the park behind Rothschild House I fell onto one of the benches and the tears burst out of me—for the scarf I had knit-ted in secret, evening after evening for a month, and for the notebook, which I copied for her in my best handwriting, and the way she had told me to get dressed and go, as if I was her Sancho Panza or something. I heard her voice whispering into my ear, "How did I deserve to be so loved by you, kiddo, I must have once done something really, really good," and I felt that I really did love her too much and perhaps she wasn't worth it at all, perhaps she only needed me so that her days wouldn't become habitual to her, like in that poem of Leah's.

It started raining, and the wind pierced me with needles through my clothes. I raised my head to let the raindrops cool my face and erase the red blotches. I don't know how long I sat there, mumbling like a mantra, I don't care about her, I don't care, I don't care. Suddenly I panicked at the thought that it must be really late, and Mother was beginning to worry and maybe she had already phoned Racheli to see if I was there, and I forced myself to get up and dragged my heavy, superfluous body home.

I opened the door with my stomach turning over and the lie already quivering in my mouth. My mother was standing at the marble counter in the kitchen and cutting up vegetables for a salad.

"Where have you been," her X-ray eyes pierced my blotched face.

"At Racheli's," the lie dropped from my lips, "I had supper there."

(Lately I've been trying to eat before or after them, and sometimes I don't eat at all, anything to avoid sitting at the table with Mother and Noam and Oren, opening their mouths wide opposite each other to reveal a mess of chewed omelet and tomato and cottage cheese, and yelling and yelling, "Gross," "What a pig," "Idiot," "Mother, tell him" "Stop that at once" "But he started" "No, I didn't" "Yes, you did," until I wanted to slap them both.)

The girl shuts herself in her room, and she sits with her back to the door, writing wounded words to you, trying to tear her treacherous love from her heart. Enough, I've had enough, let her go and live in somebody else's heart.

Soon her mother will go out, like every evening, and disappear into the maw of the white whale waiting for her opposite the house in the darkness. The girl will emerge from the prison of her room and make herself half a cup of tea, and fill it up to the brim with rum, and drink it thirstily, in great gulps, to dilute the pain and the longings, so that she can fall asleep.

Yes, Anne, your Kitty has turned into a drunk!

2.24.78

Dearest Anne,
I don't talk to her, I can hardly look at her. Yesterday she didn't teach, and I didn't call her at lunch time from my "little house in the post office" so that she would be sorry and worry about me. Today I was in two minds as to whether to stay for the literature

lesson at all. I consulted Racheli, and she said that she was sure Michaela was sorry for what had happened and that she was looking for an opportunity to talk to me. In the end I decided to stay in the classroom, because I wanted to see how she would behave to me. I pretended to be bored, I looked out of the window with a sphinx-like expression, and took no part in the lesson. Michaela tried to teach as if everything was as usual, but all the time she kept trying to catch my eye. She didn't succeed, and the more time passed the more the corners of her mouth tightened in insult. She went on talking about N'ima Sasson and her teacher, and read, too loudly, from the story: "Everyone feels the miracle in his heart. But I, please God, when I grow up, will find out how to describe this miracle, all the miracles, in writing. I have to. Otherwise my life is no life." And she said, "Who can tell us what the miracle, or miracles, that N'ima Sasson wants to express in writing, are and why she feels that her life depends on it," and she looked at me again, but I knew it was bait, a trap, and I lowered my eyes to the open book, and then Michaela said almost pleadingly, "Rivi, you write, perhaps you can tell us," but just at that moment my eyes fell on another line, that pierced my heart, and I raised my head and looked straight into her eyes and said, "Perhaps the miracle that N'ima Sasson wants to express is the miracle of love, but I think that it's a good thing that the teacher Ezekiel wasn't seduced by her love, he knew that he was much older than her and a married man, and they couldn't really be together, and she would only suffer from it, and so he says to her," and then I read the line I had found earlier and kept my finger on: "'Today, it's school. Tomorrow, life. Listen, and bear this in mind. Limits are set. We are not living in the days when there was no king in Israel and every man did that which was right in his own eyes. A certain N'ima Sasson, a certain Ezekiel Da Silva. Will they please stick to the rules. That's how it is here. And that's how we want it.'"

I raised my eyes and saw that she was pale and biting her lower lip and she didn't know what to say, and in the end she said quietly, "If it was as simple and unequivocal as you say, the story wouldn't be interesting. What makes it interesting is the complexity of each of the characters," and then the bell rang, and Michaela said that we should answer her question at home, and Gil Klein asked if it was homework, and Amnon Neuman cuffed him on the back of his neck and said, of course it's homework you idiot, and I collected my things and hurried out of the classroom, without looking at her, and ran home before she could reach Rocinanta and catch up with me.

My stomach still feels as if it's on fire and I want to cry. I miss her so much, talking to her, laughing, feeling her lips and embrace and silky hands, hearing her whisper sweet words of love. It's as if she has two Michaelas in her, the familiar, beloved one, who belongs to me, and the strange, denying one, who belongs to Yoel and all the rest. Do you think I'll be able to reconcile the two of them inside me, so that our love can continue? As N'ima Sasson says: "And still the spirit can only yearn. . . ."

Your Kitty

3.3.78

Dearest Anne,

Today, instead of the last two hours of art, we went to the university to see an exhibition by the artist Hundertwasser. To my surprise Michaela accompanied us (afterwards she told me that she had asked Nilli, the art teacher, if she could join us, on the pretext that she was a fan of the artist's work, which was true in itself, but she was really looking for a chance to speak to me). In the bus I sat next to Racheli, and pretended not to see her, even though all the way her bronze ponytail danced in my eyes over the red-and-green checks of her cape.

Most of the kids took no interest in the exhibition and rushed off to invade the cafeteria. Only Racheli and I, with a few other girls, and also Michaela, listened to Nilli's explanations about the Austrian painter, whose style was influenced by Egon Schiele and Klimt. He kept returning to variations on the subject of the spiral, his works were very colorful, and sometimes looked as if they had been painted by a child. He was protesting against the architecture of blocks of dull gray buildings, and against pollution of the environment, the water and the air. He believed that Paradise was not in the world to come, but here on earth, and that human beings were destroying it. After Nilli had finished talking, Michaela asked permission to add something, and told us that Hundertwasser's father had died when he was one year old, his mother came from a Jewish family and many of her relations perished in the Holocaust, and that in the sixties he had made speeches in the nude to emphasize his social and ecological protest. She said too that Hundertwasser saw painting, and art in general, as an irrational act that did not involve the will or the intellect, but was like walking in a dream, guided by some undefined force. As she spoke she kept glancing at me to see my reaction, and I made an effort not to look at her (and not to scratch my forehead . . .) and thought how cultivated she was, how much she knew about literature and art and music, and how clearly and pleasantly she explained everything, and I swelled secretly in pride.

Nilli let us wander freely through the exhibition, and when I was standing by myself opposite a green head whose brain was a red spiral, and trying to focus on it and be sucked into it in order not to sense Michaela's presence, and I was already imagining Hundertwasser skipping and dancing naked in his green Garden of Eden, like Gene Kelly in *Singing in the Rain*—I suddenly sensed that she was standing very close to me. Her hand shot out from under the cape, took hold of mine, and squeezed it hard. She whispered, "I miss you so much, kiddo, won't you stop punishing me now?" I whispered, "Okay, let's meet," and Michaela suggested that afterwards, when everyone went to the bus stop, the two of us would lag behind and go for a walk to our forest. I told Racheli that I wasn't returning to the Center with them, and she immediately understood and said, I knew you would make up in the end.

We sat on her cape among the trees, and Michaela apologized about what had happened and explained that she had been overcome by panic, that Yoel would catch us and everything would be finished, and she couldn't bear it to be finished, because our love was the most precious thing in her life, she was addicted to it and addicted to me. Her huge eyes brimmed over, and I dripped a bit too and said that I understood and forgave her, and so we sat there bawling with our arms around each other, two pathetic, idiotic waterworks, and again I realized how fragile Michaela was and how much she needed me, as if she were the younger and I the elder, and amid our tears we began to kiss, and what happened next you can imagine for yourself, and it was especially sweet, because of the longings and the reconciliation.

Afterwards we took a bus back to the Center, and all the way we held hands under her cape, and the houses and the trees raced downhill, radiant in the winter sun, and they looked not quite real, like the world always looks to me after we make love.

And I even managed to get home in time to heat up Oren and Noam's lunch.

So now I'm happy again, your Kitty

Thursday, March 16, 1978

Dearest Anne,

What do you think of this for a lark? Suddenly I've got a baby sister! This afternoon, when Mother came home from work, she said in that cynical tone of hers that I hate (or maybe the right word is "sarcastic," I've never been able to tell the difference), "Congratulations, I hear you have a new baby sister. . . ." And I didn't even know that my father's Batya was pregnant. Oren and Noam knew, but they never said anything to me. I asked Oren why they didn't tell me, and he shrugged his shoulders and said he'd forgotten. Afterwards he said, I didn't really forget, I thought you wouldn't be interested. I left immediately for my little house in the post office and called to tell Michaela the news. She asked if I was glad, and I said that I was unable to feel anything. She said that it was an opportunity to visit them and reconnect with my father, and I said it would never happen. I'm a little curious to know what the baby looks like, if she looks like me, and if she'll have to wear spectacles and be deaf in one ear, like me and Daddy. I'd always wanted a sister so badly, and now that I had one, I wouldn't even get to know her. In the afternoon the phone rang and I picked it up. It was Daddy. I said, "Mazaltov," and he said, "Thank you, thank you, Rivi," and it seemed to me that his voice trembled a bit. This was the first time since he left home that he'd said my name, which I thought he'd already forgotten. I asked, "What's her name?" And he said, "My wife decided to call her Orly." I thought of the annoying Orly in our class and I wanted to tell him that it wasn't a good name, and to ask him if he didn't have an opinion of his own, but then he said, "Give me your brother." I called Oren and I heard him wail, "But you promised we'd go and play football." He put the phone down, and I understood that Daddy wouldn't come for them today, because of the baby.

So I have a new sister, whose name is Orly, and I had my longest conversation with my father since they got divorced, and I'm no longer his only daughter, he has another daughter, who he'll lift onto his shoulders and teach to swim and to play chess, and check out books for in the library and tell her about Jean Valjean and Marie Antoinette, and sing funny songs to her friends, and raise till she's grown.

Good night, Kitty

Passover holidays, 4.24.78

Dearest Anne,
We celebrated the Seder at Aunt Tehiya's, with Mother's uncles and their children and grandchildren. We drove down with

Grandfather in his car, and we all slept over in the big house in Ramat Gan. It was boiling hot, all the windows were open, and the smell of orange blossom, which is the most thrilling smell in the world, hung over the Seder table and put us all in a flowery, festive mood. Mother—who always wears her smartest clothes for the Seder and has her hair done at the hairdresser's, and makes herself up like a model, in order to show off to her cousins—was absolutely radiant. Sometimes I think that nobody who knows her, pleasant and amiable and beautiful as a princess, could imagine that at home with us she's so bad-tempered and hard. (And nobody who sees me, a girl with braids and an innocent look behind her glasses, could imagine all kinds of things either . . .) We took turns reading the Haggada, and Noam, who can't read properly yet, got the best bit, which is real poetry, and which I'd hoped to get to read myself, "I have caused thee to multiply as the bud of the field, and thou hast increased and waxen great, and thou art come to excellent ornaments; thy breasts are fashioned and thine hair is grown, whereas thou wast naked and bare. And when I passed by thee, and saw thee polluted in thine own blood, I said unto thee when thou wast in thy blood, Live; yea, I said unto thee when thou wast in thy blood, Live." Every year this passage is wasted on some pipsqueak with a runny nose and his front teeth missing, who mumbles and gets mixed up and blushes, and everybody laughs. I ate until I burst and drank a bit of wine, Amos and Nathan and their sons sang enthusiastically at the tops of their voices, and hit the table with their knives in time to the tune of "Had Gadya." After we'd finished singing the songs in the Haggada we all sang together "Abanibi Obohebeb Obotabach" by Yizhar Cohen, who represented Israel in the Eurovision contest in Paris on Saturday night (and came in first!) and competed with each other in speaking the "b" language as fast as we could without getting mixed up. Afterwards they began arguing about whether Yizhar Cohen is a homosexual or not, and Mother said, "That whole Tel Aviv bohemian crowd are homos and junkies, that Uri Zohar and that singer Arik Einstein, all they can think about is sex and hashish," and Grandfather said, "A bunch of nobodies." Someone remembered that Uri Zohar had gotten religion recently and become an ultra-Orthodox Jew, and Mother said that the Orthodox were God's Cossacks, and that their fanaticism was even more dangerous than drug addiction. I couldn't resist saying, "What difference does it make who Yizhar Cohen goes to bed with, what matters is how he sings," and Uncle Amos said that it made a big difference, because Yizhar Cohen wasn't only representing himself, but the State of Israel, and we didn't want people to think that we were a country of fairies. I didn't feel like arguing with them, so I went to the kitchen to help Aunt Tehiya dry the dishes. Aunt Tehiya gave me a dig in the ribs with her elbow and asked me quietly, "Well, Monkey, have you got a boyfriend yet?" As far as she was concerned, if you hadn't met your husband-to-be by the age of fourteen and a half, you were already an old maid. She had met Uncle Moshe at the age of fourteen, in little Tel Aviv; he walked past Margalit Orenstein's dance studio, heard the piano playing, peeked through the window, and saw Aunt Tehiya dancing, barefoot like Isadora Duncan, tall and straight-backed and boyish, with her long arms and muscular calves, and her black braid down to her waist, and his heart stopped in admiration for three full minutes, which was his first cardiac arrest, and he waited outside for her and invited her for a soda or something, and from then until he died forty years later from his second and final cardiac arrest, they never parted, except for when he had to go and fight some war.

"I've got all kinds of suitors," I lied, "but nothing really serious in the meantime." I was almost tempted to tell her about Michaela, but I knew that not even Aunt Tehiya would be able to understand our strange love, and she might even tell my mother.

Now I'm back at home. The suffocating tiger-yellow haze left the porch dusty with the pine pollen that Mother hates to clean, and gave way to azure-gold skies, and Michaela and I meet almost every morning. Michaela says that the spring and the vacation make her want to rearrange the house, to try new dishes, to play the piano, to buy new clothes, and to dress up. This morning she dragged me with her on a tour of the shops in Hadar. We parked in Nordau Street and went into a boutique that specializes in second-hand clothes and all kinds of old fashioned jewelry and buttons, and Michaela always finds treasures there. The saleslady, a woman of about fifty with a wild gray Afro, wearing an embroidered galabieh, which Mother would undoubtedly have called rags and tatters, greeted Michaela joyfully, and the two of them chattered away enthusiastically. Michaela bought herself a scarf hand-painted in sunset colors, and old ivory and mother-of-pearl buttons, which she intended to sew onto a bottle-green velvet jacket she was making for herself. (Yoel had bought her an up-to-the-minute Singer sewing machine, and she was as delighted as a child with a new toy.) She went behind the curtain, tried on clothes and came out, twirling in front of me, for a moment I felt like a guy pacing back and forth outside the changing booth with his hands in the pockets of his jeans overall, waiting for his girlfriend to come out and thrill his heart. In her shopping expeditions, her sewing clothes for herself, her dressing up, she sometimes reminds me of my mother, but in contrast to my mother, Michaela also reads books and listens to music, and she has a few more things in her head.

For me we found a pin in the shape of a green clover leaf with a tiny diamond in the center, which reminded us of the song "I Met You in a Field of Clover," which we sometimes sing together when Rocinanta bears us up the mountain to the forest. We also collect words that have a nice sound, like "vibrate," "velvet," "darkness," "elixir," "spellbinding." "Clover" was the last word we added to the list.

After we came out of the boutique we went into a watchmaker's dark little alcove, with an antique wristwatch Michaela had inherited from her father's sister and which needed mending; once it had belonged to her grandmother who perished in the Holocaust. The ancient watchmaker sat there in his corner, in a suit and tie, and looked through the little tube fixed in the socket of his eye at the minute mechanism in the light of a small lamp, and his hands, with the brown spots on their backs, and the long precise fingers, didn't tremble the least little bit. He removed the monocular from his eye and smiled at us with young blue eyes through his wrinkles.

Michaela spoke to him in German, because he didn't understand Hebrew, even though he had come to the country over forty years ago. She asked him something and laughed at his reply. When we came out I asked her what they were talking about, and Michaela said that she had asked him when he was born, and Herr Heim, which was his name, said in the year 1890, and his father, who was watchmaker to Kaiser Franz Joseph and who wanted his son to follow in his footsteps, had promised him that, if he looked after time, time would look after him, and you see, time has been looking after him now for eighty-eight years.

On the way to Rocinanta we passed a jeweler's with a sign in the window saying, "Ears pierced here." I told Michaela that I was dying to have my ears pierced like hers, and she said, come on then, let's go in. The shop assistant, a peroxide blond with long purple fingernails and artificial smiles, rubbed my lobes with cottonwool dipped in alcohol, inserted them into a special kind of gun, and shot an earring into them. Michaela held my hand so I could squeeze when it hurt, and I nearly crushed her hand. Afterwards I looked in the mirror with my eyes full of tears. Two golden balls laughed at me under my braids, and Michaela peeped over my shoulder and her lips mouthed: They suit you. The shop assistant explained to me how to disinfect the holes and turn the earrings around.

I imagined that my mother would not be pleased; she had never had her ears pierced, and all her earrings had clips, but I didn't expect her to be so angry. She shot me an annihilating look that hurt a lot more than the earring-pistol, and said, "You know who had their ears bored," and I said, "No, who," and she said, "Slaves who gave up their freedom. You have mutilated yourself, and branded yourself as a willing slave forever." She interrogated me about how I paid for the piercing and the earrings, and I lied and told her that I had money left over from Grandfather's birthday present.

What am I to do with her, Anne, do you think there's any hope for our relationship? I comfort myself with the thought that you too didn't get on with your mother, who was as sarcastic and mocking and tactless as my mother and leveled accusations as wounding and painful as arrows at you every day. Once, after you quarreled, you wrote that you found her harder to bear than anything else, but that you couldn't vent your feelings about her failings, and you were obliged to be a mother to yourself, because you had an image of a perfect mother in your imagination, and in the woman you were obliged to call mother you couldn't find the faintest trace of that image. "I only wish I could occasionally receive the encouragement of someone who really loves me," you wrote, and you found some consolation in your father, who for the most part understood you, and in Peter, and in your letters to Kitty. And I find consolation in you, Anne, and in Michaela, who really loves me. She also doesn't get on too well with her mother, who forces her to call her every day, and gets angry when she forgets. And it's the same with Racheli. Maybe that's just the way it is with mothers and daughters, and always will be, when we ourselves are mothers too, and when our daughters are mothers, and so on to the end of time. But I've sworn to myself, and you're the witness, that I'll be different from her, the absolute opposite. I'll respect my children even if they're different from me, and I'll take an interest in their souls.

Yours, your willing slave, Kitty

P.S. I just remembered: We should be celebrating the first anniversary of this diary round about now! I turn to look over my shoulder and smile at the girl who last Passover vacation began to write to you on the back of the tour itineraries, and since then I've raced ahead and left her far, far behind.

5.27.78

Dearest Anne,

Yesterday morning Yoel was working on the weekend shift, and Michaela and I drove to the Carmel beach, where they have a small private changing room, which they rent together with her parents. We got undressed and put on our swimsuits. In her black bikini that shows off the whiteness of her skin, as she hung up her clothes, Michaela suddenly said, in a casual tone of voice, "I wanted to tell you, I've decided to stop taking the pill."

For a moment I couldn't understand why she was telling me this. Then I understood, and a terrible jealousy flared up inside me of the baby not yet conceived, the baby in her mind and heart, and without saying a word, with all the strength of my youth, I pushed her to the concrete floor and pulled off her bikini and lay savagely on her body, as if I was raping her, my hands crushing her flesh, which would soon be taken from me, and she bit her lower lip and her eyes filled with fear and pity for me, and my tears fell and fell on her face.

Afterwards I sat on the concrete bench, wearing the lower half of my swimsuit, the top hanging by a narrow strap from my neck, and the waves of weeping came from the depths and shook my body and burst out of me in ugly bellows and hiccups and snot.

She sat down beside me, wrapped her arm around my shoulders and tried to explain. She said that they had already been married for a year and a half, Yoel was putting pressure on her, as were her parents and his parents. She said that she was doing it for us, that she had to placate everyone so that we could go on seeing each other, so as not to arouse suspicion. She promised

164

that she would love me when she was pregnant too and after she gave birth as well.

"But it won't be the same, Mishi," I wept. "Don't you understand that if you have a baby, it won't be the same anymore."

"It's not even certain that I'll be able to get pregnant," she said quietly, "it could take a long time."

That night I couldn't fall asleep, I kept thinking of the imaginary baby that everyone was planning for her, an alibi-baby that would come into the world only so that our love could continue, and I asked myself if Michaela would have enough love for both of us, or if one of us would have to go without.

Today at break she slipped me a letter, which she had written in the kitchen last night. She writes all her letters to me to the sound of the purring of the fridge, which with first light is swallowed up by the warbling of the birds as they wake. She wrote that my tears tear her to pieces, and that my love has turned the world into a place it makes her happy to live in, a place of hope, into which it's worthwhile to bring children.

I have her letter in my hand now. Again and again I read the words and try to derive consolation from them.

Yours, Kitty

June 22nd

Dearest Anne,

It's been a long time since I wrote to you, I was busy rehearsing for the party to celebrate our graduation from Middle School, which took place yesterday evening. Our homeroom teacher Galya decided that in addition to the imitations of our teachers and similar silliness the program should include a serious part too, to show our parents that we had learned something in the past three years. She divided us into groups according to subjects, and put me in charge (how surprising . . .) of the literature group, with Racheli, Gil Klein, Yuval Shalev, Noam Bloch, and Michal Braverman. I went through all the works we'd studied in the past two years, and I couldn't find anything short and suitable for dramatization for six actors. I consulted Michaela, and she suggested something from Shalom Aleichem's *Song of Songs*, but I thought it was too long. She herself was busy preparing for the graduation party of grade 8b, whose homeroom teacher she was, and we hardly had time to meet. In the end I went back and looked through the book of ballads we had studied in seventh grade, and found Goethe's "The Erl-King." My face burned and my heart began to race, and I knew I'd found the right poem. It was short and dramatic, and had parts for three boys (the father, the son, and the Erl-King) and two girls (the daughters of the Erl-King). I myself would take the part of the narrator: the first and last verses. Everyone agreed with my choice, I didn't even have to persuade them, because none of them really cared. Michaela too said it was a wonderful idea, and suggested accompanying the play with the Schubert Lied. She gave me the tape cassette, and she even offered to lend us her checked cape for the father to hide his son from the storm. In the last two weeks of school we hardly studied, and most of the time was devoted to rehearsals. We decided that Yuval would be the child, because he's the shortest boy in the class and his voice hasn't broken yet, the wooden Gil Klein would be the father, and Noam would be the Erl-King. Racheli and Michal, who had no words, prepared a seductive dance for the daughters of the Erl-King, which came out well, because Michal has been going to ballet lessons for a million years, and she got hold of costumes with transparent scarves, like belly dancers, for them. When we were working on the last bit there was an argument: Gil and Noam said that the father and the Erl-King should fight over the child, pull him by his arms and hit each other. They claimed this would be much more dramatic.

"But there's nothing in Goethe's ballad about a fight over the child," I said. "The father doesn't even see the Erl-King, he thinks he's mist, that his voice is the wind rustling in the dry leaves, and his daughters are old willows on the lake shore. He's sure his son is imagining it all, he doesn't understand that the Erl-King is about to snatch him away—so how can he fight over him?"

"I think that the father does gradually understand that it's the Erl- King, and he is afraid of him," said Racheli, "but he lies to his son in order to protect him, he thinks that if the child doesn't see the Erl-King he may be saved, and also he doesn't want him to be afraid and to know that he's going to die."

"You may be right," I said, "but in any case, the father doesn't confront the Erl-King and fight him, he only runs away."

Gil and Noam went on arguing, until I got fed up and told them that I was the director and I made the decisions, and if they didn't agree they could direct it themselves, and they gave in.

I invited Mother and Grandfather to the play and also Noam and Oren. For a moment it crossed my mind to phone the android and invite him too, but I imagined that he wouldn't come, and I would just have my feelings hurt. I knew that Michaela would be there with the rest of the teachers, and I was quite nervous about her running into Mother.

Before the play I had to run to the lavatory about five times, and I prayed that everybody would remember their lines and that I wouldn't get into trouble with the tape. So much effort and nerves and emotion for a piece that lasted five minutes. Even though I was supposed to sit in the wings in the dark I wore a T-shirt without any buttons so that this time my mother wouldn't have any excuse to leave in the middle.

At half past eight the hall was full. Hourgi didn't spare us a long boring speech, to the effect that next year we were starting high school, and in three years time we would be enlisting in the army, and this imposed an obligation. I didn't understand exactly what the obligation was, but the audience clapped, perhaps in relief that he had finished talking at last. After Hourgi the French group appeared with humorous chansons, and then the history group in a long, boring piece about the destruction of the Temple, and by the time our turn came the suspense was killing me.

In the end everything was okay. I kept the tape at the right volume, not too loud and not too soft, and from the wings I read the first verse in a loud, carrying voice:

"Who rides there so late through the night dark and drear?
The father it is, with his infant so dear;
He holdeth the boy tightly clasped in his arm,
He holdeth him safely, he keepeth him warm."

As I read, Yuval with Gil behind him burst onto the stage riding on a broomstick and wrapped in Michaela's cape, and the audience began to laugh, both because of the broom and because of Noam's entrance from the other side of the stage dressed up as the Erl-King, a kind of green hunchbacked demon with a crown and a tail, winking at Yuval and sticking out his tongue and pulling seductive faces.

The dialogue continued, the Erl-King coaxing the child to come with him, the father trying to persuade the child, and perhaps himself, that it's all his imagination. And then Racheli and Michal came on with their belly-dancer costumes, and I increased the volume of the music just in time, and the Erl-King hissed like a snake:

"Wilt go, then, dear infant, wilt go with me there?
My daughters shall tend thee with sisterly care,
My daughters by night their glad festival keep,
They'll dance thee, and rock thee, and sing thee to sleep."

Every now and then I peeked at the audience, but the light was dim, and I didn't have a clear view, and I couldn't see my mother's face, but I was sure that she was still there. Michaela was standing at the back, in the dark, and it seemed to me that she was smiling.

In the end the Erl-King grabbed hold of Yuval and said to him:

"I love thee, I'm charmed by thy beauty, dear boy!
And if thou'rt unwilling, then force I'll employ."

And Yuval cried shrilly in his squeaky voice:

"My father, my father, he seizes me fast,
Full sorely the Erl-King has hurt me at last!"

And then Gil clasped Yuval tightly to him inside the cape
and galloped as fast as he could around the stage with the
broomstick, and I read the last verse with pathos:

"The father now gallops, with terror half wild,
He grasps in his arms the poor shuddering child;
He reaches his courtyard with toil and with dread—
The child in his arms finds he motionless, dead."

Gil laid Yuval on the stage with a grief-stricken expression,
and covered him with the cape, and then it turned out that all
the rehearsals and all the practice I gave in lying dead on the
floor had been in vain; the moron couldn't control himself and
shook with laughter under the cape and the audience laughed
with him.

In the end we lined up to take a bow and the audience
applauded us more than the other groups.

Afterwards came the imitations of the teachers. Yael Essenfeld imitated Michaela, they way she talks quietly and slowly in
her deep, melodious voice, and then she closed her eyes and put
her thumb and forefinger on her forehead and said, "Who can
remind me where we were, my train of thought's been broken
off, Rivi, perhaps you can tie it up for me, I know you got ten
out of ten for crafts," and everyone laughed, because Michaela
always calls me, and also because it's a well-known fact that I'm
the worst in the class at crafts. I felt my face going up in flames,

because Michaela usually loses her train of thought when her eyes meet mine. I turned around to look for her in the place where she had been standing, but she wasn't there.

And then everyone fell on the refreshments, and I went up to my mother, who pecked me on the cheek and said, "That was very nice," and it seemed to me that she wanted to say something else too, but she restrained herself. Grandfather put his arm around my shoulders and said, "Not bad, you have some talented artists in your class," and Oren and Noam declared that it had been boring, and asked when we were going home.

We pushed towards the exit in the crush and landed outside. I parted from my loving family, who were about to go home, and said that I wanted to say goodbye to my friends, and I would come home later. I looked for Michaela everywhere, I wanted to give her the plastic bag with the cape and the cassette, which I had been holding all the time so it wouldn't get lost in the commotion. In the end I saw her next to the gate, talking to Yael Essenfeld. They were laughing, and Michaela drew Yael towards her and kissed her on the cheek. I felt the insult and jealousy burning in my chest. I passed them with a perfunctory greeting, walked out of the gate, and started climbing the hill, looking for Rocinanta. I waited next to the car for about ten minutes, until Michaela appeared, hurrying up the hill with her face beaming at me in the light of the street lamps. She hugged and kissed me, and said in her gentle voice, "That was lovely, kiddo, Goethe must be melting with pleasure up there," and I immediately forgave her for everything. Rocinanta slid down the slope, turned into Assif Street, and stopped in a quiet lane. Michaela told me that she had seen my mother before the performance, and she had said hello, and Mother didn't answer her. She didn't know if she really hadn't seen her, or if she ignored her on purpose.

That's it, school's over and the long vacation has begun! Next week Michaela is going on a trip to London and Paris with Yoel, for six whole weeks! I'm going with Racheli to the summer camp for young art lovers in Jerusalem, but only for two weeks. I just remembered something Thomas Mann wrote, that when you interrupt your routine and travel to another place and do different things, time grows longer; whereas when one day is like the next, time grows shorter. Do you think that if I take care to do exactly the same things every day, the endless six weeks of parting will grow shorter, and seem to me like only a few days?

Your Kitty

Sunday, 7.23.78

Dearest Anne,

The middle of the long vacation. Michaela's flown off with Yoel to Paris and London, and I feel like an abandoned puppy (Dulcinea was dumped in a kennel, and probably feels just like me). Michaela left me a box of chocolates wrapped in colored gilt paper, one for each day of parting, and I eat them religiously, one before going to bed every night, and while the sweetness is melting in my mouth, I close my eyes and project the beloved face onto the screen of my eyelids.

I took the box of chocolates with me to Jerusalem too, to the summer camp. I enjoyed the classes and activities, but I missed her so much! Every night, after the chocolate melted in my mouth, I would imagine her lips kissing me, and her hands stroking me, and her smell and the touch of her skin, and when I couldn't restrain myself I would push my hand into my pajama pants and pray that all the other girls were asleep and that no one would hear my panting breath, and that Racheli, sleeping on the bunk on top of me, wouldn't feel the rocking of the bed.

Before Michaela left we went to the post office together, and she rented a post office box for me so she could write to me. My "little house in the post office" had shrunk to a tiny box with a number. (I have a six-week holiday from buying phone tokens! Whenever I go up to the counter it seems to me that Bella Blum, the postal clerk with the narrow glasses on the tip of her pointed nose and without any lips, knows exactly who I'm going to call with those tokens, and why. Lately I've begun to buy stamps too, that I don't need at all, in order to confuse her and cover my tracks.) Every morning I climb the steps with my heart dancing a rumba. With a trembling hand I stick the key into the keyhole, praying to find a blue airmail envelope addressed in the sweeping letters I love so much. When I arrived at the post office after two weeks in Jerusalem I found three letters at once! Michaela wrote a charming description of their little hotel, which for some reason was called "Le Grand Hotel" and which overlooked the heavy mansions of the Ile-St-Louis, and the picturesque square with the statues and the antique street lamps where they ate fresh croissants dipped in coffee for breakfast, and their strolls along the banks of the Seine between the stalls of the *bouquinistes*, and the exhibitions they saw—a big exhibition of the Impressionists, and one of Matisse—and the delicacies they devoured at fancy restaurants, including oysters and snails and even frogs' legs. She wrote that she missed me more than it was possible to imagine, and how good it would be if I could be there with her. I'm sure they go to bed together about eighty times a day, trying to conceive a child. It's hard to imagine his pale stringy body on top of her, and his head with its scanty hair panting in her ear, with her soft, wonderful thighs wrapped around his hips.

I go down to the sea a lot, with Racheli or alone, and lie on the beach all day with a book. (Last week I got burned all over by the sun, and now I enjoy peeling off the dry skin in strips). Before Michaela left I found Martin Buber's *In the Secret of Dialogue*. I asked her about it, and she said that it was fascinating, especially the first part "I and Thou," and she lent it to me. Buber's style is rather obscure, but Hugo Bergman's introduction clearly explains his dialogic philosophy, which I find very appealing. I have always felt inside me the I-Thou relation, which moves me and arouses in me a far more vivid sense of life

172

than the indifferent and boring I-It relation—the world as a collection of people and things lacking in uniqueness, objects to be used. And it's not only people (especially one person, and you too . . .) who are my "thou," but sometimes also the sun, the sky, the trees, the sea, God as revealed in nature, and the books and poems I love.

In the evenings I console myself with movies. Racheli and I have discovered the little Cinematheque in the basement of the university, and we go to see a movie almost every evening. Up to now we've seen Bergman's wonderful *Wild Strawberries* and *Persona*, Fellini's *La Dolce Vita* and Truffaut's *Four Hundred Blows*. I come out of there thrilled and enchanted. What a miracle it is, the cinema! I've started to think that in the future perhaps I'll study film and become a movie director, and not necessarily a writer. I told Racheli that both writers and movie directors have a free ticket on the time-tunnel, and to the mysteries of the human soul, but in the movies everything is much more tangible. Racheli said that the cinema was truly wonderful, but she still dreamed of going to study art in Paris. After the movie we sit barefoot on the steps, looking at the "freaks" with their long hair and ragged jeans and waiting for one of them to talk to us, but none of them even pisses in our direction. Maybe we look too young to them. Only Joe-ten-lira sometimes approaches us, smiles his frightening wolfish smile at us, and asks "Maybe you got ten lira?" and we shake our heads even when we have the money, because if we give him once we'll have to go on giving forever. They say that he once took an LSD trip and forgot to come back.

But all the sea and all the movies in the world can't distract me from my longings. All I want is for these painful and superfluous days to be over already, and for my love to return to me!

Yours, Kitty

Dearest Anne,

Michaela came back yesterday! This morning she went to the HMO clinic to do the "frog test," which is the test for pregnancy, and afterwards she picked me up at the Center and we drove to the Carmel. You can imagine how we fell on each other after all this time, and how wild it was, and how sweet. She brought me stockings with little angels on them from London, and a thick notebook in a coffee-colored leather binding, which I'll write to you in from the beginning of the school year.

Michaela described for my thirsty ears (my thirsty ear, to be precise) the plays and the operas they went to in London, and the old bookshops, some of which are devoted to special subjects—scientific books, detective stories, children's books—and also homosexual and lesbian literature, which Michaela, in her thorough way, went through systematically. One of the books she bought was *Portrait of a Marriage*. This is the true story of a married couple, the diplomat Harold Nicholson and the writer Vita Sackville-West, he was a homosexual and she was a lesbian, and each of them had love affairs with members of their own sex. They lived in separate wings of their house, and wrote to each other every day, and they felt deep affection, respect, and friendship for each other. Vita was the friend and lover of Virginia Woolf, and the inspiration for the novel *Orlando*, which, according to Michaela, is one of the longest and most beautiful love letters ever written. Vita appears in it as Orlando, who lives in different periods of history, sometimes as a man and sometimes as a woman. Michaela promised to look for it for me in Hebrew. *Portrait of a Marriage* was written by their son, on the basis of diaries kept by his parents. I asked her if she too wanted to live like that and to stay married to Yoel and bring up children, with each of them free to have love affairs with other people. I told her that in my opinion this was a compromise, because when you fall in love with someone you want to live with him and sleep with him and share everything with him. Michaela said that every choice is a compromise, because it involves giving up the other possibilities, and among all the other compromises this was perhaps the least bad. "Apart from which," she smiled, "it's a well-known fact that everyone falls in love with their own compromises."

On the way back to the Center I told her that I believe that women who love each other should be brave enough to live together and to bring up children together, because in any case it's the women who raise the children. And altogether, the ideal situation would be for the world to belong to women, and for the men to be kept apart on desert islands to provide semen. Michaela laughed and said, "In spite of everything, they've had a few good ideas in the course of history, and written a few good books and musical compositions, and invented a thing or two."

"Yes, wars for instance," I said, "weapons and the atom bomb."

In the end we agreed that the gifted men would be allowed to create and invent, between one ejection of semen and the next, on condition that their works of art and inventions contributed to humanity and didn't harm it.

The closer Rocinanta came to the HMO clinic, the more edgy Michaela's driving became, and I knew that she was tense because of the results of the pregnancy test. I waited for her on the steps, and she went into the laboratory and came back to me with a strange expression on her face, full of surprise. She hugged me and whispered into my ear, "You won't believe it, kiddo, I'm pregnant." I hugged her to me as hard as I could, not knowing if I was happy or sad, and told her that I loved her more than I had ever loved anyone in my life, more than I loved myself, and that I would always love her.

The long vacation is about to be gathered to its fathers, and we're planning to meet each other every day now, and to drive to the beach at Tantura, which is quite isolated and where we can walk hand in hand without fear, and sunbathe in the nude as well. Afterwards the school year will begin, and the body I love so much will widen and fatten, a new life will grow inside it, and it will no longer be mine alone . . . it's hard to get used to the thought.

> See you in September in the English notebook,
> Your Kitty

P.S. Before I parted from this notebook and hid it in the depths of the closet, I read it again, and discovered that almost the only thing I wrote to you about was Michaela and our love. But there were other things too, school, tests, grades, my mother and grandfather and brothers, family affairs, national affairs, but they all seem unreal to me. The attic Michaela and I made for ourselves is my real life, and all the rest is like some movie in which I move about in a mask and a disguise, trying to play the part of the good girl and the diligent student.

Between Mountain and Sea

I grope in the depths of my bag for the key, insert it in the lock and open the door. All the lights are burning, and a noisy advertising jingle blares from the television. Carmel has fallen asleep on the sofa, her head crowned with skinny braids lies on a pile of cushions, and her long legs in shorts are drawn up to her stomach. I stand over her, hesitating. What are you dreaming about behind the door of your forehead, my child, what do you do for hours and hours behind the closed door of your room with the sign "Carmel's room" and the picture of Britney Spears, and underneath it, in red letters, "Private property—parents keep out!"—invent pseudonyms for yourself and write e-mail letters to children whose identities are also fictitious, and who knows what hides behind them?

I touch her hot pink cheek, she opens her huge sea eyes to me and mumbles, "You've come home at last."

"Where's Daddy?"

"He went to the parents' meeting. He couldn't get hold of a babysitter, so I said that I would look after Noga," she stretches her back in its short T-shirt and yawns. Most of her molars are missing and her front teeth are in various stages of growth. In the past year her body has been developing like a nature movie in fast motion. She gained height, her limbs lengthened; a dark down, sudden as grass in the desert, sprouted in her groin and armpits; and plum-like breasts, one bigger than the other, budded on her chest. On sleepless nights I imagine I can hear the woman's body breaking out of the child's.

I get her up and take her to bed, and she curls up in her blanket with the elephant pattern. My lips grope for the fine skin of her forehead, and she wraps her long arms around me, "I thought you would never come, where were you?"

"I went to Haifa, I'll tell you tomorrow." She'll be so sorry, maybe she'll even cry, better to put it off till tomorrow morning.

When Carmel was born, you sent her a big felt picture that you had made for her; against a blue background, three green hills with sheep and cows grazing on them, and a house with a red roof, and a few cypress trees, and patches of flowers in red and yellow, and in the yard a dog and a horse and two cats. A big sun, with sunglasses on its eyes, smiling from the top corner, and a flock of silver birds gliding between white clouds. I hung the picture above the white crib, and Carmel lay on her back and looked at it for hours.

Three years ago you visited Israel for the last time, for your father's funeral. Carmel had the flu, and I couldn't make it to the funeral. Two days later I went to see you in your parents' home in Carmelia, where we had once been together when they went on holiday. The house hadn't changed, it seemed to spring to life from my memories; the heavy furniture, the paintings, the jasmine running riot on the veranda wall. Your mother, erect and aristocratic, rose from the armchair to greet me, held out her hand and pierced me with her violet look as if making an effort to remember. I shook her hand quickly and mumbled, you don't know me, once, many years ago, I was Michaela's student.

I found you in your childhood room, sitting barefoot on the old youth bed, a cigarette in your hand and on your knees a notebook filled with crowded rows of Latin letters.

"They're here," you raised a face wet with tears to me, "the bedtime stories he made up for me, he wrote them all down for me to keep."

After the week of mourning you came to visit me in Tel Aviv. Yair wasn't home. It was only me and Carmel, who was then eight. She didn't remember you from your previous visit, when she was four, but nevertheless she chatted to you vivaciously. You asked her what she was reading. Carmel confessed that she wasn't too keen on reading, she preferred watching television, playing with the computer, and drawing. You said you were sure that she would like the books by Erich Kastner, *Lottie and Lisa* and *Annluise and Anton*. Her emerald eyes sparkled, flattered by your attention.

"Were you really my mother's teacher in high school?"

"Yes, and she liked reading a lot," you smiled to yourself.

"And what was she like? Did she look like me?"

"Not really," I intervened, "I had glasses and broken teeth and two pigtails."

"So you were a nerd," my daughter exulted in the discovery, and you wrinkled your brow in a questioning look.

"A nerd is what we used to call a Yoram," I explained to you. "Yes, I was a real nerd."

Carmel hurried to her room and came back with her drawing pad, and you looked at them slowly, relating to every detail. Afterwards she demonstrated a somersault and backflip for you and insisted on playing all the songs she knew on the piano. You sat down next to her and taught her a little tune for four hands. I couldn't remember if it was the tune we had played together so many years ago, in your house in Hatzvi Avenue. You touched her fingers to correct the way she held them, and for a second my heart froze. You played together, laughing at your mistakes and the collisions of your hands, repeating the simple song over and over again, and Carmel looked at you with burning cheeks. I watched you from my place in the armchair. The triangle has remained, I thought, only the places have

179

changed. How easy it is to knead the soft, yielding heart of a child, I suddenly knew, a little girl's plasticine heart.

When Carmel went to bed she parted from you with a kiss on the cheek and asked when you would come to see us again. You held her hands—I knew the precise taste of your touch on her hands, and her touch on yours—and smiled into her eyes, "Come and visit me one day in New York with your mother."

Afterwards you told me that she was wonderful, that I was lucky. The blood flooded your lips and the familiar tremor appeared at their corners.

When Yair came home I said nothing about your visit. Neither did Carmel. She hasn't asked about you since.

But two years ago, in the spring, when I was about to fly to New York, she asked me to give you a drawing in a brown envelope. For the entire flight I refrained from opening it. You pulled it out of the envelope and smiled, and turned it towards me: a piano, a little girl playing it, seen from the back. In the top left corner the words: "To Michaela from Carmel with love."

I look at Noga asleep in her bed, her fair curls on the pillow, her lips tranquilly parted, her plump foot with its pink heel peeking out of the blanket. You never saw her. When we met in New York I was six months pregnant, and after she was born I sent you photographs of her. You sent her clothes from Baby Gap and a pink summer blanket with an appliqued cat, which Noga calls her "blankie." The blanket, which has faded in the meantime, has been dragged behind her throughout the house like a royal train. When she sleeps her little fingers play with it restlessly.

Now I'm going to make myself a cup of tea, sit at the kitchen table, and take out the third notebook, with the brown leather binding.

Dearest Anne,

"In a peaceful little town between mountain and sea, there once lived a young woman and a girl, who loved each other terribly, even though it was forbidden." If I ever find the courage in years to come to write our story, this will be the opening sentence. Perhaps I'll call the story "Love between mountain and sea," what do you think? Michaela is the mountain, my magic mountain ("Berg" means mountain in German, as you know), her warm brown eyes are the earth and the tree trunks, and I am the sea, which is blue-gray like my eyes, and stormy like my soul. The mountain slides into the sea and the sea laps the mountain. The sea loves the mountain and the mountain loves the sea. They succeed in touching each other.

The school year has begun, and I'm writing to you in my new notebook, with its coffee-colored cover, that Michaela brought me from London. Every now and then I raise it to my nose and breathe, and try not to think that it was once a cow peacefully chewing the cud in some English meadow.

Michaela isn't teaching us this year. She had planned to complete her thesis on Leah Goldberg by the end of summer and receive her M.A., which is a condition for teaching the top grades in our school; but she neglected the thesis and failed to complete it, and so she has to go on teaching in the middle school. Strange to think that I've gone up to high school, and she has remained behind, but I think that it's a relief for both of us, because at the end of last year it was getting harder and harder for us to pretend and act the parts of teacher and pupil, when all the time we knew that straight after class we were going to fly on the wings of Rocinanta to the forest. You can imagine the picture: me with my chin and cheek resting on my hand, my eyes half-shut, watching her supple body moving along the blackboard, and Michaela sending me looks after every brilliant remark, to see if I'm scratching my forehead or my nose, and occasionally getting confused and closing her eyes and holding her temples with her thumb and finger, and saying, can anyone remind me where we were, and some Michal or Anat hurries to tie the thread of her thought for her. You must remember how once, after we quarreled, I sat opposite her with a sour face, and Michaela gave the lesson in total absentmindedness and looked as if she were going to burst into tears at any moment. Towards the end of the year, we were so afraid of giving ourselves away that we decided I should stop putting my hand up and taking part in the lesson, and Michaela complained that she wasn't enjoying herself anymore because she had nobody to talk to. This year our literature and expression teacher is someone called Nira, who is also our homeroom teacher. She has tiny brown eyes and thin black hair and skin that looks like dough pricked with a fork, and a sack like a toad's hanging from her neck, and I feel a little sorry for her, because she always looks tired. At eight o'clock in the morning she's already tired. She recites passages from the textbook, and I miss Michaela's warmth and vivacity, her enthusiasm for a well-written sentence, a description, an image, her way of finding connections between details that seem random, and showing how every detail echoes another. She's supposed to give birth at the end of March or the beginning of April, and after her maternity leave it will already be the long vacation, and she won't be coming back to school until next year.

Yesterday after class she picked me up in Rocinanta, as usual, and we drove up the hill almost as far as Kibbutz Beit-Oren, and found ourselves a padded bed between the pines. I laid my head on her stomach and we rested together like two naked nymphs in a forest. Michaela's body hasn't changed yet, her stomach is still flat, only her breasts are fuller and rounder, and the haloes around her nipples are darker, the first hint of what is to come. I told her that in three years time, when I'm eighteen, I'll want us to move in together, with the baby, and we'll have to have the necessary courage—she to tell Yoel and her parents, and me to tell my mother. I told her that I would always love her, and that our love is far greater and stronger than anything people will think and say about us. We could go and live together in Tel Aviv, in a house next to the sea, she could work as a teacher and go on studying at the university, and I would find a way to get out of the army, I would work as a waitress, and start studying literature or cinema. Michaela rumpled my hair and said quietly that she couldn't think that far ahead, in the meantime she couldn't even imagine what it would be like to be a mother. Three years were a long time, especially at my age, and my dreams might change and grow with me. I stood on my knees, naked, only my hair loose on my back—she always undoes my braids when we make love—and took hold of both her hands and asked, but do you want to live with me? Just tell me if you want to.

Michaela smiled a tired, rather sad smile, and said, "Of course I want to, my kitten, I'd like to live with you all the time, to go to sleep with you and dream with you and wake up with you, and perhaps in three years time we'll live in a little house next to the sea, like Charlie Chaplin and his wife in *Modern Times*, I'll go out to work in the morning, and you'll wave a white handkerchief at me."

"You don't believe it," I said, trying not to cry, "you don't believe in us at all."

"I believe in the need to observe the commandments of life," she said quietly, "your love gives me the strength to get up every morning and go to teach gladly, and I would like my love to give you too the strength to study and write and develop."

I really have been writing a lot recently, as in a kind of fever, almost every week I write two or three poems, as if my body can't contain all my love anymore and it brims over like boiling milk, and I told Michaela that she was my private Muse. (I've discovered that the desire for a body and the desire to write stem from the same source.) But I haven't got the strength to study, especially the new and irritating subjects like physics and chemistry. Luckily these lessons are at the end of the day, and I try my best to escape them in order to meet Michaela. I feel the need to be with her as much as possible, because after she gives birth—who knows if we'll be able to go on the way we are now.

We've been together now for almost a year, would you believe it?

Your Kitty

P.S. I almost forgot to tell you—in honor of the pregnancy Michaela has stopped smoking! Completely! It wasn't hard for her to quit, because the taste and smell of the cigarettes make her nauseous. I'm so pleased. Yesterday I told her that her kisses taste much better now, they no longer taste like an ashtray.

The Sukkoth holidays

Dearest Anne,

Michaela's parents have gone to the guest house at Kiryat-Anavim (it turns out that for years they've been booking holidays in Israel and also flights abroad through Grandfather's travel agency . . .). This afternoon I drove with her to their house in the suburb of Carmelia to take their mail out of the mailbox and water the garden and the potted plants. The house looks more or less as I imagined it; dark heavy furniture and thick carpets, and the walls covered with paintings by German and Israeli artists, Marcel Janko and Nahum Gutman and Manya Katz and others, who exhibited at Michaela's father's gallery, and some of them became friendly with him and gave him paintings as presents, with personal dedications on the back.

Her childhood room has hardly changed; on the shelves the big volumes of *Art* and *Civilization* whose pages Michaela would turn and imagine that she was strolling in gorgeous dresses between the statues and the paintings and riding in carriages with velvet curtains. From the top shelf the china dolls her father brought her from his trips to England looked down at us, in all their wealth of costumes and hairdos and bonnets and parasols.

On the bottom shelf I discovered a photograph album from her childhood and I fell on it delightedly. We sat on the veranda open to the garden and breathed in the white scent of the jasmine, which ran riot over the wall. (I reminded Michaela that she had spoken about jasmine in our first lesson in the eighth grade, when she read us Leah Goldberg's poem, and her voice poured into me dark and dense as honey, and I couldn't stop looking at her. Only two years have passed since then, and it seems so long ago. . . .) Michaela opened the sprinkler, which clicked and nodded its head, spitting water onto the lawn, fainting in the heat, and on our feet.

We drank lemonade with fresh mint from the garden, and looked at the jagged-edged black-and-white photos, stuck with little transparent triangles to the black cardboard pages. Here is my beloved at the age of four or five, a slender child in a white dress, with a ribbon in her hair, pushing a doll in a toy baby carriage, her big eyes wide in surprise at the world and its wonders. And here she is in a dress with puffed sleeves and patent leather shoes, in the garden of the Ritz Cafe with her parents, who look young and smiling, her mother glamorous as an old movie star in a pleated bell skirt and high-heeled shoes, and her father in a light three-piece suit and fancy summer shoes with holes punched in them, and the child Michaela smiling without front teeth behind a stainless steel goblet with three scoops of ice cream and a triangular wafer. And here she's already older, nine or ten, in short pants and boots, with a round cloth hat on her head, standing hand in hand with her beloved aunt, a lean tanned German Jewess with short gray hair, hiking in the Jerusalem hills. And here she is at twelve, on the beach with her best friend Osnat—a lanky girl with a mane of curls and light laughing eyes—both of them flat-chested, in bikinis with the bottoms coming up to their navels, and Michaela's freckles are so prominent they look as if they're about to jump right out of the picture. And here she is sitting next to a pale blond boy with matchstick legs, in a decorated carriage drawn by a white horse, and I recognize him and almost shout, "It's Yoel!" And Michaela smiles and says, "Yes, once we went with our parents to a pensione in Nahariya. One night we walked along the beach and I tried to persuade him to swim in the nude, but he was too scared. He was already a Yoram then."

After I'd finished going thoroughly through the album, I took a few folded pages with new poems on them out of my pocket, and also the beginning of a story about a student at an art class who falls in love with the nude model, and I read it aloud to her: "In the room there were a lot of people. Quiet, each absorbed in his canvas. It was very cold outside. They were wearing sweaters but their fingers holding the paintbrushes were frozen and stiff. In one corner there was a small electric heater, and opposite its two blazing red bars lay the model, on her side, the front of her body and her face turned to the painters, and her crooked arm partly hiding her heavy breasts. He allowed her pale nakedness to seep into him through the cigarette smoke. The smell of orange peel reached his nostrils and mingled with the smell of the oil paints raging to escape their swollen tubes and create new revolutions.

"He looked at the blank canvas, ran his fingers over it, dipped his brush in the red paint and began to give shape to the woman's curls, swarming with life."

Michaela laughed at the oil paints raging to escape their swollen tubes (I swear I didn't notice . . .), and then she said quietly, "One day you'll have to start taking your talent seriously."

"Why do you say that," I was offended, and Michaela said that I was too in love with words, with the glories of language, and sometimes the words took charge of me instead of me taking charge of them. My writing would recover from childhood diseases only when I renounced grand words and learned the secret of economy.

"It seems to me that every poem I write is the last one, and I have to put everything into it, like a suicide note," I tried to explain to her, and to myself as well.

"You'll have many more years in which to write many more poems and stories, so why don't you forget about the suicide notes, and try to write a love letter," she smiled at me with narrowed eyes.

"And the story? The first lines wrote themselves, but suddenly I got writer's block, and I couldn't go on."

"Nothing that's any good writes itself," she picked a jasmine flower and crushed it between her fingers, "and writer's block is another word for laziness. The only cure is work. You have to sit and write a few hours every day, you have to regard it as a job, as work, not something you only do when you're in the mood, even if it means sitting like a dummy in front of a blank page—in the end something will emerge. You have to keep at it day after day after day. And in the end you have to organize, rewrite, and polish. Someone once said that talent is only ten percent, and all the rest is perseverance. Your talent is a rare and wonderful gift, but only if you treat it with respect will it open the world in front of you."

"And what about inspiration? You yourself once wrote me something about the muses."

"The muses are demanding and pampered goddesses," she reached for my hand over the table and held it, "when they see that someone is working really hard, they appear in her room, sit on her shoulder, and whisper one or two good lines into her ear."

What do you think, Anne? Can you see my backside stuck to a chair with carpenter's glue for hours on end, day after day? Do you think I'll ever succeed in writing good poems and stories that people will actually buy in bookshops and read and be moved?

Your Kitty

P.S. Today I forgot to phone Racheli as usual before I went home to ask if my mother had been checking up on me. When I got home she asked me where I had been, and I told her I'd gone to visit Racheli. She said she'd called Racheli's house and I wasn't there. On the spot I invented a complicated story about how I'd gone around to Racheli's and she wasn't there, and then I met by chance in the street another girl from our class, who lives next door to her, and she invited me to her place. . . . Mother studied me suspiciously for a moment, but she stopped grilling me, and I escaped to my room with my heart hammering like a prisoner on the wall of his cell. This time I got away with it somehow.

Goodnight, Kitty

11.12.78

Dearest Anne,

Yesterday was my birthday! I told Michaela that I felt more like two hundred than fifteen years old, and she said that sometimes she felt like the two thousand years in the national anthem. (Once I asked her how come the difference in our ages didn't bother her, and she said that the difference between me and her was greater, psychologically, than the difference between her and me, because the girl she once was still existed inside her, like a Russian doll, whereas the woman I would one day be was already inherent in me, but in the meantime only as a possibility.)

Mother gave me a silver ring set with a pearl, which Grandma Rivka had given her when she was my age, with a letter full of sermonizing. She hoped that I would be more sociable with the family, shut myself up in my room less, and help her more in the house. Sometimes it's hard for me to believe that my mother, my own flesh and blood, is so remote from what's happening to me, and knows so little about me.

Michaela gave me *Orlando* and *A Room of One's Own* by Virginia Woolf (*A Room of One's Own* is in English, because there isn't a translation into Hebrew yet, and I'm plowing through it with a dictionary), and a greeting card she made herself. On the back of the card she drew my face in Indian ink, with the braids but without the glasses, my eyes closed tranquilly—and inside she wrote:

"If I were taller I would adorn you with a necklace of stars,
If I could sing I would sing you songs the cherubs sing,
If I knew how I would write you love sonnets,
But all I can think of are the usual banal words:
I love you, my child,
Love that has no end or age."

She had also baked me as a surprise a chocolate cake in the shape of a heart, with candles on it. She reminded me to make a wish, and I closed my eyes and silently wished as hard as I could for me to be a writer and a poet and for us to live together in Tel Aviv.

After polishing off the chocolate cake (with our hands, like proper pigs . . .) we got into bed, and suddenly I discovered on the bedside cupboard a book of poems by Sylvia Plath, in English. I paged through it until I came to the poem "A Birthday Present" and I knew that it was no accident that I had found the book today of all days, and I forced Michaela to read it aloud to me. She stood over me on the bed as if it were a stage, naked and so beautiful with her rounded belly and her snakes of auburn hair, and read the poem aloud in her perfect accent, and translated it for me:

"What is this, behind this veil, is it ugly, is it beautiful?
It is shimmering, has it breasts, has it edges?

I am sure it is unique, I am sure it is what I want."

And so on to the end of the long poem. It was so beautiful I came out in goose pimples and there were tears in my eyes, because suddenly I knew that I would never, never be able to write like that.

Half my life is already behind me, and I feel old . . .

Yours as ever, Kitty

P.S. The Union of High School Teachers is threatening a strike beginning the day after tomorrow, and Michaela and I fantasize about how we will spend all the mornings together. Let's hope it comes true. Hold thumbs for us.

11.29.78

Dearest Anne,

The wonderful teachers' strike has been going on for two weeks already, and the end is not yet in sight. Every evening we watch the news on television and the anchorman announces that tomorrow there won't be any school again. And every morning I climb the geranium-pot stairs. We eat a big breakfast, and apply ourselves to the ritual of the bath: Michaela plugs the bathtub and runs the water and squeezes the tube of "Bat Oren" into it, and while the green liquid turns to pine-scented foam, we get undressed and look in the mirror. We marvel at the changes in her body. At the bottom of her rounding belly, between the navel and the chestnut pubic hair a delicate line has appeared, and I like standing behind her and spreading my hands on her stomach, to feel her growing between them. You know, Anne, pregnancy is such an amazing thing!

After that we sink into the mountains of foam, Michaela leans against the "good" end and I lean carefully against Michaela with my head on her shoulder. For a long time we sit like that, talking, kissing, shampooing each other's hair, letting the lust slowly charge our bodies. When we get too hot, we cool our faces with cold water, or Michaela get out and fetches ice cubes and we pass them from mouth to mouth. And then she pulls my hand to her vagina and whispers, "Feel, as smooth as moss," and we get out of the warm, scented water, already intensely aroused, dry ourselves quickly and run—our skin damp and our hair dripping—to slip between the sheets. There we hide till lunchtime, seeking new paths to pleasure. I'm ashamed to tell even you the crazy things we get up to, I'll only tell you in secret that yester-

190

day we took a magnificent peacock feather to bed with us. (It turns out that when a woman is really aroused, the gentlest touch of a single filament of a peacock's feather is enough to make her explode. . . .)

Every noon, when Michaela drives me home in time to heat up their lunch, we decide that tomorrow we'll do something cultured and educational, we'll read some book together, or go to the museum, and the next day we surrender again to the rituals of the bath and the greed of the body, which seems insatiable.

But today something new happened. Michaela crouched over me in reverse, her tongue fluttering between my nether lips, her abundant white flesh spread like a tent before me and all around me, her engorged purple vagina gaping at my face like a voracious flower, and above it a little brown spider. I breathed in the pungent smell and swallowed my saliva, and then I suddenly saw a little lump of greenish toilet paper stuck between the folds. Nausea rose in my throat, I pushed her away and sat up, and whispered, I can't. Michaela cupped my face between her hands and kissed me on the forehead and the tearful eyes, and said quietly, what do I want of you, you're still such a child.

Your Kitty

December 28, 1978

Dearest Anne,

The teachers' strike came to an end after six magical honeymoon weeks, and I walk up the hill to school every morning with a heavy heart. All the teachers pile on the homework to make up for lost time, and I'm collapsing under the burden. A few days ago I complained bitterly to Michaela about a book report that Mr. Jacobs had given us. She showered me with sympathy, and we agreed that I would write it in Hebrew, and she would translate it into English for me. I decided to write about *The Little Prince*. I read it, in Hebrew of course, and wrote a few pages of bullshit, which Michaela translated into elegant English for me. I told her that we had tamed each other like the Little Prince and the fox, and we argued about whether I was the prince and she was the fox, or the opposite. I argued heatedly that she was the fox, because her hair, and also her pubic hair, were the color of a fox's tail. In the end Michaela said that I was the lazy pampered rose, who had to have her English homework done for her.

Michaela is already in the sixth month. She hasn't gained a lot of weight, but her stomach is quite big, and sometimes it seems to me that it's swelling and swelling and that soon it will fill the whole world. When I lie on top of her I lean on my elbows and take care not to press on her stomach, and nevertheless it seems to me that I'm squashing the fetus. Sometimes I can feel it kicking, and I know that it's kicking me on purpose. I'm afraid that because of me she'll have a squashed baby with brain damage. Michaela reassures me that the amniotic fluid protects it and that I don't need to worry, but I worry anyway.

A few nights ago I dreamed that my mother was pregnant, and that she gave birth to a dead baby. I went to visit her in the hospital and saw her behind the glass of the newborn babies room. I call her, shouting really loudly, Mother, Mother, but she doesn't hear me or see me, and suddenly I realize that the dead baby is me.

I have to stop now, I have a mountain of homework in math, history, chemistry, and French.

You forgive me, don't you?

Au revoir! Your Kitty

Hanukkah holidays, 1.1.79

Dearest Kitty,

This morning I went to Michaela's house, and I found her in the kitchen wrapped in a long apron, stirring strawberry jam in a big saucepan. Her and Yoel's parents are coming to light

Hanukkah candles with them tonight, and she wants to make doughnuts with a jam center for them. The sweet smell of strawberries cooking in burned sugar pervaded the whole house. Michaela turned off the gas and went to fill the bath. When we were already in bed she went to kitchen and came back with a saucer full of that bright redness. I tasted it on my finger and my mouth opened wide to the warm, dense jam with the fleshy, grainy fruit. Michaela tilted the saucer over me and drew a transparent pink path from my chest down my belly and between my legs, and then she knelt on top of me with a voracious smile and licked from top to bottom, gathering berry after berry with her lips, and when she reached the place between my legs she went on licking the jam and stirring it around with her tongue, and the pleasure was so great that I couldn't stand it anymore and my hands seized hold of her hair.

Afterwards I took the jam and painted it around her dark nipples and up and down her belly and when I reached down there I took a deep breath and dived, and this time there was no toilet paper and I felt no nausea, and the sweetness mingled with the saltiness, like licking sea water from a shell, and Michaela writhed between my hands and screamed so loudly that for a moment I was afraid that she would die.

Sticky and sweaty we ran together to the shower, and after we had soaped ourselves and washed the soap off, I went down on my knees under her belly in order to taste her without the jam, and the taste was sourish and a little salty, different from my own taste, which is more delicate (like the difference between cottage cheese and Brie . . .).

When we returned to the bedroom we saw that the white sheets were stained with red (I remembered the poem I once wrote, a red rose in an ice city . . .), and we quickly pulled them off the bed, and Michaela switched on the washing machine.

Afterwards I helped her make the doughnuts, and I thought about Yoel and the two pairs of respectable German parents who would eat them in the evening, and praise Michaela for the delicious strawberry jam, without any idea of the sweet, scandalous pleasures it had served that morning.

Michaela drove me home, and before I got out she took both my hands and squeezed them hard and said how glad she was that I was opening up and ready to learn new things, and I said that I enjoyed learning from her, because she was a good teacher of love.

Now I'm going to light Hanukkah candles with Mother and Oren and Noam, and with Grandfather who's been invited to supper. Mother is frying potato pancakes and the smell is creeping in under my closed door and reminding me that I'm dying of hunger.

So a happy Hanukkah to you too, from me, Kitty

1.20.79

Dearest Anne,

A cold, sad, rainy Saturday, and I'm alone at home, writing to you at the big table in the dining nook. The wind is whistling like a thousand chimneys and the rain is pouring down in buckets. Neon veins are splitting the sky lowering over a sea whose face is as gray as a dead man's, and the thunder rumbles like a giant stomach that ate too many beans. Someone passes in the street below, battling with his umbrella, tilting it against the wind and twirling in a kind of bizarre ballet, but the umbrella turns inside out in his hands like a huge tropical flower and carries him away, in a minute he'll take off and fly, and then the umbrella breaks and the man supports the sagging cloth with his other hand, and runs lopsidely under it, bowed and defeated.

The weather forecast yesterday didn't predict the storm, all they said was cloudy with scattered showers, and at supper Mother suddenly announced that she had a surprise for us, and tomorrow morning we were all going on a family hike under the auspices of the Nature Protection Society, for which we had to wake up at five a.m. Oren and Noam were thrilled and asked where to, and Mother said the stalactites cave. I said that I couldn't come, because I'd arranged to spend the day with Racheli. (Yoel was supposed to be on call and I'd made a date with Michaela to go to the artists' village at Ein Hod, where we would visit the artist Marcel Janko, who was a friend of her father's, look into the galleries, and eat lunch at a restaurant, or pick mushrooms and cook ourselves a feast at her house.)

Mother said I spent more time at Racheli's than at home, and it wouldn't hurt me to go on a hike with my family for once. She had already paid in advance for the trip, which was quite expensive, and they wouldn't refund the money. "But why do you let me know at the last minute," I said crossly, "I've already made plans and that's it, I'm not coming with you."

"You are coming with us," she raised her voice, "whether you like it or not."

Against my will I began to cry. I said that I didn't give a damn for the stalactite cave, and why did I have to go if I didn't want to, and Mother retorted with her usual argument clincher, because-I-say-so. (Sometimes she adds, "When you turn eighteen you can do as you please," and I restrain myself from saying that I've been doing as I please for a long time already. . . .)

I shut myself in my room and thought that I wasn't to blame if she suddenly felt like being a family, a model mother taking her children on a Nature Protection Society hike. She never took us abroad, only her Moishele, and she also spent nearly every evening with him, and if he wasn't married she would probably prefer spending Saturdays with him too, at the stalactite cave or anywhere else—so I had a right to a life of my own as well. I put on my shoes and coat and very quietly, without anyone noticing, I slipped out of the house and went to Racheli's. It was quite late by the time I got there, and she was rather surprised when she opened the door. Her parents were already asleep. I told her about my quarrel with my mother, and said that I'd run away from home, and asked if I could sleep over at her house.

We chatted until Racheli fell asleep, but I couldn't sleep. I waited in suspense for my mother to discover that I'd disappeared, and for the phone to ring. In the end sleep must have gained the upper hand.

At five in the morning the phone rang and woke the whole house, and Racheli's mother answered it. I heard her say, "I don't think she's here, I'll go and look."

Racheli and I pretended to be asleep, and I heard the door open and close, and Racheli's mother saying in her funny Dutch accent, "Yes, the girls are sleeping like two little bears and I haven't got the heart to wake them."

She put the phone down, and I understood that Mother had given up on me, and they had gone without me.

At nine o'clock, after breakfast, I phoned Michaela, who answered in a sleepy voice. She told me in a whisper that Yoel's shift at the hospital had been canceled, and that when he woke up they were going to Tel Aviv, to visit her friend Osnat, who had invited them to eat *cholent,* and we would go to Ein Hod another time.

I told her quickly about my quarrel with my mother, and the efforts I had made to meet her, "so why can't you make a bit of an effort for me," I asked, and my voice shook.

"I make an effort all the time, kiddo," she said in a whisper, "you know how much I want to be with you, but sometimes things don't work out exactly as we wish."

"All right, goodbye," I said, on the point of bursting into tears, and Michaela whispered, "See you later, my kiddo, have a wonderful day."

Racheli went on some family visit with her parents, she invited me to come with them, but I preferred to go home (lucky I took a key). As soon as I got there it began to pour, and I thought of Mother and Oren and Noam, and if the rain was ruining their trip too, or if they were sheltering in the cave and admiring the stalactites and stalagmites in the meantime. I thought about Michaela and Yoel as well, gobbling *cholent* with that Osnat and her boyfriend in Tel Aviv. Outside the storm was howling, and they were safe inside, drinking wine and laughing, all warm and cozy.

At first I switched on the radio and listened to humorous skits, but none of the comics succeeded in amusing me, and I switched it off and sat down to write to you.

The only one left to relieve my loneliness is you. How happy I am to have you.

I've written Michaela a letter, and I'm going to slip it to her tomorrow at school. I'm copying it here:

"My Mish,
I'm not cross with you for going off and giving our Saturday to somebody else. I even told Racheli that it would be a good thing if we learned to have relationships that aren't based on obligations, like Simone de Beauvoir once said. For you pleasing "society" is obviously more important than pleasing me, and it's certainly much easier to go to Tel Aviv with Yoel, to laugh and enjoy yourself with your friends, than to tell him that you're in love and that you're with me. That's why you never let me upset the ordinary, routine life that we're "supposed" to live in any way—you continued with your married life, your job, your studies, you traveled abroad with Yoel, you got pregnant, you did everything you wanted to do and would certainly have done even if we hadn't been together. I only added the "pepper" to your life (and in quantities. It's a miracle that you don't sneeze all the time . . .).

I definitely "sacrificed" far more; all the perfection and innocence (however banal it sounds) of first love. And here I come to my wish to be free of commitment; I have to look for someone with whom I can feel complete devotion, happiness free of fear, and other things some of which you can't, and some of which you don't want to give me.

I don't regret what we had and will still have together. I loved you with the greatest passion, but now that you're going to give birth soon—in another two months there'll be a helpless little creature lying in your arms, who'll need you even more than I do—and I'm sobering up from my passionate feelings, and discovering all the empty spaces that I've despaired of filling with what you are able to give me, I feel a great need to fill them with something else, with someone else, and I'll do it soon, I'm sure.

In the meantime, as long as we're together, let's commit ourselves in spite of everything to the maximum intimacy and tenderness between us. Let's tell each other everything, and not hide any thought or pain or dream from each other, let's talk deeply and let our bodies touch deeply when they meet. It's hard for me to think of the end of the fire flower that burned so intensely between us.

> Loving you with a lot of rain in my eyes
> and my heart, Rivi"

That's it. I feel a little better. Now I'm going to make myself a cup of hot tea with rum and try to knock myself out. I'm so very tired.

> Your Kitty

> Tuesday, February 20, 1979

Dearest Anne,

Today Michaela is twenty-eight years old! I couldn't decide what to buy her, I spent hours in book shops, but I didn't find anything special or significant. I consulted Racheli, and she said there was a good secondhand book shop next to her art class.

Yesterday we went down there together and pored over the shelves, and suddenly I discovered a slender volume in a lilac cover, *The Songs of Bilitis* by Pierre Louys, a French poet who had invented a Greek woman poet, a friend and student of Sappho, constructed a biography for her, and written erotic lesbian poems in her name. When the book came out in France at the end of the last century, people were convinced that they had really been written by a contemporary of Sappho whose work had suddenly been discovered. The poems are beautiful, very erotic, and it's really hard to believe that they were written by a man. Reading two or three of the poems was enough to convince me that this was the right book. At home I read them all, and suddenly I had an idea. I went through the poems I've written recently, and found that some of them echo Bilitis's poems. I copied them out and laid each of my poems on the page with the appropriate poem in the book: my "Treetops" opposite her "The Tree"; my "Wine" opposite her "The Goblet"; my "Sabbath Eve" opposite her "The Priestesses of Astarte"; my "Only the Eyes" opposite her "Eyes"; and my "Like Flowers" opposite her "The Flower Dance." Opposite her "Maternal Counsel" I put the following poem, which doesn't have a name and which I'm copying for you because it's short:

I grew like a wild flower
from between my mother's thighs
into her hands that held me
helplessly.
The eyes did not know.
They were closed.
They wept.

Today after school we drove to the beach at Atlit. Rocinanta stopped on the sand dune opposite the sea, and I gave Michaela the book. She carefully removed the wrapping, opened it, and read the inscription: "To my Mishi, mother and sister, teacher and friend and lover," and she leafed through it and said the poems were beautiful, and then she suddenly discovered mine too, hidden between the pages, which made her even happier. A strong wind battered the car and the sea raged, and we cuddled up together on the back seat, Michaela in her cape and me in my blue parka. I undid the buttons of the cape and pushed my freezing hands into her armpits, over her sweater, and we were warm and cozy. And then I suddenly said, let's get out, and I opened the door and sprang into the wind and began to run to the sea, and Michaela ran after me with her open cape flapping behind her and with her big belly, and we stood facing the waves, which were as high as houses, like in my dreams when the sea rises and floods everything, and in the roar of the wind and the crashing waves I shouted at the top of my lungs, I love you, I'm in love with Michaela and with life, and Michaela hugged me tight, and thus we stood there, kissing in the rain that began to fall, holding onto each other so that the wind wouldn't send us and her belly flying, our coats got wet and so did our shoes and trousers and hair and faces, and I couldn't see anything through my glasses, and then Michaela came to her senses and took my hand and said, come on, let's go back, there's no point in catching cold, and we returned to Rocinanta and drove up the Carmel to a little cafe in Hanasi Avenue. We sat in front of the heater to dry out, drank hot chocolate, and shared a slice of warm apple pie with whipped cream, and all the time we looked into each other's eyes like on our first meeting, when we sat together next to the heater in her house, before we turned into two pearls in their woven robes on the ocean floor.

Michaela read a few of Bilitis's poems and was full of admiration, and about mine too she said that they weren't bad at all. I asked her if I'd been weaned of the big words, and if I had begun to take my talent seriously, and she said I was on the right road.

Now too the rain is tapping lightly on my window like a

troupe of dancers on their toes, and I'm going to turn out the light and imagine that Michaela is embracing me from behind in the teaspoon position, and try to sleep.

Goodnight, Kitty

3.27.79

Dearest Anne,

My fears have been realized: Nira my homeroom teacher called my mother in for a talk about the deterioration in my school-work and my frequent absences from the last class of the day. Mother arrived at the school at ten, after the long break. She grumbled that she hoped it wasn't going to take long, because she had a meeting at the office, and said that she simply couldn't understand how things had come to such a pass, she always thought that at least as far as schoolwork was concerned I was responsible and trustworthy. I didn't say anything, but in my heart I felt a spiteful little satisfaction at her expense, because all these years when I bought home a report full of very-goods she would pounce on one poor little fairly-good, and now she had no idea of what was about to come down on her head.

We went into the staff room together, and found Nira waiting for us there. Mother seemed to make an impression on her with her meticulous hairdo and her burgundy tweed suit and her high heels, because she tried to smile at us and to be nice. She said that in her subjects, literature, written expression, grammar, and Bible study I was actually up to the mark, but the math and physics teacher, and the chemistry teacher complained that they hardly saw me, and even when I did them the favor of sitting in their class I daydreamed or read a book under my desk, and in the last physics test I had handed in a blank page. My term grades in these subjects fluctuated between poor and very poor, which meant three failures on my report; and in English, French, biology, sociology, Talmud, geography, history, and civics the situation was far from brilliant, in comparison to the good grades I had obtained in middle school. She asked tactfully if I had any social problems, and if everything was all right at home. Mother kept quiet, and I shrugged my shoulders and said that everything was fine, and I wanted to add, except that my father had left home and acquired a new family and hadn't spoken to me for over three years, and my mother went out every evening with some married Moishele, whose real name I didn't know, and when she was at home she yelled at my little brothers, who fought all the time, and I had to bring myself up alone and also look after them, and for a year and a half I'd been having a passionate love affair with my literature teacher from middle school, who was about to have a baby any day now—the baby wasn't mine, but I was still tense, so I don't have too much time or patience for learning equations in physics, you understand, Nira, imagine what you would do in my place. Instead of this I smiled my sweetest smile at her, and said that I loved her lessons in the humanities, and intended majoring in literature next year, and I really didn't understand what use physics and chemistry would be to me in my life, which was why I didn't invest any effort in them, but that I promised to try to do better. Mother looked at me sourly and said, "I certainly hope so," apparently she felt that she hadn't contributed enough to the conversation, and Nira stood up to see us to the door, and before we left she put her hand on my shoulder and said, "You should try to realize your potential, because there's no lack of brains."

I accompanied Mother to the gate. She didn't say a word, and I too was silent. Before she left she gave me a peck on the cheek and said, "We'll talk about it at home," and I knew that we wouldn't talk, because there was nothing more to say, and because this evening she would go out and she wouldn't have time.

I console myself with the thought that the Passover holidays will soon be here, and after that two months to go till the long vacation, and next year, in the literature stream, I won't have to study those depressing and superfluous subjects anymore.

Goodnight my dear, yours, Kitty

P.S. Very important: yesterday a peace agreement was signed with Egypt in Washington! We went down to watch the ceremony with Grandfather, because it was screened in color and he has a new color T.V. I was thrilled to see Begin, Carter, and Sadat shaking hands in Technicolor. The White House is really white, but its lawns aren't gray, they're green! On Saturday they're going to show the Eurovision song contest in color from Jerusalem. "Hallelujah" by the "Milk and Honey" band has a chance of winning, because of the peace agreement.

Monday, 4.2.79

Dearest Anne,

Early this morning Michaela gave birth to a son! This afternoon I visited her in hospital, and I'm beside myself with excitement, but I'll tell you about it from the beginning, in the sequence of events. At break I waited for her in our usual place, behind the middle school home economics room, but she didn't show up. I asked a kid from the ninth grade, and he told me that their literature lesson had been canceled. For the next two hours I had a stomachache from excitement, because I had already guessed. At the twelve o'clock break I couldn't restrain myself, I ran to my "little house in the post office" and called her at home. Yoel answered and announced in a happy voice "This morning we had a son." For a moment I wondered who "we" were and why he was pushing himself into the picture, but I recovered immediately and asked anxiously how she was and how the birth had gone and how the baby was. He said it was an easy birth, and she was fine, and the baby was chubby and cute. I asked when he was going to see them (so as not to go when he was there . . .). He said that the labor had lasted all night (they let him be present because he's a doctor there) and now he was going to sleep. I congratulated him, put the phone down, and began to do an Indian war dance in the phone booth. Anyone walking past must have thought I had gone completely mad. I decided to play hooky for the last two classes (chemistry and physics) and go to visit her.

The passage in the maternity ward in Rambam Hospital, where I too had been born fifteen and a half years ago, was flooded with spring sunshine, and coming towards me on the carpet of light was my beloved, slightly stooped, in a white nightgown with little flowers on it, transparent as a dragonfly's wings around the contours of her body. She tried to smile at me, and I clasped her limp body in a tight embrace, and she embraced me too in a sudden access of strength, and our tears mingled.

When we calmed down I asked her if I could see the baby. More than I was curious to see him, I needed proof that she had really had one (her belly was quite big, as if she were still a bit pregnant), and mainly I wanted to check and see if he looked normal and didn't come out squashed because of me.

We went to the neonates room, Michaela went in and I waited in the passage, behind the glass partition. There were dozens of tiny babies lying there, all alike, in rectangular stainless steel boxes. Michaela thrust her arms into one of them and fished out a kind of giant white cocoon, with a red, very slightly squashed face. She brought him close to the glass, so I could see, and he opened eyes that were blue and shiny as beetles, and looked at me. For a long moment we examined each other, the baby and I. What would we be to each other? Brother and sister? Friends? Enemies? Michaela smiled at me almost imploringly over his little head, and I shaped the word "adorable" with my lips.

When she emerged into the passage her hands were empty, and I said, "I wonder who he looks like, neither of you have blue eyes." Michaela leaned on me, put her arm around my shoulders, and smiled a tired smile, "You know what, kiddo, he must look like you."

I accompanied her to her bed and helped her to lie down

and then I pulled the curtain so that we wouldn't be disturbed. She told me about the delivery, about the moment she put her hands between her thighs and felt the sticky head with the tips of her fingers. I asked her if it hurt and if they gave her stitches afterwards. She said yes, and that I shouldn't look. I felt a little sorry for that miraculous organ of hers, which gives her so much pleasure, and knows how to give birth too, and now it's sore and aching. I asked her if she already loved the baby, and she said "How can I, I don't know him yet, I still have to get used to the idea that he's a boy and not a girl." And then, as if she guessed my thoughts, she took my hand and squeezed it and whispered, "But I know you very well indeed, and I'll always love you." I hugged her and kissed her, I didn't care that her mouth smelled bad, and we cried a bit again, and suddenly it occurred to me that I didn't know what she was going to call him. I asked her, and she said that she was hesitating between Emanuel from *Letters from an Imaginary Journey* by Leah Goldberg, and Ido from *Ido and Einam* by Agnon. Yoel preferred Emanuel, but he didn't really care. I said that my grandfather's name was Emanuel, and Ido was shorter and more modern, and we decided that would be his name. (Each man has a name given to him by his father and mother and given to him by his mother's lover. . . .)

When I was waiting for the lift the door opened and Michaela's parents came out (I recognized them by the photographs). Her father in a three-piece suit, with a long reddish nose and bushy eyebrows that gave his face a clownish look, holding a huge bunch of flowers in his hand, and her mother very like her, erect and elegant in a matching skirt and jacket, with violet eyes and a helmet of completely white hair that looked as if it had been rinsed in starch.

I wanted to congratulate them and say they must be very happy to have a grandson at last, but I didn't say anything. They looked more anxious than anything else, consulting each other in German about the number of the room.

It was only in the bus that I remembered Oren and Noam's lunch. I glanced at my watch and saw that it was already after three, and my mother would be home at any minute. I ran home from the bus stop as fast as I could, with my heart racing, will I make it, won't I make it, and our street stretched out indifferently before me, white-hot in the afternoon sun, silently presenting me with the house that wasn't my home. I managed to get there a few minutes before my mother and to heat up the meal. When she walked in she found us sitting at the table, and she didn't say anything. After she had gone to rest, I phoned Racheli and told her. I said, "I know that nothing will be the same as it was before," and Racheli was silent for a moment and then she said, "It will be what it has to be."

Good night—I'm sure I won't sleep a wink, Kitty

4.10.79

Dearest Anne,

This evening something really frightening happened, and maybe everything is over.

Four days ago Michaela went home with the baby. Yesterday they had him circumcised, and this evening she left him with Yoel (she said she was going out to get a few things from the pharmacy), and she picked me up on the corner of Ocean Road. Rocinanta swept down the hill—an April khamsin blew into our faces through the open windows—and led us where she would, as usual, until she stopped on the sand dunes of the beach at Atlit.

We moved onto the back seat, wild to touch, to kiss, to renew the contact that had been cut off. Michaela undid her flimsy silk blouse and her bra, and I clamped my lips to her breast. I'll always remember the touch of the swollen nipple and the surprising taste that streamed into my mouth, sweet and airy. I'll always remember the scream wrung from her throat. I too came without warning, quickly and strongly. For a minute or two we went on lying there joined together, my cheek on her burning, congested breasts, her hands in my hair, when suddenly a dazzling blue light scratched our eyes. While she was still buttoning her blouse with panic-stricken fingers, the door opened and a male voice commanded, "Get out, police."

We got out, blinking opposite the flashlight in his hand, the circle of light moving from her face to mine.

"What are you doing here?" demanded the fat, middle-aged policeman, his eyes darting between the visor of his cap and his gray mustache.

"Nothing special." Michaela made an effort to sound relaxed. "Talking."

Another policeman, younger, slim with curly hair, emerged from the patrol car. The two of them looked at each other, and the younger one put his hand on my shoulder and led me a few steps away. I was afraid his hand would feel my heart that was beating as wildly as an air-raid siren.

"Aren't you afraid?" he whispered in a confidential tone.

"Why should I be afraid?" I asked innocently. "Is it dangerous here?"

"That woman, what is she to you, a relation?"

"No, we're friends."

"But she's a lot older than you, isn't she?"

"So what."

"How old are you?"

"Eighteen." Don't move a muscle. Don't bat an eye.

"You don't look eighteen to me," he examined me suspiciously. "Can I see your identity card?"

"I haven't got it with me."

"Then give me your phone number," he demanded, losing what was left of his patience.

"I haven't got a telephone."

"You haven't got a telephone either?" His voice rose angrily. "Where do you live? With your parents?"

"No, in a rented flat, with my boyfriend."

"Good," he grunted, at a loss. He was out of questions. We both listened to Michaela's interrogation, which was being conducted on the other side of the patrol car. The older policeman examined her ID card in his flashlight.

"I see you're married."

"That's right," Michaela smiled at him pleasantly, as if he were some boring old aunt who had cornered her at a family affair.

"What does your husband do?"

"He's a doctor at the Rambam hospital, an anesthetist," she explained patiently, "but now he's at home, looking after our baby."

"You've got a baby?" the policeman asked in a scandalized voice, and I asked myself in fear and trembling what they had seen. They must have seen me stealing the milk from the baby's mouth, and now they were going to take me to jail, or to an institute for juvenile delinquents.

"Yes, Ido. He's nine days old. I really must get back to feed him."

"I'll be getting in touch with your husband. What's his name?" the policeman barked sullenly, and Michaela, maintaining her ladylike airs, replied politely, "His name is Yoel, Dr. Yoel Rosen, please do call him, he'll be happy to talk to you, he's a great admirer of the police force."

After a brief consultation, the two policemen parted from us with looks of revulsion and allowed us to return to Rocinanta and drive away. For a few minutes we drove in silence on the sandy road, letting the sea breeze give us back our breath.

"I've never been so scared in my life," I said quietly.

"Neither have I," my love admitted, "my knees are still shaking."

"You think he'll call?"

"I hope not," she laughed suddenly, "Yoel has enough on his plate. All he needs now is for his wife to go to jail."

There's nothing we can do now except wait for the policeman to call, and pray for terrible crimes to take place in Haifa over the next few days and make him forget all about us.

Yours, Kitty

P.S. Five days have passed and the policeman hasn't called. It looks as if we've been saved this time.

The Passover holidays, I don't remember the date

Dearest Anne,

Racheli has a boyfriend! His name is Daniel, and she met him a week ago on the beach. He was sitting cross-legged facing the sea and playing his flute, and she felt the sounds drawing her closer and closer to him, like the Pied Piper of Hamelin, until she reached him and sat down next to him. When he stopped playing she said to him, "You play wonderfully," and he smiled at her and said, "And you're very pretty." He's twenty-two, tall, he has green eyes and long brown hair. He plays with a jazz band in all kinds of bars and sometimes, when he needs money, he plays outside the entrance to the auditorium before concerts. He lives in a shack in the backyard of some Arab house in the Sprinzak quarter, near the sea. Racheli agreed to go around to his place, because he seemed like a gentle soul to her, and also because she's attracted to him in a big way. Soon enough they began to kiss, but Racheli didn't want to go all the way because she isn't on the pill yet. Tomorrow she's going to go to the gynecologist at the HMO clinic and ask for a prescription, and then she'll be able to do it properly.

She told me that he has a gazebo covered with vines in the yard, and next to window, over the mattress he sleeps on, there's a fig tree offering its fruit straight to his mouth (but the figs aren't ripe yet). I told her it sounded very romantic and a lot of fun. Next Friday he's performing with his band at "Basement 10" in Rothschild House, and she invited me to come along and hear them and meet him. I'm happy for her, and wish I had someone like him too (maybe someone from his band?). Ever since Ido was born, Michaela is busy most of the time. She's on maternity leave until the long vacation, and I go around there almost every day (especially instead of the last lessons, chemistry, physics, and gym), and when we're in bed he suddenly begins to cry, and she has to get up and feed him and change him, and even then he doesn't calm down, and she walks around with him in her arms and sings him lullabies in her sound-box voice, hoping he'll fall asleep, but he only stares at me with his glittering blue beetles that refuse to close, as if he has to see everything, and I feel guilty for stealing his mother from him, and when he finally goes to sleep, and Michaela returns to me, my desire has escaped me, and then she's offended and sure that I'm punishing her and doing it to spite her, and she immediately begins to cry. Because of the hormones she's hypersensitive and any little thing makes her cry, and I have to hug her and reassure her. She doesn't understand that it's hard for me to share her with this strange baby, who I can't make myself love, even though he came from the woman I love most in the world. The fear of being caught, and my lies to my mother, are weighing more and more heavily on me. For a year and a half we've been enclosed in our bubble, trembling for fear of every teacher and pupil and pupil's parent who might see us and tell on us, and only Racheli—my Dutch Miep—connects me to the world. I deserve to love without being afraid and without hiding, someone who will be only mine, and I have to try to see what it's like with a man, to prove to myself that I can. A few weeks ago I had my eye on someone I sometimes see in the Center. We've never spoken, and I don't even know his name (to myself I call him "the man"), but he has the bluest most radiant eyes I've ever seen, and a brown beard, and a forest of curls. He looks to me about Michaela's age, maybe a year or two younger. Whenever I go past the Center I look for him, and he always looks at me with those eyes of his, which are like clear water reminding me of how thirsty I am, and I badly want to drink from them. The last time he came towards me I almost got up the courage to talk to him, but we only exchanged looks, and I went on walking. A few nights ago I even dreamed about him. In the dream he crammed figs into my mouth and fixed those eyes of his on me. The figs were very ripe and sweet, and he pushed more and more of them into my mouth, until I wanted to vomit, but I couldn't tell him to stop because my mouth was too full of the flesh and sticky juice of the figs.

Goodnight my confidante, yours, Kitty

P.S. Michaela has started to smoke again. At first she only cadged one here and there, but she soon began buying packets of Kent and she polishes off a pack a day, just like before she was pregnant. I tried to persuade her to stop harming herself and Ido, but she said it was too hard for her now, she was too tense, and told me to leave her alone.

4.25.79

Dearest Anne,

On Friday night I went with Racheli to "Basement 10" and met her Daniel. He really is smashing, a real freak, with pure eyes and delicate hands, and long fingers that play amazingly. It was the first time I heard live jazz, and I discovered how much I like this music, which sounds a little like human speech, as if it's telling you a story full of feeling and humor, and from time to time it winds off onto a side path that doesn't lead anywhere, but where it's nice to walk.

While he was playing his eyes smiled at Racheli, and after the gig he came over to our table and they kissed. I saw how much in love they are and how happy she is with him, and I was a little jealous. He introduced us to his friends, but I didn't fancy any of them. All of them looked a little bedraggled, as if they wash at really long intervals.

When we left, we saw the man with the blue eyes sitting in a cafe by himself and drinking beer. He called Daniel, and it turned out that they know each other. We sat down with him. His name is Dudu, and he lives in some commune in Rosh-Pina, and sometimes comes to Haifa to visit his brother. I drank quite a lot, and somehow found myself sitting on his lap. He stroked my hair, and his fingers felt gentle and pleasant. I told him that I'd seen him in the Center a number of times, and that I liked the look of him, and asked him if I could come and sleep with him. Dudu laughed and asked how old I was.

"In November I'll be sixteen," I said, "but I'm mature for my age."

He laughed again, took a telephone token out of his jeans pocket, and said, "Call me in December, I don't really feel like going to jail."

I thought of Michaela, who was ready to endanger herself and risk everything she had for the sake of our love, and I knew that he was a coward, and that in spite of his blue eyes and gentle fingers I would never call him.

Yesterday was Holocaust Day, and Racheli decided to forgo the ceremony, which in any case repeats itself every year—with Itzik the janitor, who lights the memorial torch, and Hourgi's speech about the heroism of the Warsaw Ghetto fighters—and go to Daniel's place to do it (she bought the Microgynon pills and has started taking them). She asked me if I thought it was right to lose her virginity on Holocaust Day, and as the daughter of survivors too. I told her that on the contrary, it was the incontrovertible proof of the rebirth of the Jewish people in its land. All evening I waited for her to come home and call to tell me, but she didn't call. Today she told me that she came home late, and she was so happy that she wanted to keep it to herself a little longer. She said that it was wonderful, that he was gentle and sweet and that it hardly hurt her. The first time she bled a bit and she went to shower, and after that she didn't bleed and it didn't hurt at all, and it was pure pleasure. I felt like asking her, "So, was it like reading a good book?" but I just kissed her and said, "Devil, I'm proud of you" and Racheli said, "Your turn next, Devil."

My turn next, yours, Kitty

P.S. There's only one shadow on Racheli's happiness; Daniel told her that at the end of summer he intends to take off for Europe. He hasn't got any money, but he's going to sail on a ship's deck to Greece, and from there he'll hitchhike. He intends to play in the street and earn enough to continue from town to town, for an unlimited period of time, free as a bird. She consoles herself with the thought that precisely because theirs is a love without a future and with a time limit, they can enjoy it to the fullest for as long as it lasts.

7.6.79

Dearest Anne,

I couldn't believe that it would ever come, and here it is, spread out at my feet like an endless desert of sea and sun, the long vacation! We studied to the end of June, like in elementary school, because of the long teachers' strike in winter.

For the past few weeks I've neglected you a little, because Racheli and I were cramming for exams in all the boring difficult subjects, which as literature majors we won't have to study anymore next year. Without undue ceremony I threw away my chemistry, biology, physics, and sociology notebooks. After that I decided that my room was full of things I don't need, and I spent the first days of the vacation sorting and throwing out old clothes that don't fit me anymore, drafts of poems, my collection of paper napkins and gold sweet papers from the age of eight, Arik's letters from Natanya, who I corresponded with in the seventh grade, and all kinds of other superfluous knick-knacks and junk. Children's books I passed on to Noam and Oren.

With the help of Racheli, who I recruited for the job, I also

213

threw out the scratched old desk I always hated, and the Jewish Agency bed that broke my back. I left only the two wide striped mattresses and Michaela gave me a bright orange velvet cover with fringes that she found in the flea market for them, and two big cushions with Arab embroidery that she sewed especially for me. All week long we scraped and stripped, Racheli and I, the revolting wallpaper with the flowers, plastered the holes in the walls, sandpapered them, and painted the room with three coats of white paint. We painted the wooden box of the roll-up blind in psychedelic pink, and Racheli decorated it with red spirals, and the peace sign.

Yesterday morning I drove with Michaela to the Druze village of Dalyat-el-Carmel, and bought a soft, hairy white rug, and a wicker book case, where I put my record-player, records, and poetry books. I also bought a big jar, which in the meantime is empty, but where I can put pretty thorns or peacock feathers. (I forgot to tell you, a few weeks ago I decided to clean Grandpa's apartment once a week and the office once a week, for twenty lira an hour, and so I saved a bit of money.)

Now I'm writing to you sitting on my "pad," the mattress on the floor. I learned the word from the book *Fucking Isn't Everything* by Dahn Ben Amotz, which I read recently. I spent a whole weekend in bed with it, and every now and then I heard myself laugh out loud. He talks about the subjects that preoccupy me, ageless relationships and same sex relationships. He too had a few homosexual experiences, which he writes about with courage and in detail. He has developed a philosophy of life that holds that everyone has many layers to his personality, some of them contradictory, and that you can do anything, experiment with everything, including drugs and orgies, on condition that you don't cause harm to others. Everybody is his own supreme judge, and other people have no right to judge him. He himself tries to "confront every moment in utter innocence." Nice, no? Reminds me a bit of Buber. He also explains why the Palestinians that were expelled from here in the War of

Independence, and are living in refugee camps in the territories, are entitled to a state alongside the State of Israel. He succeeded in persuading me, I never thought like my mother that all the Arabs hate us and all they want is to throw us into the sea. It's nice to discover at last a grown-up whose head isn't locked up, but is like a room whose door and windows are open, with a wind blowing through it all the time.

My room has grown around me and begun to breathe, and it gives me a good feeling. I like it that the walls are clean and white: the only pictures I hung up are my childhood portrait and a big reproduction of a Picasso painting, women on the beach, that Racheli bought me in honor of my new room.

Mother, of course, isn't pleased with what she calls my "abnormal ideas"; mainly she objects to me sleeping "on the floor." She says its not good for my back. I told her that the Jewish Agency bed was a lot worse. Then she said that she doesn't understand how I can do my homework without a desk. I explained that I could do it without any problems, on the carpet or the mattress, with a big book to write on. In any case that's how I've been doing my homework for the past year. And she snapped, "Yes, we saw how brilliantly you did at school this year." I wanted to tell her that Virginia Woolf wrote sitting in her old padded armchair, with a wooden board on her knees, and you too wrote on a tiny table, in the single hour that Dr. Dussel agreed to vacate it for you; and that the working conditions don't determine the quality of the work; but I knew there was no point in arguing with her, because she would barely listen to me and only grumble, "You think you know best about everything, you think you're the cleverest person in the world."

I wanted Michaela to see how I had fixed the room, and one morning, when Oren and Noam were at day camp, I invited her to come up for a few minutes. (She had left Ido with her parents and come to take me to the beach.) She came in and immediately said, "Wow, it's so full of light." Then she looked around and admired every change and noticed every detail. She advised me to hang a light curtain of cotton or tulle on the window, and even offered to sew it for me on her Singer machine, but I told her that I liked seeing the pine, which had accompanied me since I remembered myself, and thanks to which I had never, even on the blackest days, felt that I was alone. I was glad that she liked the room, because I remembered her previous visit, when our love had just begun and we didn't yet know what we were permitted to do with it, and Michaela sat on the edge of the bed and looked through the window and her foot revolved around itself and there was a bittersweet smell of narcissi in the room; I thought how much the room had changed since then, and how much I had changed.

I offered to show her the album of my photos from when I was little and we looked at them together. Black-and-white pictures with Mother carrying me piggyback, my hands around her neck, and she is so young and slender, and her breasts are erect and pointy. And here's my father sitting in the armchair, in a sweater and short pants, and me sitting on his lap, and we're both opening our mouths as wide as we can, to swallow life whole. And pictures of the wood behind the house—a little girl with a mop of curls and a dimpled smile and little white teeth, before they changed and before they broke, tightly hugging the trunk of a pine. And Michaela laughed, what is it with you and trees, and I said, I was in love with them, they were my best friends, especially one that I liked to climb, and once I built myself a tree house from planks between its branches, and I would hide there and read for hours. Michaela said, what a happy child you were, a face full of vitality, juicy as an apple. Suddenly I was afraid that my mother would come home unexpectedly, or my grandfather would drop in, and I told Michaela that we should go, and we went down to the sea.

We sat on the edge of the water, and I talked about Dahn Ben Amotz's book, which Michaela had not yet read. I told her that I would like to live like him and like Picasso: free of all commitments, not dependent on anyone, not giving a damn for social conventions, an eager hunter of people, adventures, and thrills, and "realizing my potential" every day. Michaela said that a life à la Ben Amotz or Picasso, however romantic it seemed from outside, was actually a life of great loneliness, which wasn't suited to everybody. To live like that you had to have a very strong and even cruel personality, and be capable of disappointing other people's expectations, and of cutting ties ruthlessly, even with the people closest to you. If I ever wanted children, I would have to be committed to them, and I would have to put their needs and welfare above my own, and therefore I would never have the freedom possessed by men, who only had one umbilical cord in their lives. She told me about an acquaintance of hers, whose children from different wives were scattered over the globe—a sculptor by the name of Amos Lev-Ari, who also, like Dahn Ben Amotz, lived and worked in Jaffa opposite the sea. Perhaps we would go and visit him together during the vacation.

The air is golden, intoxicated, dizzy with expectation, anything could happen to me this summer!

Your Kitty

7.20.79

Dearest Anne,

Since yesterday I've been wearing contact lenses! In the afternoon I went to pick Mother up at the office, I haven't been there for a long time, and everyone said I'd grown. Motti, one of the travel agents who always gives me admiring looks, said to Mother, "She's a real peach, your daughter, aren't you jealous of her sometimes?" and Mother raised her neat eyebrows and said, "How could I be jealous of her? It would be like being jealous of my own hand."

We had a falafel at the "King" in Hehalutz Street, and the tehini dripped and almost stained her Italian shoes. We laughed like a couple of little girls, and for a moment I almost felt as if I was with a friend. I wanted to ask her about Moishele, when he was going to leave his wife at last, and if she wasn't tired of living like this, taking second place all the time. But I sensed that if I pried into her soul too much I would spoil the moment. Afterwards we went to the optician who had made my glasses years ago. He hadn't changed since then: the same side-parted hair that looked like a wig. He tested my sight, and as luck would have it he had soft lenses in the shop that matched my prescription. He showed me how to put them in, and after a few attempts I succeeded. When we left Mother kissed me and said, "Now you look like a human being." Perhaps before, with the glasses, I had looked to her like Daddy, and whenever she looked at me she was forced to remember her ex-husband. We went on strolling along Herzl Street and looking in the shop windows. It was a strange feeling to see the world naked, not through two square frames, and my face felt completely exposed. When we reached the corner of Balfour she suggested going into the Atara cafe. We ordered iced coffee with ice cream, gossiped about all kinds of acquaintances, and Mother pinched my cheek and said, "How did you grow up so quickly, only yesterday you were three years old." In the last year and a half, ever since the beginning of my affair with Michaela, I saw my mother as my enemy, and perhaps I was doing her an injustice, because she actually cares about me, and even though she doesn't resemble me in any way and she doesn't really understand me she only wants me to be happy.

In the evening, after Mother went out and Oren and Noam went to sleep, I took off my clothes in her room opposite the mirror on her closet door, loosened my hair, and looked at myself like that, without glasses, the way God had created me. I saw how much I had matured since I began writing to you in this diary, when I was still a shy, bespectacled duckling. I like my hair, which comes down almost to my waist, and which the sun has splashed with pale shades; and my blue-gray eyes, which look bigger without glasses; and my tanned body, which has grown longer and thinner (when we began, Michaela and I were the same height, now I'm one and a half inches taller than she is!). I like my jutting collarbone, and the two white cones with their pink nipples; the narrow waist and the flat belly and the long, strong legs; even the hips, which are a tiny bit wider than I would wish. It's too soon to fix the broken teeth—Dr. Miller told mother the mouth only stops growing at the age of eighteen, and I'll have to wait till then to be fitted with crowns.

This morning I drove with Michaela to the Tantura beach. She left Ido with her parents, and we only took Dulcinea, who stuck her head out of the back window and smiled at the wind. I took my new camera, which we won in the Crystal soft drinks promotion campaign (you pry the cork out of the tin lid with a knife, and underneath it is a letter; you have to collect the letters that make up the slogan "Drink Crystal and keep cool;" Oren, Noam, and I collected letters for two months, sent them off, and won the camera).

We found a deserted corner of the beach, took off all our clothes, and went into the water. We clung to each other, buoyed by the waves, almost weightless, and our kisses tasted of salt. Dulcinea swam next to us, holding her head high above the water like a well-groomed woman taking care not to spoil her hairdo. Afterwards we came out and lay on the flowered sheet, abandoning ourselves to the wind, the sun caught in the beads of water on our skin, and the sand under the sheet, warm mounds shaped like a body. Michaela peered into my eyes and said, "The contact lenses have changed your look, now you can look life in the eye," and I said, "Where is it, this life, I'm dying to look it in the eye already," and Michaela laughed. I licked my thumbs and sleeked down her eyebrows mussed by the water, and then I took out the camera and snapped her in her white nudity shining on the field of flowers on the sheet, and her hand came up to hide her face from the sun. Afterwards I photographed her with Dulcinea, and she took pictures of me too in all kinds of poses, sitting like the little mermaid with my hair streaming in the wind. In the end we pressed cheek to cheek and I stretched my hand with the camera as far away as I could so I could snap us both together. When we came out to the parking lot I asked Michaela if she would let me drive Rocinanta a bit and she said yes. She showed me how to press on the clutch, the brakes and the gasoline, and how to change gears. I drove around the lot a few times and even though Michaela tried to look calm, I knew that she was nervous, and Dulcinea whimpered in the back seat too. It was fun!

At home I snapped Oren and Noam making horns at each other and pulling all kinds of faces to finish the film. I took the bus to Neve-Sha'anan, to some ancient photography shop where they don't know Mother or Grandfather or me, and gave them the film to develop. Tomorrow morning I'll go back there to get the photographs.

Goodnight in the meantime, Kitty

This morning I went to Neve-Sha'anan again to get our photos, which came out fantastically. They gave me a little album as a gift, with a picture of a man and woman kissing against the background of a sunset over the sea on the cover. Quite kitschy, but I arranged the photos in it anyway and buried it in the bottom drawer of my closet, under a pile of old notebooks.

8.6.79

Dearest Anne,

It's nearly two in the morning and I can't fall asleep. This afternoon, when I arrived at Michaela's place, Ido was awake and crying, and she put him in his "Moses basket" opposite the television. She says he can stare at the television for hours, it's the only thing that soothes him, especially the cartoons and the theme tune from the serial "Barbapapa." Then she joined me in the bedroom and we lay down and started kissing, but even before we got undressed we heard the scraping of the key and

Yoel came in. (Since the baby was born Michaela sometimes forgets to bar the door from inside.) We jumped up at once and Michaela went to greet him, while I pretended to be playing with Dulcinea on the carpet. He sent a polite, perfunctory "Hello how are you" in my direction (ever since Michaela told him that I came from a broken home, and that I had a lot of problems with my parents he tries to be nice to me). Michaela said, "We were just about to go out with Ido and Dulc to the library. I wanted to help Rivi find a certain book. But now that you're here, perhaps you'll be a sweetheart and stay with him, they're not too keen on dogs and babies there."

Yoel glanced at me and said, "Okay, no problem," and I saw that he wanted to say something else but controlled himself.

He picked Ido up and held him in his arms and cooed all kinds of babyish coos to him, and I thought that he really was a good father and a good husband, and he had no idea of what his wife got up to while he was working so hard at the hospital, and I felt a little sorry for him.

When we were at the door Ido began to cry, and Yoel asked when he had been fed and said that he looked hungry and Michaela said impatiently, "So make him a bottle," and shut the door behind us, and we bounded down the stairs like a couple of schoolgirls running away from school. Michaela burrowed in her bag and fished out the neighbors' key—the Germanns had gone on holiday and asked her to water their plants, and we went into their apartment, which resembled Michaela's, but was furnished in an old fashioned way and smelled of old age. And all the time we went on hearing Ido's screams, which grew louder and louder like a fire engine's siren going full blast. Michaela sat down on the television chair in the living room and shut her ears with her hands and said that she couldn't stand his screaming day and night anymore and she had already told Yoel that something was wrong with the baby, that they should take him to the doctor, and Yoel said that he was fine and she mustn't worry, he had simply been so contented in the womb that it would take time for him to get used to the world outside. Yoel was sure that he knew everything because he was an anesthetist, but in fact he didn't even know how to put the baby to sleep, so that she hardly slept at night, because even after Ido fell asleep at last, worn out by crying, she couldn't get back to sleep herself, and she lay there thinking about what was going to become of us. A few days ago Yoel had told her that he had been offered a post in a New York hospital to learn the newest techniques in anesthetizing, for a salary that it would take him years to reach in Israel, and she had tried to hide her alarm and asked him, what about my job and my studies, and Yoel said that in any case she earned a pittance at the school, and that she could have completed her degree ages ago, if she hadn't wasted her time on students half her age. It was nice of her to worry about me and give me the attention I was lacking at home, but it seemed to him that I had adopted her as my mother and developed a dependency on her, and that I had to understand that now she had a baby of her own.

I felt my mouth going dry with dread. I knelt down next to her on the carpet, laid my head on her lap, wrapped my arms around her, and said that she couldn't go, she couldn't leave me, I would die if she went away. Michaela stroked my head and promised that she would try to persuade Yoel to stay. She had already told him that she couldn't leave her parents, who were no longer young and not so healthy anymore and had no one but her to look after them, especially her father, who had already had two heart attacks.

Afterwards we went into the Germanns' bedroom, which was dark and stuffy, and smelled of medicines, and we got undressed and crawled in between their flowered sheets and hugged and kissed, but our bodies were sad and troubled and didn't feel like making love, and Ido's wails wounded the air, until they suddenly died down. We lay embracing in the failing light like a couple of refugees on a frosty night, and Michaela sang softly into my ear in her deep velvet voice, "Oh my love, my sweet, my tender, my marvelous love, from the dawn until the end of day, I love you still, you know I love you," and I wondered if there were any chance our love would last for twenty years, like in Jaques Brel's song.

When we left the apartment and Michaela locked the door I asked her about the plants and she laughed and said, "I forgot, I'll water them tomorrow."

So Michaela may go abroad, and I won't be able to see her or talk to her, and her body will be far away. The thought of this cuts me up inside like knives, and I feel like wailing like Ido. I'll do everything I can to prevent it from happening, and the day after tomorrow we're driving down to Tel Aviv together!

I feel a little easier now. I hope I'll be able to go to sleep.

Goodnight my faithful friend. Yours, Kitty

Thursday, 8.9.79

Dearest Anne,

I've just come back from Tel Aviv and I'm totally exhausted, after an almost sleepless night. Soon I'll take a shower and flop down, but before that I have to write to you about the trip, especially the nightmarish night I passed.

Yesterday morning we drove down. Michaela made a date for us to have lunch with her friend Osnat (she's told me a lot about her, and I really wanted to meet her), and arranged for us to go to Jaffa after lunch to visit the studio of the sculptor Amos Lev-Ari. I was curious to meet him, and in the meantime I also read an interview with him in *Days and Nights*. In his photograph in the newspaper he looks impressive, tall and broad, with a bronzed, sculpted face, intense blue eyes, and gray curls. It didn't say how old he is, and Michaela said that he must be about fifty. She met him through her father.

I told my mother I was going to Tel Aviv to visit Ayala, a friend I met at the young art lovers' summer camp in Jerusalem, and that I would be back in the evening.

Michaela and Rocinanta were waiting for me at the Center, after taking Ido to her parents. The drive was pleasant, and the elderly Rocinanta did herself credit in accomplishing her mission. On the way I asked Michaela about Osnat. She lives with her boyfriend in a little street next to Dizengoff, and illustrates children's books. Michaela told me about a quarrel they once had, when they were fifteen. "I don't even remember what it was about, only that we didn't speak for a long time, weeks or even months, and I missed her terribly, and on her birthday I decided to buy her a present and a bunch of flowers, and to simply go around and knock on the door. When I arrived, she came out of the apartment and saw me coming up the stairs and her face suddenly opened up in great joy, and her blue eyes shone, and my heart trembled in happiness, and she ran down the stairs and we embraced, we probably cried too, and I felt that I was brimming over with love for her."

"So Osnat was actually your first love," I said and something soured inside me.

"My first love was my mother," Michaela smiled over the steering wheel, "an absolutely unrequited love. And Osnat, yes, I suppose I was in love with her then, but I didn't yet know, or didn't permit myself, to call it by name."

I turned my face to the window and let the wind dry my eyes.

Osnat was really lovely. I almost fell in love with her myself when she opened the door barefoot, in short tricot pants, tall and thin, with a long inclining neck and long giraffe legs, and a narrow face with high cheekbones, and a beaky nose, and burning blue eyes, and curly hair and a gigantic smile. She hugged Michaela and shouted "Michaelush," and Michaela shouted "Osnatush," and I tried hard not to be jealous. We drank lemonade, and Osnat showed us the illustrations she was working on, which I thought were wonderful. Afterwards we went to eat at some Italian restaurant in Atarim Square, overlooking the marina and the sea. Michaela and Osnat drank wine and got a little tipsy, and reminisced to the accompaniment of bursts of laughter, but they included me too, and explained every joke, so that I wouldn't feel left out. When the coffee came, Osnat suddenly looked at us seriously and asked, "So what's the story, are you together?"

I didn't answer, I only smiled, because I didn't know what Michaela had told her about us. Michaela lit a cigarette and nodded. Osnat looked from Michaela to me and said quietly, "It's so strange."

Michaela let out an embarrassed laugh and said, "Yes, love is a strange creature that overtakes us in the most unexpected places."

"In the classroom, for example," I said, and we both burst out laughing.

"Who actually started with whom?" asked Osnat and cupped her chin in her hand.

I glanced at Michaela, who smiled to herself, and said rather proudly, "I fell in love with her first. I loved her for a whole year, and she didn't even know," and two scraps of sky in Osnat's eyes shone at me.

Michaela invited her to come with us to Lev-Ari's studio, but Osnat said that her man was coming home soon, and she wanted to be at home. She kissed Michaela and me too, and went on her way like a big bird, so at peace with herself and her life and her man and her work. And I thought that when I reached her age I would like to be like her.

On the way to Jaffa Michaela asked me what I thought of Osnat. I thought for a minute and said, "She's a sweet soul," and Michaela nodded.

When we reached Lev-Ari's studio, opposite the fishing boats, we found him in his work overalls, his sleeves rolled up above the elbows exposed tanned, muscular arms. He was wearing thick dark glasses, like diver's goggles, and holding a blowtorch, which gave off sparks when it touched the huge iron statue, on which he was working: a heap of distorted faces, guns, helmets, and amputated legs and arms. All around, along the walls, stood similar statues in different sizes. Michaela stopped in front of a statue of a soldier standing to attention on two legs amputated above the knee, and saluting. (His amputated legs reminded me of Grandpa Ya'akov, who I hadn't seen for years.) Amos smiled, turned off the blowtorch, pushed his goggles onto his wet forehead with the silver curls sticking to it, and said in a surprisingly soft voice: "I call it 'The lead soldier.'" Then he pointed to the big statue and asked: "Well, do you like it?"

I asked what it was exactly, and he said that he intended calling it "The Chinese Farm" after the battle in the Yom Kippur War.

"Did you fight there?" asked Michaela, and Amos said, "I didn't have the pleasure, but a good friend of mine lost his life there, and another friend lost his legs and his mind."

"Yes, a friend of mine lost his mind in that war too," said Michaela, and I remembered what she had told me about Shaul, her first lover.

"But the country lost it long before. That war was only the punishment," said Amos.

"Punishment for what?" I didn't understand.

"For the hubris," he said, and for the first time he looked into my eyes. "And it doesn't look as if the punishment is going to be over anytime soon, in spite of the lame peace we may have with Egypt now."

He pulled a pack of cigarettes out of his overall pocket, and offered it to me and Michaela. I shook my head, and Michaela took one. Amos said that he had finished work for today, and invited us up to his house to have a drink and see the sunset from the porch.

He shut the heavy iron gate to the studio and began walking, a few steps ahead of us. We smiled at each other behind his back, and I shaped my lips in the words "He's nice."

When we reached the stone wall, he fished a bunch of keys

out of his pocket, and opened a creaking barred gate. We climbed a few steps and reached the narrow alleys of the reconstructed old Jaffa. In the alley called "Scorpio"—my sign—he announced, "Here we are, we've reached the kennel," and opened a heavy wooden door, surrounded by a thick creeper. His kennel looked like a cave. A vast vaulted space, with Oriental carpets, and mattresses and cushions along the walls. Hanging on the walls were paintings by Israeli painters, apparently friends of his. One wall was entirely covered with pictures of Madonnas holding babies. Amos said that they were ancient icons he had collected in flea markets in Europe. An arched glass door led to a large porch, beneath which lay the sea.

Michaela and I sat down on the porch, and Amos went to shower. When he came back he was wearing only white cotton trousers, his curls were wet, and drops of water glittered in the tangle of gray hair on his mighty chest. He gave off a masculine post-shower smell, which suddenly seemed familiar to me. He was carrying three tall glasses each containing a tricolored drink, pink, orange and purple.

"My special sunset cocktail," he announced. He put the tray down on the table, stuck a glass straw in each glass, and offered them to us. The drink was cold and refreshing, tasting of various fruits, and I was so thirsty that I drank it all at once. Immediately my head started to spin, and I closed my eyes. It felt so pleasant with the smell of the sea, the sun on my face, and Michaela's hand stroking the back of my neck. I listened to their voices, speaking of artists I didn't know, and then about Brecht, and a play by Buchner called "Wozzeck," which the composer Alban Berg had turned into an opera, that had inspired one of Amos's statues, and afterwards they talked about Kierkegaard and Nietzsche, and the *Myth of Sisyphus* by Albert Camus, and *Atlas Shrugged* by Ayn Rand, which I had actually read recently, but when I wanted to say something my thoughts dissolved and my mouth became paralyzed.

The sea faded and turned silver, and Amos offered to make

us supper, red mullet and finely chopped salad the likes of which we had never tasted before.

I succeeded in saying that it was getting late, and that they were waiting for me at home (even though I was sure that Mother would go out with her Moishele, and all she cared about was knowing I had returned safely so she wouldn't have to worry about me while she was with him and also so she wouldn't have to get a babysitter), and Michaela said that she had to take Ido from her parents.

"Say you got stuck in Tel Aviv," Amos tried to change our minds, "you can stay the night here. What are grandparents for, they'll be only too happy to have their grandson sleep over."

Michaela and I exchanged looks. We had never spent the night together before.

"I can call and tell my mother that I'm staying over at Ayelet's in Tel Aviv," I mused aloud, and Amos joined in with enthusiasm, "I'll call her myself. I'll say I'm Ayelet's father and that you're in good hands."

Michaela phoned her parents and talked to them in German. I caught the name "Osnat."

"It's okay," she smiled, "Ido's already sleeping anyway, and Yoel's working tonight."

Amos called and spoke to my mother. My heart raced, and my stomach felt as if it was going to burst. He looked at me and Michaela and said, "No, it's no trouble at all, you have a delightful daughter, and the girls are stuck together like Siamese twins, it would really be a shame to separate them." Then he passed the phone to me. "I'm not too thrilled about this plan," Mother said in her dry voice, "but perhaps it's better than taking buses in the middle of the night."

I promised her that I would be home by lunch time, and breathed a sigh of relief. We would have a whole stolen night to ourselves!

We ate the crisply fried little fish that Amos prepared, accompanied by salad and white wine.

"Do you do anything with yourself apart from school?" he asked me with his mouth full. I said that I read a lot, and wrote poems.

"Her poems aren't bad at all for her age," said Michaela, and my stomach suddenly cramped.

"At her age everybody writes poems instead of living," said Amos dimissively, "Bernard Shaw said once that youth was wasted on the young, because they don't know how to really enjoy it. Live!" He raised his glass to me.

"I'm trying," I smiled at him. I liked his sardonic masculinity, and his absolute freedom.

Afterwards the two of them talked about Sinai that was about to be returned to the Egyptians, and how they had to go to say goodbye to the marvelous beaches of Sharm-al-Sheikh, Dahab, and Nueba, and Amos said, "We can always go to Nelson's village to console ourselves, they're not giving that back," and Michaela talked about the holiday she and Osnat had spent there before they joined the army, and how Rafi Nelson had started with both of them, and I thought that I really hadn't lived yet, I hadn't been to Sinai or even Eilat, and even a trip to Tel Aviv seemed to me like a great adventure.

After supper we went inside and lounged on one of the mattresses. Amos crumbled a brown lump that looked like a clod of earth, mixed the powder with the tobacco from a cigarette, and rolled it up in thin paper. Then he flicked an agile tongue over the paper, and made it into a new cigarette, which he called a "roach."

I already felt quite sleepy from the cocktail and the food and the wine, but I was curious to see what it was like. Michaela took a few drags and passed the cigarette to me. I took a deep drag and started to cough, even though I tried not to. A transparent elevator flew into my head and through its walls everything seemed sharper and clearer: Their two faces looking at me intently, and the Madonna icons with the infants all of which looked to me like Ido. As soon as we had finished the cigarette my body turned to stone and I dived into the mattress.

When I woke up I was covered with a sheet, Michaela's nakedness at my back, and her hands groping under my blouse. I understood that Amos had retired to bed. I turned to her and we started to kiss. Beneath us the sea surged as if the next minute it would be lapping at our feet. I felt full of joy that we were together, in the hallucinatory light of the moon, and I threw the sheet off us. I pulled off my clothes and clung to the warm, familiar body, to the soft, sucking lips, and when lust was already raging between my thighs I suddenly saw him, standing in the dark next to the wall and looking at us, and his white pants were stretched tight as a tent. He saw me looking and whispered in a hoarse voice, "You're so beautiful together like this, so very very beautiful." For a moment I froze, and he asked, "Can I join you?" I looked into Michaela's eyes without knowing what to say, and Michaela stretched out her arm and said "Come."

Amos quickly took off his trousers and lay down next to my legs. I felt his tongue sliding over my thigh and when it reached my vagina he stuck his lips to it like a thirsty man drinking from a spring, and groaned in a strangled voice, "So delicious, so sweet," and I didn't know if he was talking to me or singing my praises to Michaela, who went on kissing me and stroking my breasts. It was nice to have both of them stroking me like that, like a small child getting into her parents' bed on Saturday morning, and suddenly they both stopped, and Amos raised his face to me and asked with glistening lips, "Will you allow me to come into you?" I was alarmed, but also very aroused, and I felt his thick warm penis knocking at my thighs, and something in me wanted it so much, to embrace him tightly with my legs and to feel him deep inside me, and I sought Michaela's eyes, to ask her if she agreed. She knelt on the edge of the mattress and nodded at me, her body pale in the moonlight and only her pubic triangle dark—and also her nipples and hair and eyes, and her lips stretched in a strange kind of smile I had never seen before. And suddenly I knew that they had arranged it all in advance, because Michaela knew that I had been wanting to try it with a man for a long time already, and she had organized this whole trip in order to see me in my first intercourse, at the moment of penetration. Yes, she was using this man to do for her what she couldn't do for herself, and they had both brought me here and made me drunk and doped me in order to ensure the success of their plan. And a terrible nausea rose up in me, and I stood up swaying on my feet and mumbled, I don't feel well, and in that hallucinatory light, between the shadows, I groped my way to the toilet, and knelt down with my head in the bowl, and vomited the crisply fried fish with the incomparable finely chopped salad, and I shook with weeping, because it wasn't supposed to happen like this, with a stranger I had only just met, instead of someone I really loved and wanted, how could she have handed me over to him, how could she have betrayed me, how could she?

I heard her knocking on the door, and her soft voice asking, "Kiddo, are you alright in there?" and I knew that I wasn't alright, that she wasn't alright, and that nothing was alright, and I opened the door violently, so that it would bang her forehead, and returned to the mattress and found my trousers and top and put them on quickly and went to the door and opened it and went outside, and began to run down the dark lane before they could catch up with me, and her broken voice pursued me, Rivi, Rivi, and I didn't turn my head, and I passed the paved square next to the lighthouse and went into some park or other, and charged down a dirt path between dense bushes that scratched my shins, and left the park and went on running down the street, until I saw the sea, a huge blot of ink, and I went down to the sand and kept going on and on, and when I felt that I had gone far enough and there was no chance that they would find me—I fell on the sand with my heart beating wildly.

I breathed the damp salty air through my mouth to stop the racing of my heart that went on and on like some broken stopper when the race was long over already, and I realized that I was having an attack of tachycardia. I tried my breathing exercises, I held my breath and pressed down hard as if I was taking a crap, but my heartbeat didn't settle down, and suddenly I wanted so badly to be at home, in my own bed, to call Mother and tell her, my heart's going tick-tock, because I knew that only her hand would be able to restrain it.

The sky squatted over me as black as a panting dog. I thought of the two of them, perhaps taking comfort now in each other's arms, and I knew that it was all over between me and Michaela.

I must have fallen asleep, because when I woke up there was a pale light and a familiar hand was stroking my hair: "I've been looking for you all night, I was so worried." I sat up and hugged her, trembling all over. "How could you have done that to me, how could you have betrayed me like that," I choked into the hollow of her neck, " the only reason I agreed to sleep over at his place was so I could spend the whole night with you." Michaela moved my body away from her and looked into my eyes, "I know, kiddo, I didn't plan it, you have to believe me, it just happened."

I wanted so badly to believe her, and I didn't know if I could. She helped me up, and we walked slowly back, climbing up the path between the thorny bushes, crossing the square next to the lighthouse, and descending Scorpio Lane. Amos opened the door, a cigarette in his hand, his curls flattened and his eyes red with sleeplessness.

"Coffee?" he asked quietly. I wanted to tell him that it wasn't on his account that I ran away, that I liked him and he shouldn't be offended, but I only nodded my head.

We drank the black coffee on the porch in silence, watching the little fishing boats coming in to the harbor with their catch. Then we went down to Amos's studio, and he lifted the "Lead Soldier" in his arms, carried it to Rocinanta, and laid it on the back seat. "Lucky he hasn't got legs," he said, and then he said to Michaela: "Give my warm regards to your father, he's a dear man, I'm very fond of him."

"He is of you too," Michaela smiled.

"Will we see you again, child?" he asked me and looked into my eyes with his direct blue gaze. And I smiled and said "Perhaps."

And already on the drive back, staring at the racing landscape—I was too tired to talk—I knew that I would, I would return to go to bed with him, he would be my first man, but I would do it without her, I would do it all by myself, and the lead soldier on the back seat didn't stop saluting.

When Michaela stopped for me at the Center, before I got out, she took my face in her hands, kissed me on the lips, and said, "You have to believe me, kiddo, it just happened, but please forgive me anyway."

I hugged her and said, "I already have."

Luckily Mother's still at work, so her X-ray eyes can't see what happened to me last night, and now I'm going to take a shower and go to bed. I'm so exhausted I hope I sleep until morning, and tomorrow nothing will show.

Yours as always, Kitty

8.21.79

Dearest Anne,

Oof oof oof and oof again! So you'll understand what I'm complaining about I'd better tell you from the beginning:

The day before yesterday I called Amos Lev-Ari (I didn't want to get his number from Michaela, and at directory inquiries they told me the number was unlisted, and in the end I got it through the Painters and Sculptors Association). He remembered me immediately, and said that he was glad to hear my voice.

Without any introductions I asked, "Can I come to you tomorrow to say goodbye to my virginity at last?"

Amos laughed heartily and said, "I'm thrilled and delighted

233

that you've chosen me to be your first. Come, and we'll throw a magnificent farewell party to your virginity."

Yesterday afternoon I took the bus to Tel Aviv (to sleep over at "Ayalet's"). Amos was waiting for me as arranged at the clock tower in Jaffa, and he kissed me on the mouth with twinkling eyes. I hugged him, breathing in the familiar smell, and excitement fluttered in my stomach like love. We strolled through the flea market and he showed me all kinds of antiques and explained the difference between Art Nouveau and Art Deco to me and introduced me to a number of the sellers. Everybody knows him there, slapping him on the back and offering coffee or arak. Afterwards we went to eat at a restaurant called "The Courtyard." We sat under a tree and drank champagne from a green bottle that waited for us in a silver bucket while a middle-aged waitress in a plunging neckline piled more and more appetizers in little dishes on our table. At the table next to us two men in suits and two elegant women were talking French. One of the men leaned over to Amos and they exchanged whispers. I managed to overhear the man say, "*Votre fille est très belle,*" and Amos put his arm around me and said, "*Ce n'est pas ma fille, elle est mon amante.*"

"Oh, pardon," said the man, and his eyes popped out of his head as if he'd swallowed a fish bone.

"That's the French ambassador, he lives not far from here," Amos explained, and I, having understood everything except for one word, asked, "What does *amante* mean?"

"Lover," his eyes twinkled at me.

"Not yet," I smiled, "you still have a little work to do."

"I've never been afraid of work," he smiled and rumpled my hair with his hand. "What do you care if I brag? The main thing is that it sounds good."

"Yes, especially in French," I said. The champagne had gone straight to my head, and the world had turned into a light, airy balloon. I saw myself through his eyes, a fresh, pretty, adventurous young girl.

Amos took my hand in his thick hand and looked at it. "A big hand," he said, "long fingers, like a pianist's, you won't be anyone's little wife."

"No, I don't plan to be," I said, "if I ever marry I'll be a big, tyrannical wife. My hands are nothing, look at my feet." I slipped off my sandal under the table and put my foot on his thigh.

Amos looked at it between his hands as if he were looking at a museum exhibit. "You have the long narrow foot of a redhead, even though you're a brunette. What number shoe do you take?"

"Forty," I said proudly. He raised my foot to his lips and sucked my big toe. The French ambassador gave us an outraged look and coughed grimly into his white linen napkin.

Amos put my foot back on his thighs, and my big toe groped for the raging bulge between them. The lust stored up in my womb, as in an inverted jar dribbling honey drop by drop, collected in my panties. Soon I would go to bed with him, I knew, and his warm penis would make its way deep inside me.

"Come on," I said softly, "let's go to your place and do it."

He went to pay and we left. At the door we bumped into a big, bearded man, wearing a white galabieh. His enormous feet were bare and dirty. I recognized him at once, from the television and the newspapers.

"Lev-Ari, how are you," he said to Amos in a slightly hoarse voice and his blue eyes surveyed me appraisingly. "That's a lovely little girl you've got there."

"Yes," Amos smiled, "someone already said that."

"Someone said that? Before me? Never mind," the blue eyes smiled, and so did the red lips in the thickets of the beard. I wanted to tell him that I had read most of his books, and liked some of them a lot, even though they wouldn't change the world; I was especially impressed by the last one *Fucking Isn't Everything*, and I had almost written him a letter. But in the end I didn't say anything, because I didn't want to be delayed.

"Dahn is a neighbor of mine," said Amos as we walked

away, "did you see how he devoured you with his eyes? I bet he'd be happy to change places with me."

"Go on, make him an offer," I teased. For a moment I was charmed by the idea of doing it with him, with the hedonistic, humorous, romantic writer. Perhaps some of his talent and success would rub off on me.

"Do I look like a sucker to you?" Amos put his arm around my shoulders. We walked down the alleys with our arms around each other until we reached Scorpio Lane, and Amos announced, "Here we are, we've reached the stable."

"Isn't it a kennel?" I smiled.

"When I'm a dog it's a kennel, when I'm a pig it's a sty. Today I'm a horse."

"Lucky for me you're not an elephant," I said, and Amos laughed.

He went to take a shower and I climbed the two steps to the stone floor with the double mattress and got undressed quickly and efficiently, as if I was seeing a gynecologist. (I forgot to tell you, that in the framework of preparations for saying goodbye to my virginity, I stole the red HMO card from my mother's bag and went to the gynecologist to get a prescription for Microgynon, and I've already started taking it.) I lay on the mattress and covered myself with the sheet. The champagne was still fizzing in my head, and the roar of the sea was very close, as if I was holding a conch shell to my ear. I wasn't afraid of what was about to happen. I remembered how Michaela had once said that courage was a better guide than fear. I knew that Amos had a lot of experience, that he liked me and that he wouldn't harm me. I tried to guess how she would feel if she could see me now, and I told her silently that I wasn't here to cheat on her, but in order to be faithful to myself. Because only when I had proven to myself that I enjoyed being with men too would I be able to love her wholeheartedly again.

Amos emerged from the shower with a towel around his waist, and came to lie down next to me. He spread out his strong arms like a statue of the crucifixion and said, "I'm all yours, my beauty, do as you wish with me." With one movement I loosened the towel and pulled it off him. His pubic hair was sprinkled with gray, like grass whose tips are already withered, and his penis rested on his thigh as if it was half asleep, opening one lazy eye. I got up on all fours and lowered my body onto his, smelling the shaving lotion on his cheeks, and my lips sought his mouth. I rode his thigh like the branch of the pecan tree in Aunt Tehiya's garden, and thrust my nose into his neck and armpit in order to breathe in another ancient smell from the lost continent of Atlantis. Every pore of my body opened to the touch of the new skin, of the big hands smoothing my back and waist as if they were sculpting.

"Come," he murmured with his eyes closed, "take it into you, sit on it."

I lay on his penis with my legs parted, pressing my moist vagina to his smooth warm belly, flesh to flesh, blood beating to blood, and his mouth slid down to my nipples and sucked them one after the other, and I knew that in a minute I would crash onto him like a wave, but first I had to get him inside me with a single stroke, even if it hurt, and I took him in my hand and tried, but my body suddenly shrank and refused, and I tried again, like someone insisting on inserting the wrong key into a keyhole, and Amos sat up suddenly and turned me over onto my back with a decisive movement, and parted my lips with two thick thumbs and tried to push himself into me, but the harder he pressed the more I contracted, and he breathed heavily and dragged down a pillow and whispered hoarsely, "Lift up your bum," and I lifted it, and he pushed the pillow under me and stood on his knees and put my ankles on his shoulders, and tried again, and it burned like a fire, and the tears burst out of my eyes, and I bit my lower lip and silently cursed Racheli whom it hadn't hurt at all, and whispered, "It isn't working, it's burning terribly," and Amos withdrew from me and ordered, close your legs, and I pressed my thighs tightly together and he grabbed hold of my buttocks with both hands and thrust himself between my thighs again and again, his rigid body going up and down like a piston, his heart racing and his mouth panting and whispering obscurely into my deaf ear, and suddenly he froze and grunted as if he were crying or trying to shit, and my thighs were covered in a hot, sticky liquid.

His heavy body rolled off me and collapsed at my side like a stone, and I stretched out my hand and collected his sperm on my fingers, sniffed it and tasted it on the tip of my tongue, and the smell and the taste were like nothing else I had ever known, perhaps a little like carob leaves, or green almond shells.

"Do you want me to help you to come?" he asked into my hair in a melting voice, but I didn't want anything, just for this burning, treacherous body to be left alone. He turned onto his side and pulled up the sheet and plunged like a diver into his deep breaths, and I lay next to him in the dark and listened to the sea, which went on and on, indifferent to me and my failure, and the tears fell from the corners of my eyes and slid behind my ears. Unthinkingly I began to play a game from long ago, from the lost continent of Atlantis, when we drove back from Aunt Tehiya's and the little girl sat in the back seat of the Susita and breathed in the hot khamsin night with its smell of burning trash, and said some word or other to herself, which suddenly sounded strange and random to her ears, disconnected from the thing it represented, until she grew afraid that the word existed only in her head, and the thing had a different, more appropriate name, which everyone knew except for her, and if she said her word people would look at her as if she were mad, and she repeated the word over and over in a whisper so that it would reunite with the thing that it described until they were inseparable, but the more she whispered it, the more it lost its grip and broke up into meaningless syllables, ceiling, I whispered now, sea-ling, seal-ing, sea, seal. . . .

When I woke up it took me a few seconds to remember

where I was and why. The mattress on Amos's side was empty, and there was a key and a note on the pillow: "You were sleeping like a Murillo angel, I didn't want to wake you. Lock the door when you leave and bring the key to me in the studio." Without a kiss, without a signature. It wasn't the right key, I knew, and his Madonnas looked at me from the wall with the compassion of sisters in fate.

I filled the pink, peeling bathtub on the lion's paws, and had a long soak. I missed Michaela. If she were here now we would have been sitting in the bath together. I would have leaned my back against her breasts, and she would have shampooed my hair. I wondered whether to tell her that I hadn't succeeded in leaving my virginity behind in Tel Aviv and it was coming back to her with me, in shame and disgrace.

I got dressed and went out to the porch and breathed in a lungful of sea. I tried to draw the moment out, to persuade myself that I was having a good time, that the adventure wasn't over yet, but I knew that there was nothing more for me here, in this kennel or stable or whatever it was. Before I left I had a look at his books, and helped myself to the *Myth of Sisyphus*, which he and Michaela had talked about last time, because I felt that I had to take something away with me, and also so I would have something to read in the bus back to Haifa. And then I took my bag, locked the heavy wooden door behind me, and walked up Scorpio Lane. The gate to the harbor was open, and I went through it and reached the studio.

Amos was standing there in his overalls, bending over his statue, and when he noticed me he turned off the blowtorch and pushed the diver's goggles up his forehead.

"Good morning, my beauty, how did you sleep?" His blue eyes caressed me as if we hadn't failed.

"All right," I said glumly.

"Don't be sorry," he put his arm around my shoulders, "sometimes one needs a little help in these things. You should go and see your doctor, they have ways to help, and afterwards you can come back to me and we'll do it again, properly."

I won't come back to you, because your key doesn't fit, I wanted to say, but instead I said, "Perhaps I'll remain a virgin all my life like the Virgin Mary."

Amos laughed, "Remind me how old you are?"

"Sixteen in three months time."

"A dried-up old maid. Very worrying indeed." He smiled, and his eyes flashed sparks at me like his blowtorch.

"Thanks for everything," I kissed him on the cheek, "bye for now."

"Give my love to your girlfriend," he called after me, "come and see me together."

I knew that we wouldn't come back to him together, because three people can't really make love, and there was no point in just getting mixed up, like one of his statues, body parts and arms and legs jumbled up together. Love is the alchemy of two people, flesh welded to flesh, soul welded to soul, eyes welded to eyes.

That's it for the time being, I'm exhausted, your Kitty

Fourth Notebook

The Hiding Place Inside the Hiding Place

Footsteps on the stairs, the grating of the key in the lock, Yair's blue gaze. I raise red eyes to him. Crumpled tissues are scattered over the kitchen table as in a field of white weeping-flowers.

"How was the parents' meeting?"

Yair comes over to me and our lips are stitched together in a kiss. "They talked a lot, as usual. I paid the class committee."

"How's the new teacher—what's her name?" For a moment it slipped my mind.

"Hadas. Nice. Young. Twenty-seven, eight. Too-short skirt and long legs. How was the funeral?"

"You know, a funeral." The first lips I had kissed, the first body that had taught me pleasure, the first heart that had raced against mine—had been buried in the ground today.

Eleven years ago you came to Israel for our wedding. You wanted to make me up, and two hours before the ceremony you arrived in the hotel room with your makeup case that you had dragged with you from New York. Thus, your face above mine in the mirror, your fingers smearing eye shadow on my closed eyelids and outlining my lips with a pencil, Yair met you for the first time. You shook hands with each other, and you smiled at me in the mirror and shaped the words with your lips, "He has good eyes." You wanted to stand at my side under the wedding canopy instead of my mother, who had passed away a few months before, but I preferred Aunt Tehiya, who walked next to me erect and festive in the crown of her black braid. As usual she poked her elbow into my ribs and whispered in my ear, "The most important thing in a marriage is patience, a lot of patience, and it doesn't hurt to know how to laugh as well," and I thought about my parents, who had no patience and didn't know how to laugh, and through my veil I saw my father standing solemnly in a black suit next to the pole of the canopy and rubbing his eyes under his glasses with his thumb and forefinger, and then I looked into Yair's eyes shining at me, and said to myself, let's hope we can make a go of it.

When the wedding was over and we returned to the room, I told Yair our story, and it lasted all night long. When I was finished I asked, "What do you think?"

He was silent for a long time and then he said, "What does it matter what I think, I love you, and this story is a part of you. What I find astonishing," his eyes embraced me from the white of the pillow, "is that you don't know how to part, like a baby clinging to its first blanket you drag all your loves from nursery school to the grave with you."

True, I mused. Because apart from you, there were a few other ex-lovers of mine at the wedding, who clouded Yair's eyes for a moment when I introduced them.

"I suppose I understood quite early on that life, and mainly death, would provide me with enough partings without my initiating them," I said. "Anyone who's been deserted again and again needs to hang onto the ones who are willing to stay." With a swift movement I wrapped my thighs around him, mounted his big, protecting body, and buried my face in his neck.

Now he glances at the table and says nothing. I don't know if he noticed the notebooks, and perhaps nobody but me can see them.

"Have you eaten today?" His fingers in my hair.

"Yes, I had something to eat." If I tell him the truth he'll start cooking me a schnitzel now, cutting up a salad, and I have to go on with our story and reach the end.

"Then I'm going to bed. Are you coming or staying here?"

"Staying here."

"Good night," He stitches his lips to my forehead, just don't let the stitches come undone.

I listen to the humming of the fridge, the breathing of my dear one, the silent growing of my daughters. Yes, these are the sounds of my life. Once, years ago, in wakeful nights like this, in your kitchen in Hatzvi Avenue, you used to write me letters. Your windswept writing raged above and below the lines, rebelling, refusing to resign yourself to the breathing of your husband and your son, to the pupils' essays you had to correct.

Before you went away I gave you back your letters, so that no incriminating evidence would remain in my possession, and you promised to take them with you, and to keep them with the letters and poems I wrote you. On my last visit to New York I asked you to give them back to me, so that I could read them and remember. One morning, when Yoel and Ido were out, we turned your apartment inside out like a pocket, we rummaged in all the drawers, we took out packet after packet and spilled the contents on the floor. We found letters and postcards I had sent you over the past twenty years: from Haifa, from my first trip to Europe, from my basic training in the army, from Tel Aviv; and from all kinds of places in the world, some of which I had traveled to with men I loved, and to others alone. We also found rough copies of my first stories, which I had sent you in fear and trembling, waiting for your comments. But the letters from the two years of our love had completely disappeared. Had Yoel found them and in a sudden fit of rage and disgust destroyed them, without telling you? And perhaps you had hidden them too well, to conceal them from yourself as well? Only a few poems, the ones I had dedicated to you, came to light: to my surprise, you pulled them out of your handbag—yellowing pages torn from a notebook, folded in four inside a red leather purse embossed with a copper palm tree, in the old "Bezalel" style.

I unfolded one of them, and my handwriting of twenty years ago immediately turned into a time tunnel.

"I always keep them with me," you smiled, "like a charm they protect me from the indifference of the world."

But they couldn't protect you from the disease, I thought. A young girl's fragile, unripe poems, made of words and love and the smell of pines, consolations for a moment, how could they prevail over the forces of life, over death.

"Take them," you suddenly said, your face expressionless, "you keep them, I won't be needing them anymore."

Now I'll take a deep breath and open the notebook with the refined features of Virginia Woolf's face on the cover, which you gave me when I started the eleventh grade. The fourth and last notebook.

Tuesday, 9.5.79

Dearest Anne,

Again the beginning of September, again a new notebook, and in the morning, on the way to school, I dilate my nostrils to catch the first scents of autumn. This year we divided into streams, and I'm in 11c, the literature stream, thirty girls and three boys, conducted by the homeroom teacher Benjamin Keinan. Racheli isn't in my class anymore, she's a biology major, and we meet at breaks. Avshalom, who used to be in another class, sits next to me. (I wrote to you about him once, the one whose father was killed in the Yom Kippur war, who reads "Here Our Bodies Lie" every Memorial Day.) He's tall and curly haired, and he has dark lips and blue eyes, wide in perpetual surprise, behind round glasses in silver frames, and he's nice and terrific at drawing, especially caricatures of teachers. Sometimes he pushes some drawing over to me, and I have a hard time suppressing my laughter. A few days ago he drew Shoshana Ardon, the dried-up history teacher and deputy principal, lying in the missionary position with her huge square specs, whispering into the ear of the man lying on top of her: "I demand the emancipation of the orgasm." I laughed out loud and Ardon came up to our desk, took the picture, glanced at it without moving a muscle, and sent Avshalom to show his masterpiece to the principal. Hourgi warned him that if he was ever caught drawing "such filth" again, his parents would be called in for a talk, and immediately corrected himself, "I mean your mother." But Avshalom doesn't care, and he carries on as usual. Today he drew Benjamin Keinan—who grows the hair long on one side of his head and combs it over to the other side to hide his bald pate in the "loans and savings" method. In the drawing he's entering Hourgi's room, where the principal is standing on his desk in Elvis flares and playing the guitar, with his mane of hair exaggeratedly long and wild and a bandana around his forehead—and Keinan is holding a lock of his own limp hair and asking, "Perhaps you could make me a small loan?" Again I couldn't suppress my laughter, and Keinan came up to look at the picture, and then he raised his head to the ceiling and let out a huge bellow of laughter that shook his face and body, making the thick-lensed glasses dance on his cheeks. After he had recovered he told Avshalom that he had talent, and asked him if he was studying art and what his influences were, and Avshalom said that he went to drawing classes at Rothschild House and read comic books, especially Mad, and Keinan asked if he knew the courthouse caricatures of the brilliant nineteenth-century French painter Daumier. Avshalom said he didn't, and Keinan sent him to the library to find copies of Daumier's work and to prepare a lecture on him for the class.

I adore Keinan and I'm even a tiny bit in love with him (apparently it's my fate to fall in love with my literature teachers . . .). He's a "Yekke" too, he was born in Heidelberg and came here as a child. He has a deep, rich, resonant voice, and wise, lively brown eyes behind his glasses, and talks to us about everything, including politics and sex and drugs, and in literature classes he doesn't just analyze the text, but lectures us on the period, the social and political background, and connects it to developments in genre and style. We've started studying *Madame Bovary*. Keinan talked about Flaubert's ironic attitude towards Emma Bovary, the provincial doctor's wife who is influenced by cheap romances and tries to live according to them in a way that destroys her and leads to her death. I put up my hand and said that in my opinion his view was a little chauvinist, because Flaubert wasn't only ironic; he vividly and faithfully described Emma's suffering and distress, imprisoned as she is in a lifeless marriage, so that the reader, and especially the female reader, could identify with her. And besides, if Emma lived in a fantasy world detached from reality, the alternative of living with both feet on the ground was no less sad and ironic, to judge by her husband.

Keinan said that Flaubert wasn't only criticizing Emma, but also the moral hypocrisy of the petit-bourgeois society in which she lived. And I said that his readers were probably petit bourgeois too, and in order to satisfy their moral hypocrisy he chose to punish Emma for her sins and kill her at the end. Keinan smiled to himself and said that writers often killed their characters because they simply couldn't stand the thought that their creations would outlive them, but that the great characters of literature went on living after their deaths anyway.

I thought about my doctor's wife, and I asked myself if I was some Rudolph or Leon for her, a fantasy with which she tried to fill some hole in her soul, which nothing could perhaps ever truly fill.

Michaela can feel that I'm trying to distance myself from her a little, and she is afraid that I'm slipping out of her hands, so on the days that she's at school she casts caution to the winds and waits for me at the gate after classes. Sometimes we go to her place, or up to the Carmel, and sometimes I tell her that I can't go with her because I have too much homework. On the days when she doesn't teach I try to call her in the afternoon from my little-house-in-the-post-office so as not to hurt her feelings, because she says that when people are in love they have to sometimes do things even when they don't really feel like it. A few days ago we had a silly quarrel again because I hadn't called her. Michaela was angry, and her burning eyes turned into cold ashes. I told her that lately all our arguments were about who was more faithful and devoted to our love, as if that love had turned into some kind of fat demanding monster, that had to be fed and sacrificed to all the time, so that we were enslaved to it instead of enjoying it, and perhaps it meant that we should open the valve and let out a little air. Michaela cried, I cried, and we quickly found ourselves in bed.

After the Sukkoth holidays we're going to Kibbutz Ashdot-Ya'akov for a week's national service. To my regret, Benjamin Keinan isn't coming with us, but Racheli will be there, and also Avshalom, who I'm getting to like more and more every day.

Goodnight for now, yours, Kitty

Kibbutz Ashdot-Ya'akov, 10.23.79

Dearest Anne,

I'm writing to you lying on the lawn under a palm tree, in the orangey-pink light of late afternoon. We've been here three days now, and our daily schedule is as follows: five o'clock in the morning—wake up call. With half-closed eyes the herd gathers at the toilets and the taps, everyone standing in line to pee and brush their teeth. After that they drive us to the citrus grove. There we eat breakfast, and at six we're already standing on the ladders, clippers in our hands, picking grapefruit. Racheli and I stand together, take long breaks to chat, and guzzle grapefruit till our stomachs hurt. At noon they take us back to the kibbutz, and we have lunch in the dining hall. After that we have all the time in the world to swim in the pool and relax. There are big inner tubes floating in the pool, and I like lying in one of them and sailing with my eyes closed. The "national sport" is to upset the occupant of the tube, or to hang onto it on all sides until everyone falls onto everyone else in a heap. The boys get a special kick out of upsetting the girls and hearing them shriek. Racheli and I are usually left alone, because we're not part of the crowd: we've got a reputation of being aloof and weird. After supper we sit on the lawn outside the huts, Yoni from 11a plays the guitar, and we sing the Beatles and the Doors and songs from "Hair" and so on. Yesterday, when everyone started dispersing to go to bed, I pricked up my courage and asked Avshalom if he felt like going for a walk. Until two o'clock in the morning we walked up and down the kibbutz paths and sat on almost all the lawns. I asked him what he remembered about his father, and he said that he was a fat funny father with a Hungarian accent, who worked in the "Phoenician Glass" factory, and in his free time he liked fishing and cooking the fish he caught, and when Avshalom and his big sister, who was in the army now, were small, he would make them a tent in the living room, from a blanket and chairs, and on Saturday mornings they would sit in the tent in their pajamas, and he would tell them about his childhood, and read them stories from Greek mythology. I told Avshalom about my parents' divorce and about my estrangement from my father. We argued about which was better, a father killed defending the homeland, who left wonderful memories behind him, or a living father who was an android. Avshalom said that if his father had been alive, he would have done everything to keep in contact with him. He was sure that my father loved me, and I should be the braver of the two of us and ask to meet and talk. All the time he was talking the moonlight turned his hair silver and his lips glistened like a dark grape, and I wanted to move close to him, take his face in my hands, and taste and kiss, but I restrained myself, because I was afraid of alarming him. I told him that he drew brilliantly, and he said that he intended to study art and become a caricaturist or an animator. Suddenly, without meaning to, I said, draw me something on my back, let's see if I can guess what it is. I turned my back to him, and Avshalom drew with his finger on my tank top, and from time to time he slid up to my naked shoulders and to the gap between the top and my jeans. I closed my eyes in pleasure, his finger felt so good that I didn't care what he was drawing, as long as he didn't stop. His fingers fluttered over the fine hairs on the nape of my neck, and down my back to my tailbone, and I felt waves of warmth and sweetness between my thighs, and at the last moment, before I could fall on him shamelessly and wrapped arms and legs and lips around him, I said that I was on the point of falling asleep, and that we should go to bed, because in three hours time they would wake us up to go to work. Avshalom mumbled, okay, if you're tired, and escorted me to the girls' hut, but when I lay down I was too excited to fall asleep, I imagined his body on top of me and I touched myself under the blanket, and then Avshalom suddenly turned into Michaela, who appeared without permission, but I banished her from my imagination by force, because I wanted to be alone with him, and somehow I fell asleep at last.

Today I was completely out of it I was so tired, and I nearly fell off the ladder with my bag of grapefruit. Avshalom was walking around red-eyed too, and every now and then he smiled at me from his ladder. In the afternoon, instead of going to the pool, I went back to the hut and slept for three hours. It goes without saying that I told Racheli about last night, and consulted her about whether to seduce Avshalom tonight. She was in favor. What do you think?

Bye for now, Racheli's calling me to supper.

Yours, Kitty

Dearest Anne,

That's it, last night it happened, and I feel big and festive and new. I'll tell you in the order of events, as usual. Last night, when the singing died down and everyone dispersed to go to sleep, the two of us stood up and started walking together without talking until we reached the pool. We lay down on the lawn and looked up at the sky, which is much more generous with its stars over here than it is in town, and Avshalom showed me the Big Bear. I told him that the gang you formed with four of your friends was called "the Big Bear minus two." Avshalom said that a lot of the stars were already dead, only their light was still alive, and I said that there were people like that too, whose light went on shining long after they were already gone. And then Avshalom suddenly got up and asked if I felt like going for a dip, and before I had a chance to reply he had already taken off his shirt and rolled his glasses up in it, and in a few seconds he was stark naked, long and pale, and he jumped into the dark pool and started swimming with elegant rhythmic crawl strokes, like a dolphin in the moonlight. I got undressed too, and Avshalom waved at me and shouted, come on, the water's wonderful. I dipped my feet in cautiously first, to get used to the cold, and then I slid into the icy water and my whole body froze with the shock, and for a moment I couldn't breathe. I swam as fast as I could to warm up, and reached the other side, where the inner tubes were floating like herd of black hippopotamuses. I climbed into one of them and Avshalom climbed into another one, and we floated side by side in the dark, and every now and then the tubes bumped into each other, and we spun around and drifted apart, and came together again. We looked at each other and smiled, and Avshalom took my hand, and I closed my eyes and wanted the moment to go on and on, but then he suddenly pulled me out of the tube into the water, and we pressed our bodies together and started kissing, and I felt his penis between my thighs, and I whispered, let's get out, and we climbed out of the pool and dried ourselves quickly with his shirt, and Avshalom shook his curls and sprayed drops of water, like Dulcinea when she comes out of the sea, and we lay on the lawn, and went on exploring each other with our lips, and his hand carefully felt my breasts and nipples that had hardened from the cold, and my hands wandered over his chest and his smooth hairless stomach and his back and bum, and then his hand slid down, and I opened my legs a little to give it room, and his fingers stroked and danced there, in the sweetness and the warmth, and I was so aroused that I had to press up against him and come with little pants, so as not to wake the whole kibbutz; and then, when I was already completely wet, he lay on top of me and came into me, and it was lovely and it didn't hurt, as if there wasn't a hymen there at all, only the lawn pricked my back a bit, and all the time we looked seriously into each other's eyes, and it felt so natural to lie like that, completely open and penetrated, under the black sky with all its stars, alive and dead. I could feel that Avshalom was trying to move inside me as slowly as he could, so as to prolong the pleasure and make our first time last as long as long as possible, and I took his handsome face in my hands and pushed my thumb into his mouth, like I sometimes do to Michaela and she does to me, and he sucked it, and I sensed his excitement growing, because his backside began going up and down faster and faster, and I wrapped my legs around his thighs to press him to me as closely as possible, and we went on stuck together like this, without knowing where one ended and the other began, until Avshalom closed his eyes tight, and his whole body stiffened on top of me.

We lay there for a while, breathing quietly, and Avshalom slid down next to me and whispered in my ear, You know, that was my first time, and in a muffled voice I said, Mine too, and he raised himself on his elbow and said, Really? And I thought he didn't deserve to be lied to, and I said, Yes, more or less, and Avshalom smiled and said, What's that supposed to mean? And even though I don't really know him yet, I knew that I could trust him and tell him about Michaela, who at that moment seemed very far away, but nevertheless I felt the need to unburden myself of our story, of the load of love and fear and guilt, and I said, I'll tell you if you swear on your right hand never to tell anybody, because I thought that he wouldn't risk the hand he drew with, and Avshalom raised his right hand in a scouts' oath and said, "May my right hand wither and my tongue cleave to my palate and may I turn into Trumpeldor if I tell."

I told him everything, from the beginning, how I fell in love with Michaela at the beginning of the eighth grade, and loved her all year without her knowing, and how by a miracle, at the beginning of the ninth grade she fell in love with me too. I told him about our drives in Rocinanta, and our hiding places on the Carmel, and my mother's suspicions and my lies, and about Yoel and her pregnancy and Ido's birth, which had driven us apart in recent months, and my fear that I would be a lesbian all my life, and my failure with Amos Lev-Ari.

Avshalom chewed a blade of grass and listened, and from time to time he shook his head and said, Incredible, what an amazing story. He knows Michaela. In middle school she taught his class too. He said he loved her lessons, her intelligence and depth and passion, and thanks to her he had started reading more, but he had always thought that she was such a square, walking around with her big stomach like a self-satisfied duck, and he would never in his wildest dreams have guessed that she took her female students to bed.

"Not her students," I was offended, "only me, and as a matter of fact, it was me that took her to bed, she didn't even know that she loved women."

Avshalom lay on his back with his hands behind his head, and he said, "You always looked so innocent to me, with your specs and pigtails, who would have believed that at the age of fourteen, when I was squeezing pimples and masturbating, you were having a passionate love affair with our literature teacher."

He asked if what we'd just done had dissolved my fear, and

I said yes, now I knew that I could enjoy being with people of the opposite sex as well. He laughed and brought his face close to mine and we kissed, and afterwards he looked at me seriously and confessed that he sometimes had erotic dreams and fantasies about boys, and he was afraid that he was a homosexual, but it had been so good for him with me that he too felt reassured. I told him that Virginia Woolf had once written that the androgynous soul was the richest soul, and that he should try it once with a boy too, because it was a shame to renounce half of humanity. Avshalom said that he had never thought about it like that, but I was right, anyone capable of loving both men and women had enormous freedom.

At five o'clock in the morning we got dressed and went back to the huts, and a few of the kids who were already up threw out remarks like "Coming back from night field training?" and so on. I expect they're all gossiping about us already. I just had time to shower and change before they took us to the picking. When we were standing on the ladders I told Racheli, and her blue eyes sparkled at me between the branches.

This afternoon I slept for three hours, and now I'm writing to you under "my" palm tree.

What's going to happen with me and Avshalom? I love him, but I'm not "in love" with him. Do you think we could be a couple? And what's going to happen about me and Michaela? I'll have to tell her, I hope she'll be happy for me and she won't be jealous.

Do you think I'll be able to be with both of them? Life's complicated. It's a pity you're not here, I'm sure you'd give me wise advice.

And tomorrow, after picking, we're going home. Pity.

Isn't Avshalom a lovely name? I roll it around in my mouth, Avshalom, Av-sha-lom, Av-shalom.

See you at home, your Kitty

Dearest Anne,

Mother had a surprise waiting for me. I got back from Ashdot-Ya'kov in the evening, all sweaty and untidy (they didn't even let us take a shower after the picking. Lunch, pack, and out), I opened the door, and there sitting on the sofa in the living room was a silver-haired man of about fifty. Mother kissed me and said, "Let me introduce you to David, and this is my eldest, Rivi, back from national service." He stood up, shook my hand, and said, "Pleased to meet you." I noticed immediately that he was tall, much taller than my father who's six feet tall, with broad, powerful shoulders, and a strong, clean-cut face, a bit like Hourgi's, but with two deep lines running from an eagle nose to narrow lips, which turn down at the corners with a slightly bitter expression. He asked what it was like on national service, and if I had already received my first call-up notice, and a few more polite questions, to which I replied politely, but briefly, because I was out on my feet and all I wanted was to shower and go to bed.

In the morning I asked Mother if David was the mysterious Moishele, and she admitted that he was. I asked what he did, and she said that he was the director of some department in the weapons development authority, after having served for years as a high-ranking officer in the standing army, and fighting in the Palmach in the War of Independence. I remembered that afternoon, a few years ago, when I thought that he worked in a bank and looked for him in all the branches in the Center. I wanted to ask if he had left his wife at last, but I didn't ask, because Mother didn't know that I knew that he was married. I only asked if he had any children, and she said that he had twins, a boy and a girl, who were at the university, and had recently left home. She asked how he looked to me and I said, "Okay," and then she said, "How would you feel about him coming to live with us?"

For a moment I was confused. Since when did she care about what I thought, she didn't ask me when she fired Annette, or when she threw out Daddy, so why was she bothering to ask me now? I shrugged my shoulders and said "Okay" again, because I thought that it was her affair and I had no right to interfere, and anyway I want her to be happy, because then she'll be less irritable, and it will be better for all of us. I thought that David would come to live with us sometime in the future, after we got to know him, but Mother surprised me again: it turns out she'd taken leave from work and gone on a cleaning-up spree, sorting out old clothes and all kinds of junk and clearing out the closets to make room for his things, and in the evening he showed up with two huge suitcases and unpacked them, and that's that, from yesterday he's been living with us here.

In honor of the occasion Mother prepared a festive meal, and invited Grandfather too, who got all togged up in checked trousers and a cap to match, and Mother scolded him, "You've dressed up as a clown again."

She laid the table in the dining nook instead of the kitchen, with a tablecloth and the best china, and prepared all kinds of pies and salads, not the omelets with cottage cheese that we usually have for supper, and she even opened a bottle of wine. After we clinked glasses David said that he was sure we would get along well, and announced that he liked the house to be tidy, and since he had heard from Mother that we were quite messy, leaving our shoes in the living room and not always remembering to dry the bathroom floor behind us, he would appreciate it if we made an effort to maintain order, because that way it would be more pleasant for all of us and there wouldn't be any problems. He also said that in a few days the new stereo system he had bought would arrive—he was very fond of listening to classical music and he had a big record collection—and he would like us not to use it, because it was a sensitive and expensive system, and we were liable to damage it. Throughout his lecture Oren and Noam pretended to be listening, but I saw that they were kicking each other under the table and trying not to burst out laughing.

This morning, at school, I told Avshalom that my mother had brought a new father who liked classical music down on our heads, and he was silent for a minute and then said that it was hard to believe that he would be a father to me "for real," and that I should renew relations with my real father. I didn't say anything because I didn't want to get into an argument with him. He's sweet, behaves as if we're a couple, and in boring lessons we stare innocently at the teacher while he slips his hand under my blouse and draws on my back with his finger.

At break, when we were standing in the corridor and laughing at some nonsense, I suddenly saw Michaela, who I hadn't managed to call since I came back from the kibbutz. She came towards us and said, "Hello children, how was it on the kibbutz?" She looked from me to him and back again, and I could see in her eyes that she sensed something. Avshalom turned bright red and said, "It was fun, we picked grapefruit and got up to all kinds of nonsense," and I, no less embarrassed than him, said, "I'm dying to pee, see you at the gate after classes."

After school we met for only a few minutes, because Michaela had to hurry home to free the nanny, and I didn't feel like going back with her to listen to Ido's bawling. So I walked with her to Rocinanta and we talked a bit. She said that she had missed me terribly, and I said that I had too, even though it wasn't completely true. I told her about the new father who had suddenly descended on us, and I said that he seemed a bit of a pompous bore and quite strict, and I was afraid that he was going to impose a military regime on us. Michaela laughed and said that I should give him a chance. And then, making an effort to sound light and amused, she asked, "So what's the story with the boy? What nonsense have you already gotten up to?" I said, "I'll tell you tomorrow, I can't do it on one foot like this," and she said, "Oho, it must have been serious nonsense."

Tomorrow Michaela's not teaching, and Ido will be with her parents, and we arranged for me to come to her place after school. I expect we'll fall on each other, we haven't been together for almost two weeks now, and afterwards I'll have to tell her. I'll say that the relationship with Avshalom doesn't detract from what exists between us, but that alongside our love I need to start living a normal life, like other girls my age. And I'll also tell her that if I have a boyfriend it will reassure my mother, and we'll be able to go on meeting without arousing her suspicions. Michaela loves me so much that I'm sure she'll understand, and she'll even be happy for me.

So Mother has David and I have Avshalom; do you think that peace and tranquility will now descend on our home?

Yours as always, Kitty

Dearest Anne,

I'm writing to you quickly sitting on the rock under my and Michaela's pine tree, and when I'm finished I'll have to hide the notebooks and part from you perhaps forever, so the style won't be great and the handwriting will be crooked and forgive me. I can hardly organize my thoughts and understand how everything exploded in our faces, my stomach is still hurting and my heart is beating like crazy and I feel like vomiting. So what happened is that this morning in the English lesson the school secretary Bruria came in and told me to go to Hourgi's office. I made a face at Avshalom to say, "I haven't got a clue what they want from my life," and went with her, and I didn't guess what was waiting for me. In Hourgi's room my mother was sitting with a fallen face, as if she had suddenly aged by ten years, and Mrs. Hardona the deputy headmistress. On the desk in front of Hourgi's eyes, you'll never believe it, was the album of the nude pictures we took last summer on the beach, open at the one of the two of us cheek to cheek, and in the middle of the desk the three previous diary notebooks (this one was in my schoolbag in the classroom). All the blood left my body, and my knees began to tremble, Marie Antoinette must have felt like this on her way to the guillotine. Presumably in the framework of the house-

257

keeping spree my mother had embarked on in honor of the fact that David had finally decided to leave his wife, she had decided this morning to tidy my drawers too, and discovered the photograph album. She must have had a fit on the spot and conducted a thorough search to find additional evidence, and found the notebooks too, hidden on top of the closet, among my winter clothes. Actually it probably happened the other way around, she must have started tidying the closet, taken down the winter clothes, found the notebooks, and then continued the search and discovered the album too. What's certain is that she read the notebooks, and now she knows, the suspicions she had harbored long ago had been proven correct, and with all this booty she came rushing to Hourgi—without even thinking of talking to me first—and the three of them sat here and read my most private secrets, which were meant only for your ears, and in a minute they were going to interrogate me and try to get a confession of guilt out of me.

Hourgi said, "Please sit down, Rivka," without raising his eyes from the photograph, and I sat down carefully on the edge of the chair, and I felt like asking if he liked my tits that were spread out in front of his eyes on the desk, or if he perhaps preferred Michaela's. Mother lit a cigarette with trembling fingers and raised her head to look at me, and in her eyes I saw fear and confusion and helplessness—she couldn't understand how she had given birth to such a wild savage, a pervert and a traitor and a liar—and suddenly I felt sorry for her. Mrs. Hardona mobilized her friendliest voice and said that I needn't worry, all I had to do was to tell them exactly what had happened and what Michaela had done to me, and nothing would happen to me. They knew that I was a good girl and a good student, and before they had recalled the beautiful and moving essay about Anne Frank that I had read to the whole school a few years ago at the Holocaust Day Memorial Ceremony, and it was a great shame that I had chosen to use her sacred memory in order to write such things, but she understood that I didn't have anyone to tell, and now I could tell them. I was silent, only my brain was racing at the speed of light, what to say, how was I going to get out of it, I remembered the oath I had sworn to myself at the beginning of our love affair, that I would never, never betray her, and I knew that I had to do everything in my power to protect her.

Hourgi said that from what he saw in front of him it was obvious that I had fallen victim to a sexual pervert, and he was very interested in hearing the sequence of events, and if Michaela's husband too had been involved, because it seemed clear that the picture of the two of us together had been taken by a third person, and it was important to him to know if her husband too had exploited me sexually. I looked him straight in the eyes and said quietly, that I had taken the photograph myself, and that Yoel had nothing to do with it. Michaela and I were good friends, we had gone to the beach to sunbathe. We had taken a few artistic photographs, an homage to Picasso's "Women on the Beach," but she had never exploited me. Hourgi narrowed his eyes in disbelief and said aggressively that from what he had managed to read in the notebooks, he understood that sexual relations had taken place between us, and even if I had consented to them—as far as Michaela was concerned it was a criminal offense, since I was a minor and she was a teacher in authority over me, who was supposed to act as a role model. His face turned the color of borscht from all the blood going to his head, and the veins on his neck swelled, and he banged his fist on the desk and yelled that he would do everything he could to make sure that this pervert rotted behind bars, and that he personally would see to it that she never taught again in any educational institution in the State of Israel, because it was intolerable that she should cast a stain on his school and turn it into Sodom and Gemorrah.

I was silent, but the words that I wanted to shout out loud burned inside me, don't dare touch my love, what gives you the right to judge her, the only person who cared about what happened to me, the only one who saw me as I really was, and wanted to hear me and embrace me and gather up my pain and dry my tears, the only person who believed in me and told me that I was beautiful and clever and gifted, apart from her nobody pissed in my direction, not my father and not you either, Mother, always busy with yourself and your Moishele, and this school, which is nothing but a factory for turning out high marks—except for Michaela, and maybe Benjamin Keinan, there isn't a single teacher you can talk to here—so now you want to rob me of the poor man's lamb, to punish Michaela for the love that saved my life, don't you know that love is sexless and ageless and pure and holy, a gift from God like life itself, so how can it possibly be regarded as a crime?

I restrained myself from shouting all these things, because I knew that they would interpret them as a confession, and it would only hurt Michaela. I don't know how I kept cool enough to say to them quietly that everything I had written in the notebooks was fiction, I was practicing to be a writer and I made things up, in the first place I was writing to Anne Frank who had died long ago, and my name wasn't really Kitty, and that was what I would say to the police too, Michaela and I were good friends, and all the rest was the product of my fertile imagination, she was a married woman and they had recently brought a child into the world, and I had a boyfriend too, Avshalom from my class, and anyway, I thought it was a cheek to pry into other people's notebooks without asking permission, "and if you don't mind" I said, measuring the distance between myself and the notebooks, "I'll take them back now." And then, with the leap of a football goalie, I jumped for the notebooks and snatched them from the desk. The album was too far, it remained open in front of Hourgi's eyes, let him enjoy himself. I left the room and fled for my life, first I ran to the classroom and grabbed my bag, ignoring the startled looks of Mister Jacobs and all the others, including Avshalom, and raced out of the gate and went on running up Wedgewood Street without looking back, and crossed the road against the red light at the Center and was almost run over, and with a wildly beating heart I went on running through the Manya Shochat park and down Hatzvi Avenue, and with the last of my strength I climbed Michaela's stairs and rang the bell. I knew that she was at home because I was supposed to come around to her place after school, and I heard Dulcinea barking behind the door, and Michaela opened it with her radiant smile, and Dulcinea jumped on me as usual and wet my face with her tongue, and panting and gasping for breath I hugged Michaela and said, "We've been found out, Mishi, we'd better get out of here because they'll be coming to look for us soon," and Michaela didn't ask any questions and took her bag and Rocinanta's keys and we hurried out, leaving Dulcinea at home, scratching the door with her paws and whining in insult.

Rocinanta climbed the slopes of the Carmel, and on the way I told Michaela everything that had happened in the principal's office. She listened in silence and said, "They won't leave us alone now, we're a body blow, a punch in their belly, actually not us, only me, they'll fight me like a cancer, and from their point of view they're right, what exists between us goes against all their values, education, morality, common sense, for them we're not the Little Prince and the fox, not the mountain and the sea, and not kiddo and Mishi, who love each other terribly, but a teacher and her pupil. A certain Rivka Shenhar, a certain Michaela Berg, will they please stick to the rules. No, they can't afford to let such things happen."

We had almost reached Beit Oren, and Rocinanta turned off the road and stopped on the verge of the wadi. The entire Carmel range spread out at our feet, all the way to the sea, and Michaela took a deep breath and asked quietly, "What do you say, kiddo, should I start the engine now and step on the gas?"

A strange happiness seized hold of me. I imagined Rocinanta charging forward and hovering in the air for a moment, like Pegasus the winged horse, and then tumbling into the chasm in slow motion, turning over and over, until she landed on her back at the foot of the mountain, with the two of us inside her hand in hand for all eternity, and a great fire flares up and consumes our bodies in a glorious annihilating blaze. Yes, that might be quite a good solution, that would spare me having to go home and face my mother and that David of hers, who probably knows everything by now. After all, you were finished at the age of sixteen too, and up to then you succeeded in living a rich life, because your soul was rich, and you left a giant light behind you, and if I open the car door and leave my bag here, they'll find the notebooks and know that once upon a time, in the seventies, in Haifa, there was a girl who wrote and loved, I'll never know another great love like this one, and I've even managed to know a man, I won't die a virgin.

"You can't do it," I suddenly realized, "you have Ido."

Michaela nodded slowly, her gaze fixed far on the horizon, at the end of the sea.

"I won't let them hurt you," I hugged her, and the tears I had succeeded in suppressing up to now burst into my eyes, "I'll hide the notebooks and lie to the police like I lied to them on the beach at Atlit, and I'm sure that Racheli won't say anything either if they question her. They won't have any proof."

"It won't help," said Michaela, "they know the truth. I'll paint my face and wait for them at the window like Jezebel, and they'll come and take me, and I'll tell Hourgi that I intended to resign in any case, because my husband is going to work in New York and I'm going with him, and it would be better for him to let me go quietly, because if it gets into the papers it will spoil the reputation of his school."

"So that's it, you'll go away and we won't meet again?" My wet face sank into the hollow of her neck, my body shook with sobs, "after you conceived me anew and gave birth to me and brought me up, how can I not see you, not talk to you, not embrace you," and Michaela stroked my hair and whispered, "We'll write to each other and talk on the phone, and in a few years time you'll come to New York to visit me, and in the meantime you'll go on growing and learning and writing. It seems to me that I'm leaving you in good hands."

I raised my head and looked at her in surprise, how had she already guessed, and Michaela dried my tears with her thumbs and kissed my damp eyelids. "I love you as I've never loved anyone in my life," she whispered into my eyes, "and I'll take you with me always, everywhere, you and your beautiful eyes and your huge love."

We sat locked in an embrace, burrowing into each other in one last moment of consolation, of a smell as familiar as home. And then I said that in any case we should find a good hiding place for the notebooks, and Michaela remembered the warren under our pine tree in the wadi next to her house, which Dulcinea liked poking her nose into, sniffing the vestiges of the scent of the rabbits.

Michaela started the engine and drove rapidly in reverse, and we reached the road and slid down the mountainside in silence. I looked for the last time at the fields, the forest, at the scraps of sea between the curves of the mountain. Rocinanta stopped in Nitzanim Street, and we kissed for a long time, without worrying about whether anyone was watching, and Michaela squeezed my hand hard and said, "See you, my kiddo, be brave, we'll talk."

I saw her striding erect up the hill to her house to greet her persecutors, her bronze ponytail challenging the sun.

And it's not only Michaela I'm parting from now, but you too, and myself as Kitty, and the notebooks I've been writing and loving and laughing and crying and dreaming in for two and half years already, and this parting too rends my heart, but it's too dangerous, you'll have to go into hiding, I don't know for how long, but I promise that I'll come to rescue you when I can.

I found a white plastic bag with the logo "Rauch Haberdashery" in a garbage can outside one of the houses, and now I'll put the notebooks into it, and secure it with the rubber band I took off my braid, and pray that it will protect you from rodents and insects and rain.

> So that's it, my dearest Anne, my confidante, my faithful ally, a last farewell from she who will remember you always, Kitty

Dearest Anne,

Here I am writing to you again, ten months after I hid you away. I came to visit you, because I have a lot to tell you, and also because I wanted to check and see how the notebooks had survived the winter and the summer. After I finish writing this I'll wrap them in a few more plastic bags that I brought with me, and secure each of them with a rubber band, just to be on the safe side, and put you back in your hiding place.

Two weeks ago I came back from my first trip abroad! Mother is so pleased about my relationship with Avshalom (which proves to her that I'm "normal" in spite of everything . . .), and the way we studied together for our matric exams (in math, language, and civics), that she put us down together for an organized youth trip—"Classical Europe in Thirty Days." There were about forty kids from all over the country, with our guide Doron. We started in London, which I will always remember as my first "abroad," no longer the kitschy description of the advertising brochures, nor a literary fantasy, but a real, three-dimensional place, where the light has a color of its own, a kind of gray, and where the air has special smells, and its cool touch on your skin is different too.

From London we traveled by bus and ferry to France, to Paris, which is far more beautiful than in books and films, almost too beautiful, and from there to Amsterdam! I walked down the streets you rode down on your bicycle, under the magnificent tall chestnut trees, I breathed in the smell of the canals, with which you too filled your lungs almost forty years ago, and I was beside myself. We visited your hiding place, which is different from how I imagined it from your diary, lighter and smaller, especially the room you shared with Dr. Dussel the dentist, whose real name was Fritz Pfeffer. Hard to believe that you lived together for two years in such a small room. The furniture has been removed from the rooms, but the pictures of the movie stars with which you decorated the wall over your bed—some of whom, like Greta Garbo and Ginger Rogers, I knew from old movies I'd seen on television, and others, like Norma Shearer and Ray Milland, I'd heard about from Mother—are still there, just as you stuck them up with your own hands. And the same goes for the photograph of the blond girl in the white dress, her hands folded in her lap and her gaze serious above her smile (today she's the Queen of England), and under it the picture of her younger sister, she too in a white dress, and the pictures of the angelic blond children, and the pictures of the landscapes you longed for so much, and the postcard with the self-portrait of Leonardo da Vinci, and the head of Michaelangelo's "David," and the head of Jesus from the "Pieta" that you cut out of the newspaper.

Your real diary in the red-and-white checked cover with the lock that broke in the meantime, your private hiding place inside the hiding place, the holy of holies, is displayed for all to see in a glass case in one of the rooms; and in a big glass cupboard there are copies of the book in all the languages of the world.

No one in the group, apart from Avshalom, could have known how thrilled I was by this visit. After they all left and went to do their shopping in some department store, we started the tour again from the beginning, just the two of us, in silence. When we reached Peter's cubby hole, I asked Avshalom to climb up the ladder with me to the attic, where you liked to stand at the little window overlooking the top of the chestnut tree, and where you kissed for the first time. There was a sign on the ladder warning people in red letters, in Dutch and English, not to climb the ladder, but nobody took any notice, and we sneaked quickly up the rungs.

We stood next to your attic window and looked at the chestnut tree, whose fresh green leaves swayed slightly in the wind and danced in the sun, and I took Avshalom's handsome face in my hands and brought it to mine, and so we stood there—for a long moment, longer than the siren on Holocaust Memorial Day—and kissed with our eyes closed in memory of you both, in memory of your first kiss, in memory of your love that flourished for a single summer and withered like a leaf.

When we left the building we passed the Westerkerk church whose tower is crowned with a gold dome topped by a cross, and we heard the pealing of the bell, which for two years sliced up the endless time into quarter hours for you. We walked hand in hand along the canal until we discovered a little cafe with tempting cakes in the window. We ordered tea and raspberry cake, and settled down to write letters. Avshalom scribbled postcards to his mother and a few friends, and I wrote an air-mail card to Michaela in New York.

Yes, two and a half months after we were caught, Michaela left, with Yoel and Ido. In the weeks before the flight she wanted us to meet, she would phone me in the early afternoon when she knew my mother wasn't at home, and say that she had to see me, to talk to me, but I told her that it would be better for both of us not to see other again, that it was too dangerous. Sometimes, when I emerged from the school gate, I saw Rocinanta lying in wait for me further up the hill, and I took another way home, without looking back.

In the clarification to which Hourgi summoned Michaela, she informed him that she intended resigning anyway, because she was going to New York with her husband. Since I had lied to him that I had burned the notebooks, and declared that I would never give evidence against her, and Racheli too, who was also summoned to his office, vowed that she didn't know anything, he had no material proof, and he decided not to lodge a complaint with the police, but he warned Michaela that if he ever saw her face within the radius of a kilometer from the school, he would go to court and get an injunction to prevent her from leaving the country. And nevertheless she refused to be careful and one day she waited for me right next to the school gate, but luckily for her nobody saw her. We drove down to Panorama Street and sat on a bench in Allenby Park, and Michaela wept and said that I was cruel and that she was cut up inside with longing for me day after day and night after night, and I didn't even care. I cried too (tears were always our strong point), and told her that I wasn't cruel, that I loved her and missed her, but that she had to return to her life and let me lead mine. I told her that the rumors had somehow reached the kids in my class, and in other classes too, and apart from Avshalom and Racheli nobody would speak to me, and sometimes, when I walked down the corridor or crossed the yard, someone would hiss, "Here comes the lesbian." (Once someone from the other twelfth grade said it when Avshalom was standing next to me, and Avshalom looked him in the eye and said quietly, "She isn't a lesbian, she's my girlfriend, and if I hear it one more time, your life won't be worth living." I was so proud of him, at that moment I really loved him. Since then they've stopped bothering me, but they still treat me as if I'm not there.) When I walk down the street too, it seems to me that the rumor has spread, and that everybody is staring at me with a mixture of curiosity and revulsion; Greenberg from the sweet shop and Max from the stationer's and Shein from the grocery and Bella Blum from the post office and Leon from the florist, and also in the pharmacy and the newspaper stand. Michaela listened and bit her lower lip, and said that she too felt the stares and heard the whispers, and that all their friends, except for Osnat, had stopped calling. She promised that she would stop following me, and said that she wanted to invite me and Avshalom, and also Racheli—who ever since her Daniel had sailed for Greece, is quite down in the dumps—to a fondue party in honor of my sixteenth birthday.

On Friday evening the three of us went around there.

Michaela had prepared a cheese fondue in a special saucepan, bubbling on a little flame in the middle of the table. We stuck long forks with wooden handles into cubes of toasted bread and dipped them into the melted cheese, drank wine, and Michaela made an effort to breathe life into the conversation and asked us questions about school. Yoel was silent most of the time and looked bored, and picked his teeth with the prong of the fondue fork, but after a while there was a call from the hospital, and he left, and I relaxed. Michaela promised me that he didn't know anything, not even about her meeting with Hourgi, he thought she had resigned to finish her Master's at last before they left, but I had never felt comfortable in his presence anyway. The dessert—pieces of fruit dipped in hot chocolate—we ate in the living room. We were already quite drunk, and Avshalom made us laugh with his imitations of Hourgi, Begin, and Sadat, and then Michaela put on a record of dance music and we danced the waltz and tango and foxtrot, me with Avshalom and Michaela with Racheli, and then Michaela with Avshalom and me with Racheli, and finally Avshalom with Racheli and me with Michaela, who pressed me to her and looked deep into my eyes, as if she were searching for something she had lost. And then Ido began to bawl, and Michaela went to his room and brought him to the living room and warmed him a bottle of milk, but he didn't want it and he didn't calm down, and it was already late and we had to leave. I kissed her on the cheek, and she stood in the doorway and looked after us as we went down the stairs, keeping the light on for us, and I felt a little heart-sore at leaving her like that, alone with the screaming baby in her arms, and with all the dishes and the mess.

A day before they flew to America I came to say goodbye to her, and we went to bed for the last time, among the half-packed suitcases lying open on the floor. Our bodies delighted in each other like two silly puppies meeting again and not knowing that they were about to be separated forever. But after it was over we sat on the bed with our arms around each other and wept bitterly.

I hugged Dulcinea too, and kissed her on the nose, and whispered all kinds of nonsense in my terrible English, I told her she was going to turn into a New York bitch, and Michaela laughed amidst her tears.

During their first months in New York Michaela was busy organizing their apartment, which overlooked Central Park, and running around with Ido to specialist doctors, trying to find someone who would tell her why he never stopped crying and never smiled at her, or looked into her eyes, or held out his hand to touch her face, or reacted when they called him by his name. In the end she reached some professor who told her that he recognized autistic traits in Ido, but since he was only a little over one year old, it was hard to say how severe the autism would prove to be. When I read her letter I felt my heart falling and falling, because I knew that Ido was the spoiled fruit of our love, a love that was too strong and too strange, which perhaps should never have happened.

Michaela wrote that it was a good thing they were living in New York, which had one of the most advanced centers in the word for treating autism, and she had already taken Ido there and they had told her that they could help him. The center has a nursery, and she leaves him there for a few hours a day, and this month she had started teaching Hebrew in some college in New Jersey. Having this job saves her, without it she would go out of her mind.

I think about her a lot, but I have to confess that I'm relieved that she's gone. Mother and I try to be nice to each other and walk "on eggshells." We said no more about what had happened, as if we had buried the whole thing, but I know that my treachery has erected a wall of armored glass between us, which may remain there forever. I've grown used somehow to her David. Now meals have to be strictly on time, breakfast at seven, lunch at one, supper at seven again. On Saturdays he rises from his siesta at four zero-zero, opens a small packet of halva and cuts it into small neat cubes, arranges them in two straight rows on a plate, surveys them for a moment with satisfaction, maybe he's waiting for them to salute him, and then he sucks them with his coffee, suck-sip-suck-sip, smacking his lips. When Oren and Noam forget their shoes in the living room, he hides them, and the boys have to plead with him to get them back. He quarrels with them over nonsense, especially over Mother, her time and her attention, as if he were a child himself. But I suffer him in silence, because she's much more tranquil now. I like to see her face shine when he comes back from work, and how they sit and watch television in the evenings with David's arm around her shoulders, like a couple of high-school kids at the movies. (One night I even heard her moans behind the closed door, and I smiled to myself.) And at the same time the two real high-school students shut themselves up in my room, study together, listen to music, and make love very quietly (I'm sure Mother knows, and that she's glad). Sometimes Avshalom and I smoke a joint, and if anyone knocks on the door we make haste to sweep the smoke out of the window with our hands. On the last evening in Amsterdam too, which was a free evening, and everyone was walking around the street of the red windows and pointing at the prostitutes as if they were monkeys in the zoo and snickering like idiots, Avshalom and I went into some "coffee shop" and smoked and laughed until our stomachs hurt, and in the morning we couldn't remember why.

From Amsterdam we went by bus to Germany, to Munich. We were taken on a tour of the Dachau concentration camp, and while we were walking along the high barbed wire fence, dumb with dread, only our shoes squeaking on the gravel, I tried to imagine you in a place like this, terribly thin and bald, lying in striped pajamas on one of the narrow bunks, and I couldn't. I said to Avshalom that even though the Holocaust had concluded only eighteen years before I was born, I would never succeed in understanding that pure evil, and Avshalom said that the evil existed in every one of us, like a sleeping viper, and we had to be on our guard all the time not to let it raise its head.

One evening they took us to a traditional Munich beer cellar of the kind that the Nazis liked getting drunk in and where Hitler at the beginning of his career had made speeches to them. On both sides of the long wooden tables sat drunk, red-faced Germans, talking and laughing loudly, and we tried to guess which of them were ex-Nazis. Every man and woman over the age of sixty seemed suspicious to us. After two beers I had to pee. I went to the toilets and entered one of the cubicles. Apparently I should have paid the elderly woman in the gray tunic sitting at the entrance, because she banged on my door with her fist and yelled "Raus," and other words, which I didn't understand but which sounded nasty. Her language was completely different from Michaela's honeyed German. I squatted over the toilet bowl with my pants down and the pee froze in my body with fear. I had no doubt that she had once been a concentration camp guard and yelled at the Jewish prisoners like this to get out of their huts. I whispered, "One moment please," and squeezed the pee out somehow and rushed out without looking at her, dropping a few coins in the plate on her table at the entrance.

The kids in the group developed a national sport in Munich, stealing from the department stores. They said they had it coming, after everything they'd done to us, and invented all kinds of clever methods. A few of them even succeeded in stealing Adidas running shoes! I didn't steal anything, not because I'm such a saint, I've actually helped myself to a bar of chocolate in our supermarket in the Center on more than one occasion—but because no theft, not even of a thousand department stores, could possibly make up for their crimes. Only time will cover the past with another layer of life.

Now I want to tell you something terribly sad, which I put off to the end on purpose. The week after we came back from Europe, on the 19th of this month, your father died. I heard about it by chance the day after it happened. Racheli and I hitched a lift back from the beach, I was sitting next to the driver and Racheli was in the back. The radio was on the news, and at the end the newscaster said, "Otto Frank, the father of Anne Frank, passed away yesterday at his home in Basle, at the age of ninety-one." I froze. My skin broke out in goose pimples and I couldn't breathe. The first thought that crossed my mind was, I have to take the notebooks out of their hiding place and write to you, to tell you, but suddenly I knew that before that there was something else I had to do. That same evening I called my father. His wife Batya answered the phone. My heart beat like crazy, but I tried to keep my voice from shaking when I said, "Hello, this is Rivi, I wanted to ask if I could come to visit you and see the baby." Batya sounded surprised and she said, "Yes, of course, why not, come whenever you like," and then she said, "Orly isn't such a baby anymore, she's already two and a half." I said, "Yes, I know," even though somehow I imagined her as being a little baby still, as if time had stopped for her on my account when she was born—and quickly, before Batya could change her mind, I said, "Okay then, I'll come tomorrow," and we arranged for me to go there at six in the evening.

I didn't tell a soul, definitely not my mother, not even Avshalom, who has been trying for months to persuade me to make contact with them. I took the Carmel underground to Massada Street, and climbed the steps to Hillel Street. When I reached their door with the olive wood sign saying, "Batya and Yehuda Shenhar," my throat dried up completely and my palms started to sweat. I knocked softly, in case the baby was sleeping, but nobody opened, and then I rang the bell. There was a shout, "Just a minute," and after a while the door opened. Batya was standing there in a floral tunic, looking older and fatter than the last time I'd seen her on that boat trip in the summer of four years ago, and it seemed to me as if she were pregnant again. Little Orly was standing behind her, hugging her leg and peeking at me. There were red stains around her mouth from candy or jam. Her eyes are brown, not like mine at all, and her hair is brown and thin too, like Batya's. Only later, when I played with her, I saw that her smile is like mine, with a dimple in exactly the same place.

I was surprised to see that their house was completely normal—a sofa upholstered in dark brown velvet, a low coffee table, two armchairs, an orange rug, a television set, a bookcase, macramé work on the walls—as if I had expected that someone who had turned into an android would live in some enchanted castle, like in the movie *The Young Frankenstein*. I sat down on the sofa and Batya offered me coffee, and brought cookies too. She sat down on the armchair opposite me and said, "Your father should be back any minute now. He has a meeting at the university." I dipped a cookie in the coffee and nibbled it, because I didn't know what to say. She asked me what class I was in and if I was still going to the scouts. After that she asked how Oren and Noam were doing, and said that it was already two weeks since she'd seen them. I said, "They stayed with you when Mother and David went to Hawaii, didn't they?" Suddenly I felt the need to mention my mother and also David to her, so she would know that Mother wasn't alone and miserable, but that she had a boyfriend with whom she traveled all over the world and had a wonderful time. After that I said that I too had returned a few days ago from Europe, and told her a bit about the trip. Orly played with her Lego on the carpet and ignored me. I said, "She's adorable," and I sat down next to her and started helping her build. Batya said, "I see that the two of you are getting along just fine, so I'll go back to the kitchen, I have something on the stove."

Orly didn't speak or look at me, and for a moment I was afraid that she was autistic too, or deaf in both ears, but gradually she began to hand me Lego blocks and smile at me. She asked, "What's your name?" I said, "Rivi, I'm your big sister, say Rivi, Ri-vi," and she said "Ivi."

I built her a big bright house, with a tiled roof and a green door, and two pink windows with flower boxes, where she could grow petunias or geraniums or marijuana. All the time I was dying to wipe the red stains off her mouth, so I licked my thumbs and tried to wipe them off. I rubbed really hard and even scratched a bit with my nail, until her eyes filled with tears, but the stains were too sticky, and they wouldn't come off. When my father arrived he looked really surprised to see me, but Batya came out of the kitchen, her hands in a towel, and said, "I told you yesterday that Rivi was coming, didn't I?" And he said, "Yes, yes," and came up to me and put his cheek to mine, and his smell was like it used to be, a mixture of sweat and gasoline. Orly held out her little hands and called Daddy daddy er-plane, and he smiled and raised her high in the air, and swung her backwards and forwards, and said, aer-o-plane, like he used to do to me when I was small, and afterwards to Oren and Noam—and Orly laughed and screamed, more, more, more er-plane, and he did it again and again, and I thought that he was gaining time, because he knew that soon he would have to talk to me. In the end he put her down on the carpet and sat on the armchair and asked, "How are you," and I said, "all right," and asked how the meeting at the university had gone. He waved his hand dismissively and said, "It's all a mystery," and I asked if he had already been made a senior lecturer and given tenure, because I remembered that before the divorce they used to argue about it; Mother said that he didn't promote himself and didn't publish enough, and then too he said that it didn't depend on him, that it was all intrigues. Daddy said that he had received tenure and that in two or three years time he hoped to be made a professor. After that I asked about Grandma and Grandpa, and Uncle Itzik and Sima and their children. He said that they were all more or less okay, and suggested that I come with him one day to visit Grandma and Grandpa. They always asked about me and they would be happy to see me. After that he asked if I still went to the scouts, and I felt like asking him, what is it with you people and the scouts, I haven't been in the scouts for three years already, you'll never in your lives guess the things that have happened to me since I left the scouts, but I only said that I wasn't in the scouts anymore. I told him that with the encouragement of our homeroom teacher,

Benjamin Keinan, I had started going with my boyfriend Avshalom to meetings of Jewish and Arab youth at Beit Hagefen. I didn't tell him that Mother had objected, and even threatened to call the recruiting center and tell them that Avshalom and I were fraternizing with the enemy, so that they wouldn't put us in sensitive positions in the army. One evening Nizar, an Arab member of the group, came around to our house to prepare a meeting with me, and Mother opened the door to my room and asked him if it was the custom with them for a boy and a girl to sit shut up in a room together, and if his father allowed his sister to "go out with boys on her own." Nizar said that his father was a school principal, a liberal and enlightened man, and that he allowed his sister to go out with whoever she liked, because he trusted her. Mother said that with all due respect to liberalism, she would like us to leave the door open. At midnight she put the television on full volume for the national anthem, so the enemy would understand that he was a guest in a home full of national pride, and Nizar and I burst out laughing.

Daddy asked if I had received my first call-up notice, and I said yes, and told him a little about the interview at the recruiting center. After that silence fell, and I tried to think of something else to tell him. I wanted to ask him if now, when he came to see Oren and Noam, he would speak to me too, but I didn't. Batya, who apparently heard the conversation drying up from the kitchen, came out and said, "You know that Rivi came home from a trip to Europe a few days ago?" Daddy said, "Very good, very good," as if he were giving me marks for a test, and I told him that I had visited Dachau, and your hiding place too, and suddenly, I don't know why, I said, "You know, Anne Frank's father died the day before yesterday," and he said, "Really? He must have been very old," and I said, "Yes, ninety-one." Afterwards I told him that in Paris we had visited the Bastille, where Jean Valjean had been imprisoned, and I felt like asking him if he remembered how he had once beaten me violently when I wanted to be the Mapainik Marie Antoinette of the cats, but I restrained myself, and asked him if he still took part in chess tournaments. He said no, he only played occasionally, when he had a opponent, and he asked me if I knew how to play, and I said, "Of course, you taught me when I was four, don't you remember?" And I thought that he couldn't possibly have forgotten how he had saved me from the scorpion—and Daddy looked embarrassed and said, "Yes, yes."

I asked myself if Batya was going to invite me to have supper with them, but she only went in and out of the kitchen again and again, and it seemed to me that she was waiting for me to leave, so I stood up and said, "I have to go, Mother's expecting me for supper," and I kissed my sister on her head, and Daddy and Batya saw me to the door, and Batya said, "You're welcome to come again," and I said, "Thank you," and Daddy put his cheek to mine and murmured, "Come, come."

And I didn't go home but to Avshalom's, and his mother opened the door and gave me a welcoming smile, as usual, and I went into his room and he was lying on the carpet with his eyes closed listening to "The Wall" by Pink Floyd, and I lay down next to him and lay my head on his chest, and sniffled into his neck, "He isn't an android at all, he simply started a new life with his new wife and his new child, and left me behind," and Avshalom didn't say anything, only stroked my hair slowly.

Soon I'll pack the four notebooks up in the plastic bag from the "Rauch Haberdashery" and secure it with a rubber band, and wrap it up in the plastic bags I brought with me, and return the package to its hiding place and cover it with a lot of earth, in order to keep you safe for as long as necessary, and so that the words won't burst out suddenly like a geyser and set the Carmel on fire. Then I'll walk up Hatzvi Avenue under the canopy of pines, and go past her house, with the honeysuckle twining around the bars of the gate and the geranium planters on the railings of the stairs—and I'll continue on my own. That's it. I don't want to hide behind Kitty anymore. Kitty will rest under the pine, and I, Rivi Shenhar, will go on from here on my own.

■

And the end too must be written. And I take up my pen, which was never so heavy, and continue:

In the autumn of 1988 I parted from Yigal, my much older lover who decided to break off our two-year affair—after his wife found the receipt for the air tickets to Spain and he, already overburdened with guilt, confessed everything. I decided to fly to you like someone fleeing to a sanctuary, and Yigal insisted on driving me to the airport.

You were waiting for me early in the morning at the Kennedy airport, with a bunch of flowers and a smile, and after a long embrace—again your body, your smell, the touch of your cheek—we dragged my luggage to your car, a shiny white Chevrolet. I asked you what you called it, and you laughed, "Automobile. It's hard to give a name to a car without a personality." On the way to Manhattan you said that Yoel had gone to work at a hospital in Chicago for two weeks, and I felt relieved. I knew I wouldn't be comfortable staying with them for ten days with Yoel and Ido. Ido was at his special school till four, and then in his room, watching cartoons. It's as if his time is frozen, I thought, as if nine years haven't passed since he was a baby in a Moses basket and you set him down in front of the television so that we could go to bed and sink into each other. I knew that this time we wouldn't go to bed. My body wasn't weaned from Yigal yet, and our love had already receded into the distance and shrunk in size, like the view from the back window of a car.

On the other side of the river the emerging skyline of Manhattan came into view, and for the first time I felt the joy of travel awakening in me. I still didn't know how deceptive this city is. In the distance it looks like a postcard stretched to fill your field of vision precisely. Even when you look down at it from a height it seems as if it can be contained in one look around—the sea, the river, the huge bridges, the towers with their tiny embrasures and the yellow metal insects scurrying between them—but after a short journey into its innards, or a minute long descent in the elevator, it is already towering high above you and swallowing the sun. Forcing you to feel alternately like God or an ant.

We drove along Central Park West, and I exclaimed admiringly at the foliage shot with red and gold by autumn. You suggested that we take my luggage up to your apartment, have breakfast, and then go for a walk in the park with Nana, the Cocker Spaniel puppy you adopted after Dulcinea died of old age. (Did you name her after the nanny-dog in Peter Pan? I never asked you.)

The doorman hurried to open the glass door for us and took the suitcases to the elevator that had a sphinx etched on its gilded doors, cut in half down the middle.

When you opened the heavy wooden door at the end of the passage a smiling black dog jumped onto you wildly wagging its tail and almost pulled your dress off. You went into the kitchen, to switch on the coffee machine, and I wandered through the rooms, becoming acquainted with the face of your new home, its smell and character, my eyes seeking the old furniture and pictures from Hatzvi Avenue. Max Liebermann's painting of the nurse and child caught my eye at once, glowing in green and white above the sofa. The carpet with its black-and-red diamond shapes, our first bed, now lay in your study, at the foot of the *secretaire* you bought in the flea market in Paris the year you were with Phillip. On top of the *secretaire*, in a bamboo frame, stood an old photograph I had never seen: a fair-haired baby holding onto a table with his hands and staring into space with his mouth open, a cardboard clown's hat on his head, in front of him a decorated chocolate cake with a candle stuck in the middle, and you and Yoel blowing out the candle on either side of his head. Your appearance then struck me with a blow of memory and surprise—so young and slender, in your lilac-colored dress with the little flower pattern. At the edge of the picture, on the pale sofa, Dulcinea's chestnut tail. I quickly worked out the date: Ido was born on the second of April in 1979, a date I shall never forget; in other words the picture was taken in the spring of 1980, two months after you arrived in New York, a small family making an effort to celebrate, father, mother, and a child whose blue eyes are blank.

Later on we sat on a bench in Central Park, under a maple tree whose golden leaves spun in the wind and landed at our feet, and I cried to you about breaking up with Yigal. Nana embarked on an enthusiastic sniffing dance with a charming Golden Retriever, while a bare-chested young man on a skateboard and a Barbie doll in a tracksuit plugged into a Walkman passed before our eyes. A thin man in a gray suit handed out leaflets showing the solid picture of George Bush senior, and the smiling face of Dukakis in tricot stretched over a blond girl's big breasts.

"I adopted you long ago as a mother substitute, and I adopted Yigal as a father substitute," I reflected aloud, and you smiled behind the cigarette smoke and said, "You should introduce us one day, maybe we'll get married and bring you up together as a substitute daughter."

Right, I thought, you both have only sons, and me.

"I'm not sure he'd like it," I said, and remembered how two years ago, in a restaurant in Florence, emboldened by the wine, I told him our story, and from moment to moment his face grew grimmer. I was surprised: other men with whom I had shared our secret were aroused and curious about the sex—what did we do, how did we do it, how much did we do it—but Yigal said that you were depraved, and that if anyone, a teacher or any other adult, had done something like that to his son, he would smash his face in.

I defended you with all my heart. I said that at the age of fourteen I was already a grown person with a adult mind, and I repeated what I had said to myself for years, that I fell in love with you with a love so tremendous that it swept you in like a river. My love was like a force of nature. It didn't leave you any freedom of choice.

"Actually," I told him, "I started with her. She had just gotten married, it didn't even occur to her. It's a fact that she had never had an affair with a girl student, before or after, or with any other woman. She isn't a lesbian at all, it hit us both like a bolt of lightning. We were a private and unique case of love."

"Romantic adolescent bullshit," he said contemptuously, "she was an adult in authority over children, and she took advantage of her power to satisfy the instincts that her husband was apparently incapable of satisfying, and wrapped it up for you in pink cellophane, and that's all there is to it."

"Why do you think that she didn't fall in love with me?" I protested. "You yourself fell in love with me. It's exactly the same me, except that then I was a little younger. You see me as a victim, as her object, but she didn't see me as an object, and I too can see myself only as a subject. The choice was mine, and I made it with all my heart."

I tried to convince him that no harm had been done to me, on the contrary, when our relationship started, I was a shy, bespectacled ugly duckling, and within the space of two years I turned in your hands into a swan full of pride, confident of my ability to charm whoever I wanted to, to realize any dream, and to conquer the world.

"And I even became straight as a ruler, fit to be a wife and a mother, and to produce soldiers for the Israeli army."

Yigal said that even if the damage hadn't been great in the end, you couldn't have known that in advance, and you had no right to take the risk. "Walking around with a secret for years is a heavy psychological burden, and I'm sure that it damaged your relations with your mother, and perhaps your relations with other people too."

I tried to explain to him how good, how right it was to discover the continent of sex for the first time with a woman, "No man and no frightened boy could have been as gentle and generous with me as she was."

"When we get back to Israel I'm going to write to the Minister of Education"—he smiled into his beard but his blue eyes were boiling—"I'll give you two as an example and recommend that every school has a woman teacher to give the girls practical lessons in oral sex. At the end of the term she'll give them grades on their reports too."

"And dragging a young girl to Europe to fuck her when you're twice her age and married, that's moral?" I countered, insulted, "Perhaps you're angry with her because you're angry with yourself?"

"Taking you to Europe is indeed an immoral act on my part," he said quietly, "but towards other people I have obligations to, not towards you. There's also a difference between a young woman of twenty-three and a child of fourteen, and I was never your teacher."

"At that time she was the only person who cared about me," I said heatedly, "if I'd had parents like you, who were ready to smash her face in, perhaps I wouldn't have needed that love to start with, but Michaela was the only person who wanted to listen to me and hug me. For me her love was like a jerrican of water for someone dying of thirst in the desert."

"She could have listened to you and hugged you without getting you between her legs. She exploited your neediness and your weakness, and the fact that you had no backing at home."

"You're just jealous," I retorted, "you men are sure that everything revolves around your prick, and you feel threatened when it seems to you that we can get along without it. Only I know if I was abused or blessed, no one else can judge, your own soul chooses what story to tell itself, a story of exploitation or a story of salvation, and I choose the story of blessing and salvation, which is above all a story of love."

I told you all this now, waiting for your reaction. I didn't tell you how much I loved Yigal that night, in the wrath of his love for his son and the wrath of his love for me—even though like with Escher's famous picture of birds, he could only see the black birds, while I insisted then on seeing only the white ones.

You were silent for a long time. You were then thirty-eight years old, my age today. With a pang in my heart I noticed for the first time the threads of silver in your russet hair that had grown longer and was gathered into a black velvet ribbon on the nape of your neck; the wrinkles on your neck and around your lips and eyes; the thickening of your thighs and arms. Today I see all these things in the mirror.

"I've often asked myself if there's only one kind of morality," you finally said, "Freud argued that morality is masculine, and that in women the superego is flawed. The great moral philosophers too were men, and their theories didn't help humanity to prevent injustice and war and mass slaughter. Perhaps women have a different morality, more psychological, relative, that flows with life and for life. According to Freud and your friend I really am an immoral person, and because of that I've been living for eight years now in this padded exile, and longing for the air and the pines of the Carmel. Yes, there's no doubt that I have already received my punishment."

"You were very young then yourself," I tried to defend her, "today you probably wouldn't permit yourself to be drawn into something like that."

"You know what, kiddo," you turned a weary smile to me, "how did the poet put it, if it should happen a second time again—let it be the same as the first."

And then she told me about Joanna, one of her students. "She's not as young as you were, she's nearly nineteen, and she writes too, a poetic soul, and in class she gobbles me up with her huge eyes, and I feel like taking her face between my hands and kissing it and kissing it, and I know that she wants the same thing, she looks for opportunities to approach me, talks to me about books, shows me poems, but I hold back, I've been holding back for a year now, and it's so hard," you gave me your helpless look, which always made me want to put my arms around you, "You remember that once you said you felt as if I was living in your heart? Well Joanna has settled in my heart, and I don't know what to do, and I'm afraid. If something happens between us and they find out about it at the college, I'm finished."

I was silent, trying to digest the "second time"—the knowledge that I was the first for you but not the only one. A black guy walked past us with his hair in Rasta dreads carrying a huge tape recorder on his shoulder. "Don't worry, be happy" blared to the rhythmic beat we were hearing everywhere.

"Are you angry with me?" you asked suddenly, and your eyes grew damp.

"What about?" I didn't understand. "About Joanna or what happened then?"

"About what happened then."

I said I wasn't. I wasn't angry and I never had been. Not even for a minute. I was always grateful.

"I'm glad," your eyes closed and your forehead creased in pain. "All these years I was afraid that you were angry with me."

I put my arms around you and rested my forehead on your temple. "How could I be," I whispered into her ear, "You gave me what I wanted most, what I had never dared to dream of. Being angry with you would be to betray myself."

We stood up, you whistled to Nana, and she parted without regret from the golden dog and raced ahead of us, black and swift as the wind, as if Dulcinea had burned until she turned into charcoal.

As we strolled back you told me that not long ago you and Yoel had marked your twelfth year of marriage. I asked how you had celebrated, and you said that you hadn't felt the need to celebrate. For a long time now you had lived your own lives, and only the daily care for Ido obliged you to stay together. I said that I remembered how you had come into the classroom after your honeymoon, tanned from the sun of the Greek islands, and how the girls had surrounded you and asked to see your wedding ring, which was still on your finger now, and how my heart had gone out to you. Hard to believe that twelve years had passed since then, and that I'm almost as old as you were when we met. And it seems strange to me too, that you could love another woman besides me. All these years I thought that your love for me was unique, not because you loved women, but because you loved *me*. If I hadn't been absorbed in the agonies of getting over Yigal, perhaps I would have been jealous.

You asked if I hadn't fallen in love with other women during the course of the years. I thought for a minute and remembered that after you there had been a few little yearnings, faint ripples left behind in the wake of our love. There was Ella, a tall redhead from Tel Aviv I had met in Sinai the summer before I was drafted. All night long we sat on the beach, curled up in our sleeping bags, smoked joints, and talked, and when the dark began to pale I had an urge to kiss her chapped lips. And there was the beautiful section commander on basic training, who I loved looking at as she demonstrated the drill, without a single strand of her blond hair straying under her beret. And in my first year at university there was a film student, with golden tiger eyes and wild brown hair, at whom I stole frequent glances during lectures, but nothing came of any of this, until the ripples too subsided.

"Apparently it's buried somewhere deep inside, locked away in some cellar like a sleeping animal, but I lost the key long ago," I mused aloud, and you added, "Until some woman comes along and breaks the lock and wakes the animal with a kiss that will turn it into a princess again."

"I don't think it will happen," I said to you on that autumn evening, and I'm writing it to you again, on the night after your funeral, on the blank pages left at the end of Anne's last notebook. "You were the only woman in my life. You were all women to me."

Yes, for years this was the story that I told myself: I fell in love with you with a great love, which swept you along like a river.

My love was like a force of nature. It left you no freedom of choice. Later on came a time when I understood that you were free to choose. I said to myself that when I reached your age, I would understand how you allowed yourself to choose the way you did. And when I reached your age then, I knew that I would never allow myself. And I was still grateful.

And then I thought that when I reached my mother's age, and I was perhaps the mother of a daughter myself, I would be able to take in the whole picture with a panoramic look. Today, approaching my mother's age then, and a mother of two daughters, I understand: a girl whose father denied her, and whose mother was absorbed in herself, found a young woman who was ready to listen to her, who wanted to embrace her and tell her that she was beautiful and worthy. And the young woman, recently married, perhaps fell in love with her own reflection, with the youth she was still mourning, even with the unripe artist's soul she recognized in the girl. Because from an early age the girl had learned to steal hearts by means of words.

But even today I have difficulty in seeing the whole picture, as if we were trapped in a drop of amber: in our triangle I am sentenced to remain forever fourteen, you will be forever twenty-seven, and my mother forty.

Now I no longer try to understand. All I want is to go back to the dark days of my life, which are also the brightest ones, to shed the skins of maturity added to me by the years, to descend through all the layers of time, to reach rock bottom, and to touch again, if only for a moment, those clear waters. I look into them and seek my reflection—the flaming face of a young girl, her eyes radiating love.

And perhaps only the ripples spread by the stone hitting the water are important, our choices and our flights: you fled to New York and chose to love women. I chose Tel Aviv and to love men.

■

In the months after my return from New York you wrote to me about Joanna, about your first kiss in a hidden corner of the park, your first lovemaking, about the for-women-only bars you discovered together, about the difficulty of pretending in class. And after a while—about Joanna falling in love with a girl of her own age, leaving you with an aching, trembling heart. I wrote to you about my mother's illness, about the melanoma, which at first ate away at one of her X-ray eyes until it had to be removed and replaced with an artificial one, but a few months later it went on invading her body and sent metastases to her liver. For many days I sat by my mother's bedside in the hospital, checking the level of the infusion bag, adjusting the angle of the bed, plumping the pillows, coaxing her to eat, pushing the bedpan under her and emptying it, massaging with fragrant cream her feet, which were swollen from the aggressive treatments, and her bloated hands, whose unpainted nails were yellow; and Mother tried to open her single eye and smile at me, what good hands you have, like a professional masseuse, and for a moment I was happy, no more two left hands, no longer Butterfingers, and I knew that the disease, which had distorted beyond recognition her body and the face that had once been praised as the most beautiful on the Carmel, had also brought down her defensive walls, the criticism and the suspicion and the sarcasm, and suddenly we became close, body and warmth and smell, like in the swaddled days before the words, before the beginning of memory, in the lost continent of Atlantis. And only one wall of armored glass, which we both knew stood between us, and neither of us dared to touch or even to breathe on, refused to fall.

One evening—we were alone in the hospital room, the sun was setting slowly behind the mountain—Mother looked at me gravely with her one eye and said, "You know sometimes I think I wasn't a good enough mother to you and your brothers;" and I held her hand and said quickly, "What are you talking about, you were fine," and I bit my tongue, how could I have slipped up and spoken about her in the past tense, and added, "You're a good mother, you always were, but you had to bring up three children by yourself, without the help of a husband or your mother, and you didn't want to sacrifice yourself, your life."

"No, no I didn't want to sacrifice," she smiled sadly, and her swollen, so familiar fingers—practical and industrious fingers, which peeled and cooked and sewed and ironed and unpicked, and were perhaps bitten in a white car, fingers, which tidied cupboards and turned over the pages of a diary without a lock—hesitantly stroked my hand on the blanket. "I knew it was over too quickly, life, and you had to get everything done at once, because afterwards there wouldn't be any time left. I may have neglected a few things on the way."

And on the spring night of her death, after I returned, with Oren and Noam, to our dark and empty childhood home, I buried my boiling face, sore with crying, in her blue robe, sour as the smell of the illness—David remained behind in the hospital to make the arrangements, since death is a more pedantic bureaucrat than any income tax assessor—and even before calling Daddy and Aunt Tehiya and Racheli and Yigal and Avshalom (who was then studying art in Jerusalem)—I called you.

In New York it was an early April afternoon, and the trees in the park under your study window had presumably already began to blossom. I said quietly, it's over, Mish, she's gone, and you were silent for a long moment, I could hear your heavy breathing on the other side of continents and oceans, and then you said in a cracked voice, I'm sorry, kiddo, I'm so sorry, I wish I could be there now to hug you.

After that Daddy arrived, knocking hesitantly at the door, and wrapped a clumsy hug around my shoulders, and placed his big hands, like mine, on Oren's and Noam's shoulders and mumbled, "I'm very sorry for your loss," and he took a chair from the dining nook and sat with us in the living room. We sat there in silence, the four of us, each with his feelings and thoughts, Oren staring straight ahead with a frozen face, as if refusing to believe it, and Noam, so young, not yet twenty, resting his cheek on his hand and biting hard on his little finger, and from time to time gasping for breath, and Daddy rubbed his eyes under his glasses with his thumb and forefinger, and in a low voice began to tell a distant legend, about a young man who was poor but hard-working and ambitious, who met a beautiful young blond from the Carmel at the university, who had just lost her mother, and he invited her to go with him to the Purim ball at the Technion, and his voice broke, "You should have seen her dance the twist, with a cat's-eyes mask. People whispered, it isn't two weeks since her mother died, but she said, they can all kiss my ass, and pulled me into the middle of the floor, and then she got pregnant, and that was it," he stood up suddenly, as if someone else was controlling his movements, "I have to go," but he hovered over us for a moment longer and said in embarrassment, "I know this isn't the best time, but next Saturday we're celebrating Orly's bat-mitzvah in our garden, and Batya and I would like you to come." His red eyes sought mine as if to ask, "Will you come?" and I remembered another bat-mitzvah, a girl with square glasses and her hair in bunches watching her parents dancing together, and I thought that Mother had known then that this was their last dance, but he didn't know, he only took care not to tread with his big sandals on her toes in their pointed pumps, and afterwards he was suddenly torn from his family like a figure in a photograph, and returned to his parents' home with a single suitcase, his heart already bitter against his wife who had turned her back on him, and his daughter who had turned her back in the wake of her mother. And I knew that now, with nobody standing between us, I was permitted to take part in my sister's bat-mitzvah—who I hadn't seen since that visit nearly ten years ago—in the new house they had built and which I had never visited. And I looked him in the eye and said, "Yes, I'll come."

And the next day, in the old cemetery between the mountain and the sea, I forced my eyes to look at the body that had given me my life sliding into the pit and being covered with earth, and I knew that with it the treachery and the guilt were being buried too. And the cypresses, like long memorial candles, stabbed the burning blue sky with their points, and the birds didn't stop their singing.

In March 1999 I called to tell you that I was pregnant and that I was planning to come to New York at the beginning of May, because after the birth I would be grounded for God knows how long.

"That's wonderful," you exclaimed. But your voice sounded dull, drained of its usual vitality. You said that you were going through a difficult patch, you were working hard, you felt like a plucked chicken. I was afraid that you were hiding something from me, unrequited love for a student or an affair that had come to an end, or perhaps something connected to Ido, but I didn't ask any further. I knew that soon we would be strolling in the park with Nana—who on my first visit was still a frisky puppy and by now must be an old lady—and we would fill in all the gaps.

Worn out after an uncomfortable flight—my pregnant belly pressed against my thighs without any possibility of stretching my legs out in the narrow space between the seats—I looked out of the cab window. This time Yoel was home, and I took a room in a little hotel not far from Washington Square.

After unpacking and taking a long bath and lying down for a quick nap, I phoned home, seven in the morning Tel Aviv time.

"Hi," his drowsy baritone, "how was the flight?"

"Horrible. The baby didn't have enough space and I think she got a bit squashed. We'll have a squashed banana baby."

Carmel snatched the phone away from him.

"Mommy," she breathed heavily, "did you give Michaela my drawing?"

"No, I haven't seen her yet."

"Do you think it got creased in the journey?"

"It isn't creased. I looked after it."

"And you didn't peek into the envelope, right? Because it's a secret surprise just for her."

"No, I didn't peek." How easy it is to knead the soft yielding heart of a child, the plasticine heart of a little girl.

"Okay then, I'm going to school. Bye."

"Kiss," basting-stitch.

"Kiss," chain stitch.

After that I called you. We made a date for you to come to the hotel at eight, and we would go out to eat.

"I have a little surprise for you from Carmel."

"Really?" You let out a strange laugh, "I have a little surprise for you too."

At eight on the dot you knocked on the door in a long, black cape, smiled at me from a tired, sunken face, with your fingers gripping a bottle of whiskey. We embraced. Even through the cape I could feel how thin you were, your body between my arms weak and brittle, and perhaps it was me who had grown fatter because of the pregnancy, and I had always felt bigger than you anyway, stronger and more masculine.

"We'll have a drink in a minute," you put the whiskey on the table, "have you got ice here? Glasses?"

"I have everything," I said and handed her the brown envelope, "here's Carmel's present, before we forget."

You opened the envelope carefully and took out the drawing. The familiar tremor appeared at the corners of your lips. You turned the page towards me. A woman and a little girl playing the piano, shown from the back. And on top: "To Michaela from Carmel with love."

"She's wonderful, your Carmel," you smiled at me and your eyes lit up for a moment, "and soon she'll have a brother," you slid your hand over my belly.

"A sister," I said, "according to the ultrasound."

"Even better. So let's teach her to drink already."

You took off your coat and laid it on the chair, and I bent over the minibar and took out all the ice and remembered how twenty years ago you walked towards me down the corridor of the maternity ward, and how you showed Ido to me from the other side of the window of the neonates room—a baby with his face scowling in insult and his blue eyes blank. And how disappointed you were that you hadn't had a girl.

You poured the whiskey and said, "I want to show you something, but first drink," and you lit a cigarette and took a deep draw. I rattled the ice in my glass. The cold turned to heat at the bottom of my throat, and the bitterness to the forgotten taste of the cherry brandy, of rum in a teacup.

You tilted your head back and drank until the ice hit your teeth, and you slammed the glass down on the table, and with urgent fingers you undid the buttons of your brown silk blouse. In astonishment I watched your fingers undoing button after button. You took off the blouse and threw it onto the chair, the seams inside-out and the sleeves dangling helplessly. Then, with a decisive movement, you put your hand behind your back, undid the hooks of the green satin bra, and quickly, before you could regret it, you removed it and stood facing me. I remember that it took my brain a few seconds to translate the sight and to understand that in the place of your left breast—which I had sucked one sweltering evening after Ido was born, before the police caught us—there was now a long pink scar.

For a moment that young girl rose up inside me, wanting to touch the scar with light fingertips and ask, does it hurt, but I only raised my tear-filled eyes to you and said, "What a rotten friend you are, why didn't you tell me?"

"I didn't want to spoil things for you," you said quietly, "you called to tell me you were pregnant a few days after I came out of the hospital, and said that you were coming to New York, so I decided to put off the glad tidings for a while."

We can never do things together, I thought bitterly, watch-

291

ing you hiding the scar under the padded cup of the bra, and buttoning the blouse over it. You're always ahead of me, showing me the way. When you were pregnant I was still a child, and now that I'm pregnant, you go and get cancer.

"You know," you poured more whiskey into your glass, "after the doctor gave me the results of the biopsy and set a date for the mastectomy, I walked out of his clinic and sat in the nearest Starbucks. I breathed in the smell of the coffee with the cold smell of the air, and everything, the trees, the buildings, the dogs, the clouds, the people walking past in bright coats and hats and scarves, everything was bursting with life, like when I was a little girl and the world was exciting and full of hints, sending me secret signs, the promise of adventure, of love, of distant journeys," you fished a tissue out of your bag and blew your nose until it turned red, "and then I said to myself that if I went back in my thoughts to the place where memory begins, perhaps I would be able to discover where the little knot of the tumor was tied, in what the doctor called a space-occupying lesion. What space did it occupy? What was taken away from me in order to give it that space, what part of myself did I give up, where did I lie in my soul, bend it, tie it like a thread, without knowing that the knot would not come undone, but only thicken? In my marriage to Yoel? My love for you? My pregnancy? Moving to New York? Once, a long time ago, soul and life were one and the same, don't you remember?" You held my hand in both your hands, your eyes imploring.

"Yes," I nodded with my throat choking, "of course I remember."

"So sometime or other, in a moment of distraction, I let my soul drift away from my life, like a continent dividing in two. I told myself that if I went back in my thoughts and found the point of separation, the place where my breathing stopped being deep, the breathing of wind and smells, and was replaced by shallow, superficial breathing, solely in order to survive—perhaps I could help myself heal."

"And did you find it?"

"I love your practicality," you shone the smile that the sickness couldn't defeat on me. "The doctors have given me time to recover from the surgery, and next week I'm starting chemotherapy, in case a few cells have decided to jump from my tit and settle in some other place, and that includes nausea, hair loss, the whole thing. Will you come with me to Brooklyn to choose a wig?"

The end of your bronze ponytail, defiantly refracting the sun. "Of course, of course I'll come with you."

That night we didn't go out to eat at a restaurant. We ordered sandwiches from room service and emptied the bottle of whiskey. Heavy and drunk we lay in our clothes on the bed.

"Sleep here," I said, "you shouldn't drive like that."

"What difference does it make already," you said with a dark laugh, "tonight or tomorrow or next year."

You buried your face in the pillow. Your slender shoulders shook, and I put out my hand to stroke your hair carefully, as if it was already about to fall out. Don't give in, I said to you in my heart, fight, don't sink into self-pity, in your blood you shall live. I raised your face, bathed in tears and snot, to mine. You asked, "Can I embrace you, kiddo, the way we once did, like teaspoons?"

"You're still a teaspoon, I've become a soupspoon, a soup ladle," I tried to joke. I turned on my side and you embraced me from behind, your stomach on my back and your thighs under mine, as if it had never been any different, and your hand on my belly, holding the fetus beating against the walls of the womb.

And if I had turned to face you, my eyes on yours, and if I had taken your face between my hands, and kissed your soft lips tasting of whiskey and cigarettes and tears, and comforted your lacking, insulted body, with my full-moon body?

And perhaps that's what we did on that night, two grown women overcome by alcohol, more sober than we had ever been in our lives, our limbs seeking the familiar depressions, nostrils

293

sniffing for the familiar smells, skin thirsty for skin, blood pulsing to blood, and a fetus separating us, kicking in protest, as if twenty years hadn't passed.

We spent most of that week together, scouring dress shops and shoe shops in Soho, dropping into art galleries, buying delicacies at Dean and Deluca. One evening we went to the theater to see *Amy's View* with Judi Dench, and afterwards we drove to Tribeca and sucked frozen margaritas, lounging in old armchairs in a pub. You talked about Yoel, the new, hesitant closeness that had come into being between you with the sickness, "A few nights ago we even made love," you laughed, "We haven't done it for years, you know he was never a great lover, or maybe it was me who never gave him a chance, and suddenly I had an urge to climb on top of him while he was sleeping, and he got a hard-on immediately, from the shock."

You talked about your concern for Ido, who had difficulty in adjusting to the slightest change in his daily routine, and who was angry when you were in hospital for the surgery, and it would probably be the same now, when you would have to be away from home frequently for the treatments.

"I always grieved for the fact that he would never marry, that I would never have grandchildren; now all I want is to get better and go on giving him whatever he needs, not to leave Yoel alone with that heavy burden."

Afterwards you asked how things were between me and Yair.

"We've been together for ten years already," I said, "you know how it is. You remember how I once wanted to be like Picasso and Dahn Ben Amotz?"

"May they rest in peace," you smiled.

"In the course of time I discovered that the expectation of life being exciting and full of surprises had given way to the realization of how fragile everything is, and the wish for everything to stay the way it is, without any catastrophes. Because catastrophes will happen anyway, one of the four of us will die one day, and then the second, and the third, and the last one to remain, in the normal course of events the unborn baby in my belly, will have to cry for the three of us, and about the abnormal course of events I can't even think. Apparently from the minute you have children fear becomes your guide, and you can never be completely happy, like you once were, in blissful ignorance, not even for a single moment, because that fear is always stalking you, like a shadow."

"You've grown old and mature, kiddo, welcome to the club."

"Yes," I mused aloud, "my soul has faded like a blanket forgotten in the sun. I remember those nights when I was a child and I couldn't fall asleep because of the anticipation for something that was going to happen the next day, a holiday, a trip, a birthday, and the excitement was so intense that the event itself paled in comparison. And the anticipation of life too, in the last resort, was stronger and sweeter than life itself."

"Life is very sweet," you grew suddenly somber, "and apparently we feel it most strongly not in anticipation, but in parting. How does all this fit in with your writing?"

"It's lucky I once had the courage to live. Now I only have to mobilize the courage to write, and then I write as if to myself, as if nobody in the world will read what I write, like I once wrote the diaries."

"Even for the most ordinary bourgeois life you need courage," you said slowly, "look at them," you pointed your chin at two young women, almost girls, kissing on the sofa next to us, totally absorbed in each other, their legs intertwined. One was broad-shouldered, in a black leather jacket, her hair cropped, and the other more slender and delicate, in jeans and a white tank top, with a butterfly tattooed on her shoulder.

"I envy them," you said, "sometimes I think that if I had been twenty or thirty today, when so many women live together and have children from sperm donations, I might have made different choices, and my whole life would have been completely different. But then there was nothing we could hold on to, two good little girls from Haifa like us, there was no one to tell us who we were, we had nowhere to read about ourselves, we were so deviant, so lonely in our love, our fear, our secret."

"You know," I said after a short silence, "sometimes I try to imagine how I would feel if in a few more years I were to suddenly discover that Carmel was having an affair with a woman teacher, and I choke. I don't regret what happened, but I simply can't understand how you permitted yourself. To kiss a student who wasn't yet fourteen years old, to strip her of garment after garment, little by little, over a period of weeks, so she wouldn't take fright, and to continue this impossible affair for two whole years, as if we were two nymphs in the forest and nobody else existed, as if we wouldn't have to pay a price. How did you dare?"

"Apparently I had a tremendous, primitive, childish need to be everything for someone," you said quietly. "And there you were, my most gifted student, a clever, sensitive girl, with a sweet, vulnerable face, gazing at me with eyes like bottomless wells. So I told myself a fairytale, I turned you into an orphan princess, without a father or mother, completely abandoned, an open wound, with all the sorrow in the world on her shoulders. I wanted to bring the light back into your eyes, I wanted to bring you up, to teach you things, perhaps to live through you too, like a ventriloquist talking through somebody else. It was all done from love, arrogant and selfish perhaps, because no one can be everything to someone else, but boundless love, and how is it possible to know where to draw the line between love and lust, between giving and exploitation?"

"It is possible to know. The line is drawn where the feelings of guilt begin."

"Yes, and to escape from their claws, and because I knew that I didn't have the strength to part from you, I got myself pregnant. I said that I was doing it in order to protect the relationship between us, but perhaps unconsciously I really wanted to destroy it."

"You succeeded then in being everything to me," I said, "and precisely because of that you should have protected me, from other people too, because it was clear that they would never have let us get away with it, but mainly from yourself; but you didn't protect me, whereas I always protected you, at the end, when they caught us, and also, out of some loyalty that I don't completely understand, in all the years that have passed since then."

"They wouldn't have found us out if you hadn't had to write everything down," you winked at me over a drunken smile, "I'm sorry that I wasn't able to protect you. I wasn't able to protect myself either. We were both sitting on a merry-go-round that was spinning around wildly, completely out of control, and I didn't know how to stop it."

You can't blame people for what they say when they're sick, I thought, sucking up the lemon margarita through the straw, you can't blame people for what they do when they're in love. In those days we both believed that love justifies everything, and since then each of us bears the cross of her own story, of which she is the heroine.

One morning we drove to Brooklyn, and there, in an elegant shop, we fitted you with an auburn wig, resembling the color of your hair.

"What do you say," you smiled at me with pale lips under the alien, too tidy, hair, "should I become an Orthodox Jewess?"

"He won't accept you," I rolled my eyes to heaven, making an effort to smile at you in the mirror, "too many sins."

While you were paying for the wig I went into the shop next door and bought myself a pair of sunglasses, which had caught my fancy before, when I looked into the window as we walked past.

"They suit you," you said to me on the sidewalk outside, and immediately, with the eagerness of a child, "let me try them on."

I handed you the glasses, and you put them on. "Have you got a mirror?"

"No I haven't." The days had passed when we served each other as magnifying mirrors. "What's a narcissist like you doing without a mirror?"

"A narcissist doesn't need a mirror," your face suddenly shone at me with a dazzling smile, "the whole world reflects her."

Afterwards we drove in your car to the college in New Jersey. In recent years you had taught a few of my stories that been translated into English, with the English text facing the Hebrew, and you asked me to come and meet your students.

"I told them that more than twenty years ago, before they were born, you were a student of mine at a high school on Mount Carmel," you said out of the corner of your mouth, a cigarette between your lips and your head turned back, as you maneuvered the car into a parking spot in reverse. "They're nice kids. They were so concerned about me when I was in the hospital for the surgery, they even organized a deputation to come and visit me with chocolates and flowers. I hope I'll be able to complete the year somehow between one treatment and the next."

We entered the classroom where about forty youngsters were sitting, you first, showering them with your smiles, and me behind you. Again we were in a classroom together. You introduced me to your students, proudly listing my books and achievements, while I let my eyes wander over the faces, fair, dark, amiable, suspicious, not yet fully formed—what kind of childhood lay hidden behind those faces, what kind of youth— looking for the curious and trusting pair of eyes to which I would direct my words. And to which of these eyes do you talk, I suddenly wondered, and which eyes talk to you?

"I haven't prepared a lecture, your teacher took me by surprise," I said, rolling around my tongue the English I had accustomed myself to using, even though it always remained tasteless, without flavor or color, "but I would be happy to talk to you and answer any questions you would like to ask."

"I'd like to ask," opened a smiling girl with a coffee-colored complexion, "how much your writing draws on your real biography."

Practiced in answering this question, which comes up in almost every meeting with readers, I spoke about three kinds of characters: the kind I try to copy from real life, only exchanging true details for fictional ones to disguise their identity, putting a mask with a long nose attached to spectacles and a mustache on their faces. Others, who suddenly pop up out of nowhere, I have never known, and only after putting them into writing, I look for them among the living, suddenly recognizing them in the street; and seminal characters, who were branded onto my soul, and who come back again and again in all kinds of incarnations and disguises. Take for example—I restrained myself from saying—your teacher, if you look hard, you'll find her traces in more than one of my stories, because I wrote about her, and about those days, in disguises, in masks with spectacles and mustaches. One day, I knew, I would write as close as possible to the skin, in the scars that became the paths along which I led my life.

I spoke about the skeletons of fictional and semifictional plots, on which I laid, layer after layer, saved-up sights and sensations. I said that reality was a meat-hook upon which to hang the pieces of a story, and that I was interested in stretching the borders of reality, to play with what-would-have-happened-if, more than documenting events as they actually occurred. I knew that this statement too was a mask, since writing often seeks to jell life, to erect a monument to it, to stick pins in it as into dead butterflies, and sometimes it seeks to exorcise the demons from it, to straighten out the folds of time by force and correct it, like the old German Jewish watchmaker I once knew.

"In the course of time I discovered," I smiled at the young girl, whose name, she told me afterwards, was Grace, "that when I try to write a fictional story what comes out is an autobiographical story, and when I write something autobiographical, what comes out is fiction, so that I always find myself in the strange no-man's-land between deceptive memories and fiction."

"I think," said a girl with short, straight blond hair who reminded me of Racheli, "that even someone who means to write autobiography as close to truth as possible has to fill in gaps in his memory and invent some of the details. He writes from a certain perspective, which might be different at another point in time, and in any case, he chooses what to look at through a magnifying or minimizing glass."

"He usually looks at himself through a magnifying glass, and through a minimizing glass at everybody else," said a bespectacled boy sitting in the back row, and everybody laughed.

"Autobiography can be full of falsifications and even wild lies," I said, "and we can never know. And the same goes for a story that seems autobiographical. Take for example *The Lover* by Marguerite Duras, ostensibly an autobiographical novel, but how can we possibly tell if the writer had an affair with a Chinese man at the age of fifteen, and if it happened in precisely this way? She herself, from the distance of the years, couldn't have remembered all the details exactly. And it doesn't matter anyway, what matters is the response to which the story gives rise in the readers."

"So the most reliable autobiographies are diaries, because they are written in real time," said Grace, "anyone who lies in his private diary is only lying to himself."

The diaries, I felt an inner shock, like a rock shaken by a distant earthquake. I glanced at you, sitting next to the wall, looking at me and your students from the distance of your twilight, with your eyes streaming towards me all the time.

"Diaries aren't always truthful either," I said, "sometimes they're only fiction or fantasy; the writer is always liable to invent details, to make them up or to correct them. And sometimes a diary is only a way of writing, years later. And even when it's authentic, someone in the family can censor entire pages, like the poet Ted Hughes, who destroyed the last part of Sylvia Plath's diaries, or Otto Frank, Anne's father, who withheld many passages that have only recently been published."

I spoke about Anne Frank's diary, about the figure of the child-writer who was the first in the collection of writers I harbored in the secret of my childhood and girlhood cocoon, to give confirmation to my lust for writing.

"Anne Frank couldn't have known that her diary would become the most important and symbolic document of the Holocaust," I reflected aloud, "and nevertheless she did everything to ensure that it would be found and read. She could have taken it with her when they were caught, and continued to write in it—presumably she went on feeling the need to write—but she didn't take even the last notebook. She knew that the safest thing would be to leave it in the hiding place, and this proves that she was a true writer, because a writer isn't known only by her drive to write, or her talent, but also by the desire for other people to read what she writes. Sometimes I wonder what would have happened if Anne Frank had survived and returned to Amsterdam and discovered that her precious diaries had disappeared and been lost. She would probably have written a novel about those two years in hiding, conjured them up from the dark basements of her memory, and perhaps she would have chosen to write her novel in the form of a young girl's diary. But the diaries survived and she perished, and in her lifetime she didn't have a single reader, and even though she didn't live to grow up and become a writer, her diary has been read and will be read far more widely than the works of writers who enjoyed long and illustrious careers."

Towards the end of the meeting a freckled girl with red-gold hair—she looked like the actress Isabelle Huppert, and a little like you—put up her hand and said with a shy and perhaps provocative smile, "Mrs. Berg told us that a long time ago you were her student in Israel, and now you're a writer. Perhaps you can tell us what you learned from her, that helped you in days to come?"

We exchanged glances and smiled. What did I learn from you. To kiss. To make love. To scream when I come. To take my clothes off in the sun. Clothes are intended only to cover us, but in words we reveal ourselves. To be kind and friendly to everyone. To dance the tango and the foxtrot. To lick strawberry jam from your body. To worship Aphrodite and the muses. To listen to music. To love dogs and Virginia Woolf. To work hard, because talent is only ten percent. To always follow your heart, and to be prepared to pay the price. To observe the commandments of life. And what was I going to tell them now?

"Mrs. Berg is an excellent teacher, and I learned a lot from her," I said, and you leaned your head on the wall and waited. "The most important thing I learned from her was willpower. Every ambition and every love begins in a yearning, in a dream, and if we dare to want something or someone with all our might, we will almost certainly get what we want in the end, even if it seems unattainable."

The girl thought for a moment and said, "That's optimistic," and you smiled at me, scratching your forehead with your left finger and your nose with your right finger, to signal "Right but banal." Then you stood up with a weary smile, thanked me, and said to your students, "On this optimistic note we'll say goodbye until we meet again next week," and we both knew that it was doubtful you would have enough willpower to come here and teach after your chemotherapy.

In the car on the way to Manhattan I asked you if after your short affair with Joanna you had fallen in love again, and you confessed that a few years ago you had courted a brilliant student with suicidal tendencies, that you wanted to save her from herself, but that she had rejected you aggressively and threatened that if you went on writing her love letters she would report you to the college authorities.

"That was the last time," you smiled sadly. "Sometimes a pair of eyes succeeds in igniting the old flame in me—the tragedy isn't that we grow old, but that we remain young—but I'm already thirty years older than my students, and sick, and I don't want to be a pathetic old lesbian."

The evening before I flew home you invited me to come to dinner. I couldn't think of what to buy Ido for a present. What do you get a boy whose twenty-year-old body hides a child of five? I spent the day buying clothes and toys for Carmel, and at the "sales" counter of a big department store I quickly chose a sweatshirt and scarf in the colors of the New York Knicks for Ido.

At half past seven I knocked on the door, bearing the gifts and a bottle of wine. The door opened and a furry black ball leaped at me, with two forepaws raised to come to rest on my stomach.

"Stop it Nana, leave the guest alone," scolded Yoel in pale brown corduroys and an olive jersey with the sleeves rolled up to his elbows. I hadn't seen him since the fondue party before you left for New York. He hadn't changed much, apart from his hair, which was thinner and combed back, and the spectacles in narrow blue metal frames. He surveyed me with a faint smile.

"You've grown," he said, and I, reverting under his gaze to my sixteen-year-old self, said, "I know, you're not a child anymore yourself."

I held out the bottle of wine, and he glanced at the label and said, "Hmm, that looks like a good wine," and went to put the bottle on the big glass table in the dining nook, which was beautifully set, with a bunch of pink and purple wild flowers in the center, and next to the big white Rosenthal plates I remembered from Hatzvi Avenue, on four rectangular straw place mats, long-temmed crystal wine glasses and purple table napkins in elegant silver napkin rings, whose likes I had seen in the designer shop next to the Museum of Modern Art. From the kitchen a warm smell of baking rose into the air.

"Michaela's changing," Yoel replied to my unasked question, "and Ido's watching television in his room."

"I brought him something," I lifted the plastic bag, "how does he feel about the Knicks?"

"We'll call him and you'll see for yourself," Yoel smiled. He went to Ido's room at the end of the passage, knocked on the door, and said something to him in English. Together they came back to the living room. The last time I'd seen him he was nine, and when I was staying with you then I tried to avoid meeting him—I went out for long walks when he was due home from school, and came back late in the evening when I knew he was secluded in his room, watching television or sleeping. On the few occasions when we met he looked right through me, without any sign of seeing me. Now he was as tall as his father, and his fair hair receded above his forehead in two pinkish bays, just like Yoel's in the period when I first met him, when he was only a few years older than his son was now.

"I'm Rivi. You probably don't remember me," I held out my hand to him in a clumsy movement, and he took it in his damp one, and gave it a quick, mechanical squeeze, his eyes staring straight ahead.

"This is for you," I offered him the plastic bag. Ido snatched it jerkily from my hand, took out the package, and impatiently tore the tissue paper. And then he pulled out scarf with its blue, white, and orange stripes and hung it sloppily around his neck.

"Patrickewing," he grunted, "patrickewing."

I turned questioningly to Yoel, and he explained that Patrick Ewing was the star of the Knicks.

You came into the living room, first your Cheshire cat smile, and then the rest of you, in a black velvet dress with purple flowers, and after we had kissed cheek to cheek you stroked the scarf dangling down the chest of your son who was a head taller than you, and said, what a lovely scarf you got from Rivi, and I suddenly remembered another scarf, of blue-and-brown wool, knitted in secret for weeks and wrapped around your neck on your twenty-seventh birthday, before Yoel came home and almost caught us.

"Come to the table, children," you ordered and disappeared into the kitchen with Nana at your heels.

I sat down next to Ido, so that I wouldn't have to look at him, and he reached for the vase and broke off a purple flower with stiff fingers and pulled the petals off one by one, as if trying to discover whether some girl loved-him or loved-him-not; and afterwards he arranged them at equal distances from each other around the edge of his plate. During the meal he held his knife and fork in a stiff-fingered grip and ate in silence, with the trained movements he had learned in the Lovass "applied behavioral analysis" method. From time to time he put his knife down and compulsively stroked his new scarf. So that's how you are, my heart contracted, father and mother and silent twenty-year-old child who you will always have to look at from behind the glass of the neonates room in the hospital.

You, as usual, did your best to animate the conversation, and told Yoel about my meeting with your students. Yoel asked me a few polite questions, and I, my face flushed with wine, answered at length, and in the end I asked him about his work.

Yoel said that the day before he had anesthetized a gigantic man who had a vibrator stuck in his rectum—he explained to anyone who was prepared to listen that the vibrator belonged to his wife, and all he did was sit down on it by mistake when he got into bed. Afterwards, encouraged by our laughter, he told us how a few months before he had anesthetized a famous, successful lawyer, from whose intestine they had removed a string of pearls from Tiffany's.

"You can take your stories and stick them up your ass," you said in a voice thickened by alcohol; we had already polished off a second bottle of wine. "My husband anesthetizes anything that moves, but when I asked him to promise me that if I reached a terminal stage he would help me, he turned chicken."

"That's enough, Michaelush," Yoel reprimanded her quietly, "the child."

"The child?" you laughed bitterly and patted Ido on the back, "the child hasn't got a clue, have you, child?"

"Patrickewing," Ido grunted at his plate.

"You're absolutely right. I'm going to make herb tea."

"She's been a little stressed since the surgery," Yoel felt the need to apologize when you disappeared into the kitchen, "she drinks quite a lot."

"It's alright."

Ido rose abruptly from his seat, crossed the passage without a word, and disappeared into his room.

"He's always the same," explained Yoel, "he can't sit still for long, and he doesn't like sweets."

We drank the herb tea with the bought cheese cake in the living room. Afterwards you lay on the big sofa under the picture of the little girl and the nurse, closed your eyes, and lifted your hand to your forehead. Nana curled up at your feet and looked at you with a wistful look. The fetus woke up and began to move, gently stretching the walls of my womb. I have to go, I said, my flight leaves early in the morning, and I haven't packed yet.

"Yoelshin, be a dear and take Rivi to the hotel," you requested, "there's a sword dance going on in my head."

I said I would take a taxi, but they both objected strenuously.

You saw me to the door, hung on my shoulders, and whispered, "You'll always remember me, won't you kiddo? You won't forget."

"I'll remember until Alzheimer strikes," I clasped your body to me, my first body, which in a few days time would be filled to nausea with the liquids of the chemotherapy, "after that I can't promise anything."

"And one day you'll write our book," you whispered in my ear, "it will have blue-and-brown pages, which will whisper to each other like the sky and the earth, like treetops and stars."

"And afterwards we'll make it into a movie," I made an effort to smile at her, "Isabelle Huppert will play you, or Emma Thompson."

"I drank too much, as usual, and had an attack of sentimentality," you smiled too, wiping away with two fingers the mascara smudged under your eyes, "I'm going to bed."

We went down in the elevator, Yoel and I, facing our reflections in the mirror; a pregnant woman with a tired, swollen face, and a tall, balding man, with deep shadows under his eyes, which I only noticed now, in the bright neon light.

"I know that it's hard for you too," his figure in the mirror suddenly blurted out, "you were once so close."

What does he know about the closeness between us? My insides turned over and I made an effort to meet his eyes in the mirror, what did he know then?

"I'm not such an idiot," said the man in the mirror bitterly, "in order not to see and not to hear I would have had to be Helen Keller."

"And how did you feel?" asked the swollen woman at his side, my mouth dry and my heart racing.

"How did I feel?" he turned abruptly to face me, "How do you think a man feels when the wife he's just married prefers to go to bed with a fourteen-year-old child who hangs around his house all day?"

"So why didn't you do anything?" the blood drained from my face. I always preferred to empty him out, to leave only a hollow shell, a role, a title, "your husband," but he was there all the time, he saw and said nothing.

The elevator door opened and we stepped out into the car park. Yoel pressed the remote, and the car responded with a beep.

"I kept hoping that it would somehow end of its own accord.

I pressed her to have a baby, but it went on during the pregnancy, and after the birth, and then I started looking for a hospital as far away as possible from Haifa and from you, that would take me on, and in the end there was the big scandal with the school principal too."

"And why didn't you say anything to her all that time?" I felt nauseous. I took a deep breath of the stuffy underground air, trying not to vomit up the meal and all the wine I'd drunk.

"I suppose I was afraid to lose her." Yoel opened the door of the car for me and slid in at the other side, "Look, I'm an ordinary person, my imagination is limited, and she, when we were still children, she had a passionate, romantic soul; she painted, she played the piano, she danced, she wrote poetry, she had big dreams. I remember once, when we were twelve or thirteen, we went to Nahariya with our parents for the Passover holidays. We sat on the beach at night, just the two of us, there was a khamsin, the sea was completely calm, and she recited from memory a poem by Leah Goldberg that they had studied at school, something about a khamsin in April. I don't remember the poem, I only remember that it was very sensuous, and I remember her voice in the dark, deep and dramatic, and her eyes, blazing with some inner fire, like Audrey Hepburn's eyes. After that she talked about how every day should be special and festive, because we didn't have too many days left to live, she made a calculation that even if we lived to be eighty we would have less than twenty-five thousand days to live. I said that it was a lot, and she said that it wasn't enough for all the things she had planned. And then she said that we should go into the water and I said that we couldn't because we didn't have swimming suits, and she laughed and took off all her clothes, and her body, which had just started to develop, shone above me for a moment and was immediately swallowed up in the sea, and she shouted at me to come in, but I was too shy, and I knew that there was no chance in the world that she would love an ordinary boy like me."

"She never told me all that," I said quietly, and I remembered the photograph album of your childhood, a girl with freckles and a pale boy in a decorated carriage drawn by a white horse, and I knew that little girl had never really grown up, she had only wrapped herself in a borrowed cloak of adulthood, and her longings for herself had compelled her to seek her own reflection over and over again, and curl up with it without knowing who was the child and who the parent, and I thought that if I had been the teacher of that little girl, I might have fallen in love with her.

"Yes," Yoel laughed bitterly, "there were a lot of things she didn't tell me either."

For a while he drove down Broadway in silence, and suddenly he said, "She has metastases in her lungs and bones. She doesn't know. In the meantime she isn't in pain, and I've asked her oncologists not to tell her. They're going to give her intensive hormone treatment and chemotherapy not in the hope of a cure but in order to alleviate the pain and improve her quality of life in the time that remains."

At the beginning of September I gave birth to Noga, and you sent me baby clothes from Baby Gap for her: a tiny white dress with a butterfly print, a Kangaroo overall in peach velvet, a blouse with an embroidered yellow rabbit, a little red hat and matching stockings, a pink summer blanket with an appliqued cat—a sweetness that wrung my heart. In my mind's eye I saw you going into the Gap branch close to your house, the too-neat auburn wig on your head, feeling the little dresses and soft overalls on the infant shelves with your transparent fingers.

In the winter I got connected to the internet, and we began to correspond by e-mail (who would have guessed that my "little house in the post office" would turn one day into a virtual mailbox . . .). Every day I switched on the computer in anxious expectation, and every few days I found a letter from you waiting for me. Sometimes, when you returned from the hospital, and you didn't feel well, you only sent a few words. You tried to cut the descriptions of the treatments and their side-effects short, and when I asked you, you wrote, "Forget it, it's too boring and depressing, and you've already had enough of it with your mother. The worst is the envy. It's as cruel as hell. I envy every homeless person on a bench in the park, every child, every dog and cat, I envy the doctors taking care of me, Yoel, even Ido, everyone who dwells in the land of the living and not in this twilight zone, which is more terrible than death, and I want to scream, put the clock back, give me back my life, you have no right to deprive me of it, I want to live it over again, from the beginning, all of it."

Worn out by sleepless nights, absorbed in my new love: in my selfish and callous maternal happiness—I tried to find encouraging words for you, and mostly I wrote to you about Noga, about the many hours we spend joined together, refusing to separate and turn into two; I lie back in the armchair and she lies on my stomach, her tiny head buried in my bosom and my nose straying over her downy hair like a caterpillar in a field of flowers. You wanted to know everything about her. And you asked about Carmel too, what she was reading and what she was drawing, and how she was finding her place next to her new sister, and I made an effort to give you details, imagining that I was throwing you a rope over oceans and continents, turning the line connecting us over the internet into an artery of life for you.

Last summer, in the interval between treatments, Yoel surprised you with airline tickets to Paris, from which you continued to a long holiday in Tuscany, and you wrote to me from your laptop:

"Opposite the second-floor window of the wonderful villa Yoel found for us the hills curve green and gold and the olive trees are silver. I have nothing to say to all this beauty, and I drink to dull the pain. In the garden downstairs Yoel and Ido sit side by side in wicker armchairs, gazing at the dazzling blue of the swimming pool, the bougainvillea bleeding over their heads, and they look so lonely."

In autumn, when you returned to New York, I told you

about the studio I'd rented outside the apartment, since my study has been painted sky blue with clouds and become Noga's room: "I'm sure that good old Virginia is proud of me up there, not only a room of my own, but a whole apartment!!!"

And then Yoel wrote me that you were having severe pain in your pelvis, and were under the influence of a cocktail of painkillers. He asked me to go on talking to you on the internet, even though you couldn't reply, and promised to read my e-mails to you. And I, who have never known how to do anything else, went on, with the diligence of an eternal student, writing beautiful compositions for my composition teacher.

And early one Saturday evening—Noga and I were in a bubble bath among the fish and the seals and the yellow rubber ducks; in the background the noisy Hebrew dubbing on the children's channel—the telephone rang, neutral, anonymous, and his withdrawn voice, Rivi, she's gone, the funeral's in Haifa on Tuesday.

And here they are, waiting at the Cypress gate of the new cemetery. Yoel, whose face has gone very gray and whose long body seems to have shrunk; Ido, his head bowed and his shoe turning a little stone over and over again; your elderly mother, erect and alert in a wheelchair; and a handful of relatives and friends from your youth, whom I don't know. Of all your former students I am the only one who came; Racheli, whose tears choked her when I called to tell her, was unable to find a baby-sitter, and Avshalom—so his mother told me—was traveling in Australia with his wife and two children.

And I go up to your mother—her grief-stricken eyes wander over my face—and press her hand in mine and say, I'm Rivi, I was a student of hers once, she was a remarkable teacher. And then I quickly touch your son's limp hand, unable to bring myself to look into his face. And in the end I go up to Yoel, raise my cheek hesitantly to his and whisper, I brought the poem, and Yoel nods, yes, read it.

And after your still, small body, sixty-four inches swaddled in white, has been cast into the pit, and after Yoel and your son stumble through Kaddish together, Yoel mumbling the obscure words and Ido echoing him, and after the cantor wails, "*El-malei-rahamim,*" and after they piles the earth on you and lay the flowers on top—I stand next to the little mound, my back to the sea and my face to the mountain, and take the folded page with the poem written on it out of my bag.

"At the beginning of September, twenty-five years ago," I say quietly, "a young teacher walked into our classroom, sat on the edge of the desk, and read us her favorite poem, a poem by Leah Goldberg, 'April Khamsin.' I would like to read it to you now."

The paper is like a shaking leaf in my hand, but the blinding tears and the tremor in my jaw don't prevent me from reading:

"I knew that day was a day that had no parallel.
a day when nothing happened, nothing at all,
and what distinguished it from other days
no evil omen, no sign of grace could tell."

And my eyes wander over the attentive faces, clenching their lips so as not to cry, of those who had known and loved you less than me, and of the one who had loved you more:

"Except that the sun gave off a jasmine smell,
except that the sands of the shore had lips that kissed,
except that a heart in the stone pulsed as in a wrist,
except that the evening burned like an orange's golden shell."

And I remember, how could I forget, your velvety voice, and your fiery eyes, and your lips on mine, and the sun that streamed in my veins like grace.

"How to remember that day—anonymous, vague as mist?

312

How shall I preserve the grace that suddenly fell?
How shall I believe that on that day alone
every flutter and scent came from my marrow bone?"

And above me rises the tranquil, respectable city, which all those years ago had vomited you out, and which is now receiving you back to rest at its feet, and I close my eyes and raise my voice until it is almost a shout:

"For every tree in the wind was a trembling sail,
and silence had the eyes of a little girl,
and tears the odors of the blossoming grove,
and the name of the mountain resembled the name of my
    love."

I open my eyes and look at Yoel, did he notice the change I permitted myself to make in the last line? And in his face I see the girl who created the words with her voice opposite the sea on the Nahariya beach, on a khamsin night in April, and then took off her clothes in front of his thrilled eyes and threw her pale body into the surf of the waves, the girl who calculated that twenty-five thousand days wouldn't be enough for her, and didn't know that she would be given far less.

And I go up to him and shake his hand in farewell, and the question shoots out of my mouth, I can't stop it, did you help her in the end like she asked you to? And Yoel is silent, and I try again, almost begging, I know you loved her enough to forgive her, but I don't know if you loved her enough to let her go, so that she wouldn't suffer, and Yoel looked me in the eye, and for a moment I saw anger and hostility in his look, what have you to do with our love, what have you to do with our lives, invading them all these years like an uninvited guest, and then he says quietly, don't worry, she didn't suffer.

■

And already the dawn is turning the sky pale between the slats of the blind, and the birds are waking up in a great commotion, and in a little while Noga will appear in the kitchen, noiselessly tottering on bare feet, her eyelids half shut and her dimples laughing at me from either side of her pacifier, dragging behind her a faded pink summer blanket with an appliqued cat, and I will seat her on my lap and bury my face in the nape of her neck. And then Carmel will wake up too, and I will have to tell her about you, and her emerald eyes will turn black with grief when she says, I loved Michaela too, she was really, really nice. And then she'll ask, but what did she die from, and I'll say, cancer, breast cancer, and she'll look at me in horror and whisper, you know mommy, sometimes it hurts me there, maybe I've got breast cancer too, and I'll press her to my body and whisper in her ear, those are only growing pains, children can't get breast cancer, and she'll ask, how do you know, and I'll say, a doctor told me once, when I was your age.

And then Yair will appear, his eyes blue slits in his face swollen with sleep, and grunt good morning, and bend his big body and stitch his lips to ours in three kisses smelling of toothpaste, and he'll heat up a bottle of milk and a glass of chocolate, and make two cups of coffee, and sit down opposite me like he does every morning, and tell Carmel about the teacher's meeting, and I'll ask, so what's she like, the new teacher Hadas, and Carmel will say, she's a sweet soul.

And now, before they all get up, I'll gather up the crumpled flowers of my tears and throw them into the trash, and open the kitchen window and let Escher's birds fly out of the story and take off, against the background of the sky, with a beating of black-and-white wings, and say goodbye to this hiding place, which I have been carrying inside me for twenty-five years now, and which is the secret of my weakness and the secret of my strength, and allow the young woman you were, and the girl I was, to rest forever between the folds of time, which no watchmaker and no writer will ever be able to mend.

Tel Aviv, 2001–2003

Afterword

Reading *Dearest Anne*: The Novel as a Historical Document

I first read Judith Katzir's latest novel, *Dearest Anne*, in two sittings. I remember gulping it down, reading well into the night, unable to wait until the morning. The coming of age of Rivi Shenhar—the protagonist and narrator of the novel—struck me with immediacy. I felt as if I myself were being transported back in time to late-1970s, middle-class, Ashkenazi (occidental), preintegration Israel. I recognized it all: The school gatherings, Holocaust memorial services in white shirts and blue trousers (the colors of the national flag), Arbor Day (attesting to Israelis being people of the soil), National Book Week (attesting to Jews being the people of the book); National Service Week in high school that included collecting fruit; the scouts, of whom good kids who were not hooligans were a part. The novel conjured up my ghosts, brought them to light, and allowed them to be laid to rest quietly once more in a manner mirroring that of the protagonist's life. Growing up bespectacled with a Diasporic name in a Zionist age[1]; conversing about how best to live life; smoking and telling stories of developing sexuality with my best

315

girlfriend at the time who was, coincidentally, the (wonderful) translator's late daughter Noa; the awareness of growing up and coming of age in a time of great cultural historical and national importance all flooded my consciousness, filling me to capacity. Although I am a Jerusalemite and the novel is set in Haifa, the setting of *Dearest Anne* felt like déjà vu for me: Cypress trees, pine trees, open fields in which one could find solitude and think, the feel of a hot Khamsinic day or the winter driving rain shaking the trees alive, the feeling of affinity with and belonging to an anthropomorphic natural world, family dinners of finely chopped vegetable salad, omelets, and spiked tea, all combine to bring my past alive in a most palpable and synesthetic manner.

The evocation of the past was made complete for me by Katzir's masterful embedding of historical fact in fictional Rivi Shenhar's diaries. *Dearest Anne* recounts with exactness what Israelis ate; which television programs they saw; the national and religious holidays they celebrated; the way public medical insurance worked during the 1970s; the brand name of the contraceptive pill a girl was likely to take in a pre-AIDS age in which sexual responsibility meant going on the pill; the contemporary music, foreign and local, they listened to; the popular holiday resorts they visited; and the nature of Israeli social stratification. Thus read, the novel constitutes a time capsule of Israeli society at a pivotal time.

The novel also evokes some of the most formative political events of late-1970s Israel as the backdrop to Rivi Shenhar's tale of the development, fruition, and dissolution of the impossible (and improbable) love affair with her junior high school literature teacher. Israeli Prime Minister Rabin's resignation when his wife's illegal foreign bank account became known, the resultant political turnover when Begin ascended to power and thereby ended the Labor party's traditional hegemony over Israel and began a postsocialist, New Right era in Israeli politics and society, appears in the novel, as does Egyptian president Sadat's historical visit to the Knesset (Israeli Parliament) and the ensuing peace contract between Israel and Egypt. These events are important, worth noting, but remain in the periphery of Shenhar's experience. Israel's two wins of the Eurovision song contest and the Maccabi's taking the European basketball cup adds to the optimistic, at times euphoric, feeling that Israel was becoming a nation like all nations. Rivi Shenhar describes her enchantment with both the life and work of such historical cultural icons as Dahn Ben Amotz alongside her interest in how her best friend Racheli finds and acts on her first love. The interaction of Rivi Shenhar, Michaela Berg, and the fictional artist Amos Lev-Ari narrate the ascendancy of a new, hedonistic, sensuous, and individualistic, hippie-influenced, anti-nationalist age replacing the old, monolithic, nationalist, Holocaust-generated Israeli narrative espoused by such characters as her school principal, Hourgin, a parody of hegemonic cant. Shenhar also hints at further historic developments such as the large-scale return to religious fundamentalism and to the development of new ideas about lifestyle, as evidenced by the adult Racheli's chosen way of life.

The one element lacking in the full spectrum of the depiction and recreation of Israeli society in the late 1970s pertains to the ethnic aspects of Israeli social stratification. Katzir portrays ethnic tensions between west European and east European Jews when Carmela (Rivi Shenhar's mother) immediately dislikes and mistrusts Michaela Berg because of her assumed German derivation (Carmela calls Berg a *Yekke-putz*, a derogatory term for Jews of German origins), even before she suspects illicit interactions between Berg and her daughter. In this same scene, Carmela remembers the dismissive treatment she received as a young girl from German-born grocery shop owners. In another scene, when Shenhar invites Nizar, an Arab peer who participates in a Jewish Arab dialogue group, to her house, Carmela's somewhat paranoid and absurdly nationalistic behavior highlights tension between Jews and Arabs in Israeli society. However, tension between Asian or North African and Ashkenazi Jews is not mentioned. The only non-Ashkenazi women in the novel are Annette the maid and a fictional character—the protagonist of a short story who is infatuated with a (male) teacher who does not reciprocate her love. This is a curious omission in a novel dedicated to describing Israel during the 1970s, a time rife with ethnic tension, in which for the first time eastern Jews challenged the narrative branding them as passive primitive others, fit for plebian existence only, and in need of surveillance and educational intervention. Katzir has stated that her intention was to include in her novel only that with which she was familiar; thus, the novel is one of Ashkenazi, middle-class, bourgeois, or bohemian narratives and experiences (Granot 2004, 38–39).

The national and international historical landmarks bejeweling Rivi Shenhar's tale embed it within historical events and lend truth to her narrative. Her growing mistrust of grand narratives, national stances, and figures of authority mirror the changes in Israeli society at large. After the disillusionment of the 1973 war during which national leaders were exposed as deluded, self-serving, out of touch with reality, or corrupt, the grand narrative of national renewal began to fracture. The break was evident in the growing fragmentation within Israeli society; its ensuing and numerous identity politics agendas; the importation of foreign cultural influences, such as the 1960s counter-culture and second-wave feminism; and the Israeli shedding of its socialist ethos and adoption of liberal capitalism after the 1977 Likud takeover. Youngsters of Rivi Shenhar's (and Katzir's, and my own) generation were presented with options and dilemmas that simply did not exist before. They grew up in times of less cohesion, and less trodden paths appeared before them. Rivi Shenhar's narrative—cataclysmic, mocking, and dismissive of authority, while meticulously assembling a new canon, lore, standards of behavior—is made all the more credible by its historical setting.

Recalling Anne Frank

Dearest Anne functions not only as a time capsule, but also is in constant dialogue with literary and historical precedents. The historical contextualization of Rivi Shenhar's narrative, which intertwines her experience with mainstream Israeli experience, reveals how subversive and at times disturbing the novel is.

The title *Dearest Anne* refers to Katzir's decision to model Rivi Shenhar's journal after that of Anne Frank's. There is a critical difference: Where Anne Frank wrote to an imaginary recipient, Shenhar writes to the historical Anne Frank. The original Hebrew title of the work, translated as "Here I Begin," is a quote from the opening of Anne Frank's diary, attesting to how well known Frank's text is in Israel, as well as to the formative quality of Rivi Shenhar's experience.

Thus, in a daring and deliberate manner, Katzir places *Dearest Anne*, a novel depicting explicit sexual content, statutory rape, intergenerational lesbian love, pot smoking, teenage sexuality, and subversion of authority, within the same literary tradition as Anne Frank's diary, one of the most canonic texts in the traditions of Holocaust and Israeli young adult literature and Zionist justification.

The Holocaust is taught in the Israeli school system to emphasize the numbers of Jews killed and the barbarity of it, the silence of the world as it happened, and the resultant absolute necessity of a strong state of Israel to ensure that such an event shall never occur to the Jewish people again. Holocaust Memorial Day takes place exactly one week before the Remembrance Day for all soldiers who fell in the line of duty, which in turn brings in the celebrations of Independence Day. The Holocaust is thus deliberately juxtaposed with national revival in the minds of Israelis from a very early age.

Katzir is playfully aware of this inescapable national doctrine. Her novel contains not one but two Holocaust Memorial Day school ceremonies. During the first ceremony Shenhar reads a letter dedicated to Anne Frank to all the gathered students. In her letter, she writes about the individual Anne Frank and the general humanistic lesson to be learned from her experience. Hourgin, the school's principal and the novel's hegemonic mouthpiece, is outraged. He would have preferred honoring Anne Frank in a way that reinforced the need for a strong state for the chosen people. His sense of moral outrage is exacerbated by the fact that Shenhar's objectionable paper has been selected by a female junior teacher. The clash over the matter between Hourgin and Michaela Berg simultaneously highlights generational and gender differences, as well as tensions about the relationship between the Holocaust and nationalism. How Shenhar views this clash, and how she retells the story to us in diary form, provides a perfect example of how Katzir peripherally records moments of social change in *Dearest Anne*. Shenhar notes the second Remembrance Day, two years later, as the date her friend Racheli (a second-generation Holocaust survivor) skips school and the requisite ceremony to lose her virginity. Rather than seeing Racheli's actions as inappropriate, Shenhar defends them as particularly appropriate: Racheli is celebrating the renewal of life and all the things denied actual Holocaust victims.

When asked by a school inspector during an interview whether the evocation of Anne Frank's diary in her novel is blasphemous, Katzir strongly rejected the accusation. Like her protagonist, Katzir prefers individual respect for individual victims rather than a national harnessing of mass trauma. In turn, she questions whether groups adhere to grand narratives and national ceremonies in order to shirk personal ethical dealings with the past (Granot 2004, 39–40).

Instead of ready-made descriptions of Holocaust victimhood and masculinist narratives of national renewal, Katzir has Rivi Shenhar invent her own ceremonies of remembrance and personal growth. By dedicating her diary to Anne Frank, Rivi Shenhar widens and reinterprets the notion of hiding, safekeeping, and survival. Her diary is her first major hiding place, and later the ground in which she places the diary is a hideaway within a hideaway until its rebirth/disinterment.

Hiding and interment are also the fates of both Rivi Shenhar and Michaela Berg. They hide, blend, and suffer different kinds of death. When Shenhar visits Anne Frank's hiding place in Amsterdam, she and her boyfriend sneak up the ladder to recreate the kiss between Anne Frank and Peter Van Daan of nearly forty years earlier. Shenhar's sexual experimentation can be viewed as bringing life to the story of Anne Frank, a girl of enormous sensibility and talent who was only able to begin, but could never follow through. Rivi Shenhar gets to develop her life to fruition (and disillusionment). The directions that she follows in her narrative—writing, sexuality, and motherhood; a coming to terms with her past, her mother, and Berg—are precisely the paths that were denied Anne Frank by her untimely tragic death. Hints of Frank's developing sexuality—a desire to touch her friend's breasts, being moved to the core of her soul by the female nude, her kiss with Peter Van Daan—remain unrealized. Thus, Anne Frank is not an icon of budding sexuality but of truncated experience. Placing Shenhar's tale within the same canon or literary tradition as the text most symbolic of the Holocaust normalizes and individualizes Anne Frank's memory. It also dignifies and gives personal direction to Rivi Shenhar's tale as it lays the foundation for a new woman-based literary canon and historical tradition out of which Shenhar can grow.

Other Literary Allusions and the Bildungsroman

Anne Frank's diary is only one of the literary texts and traditions embedded within *Dearest Anne*. In this coming-of-age bildungsroman, or, to be more exact, *kunstlerroman* (in that it delineates the coming of age and formation of a writer), Rivi Shenhar invents in a Woolfian manner her own foremothers, literary precedents, and canons. As is the case with the novel's treatment of the narrative of national renewal, or the narrative of the Holocaust, here too the canon of Hebrew literature is decentered and reorganized along female, feminist, humanist, and romantic lines. Rivi Shenhar falls in love with her teacher to her recitation of a poem by prolific Hebrew poet Leah Goldberg. (Only later does she learn that the poem functioned to a great extent as Michaela Berg's come-on line, which brought about Yoel's enchantment with her as well.) Shenhar also reads her variation of that same poem as Berg is buried. Throughout the novel Shenhar recites, parodies, makes immediately and personally accessible a poem by twentieth-century Israeli poet Zelda about naming. Shenhar reads Israeli poet Dalia Ravikovitch and has her poems alongside Anne Frank's diary by her bed. Berg teaches Shenhar a short story by Israeli author and producer Amalia Kahana-Carmon about a young girl enamored with her teacher. Shenhar reads Woolf and is introduced to more Woolf by Berg. Michaela Berg's dog and car are named after female characters in Don Quixote.

The Israeli mainstream literary canon, however, especially the literature most revered in the 1960s and 1970s, is missing from Rivi Shenhar's bookshelves and is not represented in her affair with Berg. When young Shenhar writes, she does so from within a feminist consciousness that goes against the national grain. In addition to writing as Anne Frank's Kitty both privately and for an audience, she writes a poem commemorating the outcast, damned, biblical Jezebel, which honors Jezebel's experience.

At the same time that Rivi Shenhar embarks on the feminist project of finding her literary foremothers and creating a female tradition to follow, she also participates in an opposite, complementary, humanist, gender-erasing program. She reads Thomas Mann's *The Magic Mountain* and identifies with Castorp. In so doing, she identifies with bildungsromanesqe enculturation along humanist, liberal, gender-free, but ultimately "male-stream" values. Going perhaps even further in this direction, Shenhar and Racheli call each other "Devil," a subversive, nonhuman appellation that allows them to speak to each other using masculine forms, thereby escaping female identification and limitations.

Nabokov's *Lolita* is another unacknowledged, intertextual influence in the narration of *Dearest Anne*. At times, reading the novel feels like reading a gender-inverted narrative of *Lolita* in reverse. In the case of *Dearest Anne*, the first-person narrator is a young aggressor in a story of pedophilic intergenerational love.

The generic milestones of a bildungsroman include a description of the protagonist's formative years, strife with parents, finding a teacher for life, acculturation, sexual experimentation—usually the protagonist's experience of two sexual relationships, one degrading and the other exalting—finding a life partner and a vocation. In *Dearest Anne*, the markers are all generated from or in response to Michaela Berg. Shenhar undergoes all the processes of receiving an education, finding a vocation, being degraded and exalted in love, and feeding the mind and body with Berg. Her enculturation of the mind comes along with an erotic education. This collapsing inwards is representative of the solipsistic/narcissistic quality of their relationship, also of its hermetic and hermeneutic circularity. Each is the mother and daughter to the other. They feed each other and feed off each other. They trade positions of age, power, responsibility, birth, rebirth, and interment.

As her narrative criticizes the relationship, Shenhar insists on the totality of her experience, and demands that it be appraised as such. She does not doubt or reject any of the components in the equation. Even later, as a mother, watching Berg interact with her daughter Carmel, Shenhar is horrified and outraged at the ease with which Michaela Berg, or anyone for that matter, can access the malleable heart of a child, but she insists that her experience is what made her whole and complete, for better and worse. She holds onto and affirms her past, even when she cannot get far enough from it, while Berg is trapped in a reenactment of past patterns of behavior. The past is further glorified when compared with Rivi Shenhar's present, when she stitches her life together, laying bare her continual fear of imminent loss.

The bildungsroman is generally a genre of acculturation and social belonging. In the hands of Katzir it becomes something somewhat less positivist, linear, or celebrative of the existing social order and its institutions. Rivi Shenhar grows up against the grain, very critical of the people, institutions, and norms around her. She expresses strong sentiments at an early age. Alone and with Berg, she participates in reinscribing events and deconstructing traditional values in an enabling, feminist, countercultural, self-absorbed manner.

All along the young Shenhar is critical of Michaela Berg's choices in life. She sees Berg's inconsistencies, the places where her actions are self-serving (such as her desire to have a child in order to better cover up the lesbian affair). In the end, Shenhar is reabsorbed into mainstream society. Although she defends and upholds her past and Berg's part in her making, she condemns Berg's actions. "How did you dare?" Shenhar confronts Berg toward the end of her tale. The narrative itself is even more punitive, judgmental, and moralist than its protagonist. Shenhar finds men, motherhood, and a vocation; and the overreaching red-haired Berg, who had tried living through others, gives birth to an autistic child and develops breast cancer. Her creation, a child, is flawed, noncommunicative, and will never share or be appreciative of her literary sensitivity. Her body becomes diseased in the very organ that was central to her adultery (Adivi -Shoshan 2003, 20). The existing social order is restored.

Berg dies or rather is reborn back into the soil, swaddled in a shroud like a diapered baby. Rivi Shenhar, who once could not get enough of life and the experience offered her, now spends her energy fearfully avoiding experience that brings loss. When watching Michaela Berg interact with her daughter Carmel, Rivi Shenhar understands that, despite her journey, she has come to occupy the position of her mother. She has come full circle rather than participating in a progressive, humanist, linear tale. She has been reenmeshed in the fabric of society—a bildungsromanesque achievement—but not in an empowering manner. She has been decentered in her own tale.

Reception of the Novel

The historical setting of *Dearest Anne* and the insertion of landmark events in Israeli society into its plot; the technical mechanism of diary writing and the resultant immediacy of the protagonist's experience; the intertextual use of literature generally and Anne Frank's diary specifically, all combine to create a suspension of disbelief so palpable that the distinctions between fact and fiction blur, and thus readers are baffled and disturbed by questions of moral import, political correctness, and desirability of the narrative.

Dearest Anne received serious critical attention in literary supplements and critical journals in Israel. Some of Israel's most successful contemporary writers, including Amoz Oz, Haim Be'er, Shulamit Lapid, and S. Yizhar, hailed Katzir's masterful deployment of literary conventions themes and technique.[2] Dalia Ravikovitch, cited in the novel, commented on the sweeping effect the novel has on its readers. "I read the book with bated breath," she says. Many critics cited especially Katzir's delicate and truthful treatment of love. But critics found Katzir's embedding of Anne Frank's diaries in a plot dealing with a lesbian love story between teacher and pupil disrespectful of the Holocaust. Some found the precocious protagonist, Rivi Shenhar, and, by extension, her creator, too preoccupied with glitter and creating an effect. One critic, Yehudit Orian, accused both Rivi Shenhar and Katzir of popularist commercialism. On the whole, though, *Dearest Anne* was very well received.

Perhaps the most interesting aspects of the novel's reception transpired within the gay and lesbian community. Although this novel was targeted to a mainstream Israeli readership, it drew a large gay, lesbian, bisexual, and transgender readership.

Gay and lesbian internet portals and forums such as gogay.co.il and the lesbian forum at nana.co.il were abuzz when the novel was released. In late 2003 and early 2004 it seemed that every literate Israeli lesbian was reading the novel and sharing her thoughts about it on the Internet. The reception by gay and lesbian readers was charged and predominately negative. They spoke of disappointment, a misrepresentation of lesbianism, and a return to 1950s sacrificial lesbian novels in which evil lesbian protagonists were punished in denouements that included suicide, madness, or a recuperation of heteronormativity.

Most complaints about Katzir's representation of lesbianism focused on the protagonist's reabsorption into heterosexuality and the issue of pedophilia. They protested the pedophilic taint upon lesbianism for two reasons. First, they viewed it as partly replicating and partly demonstrating against a variety of "homosexual panic" as described by Gayle Rubin—the association of gay practice with pedophilia in order to keep gays and lesbians in check. Second, a year before the original Hebrew publication of *Dearest Anne* in 2003, a biological woman living as a man was arrested and tried for fraudulent receipt and statutory rape of young teenage girls. It was claimed that Hen Alkobi, using the male name Kobi, preyed on the girls' relative innocence in order to have sex with them. The novel was published just as the trial ended and Alkobi was convicted. The trial split the Israeli GLBTQ community along the lines of consent versus transgender rights. Some of the agitation no doubt caused the court case and its implications to spill over into readings of the book. Lesbian readers discussed the novel in terms of a return to what Adrienne Rich has called compulsory heterosexuality, and most GLBTQ readers found the pedophilic content of the novel particularly objectionable.

Most gay and lesbian readers concurred that *Dearest Anne* was not lesbian fiction, mirroring in reverse the fictional Hourgin's reaction to Rivi Shenhar's diary letters to Anne Frank. Thus, Katzir's work inadvertently finds itself embroiled in yet another struggle for narrative hegemony, this time with gay readers. A reading of the novel as nonlesbian fiction might be the only way to assuage representational fears. Rivi Shenhar and Michaela Berg's love story is as destabilizing of the grand narrative of liberal progressive gay assimilation in Israeli society as it is of the grand narrative of communal physical and national renewal. Disturbing, threatening, or destabilizing as the pedophilic content of Katzir's novel may be, that is not the point of her work. The point lies elsewhere, in respecting, recapturing, and telling individual experience for its own sake and integrity, without harnessing it to a greater cause.

Recurrent Themes and Settings in Katzir's Works

Katzir's protagonists tend to resemble her. They are female, born in Haifa, and move to Tel Aviv as adults. Her literary corpus to date consists of meticulous and obsessive rewriting of family situations. Glorious if unfaithful mothers dying young of cancer, motherly and daughterly betrayal, and absent fathers recur in her work. Her protagonists tend to be ugly duckling, blond, bespectacled, outsider daughters; they are loners, women who march to the beat of a different drum, who are peripheral to the world around them, but maintain a belief in their own importance. Relations between Israeli descendants, German and East European Jews, between the bourgeoisie and the lower middle classes are also repeatedly dealt with in her fiction. Memory, the importance of writing to record, and the importance of making sense of lived experience are central themes. Her writing often centers on unusual love attachments: Two young adolescent cousins sexually experiment in her first published short story, "Schlaffstunde"; a young woman has a much older married male lover in *Matisse Has the Sun in His Belly*; and a fourteen-year-old student has a love affair with her twenty-seven-year-old married female literature teacher in *Dearest Anne*.

Matisse Has the Sun in His Belly and *Dearest Anne*, Katzir's two novels, can be viewed as a continuum. Where the earlier novel, *Matisse*, tells the story of Rivi Shenhar's twenties, *Dearest Anne* focuses on her adolescence and adulthood. To be sure, the novels do contain biographical differences: Shenhar's father is a doctor in one novel and an academic in the next; the identity of Shenhar's first lover shifts from a female peer in *Matisse* to her teacher in *Dearest Anne*. Shenhar's central love affair in *Matisse* is with an older male academic; in *Dearest Anne*, the affair with her female teacher remains central. Nevertheless, as Katzir has indicated, the protagonist is, essentially, the same in both novels.

The similarity between the two Shenhars is further complicated by the similarities between Rivi Shenhar, the character, and Judith Katzir, the author. Shenhar and Katzir are the same age and are from the same place and social milieu. They received the same schooling. They are products of single-parent households, following parental divorce. Both Shenhar and Katzir lost their mothers to cancer while still in their twenties. The protagonists' relationships with their mothers is strained in both novels and in Katzir's short fiction as well. Katzir confirms that the same was true for her when she describes her stories as a rewriting and reinvention of her relationship with her mother (Katzir 2006, 295). Katzir and both Shenhars had affairs with older lovers—affairs that were based in tutelage; affairs that were constitutive to their careers as writers.

But readers looking for absolute biographical correlations between protagonists and their creator are bound to be frustrated when reading Katzir's work. Katzir's response to prurient questions focusing on biographic authenticity, both in person and through the use of her literary persona, Rivi Shenhar, remains uniform. In *Dearest Anne*, when asked about the relationship between her life and her writing, the fictional middle-aged Rivi Shenhar explains to Michaela Berg's students that there are three kinds of interactions between reality and invention in her work: There are real people whom she disguises to protect their privacy; there are figments of her imagination whom she searches for in real life only after she has affixed them in writing; and there are her obesessional "seminal characters," who were branded into her soul, and who come back again and again in all kinds of incarnations and disguises. Elsewhere, in her article in the literary supplement of *Haaretz*, Katzir talks about a protagonist who is and is not herself, a mother who was and was not her mother, and what really transpired between them but never really happened (Katzir 2006). In both cases the slippery relationship between art and life remains. Art may banally copy life; following the footsteps of Oscar Wilde, art may prefigure life; but what is most interesting is when art exorcizes life in sundry and various incarnations. The narratives of Katzir's Rivi Shenhar do just that. They review and recycle experienced life in an attempt to give it coherence, meaning, and lay it to rest.

About Judith Katzir

Judith Katzir is a contemporary, award-winning Israeli author who lives and works in Tel Aviv. She is the married mother of two daughters, gives courses and workshops in creative writing, and works as a reader and editor for the Hakibbutz Hameuchad/ Siman Kriah Publishing House, which has published all of her works.

Born in 1963 in Haifa, Katzir is, on her mother's side, the descendant of Yoel Moshe Solomon (1838–1912), one of the first Jews to found neighborhoods in modern Jerusalem, outside the crowded safety of the old city. Solomon was also one of the founders of Petah Tikva, one of the first agricultural settlements in Turkish Palestine. Katzir's lawyer parents separated when she was twelve. When Katzir was in her twenties, her mother died of cancer. Her diagnosis was Katzir's impetus to embark on a career in writing.

Still a student of comparative literature at Tel Aviv University, Katzir won the attention of leading Israeli publishers with the publication of her first short story, "Schlaffstunde," in the Israeli literary magazine *Iton 77*. Encouraged by this publication and the stir it caused, Katzir began to spend more time on her writing, and less on her studies. When she approached her professor, Menahem Perry, for yet another extension on one of her assignments, Perry convinced her to let his publishing house, Hakibbutz Hameuchad/Siman Kriah, publish her work. Katzir has stated that she chose this house because they were the only publisher to offer her an advance, which she used to travel and write. Soon afterward, her first collection of short stories, *Closing the Sea* (1990), was published to instant success. Five years later, Katzir published her first novel, *Matisse Has the Sun in His Belly* (1995). In 1999, she published a novella, *Inland Lighthouses*, and in 2005, a selection called *Haifa Stories*. She also wrote children's books, including *Amalia's Picnic* (1994), and *Bubble in the Wind* (2002); and one historical play, *Dvora Baaron* (2000). *Dearest Anne*, originally published in Hebrew in 2003, is her second and most recent novel.

Katzir's work, published by a literary publisher, is canonic and has been widely translated into such languages as English, French, German, Dutch, Spanish, Portuguese, and Turkish. Even her first published story, "Schlaffstunde," has become required reading for Israeli high school students who are matriculating in literature. Katzir was awarded the Prime Minister's Literary Award for Hebrew Writers in 1996 and 2007. She is presently working on another novel.

Hannah Ovnat-Tamir
Jerusalem, Israel
January 2008

Notes

1. The fathers of modern Zionism conceived of the project of Jewish national revival as involving both political and physical renewal. Thinkers such as Binyamin Zeev Herzel or Max Nordau conceived of Zionism as a cure for

the physical and mental ailments of Diasporic Jews. Accordingly, Jewish settlers were conceived of as becoming paragons of humankind, standing straight and tall, developing muscles, becoming tan. Spectacles have the aura of the ghetto upon them. More on early Zionism as a physical eugenic program can be found in Gluzman (1997), Hirsch (2001), Boyarin (1997) or Kamir (2004).

2. All the appraisals of *Dearest Anne* by contemporary Israeli novelists were supplied courtesy of the Institute for the Translation of Hebrew Literature. Quotations from these authors are available on the "Praise for *Dearest Anne*" page that opens this volume.

Works Cited

Adivi-Shoshan, Esti. 2003. "Eicha Eshmor Hasdo Hapitomi?" [How Shall I Preserve His Sudden Grace?], *Iton* 77(285):20–25.

Boyarin, Daniel. 1997. "The Colonial Masqued Ball," *Theory and Criticism: An Israeli Forum* 11(Winter):123–144.

Gluzman, Michael. 1997. "Hakmihah Lehetrosexualiut: Tzionut, ve Miniut BeAltneuland" [Yearning for Heterosexuality: Zionism and Sexuality in *Altneuland*], *Theoria ve Bikoret* 11:145–162.

Granot, Moshe. 2004. "Hatzorech Lehitboded Im Hazikaron Beofen Ishi" [The Need to Cope with Remembrance Personally], *Moznaim* 78(2):35–40.

Hirsch, Dafna. 2001. "Banu Hena Lehavi Et Hamaarav: Hasiach Hahigieni BeEretz Yisrael Betkufat Hamandat" [We Have Come to Westernize: The Hygienic Discourse in Eretz Yisrael During the British Mandate], *Zmanim* 7:107–120.

Kamir, Orit. 2004. *She'ela Shel Kavod: Yisraeliut Ukvod Haadam* [Israeli Honor and Dignity: Social Norms, Gender Politics and the Law]. Jerusalem: Carmel Publishing House.

Katzir, Judith. 1990. "Schlaffstunde," *Sogrim et Hayam* [Closing the Sea]. Tel Aviv: Hakibbutz Hameuchad/Siman Kriah.

———. 1995. *LeMatisse Yesh et Hashemesh BaBeten* [*Matisse Has the Sun in His Belly*]. Tel Aviv: Hakibbutz Hameuchad/Siman Kriah.

———. 2006 [orig. 2005]. "I Shall Never Forget the Tearing Eyes of My First Reader" (translated by Nili Gold), *Hebrew Studies* 47:295–298.

Permissions